Cam Habersham is having a hell of a time keeping up with his fae studies in the Ancestral Lands because a certain werewolf constantly interrupts his thoughts. Everton Lilch is the wolfen beast who follows Cam around, but he pushes Cam away every time things get steamy.

The queen of the fae has had enough and tasks Cam with an impossible feat, an undertaking only Everton can help him accomplish.

Without his coven, Sparks Gemmell is a lost witch. In desperation, he casts a spell, hoping to reunite his brothers. But he doesn't count on the wayward route magic often takes. He finds himself wrapped up in a mandate of the horned god and inserted into his Shadow Brothers' relationship in order to protect his city from the darkest elements of the Shadow Realm.

As the darkness of the Shadow Realm descends, Cam and his werewolf, along with Sparks and his coven brothers, confront wraiths, mutant werewolves, and witch law enforcement. Chaos erupts in an effort to please queens and gods.

After all, it comes down to the ley of the land.

CURSED

Magus Malefica, Book Two

J.P. Jackson

A NineStar Press Publication

www.ninestarpress.com

Cursed

© 2022 J.P. Jackson
Cover Art © 2022 Natasha Snow

This is a work of fiction. Names, characters, places, and incidents are either the product of the author's imagination or are used fictitiously. Any resemblance to actual persons living or dead, business establishments, events, or locales is entirely coincidental.

All rights reserved. No part of this publication may be reproduced in any material form, whether by printing, photocopying, scanning or otherwise without the written permission of the publisher. To request permission and all other inquiries, contact NineStar Press at the physical or web addresses above or at Contact@ninestarpress.com.

ISBN: 978-1-64890-485-1

First Edition, May, 2022

Also available in eBook, ISBN: 978-1-64890-484-4

CONTENT WARNING:
This book contains sexually explicit material which is only suitable for mature readers, death of a secondary character, gore. This book is part of a series and should be read in sequence.

To all the fans of the Magus Malefica.

Chapter One

"I AM NOT wearing this."

Cam tossed the skimpy garment onto his sun-dappled bed while Sen, his man-in-waiting, a Kijimuna tree sprite, wrung his long-boned but tiny hands. Sen glared at Cam, but his nervous hand wringing never stopped. Cam returned the stare, hoping his stubbornness would win.

Eventually, Cam broke the connection and focused his sights on the far wall of his room. A new tendril wove its way up the wall.

Everything the fae used or constructed was in harmony with the environment. The bed had been crafted from woven tree roots. The mattress pillowed from being stuffed with a combination of dried grasses, tufts from animal pelts, and down. All the textiles were handwoven, and when the summer night air had a chill to it, more skins were brought in for comfort. Extra blankets hadn't been necessary this summer. Despite the bed's lumpy appearance, Cam had never slept so well. Although he still wasn't used to the massive horns on his head or the protruding wings from his back.

The walls and the furniture were constantly changing,

but when one lived inside a massive tree, one had to expect the unexpected. As the tree continued to grow, so did the interior of his assigned bedchamber.

"Your Grace, the loincloth is traditional clothing. You were scheduled to meet with the queen, and certain conventions must be upheld. You need to get down to the court room." Sen tried his best, but Cam's tenacity would eventually wear out the tree sprite.

"It's nothing more than a jockstrap and I am not parading around in front of the entire Royal party in nothing but a G-string!" He pointed to the discarded underwear while scrunching his mouth to one side and crossing his arms.

"But Your Grace—" Sen licked his lips while he continued to rub his hands together.

Poor thing. Cam hadn't made his summer an easy experience. The tree sprite had been assigned as Cam's manservant as part of an international exchange program meant to expand the knowledge of cultural traditions and court customs from various fae clans around the world. Cam had seen and met Chaneques from southern Mexico, and Menehune from Oceania. Sen's vibrant red hair, a characteristic of his tribe, contrasted starkly with his paper-birch complexion. Sen's frame imitated the slender branches of a sinewy willow, so slight Cam mistakenly judged him to be frail, but he discovered otherwise. Fae could be inhumanly strong and there had been more than one occasion when Sen had managed to wrestle and hold Cam still during his magic training.

Sen's Japanese ancestry meant his tolerance did not allow for the wild range of temperatures inherent in a Canadian prairie summer. Cam had witnessed the creature either shivering to death on the rare cool summer evening or wilting in the August heat which regularly coalesced beneath the dense forest canopy. Sen's homelands were far more temperate and kinder on a body. Despite Sen's constant battle with the elements, his elongated limbs and fine features meant he was nimble and quick, which made him an excellent tutor for Cam's induction in the ways of the fae. Escaping wild and out of control fae magic spells gone awry required additional agility. The fae were supposed to be nimble, graceful, and eloquently able to slip in and out of the shadows when required, a magical talent Cam had not mastered, along with several others. Sen's intelligence, however, proved the Eldritch clan fae outwitted and outsmarted Cam's constant manipulations.

Cam struggled with his fae classification and history. The amount of concentration required to take in the volumes of documentation given to him bested his attention span. The antiquity of the clans spanned the course of human existence, and beyond.

Each fae belonged within one of four houses, although there were multiple species within each camp. Earth fae belonged to the clan of the Eldritch, like Sen and Cam. Air fae were the Aethers and Corvins. Their feathered wings and skin made for unusual flying creatures who lived above the clouds. Cam latched on to the name for water fae because he found out Atlanteans were real. But he couldn't recall what fire fae were called, and at this point he simply didn't care.

Cam had made the first few weeks frustrating for them both. He refused to study, and his wayward use of fae abilities had resulted in wanton destruction within the village, which landed him in hot water with the Ancestral Lands queen, Lady Aine.

In his defence, Cam had demonstrated his ability to become invisible, and he regularly used probability spells to favour his penchant for doing nothing in the hot August afternoons.

Cam stood beside his bed, naked, staring at the wall and contemplating how he had managed to get here. He had his best friend in the whole wide world to thank for all of this. Devid Khandelwal and his cockamamie summoning board had been the catalyst in forever altering Cam's humanity, and subsequent captivity within the Ancestral Lands of the forest fae. Granted, his home in Edmonton wasn't far away, but until Cam had, at a bare minimum, mastered the art of a human disguise, Lady Aine would never let him leave.

Grasping the concept and maintaining the illusion proved inordinately difficult. He had to completely change his new horned and winged form into the way he used to be. That meant being able to maintain the image he wanted to project in his mind's eye, all while holding conversations, or carrying out mundane tasks like household chores or visiting the local market. Illusions proved to be impossible for Cam, but public appearances with massive, curved horns and a slender furry tail would expose the Shadow Realm and its inhabitants to the mundane world. Exposure was something the entire magical community, fae, witches, beasts, and spirits alike, avoided at all costs.

Cam's membranous wings sputtered. The appendages had a life of their own, and often reflected his emotional state.

"May I point out you're not wearing anything right now, and yet I'm here. What's so different between your nudity right now and satisfying the queen with your presence in clothing which is customarily worn by males?"

"Sen, you've seen me naked every day, several times a day. You bathe me, not my choice. You dress me, not my choice. You wake me in the morning, also not my choice. And speaking of morning, where is my required cup of coffee?" Cam's tail flicked from side to side as he glanced around his room, his wings flapping in annoyance. Camila, Cam's alter ego and super bitch, showed up when the caffeine levels were bottoming out. The fae folk didn't consume coffee, and Cam hadn't had a good cup of velvety deliciousness in weeks. His irritability lately had known no bounds, but the community had made exceptions considering his most unusual initiation into the Ancestral Lands—coffee being one of them. The elders of the Ancestral Lands had commented on Cam's oddness. His fae body held on to the addiction of caffeine when his stomach no longer tolerated anything more than meat. Protein, and lots of it, was a daily requirement.

In short, Cam moped and perpetuated his miserable mood to everyone around him. His normal routine had been turned upside down, his dating life had been non-existent, and as much as he had relied on Dev for so much of his past life, he had to cut the guy some slack. Dev was going through his own adjustments, what with becoming a witch and getting a boyfriend in the deal.

Cam pursed his lips while deliberating his best friend's relationship status. Dev getting paired off before Cam had to be the cruellest twist of fate ever. If you'd asked anyone, Cam should have been the one to end up with a hot boyfriend. Not that Dev didn't deserve what he'd got. But Cam had always been more willing to date and play the field, so the odds were more in his favour. And yet, things had not panned out.

Cam slumped into himself, his mouth pulled down, as his tail came to rest hanging directly down and still.

Sen walked over and handed him a steaming cup of what they were passing off as coffee. His attendee attempted to make nice.

"Come, sit. Drink your hot brown water." Sen picked up the material Cam had thrown on the bed. "You know it's called a loincloth. Have you ever worn one? They are extraordinarily comfortable. Feel this." Sen thrust the fabric toward Cam.

Reluctantly, Cam let his fingers stroke the silken material while he cradled his precious cup of coffee in his other hand.

"It is delicate and soft, isn't it?" Sen tried to make the skimpy item of cloth enticing.

"Yeah, but it's brown. Doesn't it come in any other colours? I look hideous in brown. What about aubergine? Dark purple would be an amazing contrast to the green in my hair." Cam sat on the edge of his bed, absentmindedly fondling the loincloth.

"That's enough, Sen. You've tried." A voice startled them both. From the doorway, a woman draped in several layers of sheer muslin embroidered with tiny white leaves and flowers, spoke with iron in her voice as she crossed her arms.

Sen bowed, then retreated through the back doorway, leaving a naked Cam in front of Lady Aine. The sunlight caught within the folds of her dress reflected sparkles toward Cam, creating an aura around the queen. Shimmer light twinkled and beamed—a fairy thing.

She embodied etherealness and unmatched beauty. Lady Aine's transcendent appearance belied her strength. She maintained patience and fairness but held a reputation for delivering swift and often violent justice when required.

"Cam, you must be more cooperative. Poor Sen is going to return home in a few weeks with nothing but tales of your insolence. It's going to make us all look incompetent."

Cam stared wide-eyed at the queen and grew clammy as all the blood drained from his head. He was bare-assed naked in front of the highest ranking fae within the Ancestral Lands. He glanced around for anything that would cover him up. While still gripping his coffee mug, he snatched a pillow from the head of the bed where he sat and hastily positioned the cushion across his groin.

"You're far too modest. It's not like I haven't seen a man before."

"I'm sure you have, but you have not seen me, and I would personally like to keep it that way."

"Yes, well, not seeing you is one of the reasons I've come to your quarters. You wouldn't grant me an audience, so I've come here instead. You were supposed to be in my court an hour ago."

"I wasn't going to show up in nothing but a jockstrap."

"It is also customary to stand when someone who out-ranks you enters the room in a casual setting such as this, or at a formal affair, kneel to them if you are standing." Lady Aine arched an eyebrow. Her face instantly morphed into one of those looks mothers give their misbehaving children. Cam noted the disapproving glance and raised himself from the bed, still clutching both his beloved filled coffee cup and the pillow he pressed against his nether region.

Lady Aine snapped her fingers.

The pillow exploded into a flurry of tiny feathers. Some wafted gently to the floor of his room, while others landed in the vast amounts of hair Cam's body had grown over the last few months. He'd always been a fuzzy guy but being El-dritch—of the earth—he took after the animals of the forest and therefore his hair had thickened into more fur. Basi-cally, his body hair had grown into a pelt.

Without the pillow to protect his twig and stones, Cam used the only thing left to him and awkwardly cupped his palm and placed his hand over his groin.

"That's not necessary. As I've said, I've seen a man be-fore, Cam. Yours is bigger than most. Something you should want to flaunt, not hide, which you're not doing well right now anyway."

Heat crawled up Cam's neck, blossomed across his chest, and made his cheeks flush. Beads of sweat appeared on his forehead. His brow glistened.

Please make this be over soon.

"I've come to tell you you're running out of time. I know you're not comfortable here, and you want to return home. I can't let your release happen without a few things transpir-ing first. Namely the illusion mastery, and more im-portantly—"

"Please, not this again. I've told you before, I will not be anyone's father."

"No one is asking you to be a parent. I can't see you being beneficial to any progeny. However, it is your duty to ensure I end up pregnant. Have you seen any other Royal male fae around, Cam?"

The queen stood still, and Cam sensed her irritation, making him prickle with discomfort.

"No."

"Do you know why that might be?"

"Ah…" Cam squirmed as his tail twitched. Damn thing gave his discomfort away. He swore the appendage was the faerie equivalent of a mood ring.

"For the love of all the Gods. Have you not been paying attention during your lessons?" She shook her head as she seemingly floated over Cam's study desk. Lady Aine tossed several books aside until she found a particularly large tome. She tapped the book a few times, then grasped its thick spine and tossed it over onto Cam's bed.

Cam peered down at the textbook.

Anatomiae Biological Mediocris de Speciebus.

"You should have this memorized by now. Cam, I understand our ways have been thrust on you, but we all know you are never going to return to a human body. We were as unprepared for you as you were for us. But whereas our young are schooled and live many years seeing tradition performed in front of them, you've missed centuries of development the younger fae get as they mature within our community. You must catch up. If you don't, you're putting us all in danger.

"So I'll make this short and sweet. You are the youngest Royal male in the village which means the last fertile male has lost his potency and has now joined the ranks of the elders. They cannot produce seed. You are the only one who can ensure continuation of the clan. Every generation this happens. I've had several mates, Cam. Congratulations, you're now it. So, get with the program."

Lady Aine's hair fluttered out behind her from an unseen gust of magical air. Her gauzy dress responded similarly.

"As much as I appreciate the current situation, I don't think you understand the gravity of my predicament," Cam snapped, tilting his head to one side and suppressing a snarl.

"Careful, Cam. I will rip you apart and feast on your body parts. Don't think I haven't eaten my own kind before. And I do understand."

"I don't think you do. It's not a matter of wanting to ensure I carry on tradition or not. The fact is, I can't. There's no way I'm going to get you pregnant." Cam waved his hand dramatically through the air, sloshing brown liquid out of the cup and onto the floor. After realizing what he'd done, he peered down at his much needed and loved coffee, now lying ruined and undrinkable in a puddle on the floor. "I'm sorry. I don't know what to tell you. Sex with a girl would be like trying to shove a marshmallow into a piggybank." Cam glanced down to his now exposed bits. "It doesn't work for the lady kin." He glanced at the queen and stared as hard as he could, trying to get his point across.

"Oh for the Gods..." Lady Aine shook her head. She opened a fold of her voluminous dress, plunged her arm into an unseen pocket, and pulled out a whimsical glass vial. The vessel had a pearlescent sheen, which cast prisms of dancing rainbows, depending on how the light caught the undulations in the surface. "I know you're gay, you fool. You think being gay is a rarity within the fae? Or that any of us would judge you differently or harshly for your sexuality? How long have you been here?"

"A couple of months." Cam glanced down as the whispered words barely escaped his lips.

"And have you not seen an assortment of couplings within our village? Honestly, I should toss you out and let

Gaia have her way with you. All I need from you is your seed. Fill this, and then bring the vial to me. There's only one rule. Whatever comes out can't be done by your own hand. Your orgasm must be the result of a mating. Preferably one where there's an investment of emotion. Get your wolfman to do the deed.

"But hear this, Cam. Your time is running out. I need to be carrying before we go underground for the winter. The new generation will be born in the spring as has always happened. Which means I will gestate our offspring over the course of the winter while the entire village rests underground, safe from the winter snows."

Cam grimaced after she uttered the word offspring.

"I swear you act like a self-conscious preteen. For someone who has been driven into a prodigious position, you'd think you would feel some sense of obligation, or at the very least, self-importance. Your time is ticking away. It's already late August, and judging from the trees, our descent into the earth will be earlier than normal. You have less than a month to return this to me. Get with your wolf and get busy."

"Yeah, that might be a problem."

"What do you mean, a problem? He's here all the time. Another concession I have made. We generally don't let his kind anywhere in the village. Bad things happen when werewolves lose control. I've been graciously patient with your dalliance with this creature as I assumed the relationship would net me the seed I require. What's the problem?"

"Everton and I haven't—"

Lady Aine rolled her eyes.

She glared at Cam who stood still with his head hung.

"You are impossible. Well, if it's not your monster, who's been calling on you for the past two months, find someone else. But let me make one thing painfully clear to you. Fill the vessel before Groundswell, the winter descent, or I'll personally exile you. You will not be welcome here. Ever."

"But I thought fae cut off from their clan die? And besides, I haven't learned everything yet!"

"Whose fault is that?" Lady Aine's lips were thin lines. She turned to leave the room, but she tossed parting words at Cam over her shoulder. "And yes, severed fae rarely, if ever, flourish. They always seem to return home seeking forgiveness. Something I do not dole out willingly." Then she evaporated into sparkles and prisms.

Cam flopped onto the bed and covered his face for a moment, then let his arms splay out beside him. Sunlight streaming in through a makeshift window highlighted the grass-green fur on his chest. Cam shifted his weight, keenly aware one of his wings pinched from being awkwardly bent and tucked. He pushed himself up on one elbow.

In the quiet of his room, Cam picked at some lint on his bedspread as he considered his time over the past few months with Everton. There had been so much flirting, so many promises of a good time, and yet nothing. The wolf-man had pulled away from him on every occasion that may have turned into something more. Everton held Cam in a wolfen thrall, but now Ev's unfulfilled promise of a "night in heaven" left Cam with confusing emotions. Had Ev spoken nothing more than empty words?

Was Everton visiting out of a sense of obligation for being rescued from the witches' dungeon?

All of this stemmed from Dev's damn fascination with the occult. One stupid spell and an invocation to some Djinn had undone his mortal, human existence.

That's the fire fae. Djinn.

"I fucking hate my life. I swear I'm cursed."

Chapter Two

SPARKS GEMMELL PICKED up a bottle of wine from the end of the counter and twisted the magnum one way and then the other, trying desperately to find something that would be the perfect accompaniment for his rendezvous dinner. He stared at the label hoping an image, spur, or trigger would tell him this bottle was the best possible choice.

"All you had to do was ask for help rather than manhandling every damn bottle."

Sparks jumped at the sound of another's voice. He almost dropped the wine he held.

Spinning on his heels, Sparks found himself staring at the top of a shaggy head of hair. Naggen, the owner of Spirited, stood directly behind him. He never respected personal space, a characteristic typical for the Clurichaun. Sparks took a step away, which allowed him to take in the shop owner. His frizzy black beard neared the centre of his chest, but he kept the facial hair meticulously well-tailored. Sparks couldn't help but notice his reddish nose, which told of Naggen's nightly indulgence of the store's contents. If someone would ever corner him, though, he'd have told you the vibrant red veins were rosacea, inherited from his mother's side of the family. Naggen, or Naggy, as his more regular patrons called him, smirked at Sparks, noting the blue bolts of electricity still erupting and travelling up the witch's arm.

"You take too much delight in scaring the shit out of me." Sparks placed the bottle he held back on the shelf, then rubbed his bare arms, trying to disperse his wayward magic.

"True, but I enjoy the light show. It entertains me."

"You can be horrible, you know that, right?"

"I do. Again, it's amusing. Now, stop picking up everything in sight. You're ruining my displays. What exactly are you looking for?" Naggy didn't win the height prize. Sparks had referred to him on more than one occasion as an alcoholic pocket bear, which wasn't too far from the truth. Clurichauns were related to leprechauns—distant cousins of some sort—and the man loved to play pranks on those he considered friends.

"I'm going over to Dev and Tully's tonight for dinner. I haven't seen them in forever—you know, since *the incident*?" Sparks spoke the last few words in a hushed whisper. There were others in the store, although none of them were paying him or Naggy any attention.

"Everyone has been talking about that although you *still* haven't given me the deets. I also know the Guardians haven't met for a while, and at first, I expected to see the wraiths and demons emerge, you know, without the Night Grove's witches protecting the ley lines and all, but I haven't seen a thing." Naggy shrugged. "Makes me wonder what the hell they've been doing for the last hundred years. Here, you might want this." Naggy turned, scanned the shelf in front of him, crouched down, his knee joints popping as he did, and pulled out a bottle of merlot from the shelf nearest the floor. He blew the dust off the glass and stood. He handed the bottle to Sparks. "This is from a special winery, run by our kind. See the triangle on the bottle?" Naggy pointed to an embossed diamond at the juncture of the neck and the body. "The blank spot is an augmentation receptacle. You put any witch rune in there with the right focused intention and whoever drinks the wine will be spelled."

"Who says I wanted to spell them? They're friends! I wanted a nice bottle of wine to take over for dinner. Jeez, Naggy, what gives? Enchanting my buddies? That's a little dubious."

"Oh, please, don't lecture me." Naggy waved a gnarled, fat finger in Sparks's general direction. "I can smell the desperation on you from here."

Sparks could count on one hand the number of folks who were either full fae or admitted to having fae in their bloodline. Witch families tended not to talk about the hybrid children in their family trees, but almost every family had some relative who had participated in questionable romances.

Naggy was full fae. And the fae had the ability to read a room and sense the emotions of those around them.

"What do you mean, desperation?" Sparks's cheeks flushed hot. Of course, Naggy's summation described his emotional needs accurately—desperate for the coven to start up again. He couldn't wait to get over to Dev and Tully's place and subtly suggest as much. But after cleaning up two dead bodies and taking their coven's high priest to the hospital with near mortal wounds, there hadn't been any meaningful contact from his blood brothers. Awkward and random texts didn't count. Sparks needed the contact, the face to face visits, the group spellworking. He longed for the deeper connection to the Shadow Realm the coven provided. A sense of community which had been yanked away from him after *the incident.*

Naggy had hit the proverbial nail on the head on his current emotional state.

"Just spell the bottle for unity. That's what you want, right? For your witch boys to get together again? Tell me—

I've heard rumours—is it true you do all your coven gatherings naked?" Naggy leered at Sparks with a lewd grin plastered on his face.

"Oh my Gods, Naggy, you're incorrigible. No. I mean… just…how much for the bottle?" The heat from Sparks's face raced to the top of his scalp. He would have sworn his hair had been lit on fire.

"Fifty-six dollars, eighty-nine cents."

"What?" Sparks's jaw dropped.

"I told you the wine comes from a special winery."

"You're the worst." Sparks handed over three twenties, snatched the bottle, stuffed his purchase into his backpack, and walked out of the store. As he glanced back, Naggy, already ringing up another customer, peeked at Sparks, smiled, and winked.

THE WINE SAT on Sparks's busy and cluttered counter. Unattended mail, this morning's breakfast dishes, and jars filled with questionable witchy contents left little room for the prized purchase for tonight's dinner. He leaned against the other side of his galley-style kitchen, eyeing the bottle and focusing on the diamond augmenter area.

"I shouldn't do this," he mumbled, shaking his head. "Nope, it's wrong."

His long, dirty-blond hair—the envy of everyone—waved in time with his head motions.

Sparks pushed off the counter and left the kitchen while pulling off his tank top. He pitched the sweaty garment into his room as he passed, then stopped and stripped off his shorts. He didn't wear underwear. The shorts ended up in a pile on the floor near his tank top.

He took a few more steps down the hall, flicked on the bathroom light as he entered the small room, grabbed the towel hanging from a hook on the back of the door, and threw it near the base of the shower. He opened the shower stall and turned the faucet toward the *H* so the water would be scalding hot for a nice, long wash.

Sparks intended on getting properly attired for this evening. Hopefully, the guys would notice he had put some effort into their dinner meeting.

As steam billowed out of the shower stall and fogged up the bathroom, Sparks turned the exhaust fan on, then stared at the droplet-laden mirror—which wasn't reflecting anything from all the steam—and drew a simple rune on the flat surface.

Laguz.

It looked like an upside-down *L*.

Sparks stood a few steps away and studied the symbol. *Laguz* meant a number of things, but imagination, psychic powers, and dreams were the more standard intentions used with the rune.

But the rune also stood for unity. The collective memory of a group of people. Like a coven.

Sparks mashed his lips together and furrowed his brow. With a swipe of his hand, he obliterated the steam on the mirror and the symbol along with it.

He jerked open the shower stall door and stepped in.

Hot water scalded his freckled shoulders, burning away some anxiety. He inhaled the clouds of steam, trying to de-stress.

With closed eyes, Sparks remained motionless, allowing the water to cascade over him, and waited for the heat to melt away his worry.

The white noise of droplets splashing up against the walls of the enclosure, the drips falling from collected water on the shower rack, and the gurgle of liquid swirling down the drain made the world stop, if only briefly…

Sparks yanked the shower door open and bolted, naked and dripping wet, down the hall, into the kitchen. He snapped up the bottle and drew *Laguz* in the augmentation receptacle. Pulling forth his natural element, thinking about the last thunderstorm he had stood out in, getting soaked while watching the lightning bolts streak across the sky—which always triggered his abilities—he uttered the word as the symbol glowed silver.

"Laguz." Sparks spoke with confidence and a stiff set spine and squared off shoulders. Bolts of electricity erupted and travelled from the base of his neck, across his shoulders, and danced down his arm and through his fingers until the current lit up the rune. Electricity hummed as arcs of jagged, forked energy encircled the bottle.

The wine bottle tilted slightly, wobbled back and forth, and finally righted itself.

Sparks squinted as the bottle settled, ignoring the dripping water from his body which had created a fair-sized puddle on the linoleum.

The wine had been magicked. No taking the spell back now.

AN HOUR LATER, he stood outside a monstrous old house located in the heart of the Old Strathcona neighbourhood, close to the University of Alberta. Everyone in the magical community called the sprawling mansion "old Uncle Bart's house." Sparks had met the man several times. Uncle Bart, a sweetheart of a gentleman, always came to the party with loads of stories. Tully's family held a prestigious position in the community and were something of an institution in Edmonton. Most of the male witches from his lineage had, at one point or another, been part of the most well-known, all-male coven in the city.

The Guardians of the Night Grove had been responsible for ensuring the magical energy within Edmonton and the surrounding vicinity was regulated in order to prevent the darker elements within the Shadow Realm from gaining too much power. Since the infamous night a few months ago, with the Night Grove's current high priest hospitalized and presumably dead within a year from a werewolf infection, Sparks assumed the coven had been dissolved. There had been no continuance, no calls, and no plans for succession. Nothing.

No high priest to lead them.

No knights being promoted to fill the spaces Eddie and Gus had held. Sparks's memory of shovelling up Eddie's intestines had not been a pleasant one. The grating sound of the shovel's blade against the concrete basement floor and the wet *slush* of the organs as they slipped into the garden tool had haunted his dreams ever since.

Despite the horror he'd dealt with, he would have done anything for Dev and Tully. Most people would have agreed Sparks had fulfilled any obligation potentially owing to the two men.

But after becoming Dev Khandelwal's blood brother during his initiation into the Shadow Realm, a bond formed. A tie that went so deep the physical distance between himself and his Shadow Brother caused sleepless nights, aimless wanderings, and wayward magic. The lack of grounding Sparks normally gained from a simple meditation, along with the other symptoms were all telltale signs he needed connection. He missed his people. The camaraderie of the coven had always made him feel safe, connected with a sense of belonging. The last couple of months he'd spent most of his spare time alone.

And Sparks hated being alone.

But Dev exuded a mysterious special magical energy. Sparks had sensed a deeper attachment to the man in his bones. Dev had a bigger role to play in his life. The vibrating excitement, like a cellist plucking a bass string, ran through his bones, prompting Sparks to step up during Dev's initiation into the Realm. They were tied together, linked, but Sparks struggled to define why. Then disaster had happened, and he hadn't had any time to figure out what made Dev so special.

Then there was the bear of a man, Tully. Before Dev had shown up, he and Tully had been assigned homework and spell craft tasks from their ex-high priest. Sparks recalled only the best of memories. Tully made him laugh, and together, anything Sparks and Tully set out to do never weighed on them like a chore. They were so in sync other coven members commented on the uncanny way their work melded so well. Even their magic weaved together albeit in an unconventional pairing; metal and lightning—truly an odd couple.

The coven had been home. But Tully and Dev had made an indelible impression on Sparks. Like a tattoo, his relationship with them had created a deep, enduring mark that anticipated years of witch holidays, coven meetings, and spellworking spent together. But after that night—*the incident*—there had been nothing.

Byron had gone and messed up everything.

Sparks yearned for their continued work within the supernatural community.

So he had taken the task upon himself and called Dev and his musclebound redheaded boyfriend, and fellow brother, Tully, and asked if they would be up for a dinner. Sparks needed to start up the coven again.

Maybe not the Guardians, but something. Anything. Something to fill the magical hole left in his heart. He clutched the bespelled bottle of wine, still uncertain if enchanting the wine had been the right thing to do. His knuckles were white, and his palms were sweaty.

Sparks had hoped the guys would meet him for a coffee or drinks.

He had literally jumped with nervous excitement when both of them had enthusiastically agreed to meet and, in fact, offered to cook, inviting Sparks over to their home for dinner.

He rang the doorbell, again, and chewed on his bottom lip while his hands—and everything else—continued to perspire. He had also bought a monstrous bouquet of late-season flowers. Massive white spider asters were clumped together with vibrant yellow calla lilies, all punctuated by shocking red sprays of celosia. The flowers had cost him a pretty penny, but he wanted to make a good impression. He glanced down at the bottle.

He shouldn't have spelled the wine. Should he take it upstairs?

Or should he leave the damn thing in the empty baskets the boys left on the porch? Spelling your friends—such a no-no. Maybe the basket would de-spell the wine? The wicker containers were a common feature outside witch homes. Custom dictated anyone who entered the threshold should leave their troubles and worries in the offered receptacle. The wind would blow all the troubles away.

Maybe between the wind and the basket, the spell would be blown away.

Sparks hoisted the bottle up so he could look at it. Maybe the spell wasn't so bad.

Besides, he'd spared no expense on this purchase to make a good impression. He wanted to convince the guys that starting up a coven was the right thing to do.

Grasping the wine tighter, Sparks flipped his wrist to look at the time. He had arrived a tad early. Despite his premature appearance at the boys' front door, the wait for someone to answer seemed long, like he'd been standing on the stoop for an hour.

Maybe they don't want to see me.

The heat was unusual for the end of August. Rivulets of sweat ran down his spine despite the loose-fitting linen shirt he wore. Even with a few buttons opened in the front, the lack of an evening breeze made the air close and his skin sticky. He'd even put his hair up and used his favourite hair fork engraved with runes. A solitary amethyst had been embedded into the wood at the bend of the tool—his birthstone—but with the sheer volume of hair Sparks had grown out over many years, the late summer heat still clung to him like a desperate lover.

Maybe it's nerves too.

The time he'd spent on the front porch of the rambling old mansion winnowed away his confidence.

With knots of disappointment in his gut, having rung the bell twice, Sparks turned away from the front door. Bursts of static electricity danced across his skin—something that happened when his emotions ran high.

Complicated emotions.

Disappointment, need, emptiness, longing to—

"Sparks?" Lost in his own negativity, Sparks hadn't noticed the door open. He spun toward the voice, coming face to face with Tully and his beaming ear-to-ear grin. His mop of wavy red hair had recently been trimmed, but his beard had grown out. A tight white tee stretched across his chest, displaying his enormous stature, and a robin's-egg-blue pair of shorts spoke of the August temperatures. "We thought we heard something down here, but I probably forgot to mention the doorbell doesn't work."

Instant relief.

"No, well, if you did, I didn't remember. Ha!" He grinned awkwardly.

"It's been forever. Come on upstairs. Dev is setting the table." Tully threw his arm around Sparks's shoulder and led him inside, which was a bit of a feat as the entrance and foyer were close quarters. Tully never took into account another person's space, much like Naggy, but the moment Tully's bearish arm wrapped around Sparks, all his twisted emotions smoothed out, righting his head.

"It's been too long, Tully. I miss everyone."

"Yeah. I know. Us too. Come on. Are those for us?" Tully pointed to the flowers and wine Sparks still had in a death grip.

"I wanted to show you how much I appreciate the invitation."

"These are beautiful! Dev's gonna love them."

They ascended to the second-floor apartment. Sparks had been here before, and knew the territory, but hadn't visited since Dev and Tully had become an item. From the moment Sparks had met Dev and seen him interact with Tully, he conjectured the two would end up together. Through their sporadic electronic communication, he had found out the two had moved in.

Tully swung open the front door to the apartment. "Look who's here!" Tully's grin continued. Sparks had rarely seen him without a smile. The man epitomized optimism.

"Sparks!" Dev, wearing tight beige shorts and an equally snug-fitting maroon tank top, dropped the cutlery he held to set the table and grabbed Sparks by the shoulders, then pulled him in close, and embraced him tightly.

Sparks sighed as he sank into the gesture.

"Look what he brought." Tully held up the massive bouquet.

"Wow, those are gorgeous. You didn't have to go to the trouble."

"I wanted to. I've missed you guys so bad."

"These need to go in water. This heat has been unbearable." Dev released his bear hug on Sparks, walked over to the row of kitchen cabinets, pulled open a cupboard, and fished out a vase large enough to accommodate the flower stems. Tully handed him the bouquet. Dev spent the next few minutes removing the floral paper and arranging the blooms so the gift appeared as amazing and impressive as Sparks had intended.

"I brought wine too. But now that I'm here, and it's so damn hot, I don't think red wine fits the bill for an overheated August night. Cold beer would have been better." Sparks's cheeks reddened while thinking about his beverage selection—and what he'd done to it—as he pulled out a stool from the kitchen island and had a seat.

"Nonsense." Tully accepted the bottle and turned the wine, studying the label. "Oh, nice choice. Dev, isn't this the same wine we had at that river restaurant—what was it called—Riverside Bistro? You know, the one we went to on our three-month anniversary dinner?"

"You guys are not seriously doing the monthly anniversaries, are you?" Sparks chided them.

"Damn right we are," Dev replied, setting the flower vase on the table, but off centred so when the three sat down for supper, the flowers would be a centrepiece and not an obstacle.

"Good for you." Sparks chuckled.

"Well, our first week together was traumatic, and I promised Dev I would make it up to him. I wanted to show him that being a witch and part of the Shadow Realm wasn't all blood, death, and destruction." Tully stared at Sparks with a bit of a goofy face, which made him laugh. Sparks appreciated the effort of trying to make light of the night where Byron had almost died trying to save his werewolf-infected lover, Addas. They'd lost Gus and Eddie.

Sparks's nightmares had subsided to one or two a week after being called in to clean up the mess.

"And we owe you an apology, and something cold to drink. We are definitely drinking the wine with dinner. What would you like? A beer, a spritzer, or I think we have some chilled Perrier." Tully placed the spelled wine on the table.

"A beer would be great. And an apology for what?"

"Really?" Dev shot Sparks a side-eye glance over his shoulder while opening the fridge and pulling out a cold bottle of brew. He popped the cap and set the beer down in front of his guest. "We were part of a night of carnage that we called you in to help out with, and it's been almost four months since, and we haven't got together until now? That's what the apology is for."

Sparks waved his hand, dismissing Dev, and took a long swig from the bottle. The chilled hoppy beverage numbed his throat. It had a deep grainy taste to it with just the right amount of sweetness.

"No, seriously, Dev is right. We've been awful, and when you called, Dev and I immediately wanted to have you over. It's been—"

"I get it. You don't have to apologize. After scrubbing up as much blood and guts as I did, I expected you to take some time to recover. But truthfully, I've been terribly out of sorts. My whole life revolved around the coven. I had placed a lot of loyalty in Byron, like many of the others had. I just...I'm..." Sparks put his head in his hands. "I'm struggling without everyone. My abilities are a mess. Working in a hospital when your electrokinesis is being wonky is not a good thing. I've had a few near misses with people seeing things they shouldn't. Not to mention a few close calls with patients' heart monitors and the dialysis machines. I'm an incoming hurricane capable of erupting into a wild electrical storm at a moment's notice."

Tully grabbed a seat next to Sparks and put his arm around his shoulder, again. Sparks leaned into it. He needed the comfort. He needed his brothers.

Dev quit fussing with the dinner they'd prepared and leaned in close to Sparks and his boyfriend. "I forgot you worked in the hospital. Have you seen *him*?"

Sparks nodded and grimaced.

"Damn, I don't know what I would do if I saw him. I'm still upset with how everything went down."

Sparks let out a huge breath. "He looks like he's hurting though. Physically for sure. Those were werewolf wounds.

I've seen them before." Sparks shuddered but noticed the side-eye glance between Dev and Tully—as if they were having a private conversation between them. "But his face is drawn. I think he's emotionally a wreck too. I can only assume Byron had some kind of participation in that night's events when Eddie and Gus were mauled. And I'm gonna assume Addas was the culprit—I mean, come on, we all knew, right?"

Dev and Tully were quiet.

The timer went off on the oven.

Sparks had literally been saved by a bell.

"Come on, let's eat." Dev changed the topic.

The three sat around a magnificently decorated table, dominated by Sparks's floral contribution. Dinner went smoothly as the topic of conversation revolved around how their magical lives weren't the same without the group of guys. Mabon, the next holiday in the yearly cycle, wasn't for another month. The celebration of the harvest might be the perfect opportunity to invite some of the guys over and perhaps rekindle some semblance of what they had created within the Guardians of the Night Grove.

Tully popped the cork on the wine and poured everyone a glass. The platters of food Dev and Tully had prepared were passed around. Sparks ended up with a monstrous plateful of smoky BBQ chicken, grilled asparagus drizzled in garlic butter and lime juice, a fresh-from-the-garden spring salad, and a homemade dinner roll. Not to mention a generous helping of potato salad. Sparks squirted some mustard on it. The tangy yellow sauce added an extra punch which pushed the summertime picnic favourite into being one of Sparks's preferred salads.

When everyone was ready to tuck into their dinner, Tully raised his glass.

"A toast. To brothers. Let it not be this long again before sharing our homes with each other."

"Cheers!" Sparks said. The three raised their glasses, filled with the spelled wine, and clinked the vessels together.

As the edges of the glasses connected, jolts of energy blossomed from the contact and travelled through to each of the men's hands, gently biting them with a static shock.

Tully laughed. "You are out of sorts, aren't you?"

Dev's mouth twitched up in a silly half grin.

Sparks tensed, reliving his guilt and horror knowing the spelled wine was about to set in. He bit his bottom lip then mumbled, "Sorry."

"Nonsense. I totally get it." Tully took a sip from his glass, closed his eyes, and let out a hum of appreciation. "Damn, that is good."

AS SPARKS ATE the last bite of the frozen berry dessert Tully had made, he rubbed his belly, leaned back in his chair, and stared at his hosts.

"So, whaddya think? Should we? I mean, rustling together a ceremony so quickly is tough. You can't do Mabon on the spur of the moment. We'd have to see if the others would be interested and plan out an appropriate ritual together."

"True, although I'd expect they'd jump at the chance."

"Well, I know Wiatt would be in, I've talked to him on and off." Wiatt was Sparks's necromancer brother. "He's been hiding out in his basement, playing with his dead things. Honestly, he needs human interaction. And I'm not being mean, even he'll tell you the same thing. So, I know that's at least one more."

"I say we invite everyone. After all, the old guard from the Guardians are either dead, missing, or convalescing in the hospital. I think it would be good to bring the boys back together again." Tully cocked his head as he stared at Dev.

"But you don't have the history of the coven brotherhood like Sparks and I did with everyone else. What do you think?" He leaned across the table and grabbed his lover's hand, gently squeezing it. "I know how you feel."

Dev rolled his eyes. "I suppose you're right. I only had a night with everyone. It would be good to see them again." He glanced at Sparks. "He keeps regaling me with stories, but I'd kind of like to get to know all the guys."

"Well, I think we're safe inviting them. I can't possibly fathom any of the others having involvement in Byron's scheme—except for Eddie and Gus. They were his right-hand men and well, those are all empty positions now." Tully spooned in the last bite of his dessert after he'd spoken. Sparks squinted, confused about a mention of a "scheme," but let the words go.

"Where would we celebrate? It's far too small here for all the guys," Dev said.

"Why not at the coven house? All the supplies are there." Sparks canted his head to one side.

"I don't know." Dev scrunched his eyebrows together. "I mean, that's *his* house."

"Technically, it's the Guardians of the Night Grove's. Byron and Addas got to live there. All the books, robes, and witchy stuff belongs to the coven, not Byron."

"Wouldn't waltzing into their house be trespassing? Would kind of feel like it. Besides, the energy of the whole place..." Dev frowned, clearly not happy about this decision.

"Trespassing? Not at all. Sparks and I are both coven brothers. Coven property is communal, making the space and all the resources just as much ours as his. But I completely agree about the vibe."

"You know, if you want, I'll ask Byron since you're worried about using the house." Sparks offered, although as soon as he spoke, he immediately regretted it.

A palpable tension filled the space between Tully, Dev, and Sparks.

"You know what, screw him. He fooled us and used us. He tricked everyone into drinking dead fae. I say we use the space and anything else we need and bring the guys together. The coven doesn't belong to Byron. We are as much part of that house as he is." Tully raised his wineglass and bobbed his head once, reaffirming his statement.

"Hold up. Drink what now?" Sparks wasn't about to let the last statement go without an explanation. He glared at Tully.

"Oh shit. Yeah...I guess there's a few things you don't know." Tully grimaced as he looked at Dev. "This is another reason why we owe you an apology. We discovered some stuff...things Byron had done, and we should have told you and everyone else. Remember the bubbly green juice Byron used to pull out on special occasions, and after we all drank some of it, we were all, like, super-witchy? That fluid came from the spinal column of fae. Byron captured them and used them in experiments to try and fix Addas."

"Shut. The. Fuck. Up. Fix Addas, you mean...trying to undo the werewolf infection?" Sparks's mind flipped, doing mental leaps trying to piece everything together. The guys had never told him the whole story.

"Yeah. So, again, sorry. We should have told you all this a long time ago. Everything happened so fast, and afterward I didn't want to revisit any of it." Dev glanced at his empty dinner plate. "Which wasn't fair to you."

"No, I get it. After cleaning up that mess? Dev, I didn't know exactly what had happened but judging from the gore—well, clearly the night had been a rough one. I hoped you guys would eventually tell me. But we're bonded brothers—I would do anything for either of you. No questions asked. But you gotta tell me now. What the hell happened?" Sparks honestly didn't hold a single judgement against his witch brothers. Sometimes they got called in to do things ordinary humans would never face. The Shadow Realm could be glorious, but it could be ferocious.

"So, long story, short version? I think we all knew Addas had been bitten by a werewolf. No adult male grows six inches taller in the course of a year unless…" As Tully uttered the confession, Sparks nodded his agreement and rolled his eyes. Addas's infection was the worst-kept coven secret, despite Byron trying to hide it. "Dev and his bestie, Cam, used the summoning board the coven had created—remember those? They used Desires, and the ritual catapulted Dev toward the Shadow Realm. He was bound to get here, but the use of the board quickened the pace. Unfortunately, Cam ended up on the wrong side of his wishes."

"That was the board we fused a Djinn into, wasn't it?"

"Yeah, that one."

"Someone made a wish…didn't they?" Sparks frowned. "I knew those boards were a bad idea. The whole idea—binding a creature to the board. Sketchy shit."

"Yup. Both Dev and Cam made wishes. But Cam got the short end. He turned into fae. Byron captured him and used Cam's newly formed body in experiments and extracted his spinal fluid—apparently fae juice has properties—and we've all drunk a little of Cam. Which means we all have fae in us." Tully half grinned, again, trying to make light of the situation.

"Oh my Gods, and once touched by the fae…" Sparks started.

"You're never quite the same ever again." Tully completed the thought. "So, we're witch-fae. Addas imbibed the goo, too, so with the infection—"

"Holy shit. He's witch-werewolf-fae!" Sparks sat there shocked at all this new information. "Do you think he survived his transformation?"

"Wouldn't surprise me if he did, but we have no proof either way. Just a set of paw prints leading away from the house. I mean, who knows?" Dev raised both eyebrows and twisted in his chair, obviously uncomfortable. "I can't begin to tell you how many times we both said, 'We need to call the guys.' But how do you even start that conversation?"

"Wow." Sparks took the last sip of his wine. "Well now, that puts a whole new spin on Byron. I mean, who would torture other living creatures?" He glanced at Tully. "I don't know. Maybe we shouldn't use the Night Grove's witch things. Now the thought of anything from that night seems tainted."

"True. There's some bad mojo. Maybe we should leave it all behind." Tully's continual optimism waned as the statement sat heavy on the table before them, a rare instance where Sparks witnessed Tully in such a state. "But there are things at the coven house that would be useful, and a few items there are mine...or belong to my family."

"We should get them," Sparks replied with a devilish grin.

"Sorta feels like stealing, no?" Dev pinched his eyebrows together.

"Hardly stealing if it's ours." Tully grabbed his boyfriend's hand. "It would only take a few minutes. Sparks and I could go, gather the things that belong to us, and I can think of a couple of other items the guys might want. Then I think we call it quits on the Night Grove."

"Should we strike up our own coven?" Sparks cocked an eyebrow and sat up straight, filled with excitement.

"Oh, I do like that." With his other hand, Tully placed a bearish mitt on Sparks's shoulder. "And you never got the chance to be inducted into the coven either. Whaddya say, Dev? Our own all-boys group?" He squeezed Dev's hand.

The conversation made Sparks's heart happy.

"I think we need to declare a new high priest." Tully let go of Dev but locked his gaze on him as he emptied his wineglass in one gulp. He picked up the bottle and poured what remained into everyone's glass. "Whaddya say, boys? Time to reunite the guys but under a whole new coven?"

Sparks tried his hardest to suppress his giddiness. His hopes had manifested themselves. Damn Naggy and his special bottle of wine. Who would have guessed the evening would have worked out so brilliantly.

Chapter Three

DEV CLOSED THE door to the apartment as Sparks left for the evening. After a few drinks and a couple of bottles of wine, he was a tad tipsy, but feeling happy.

"So, what do you think?" Tully asked while putting the used dinnerware into the dishwasher.

"I think we waited too long to have him over and tell him the truth about what happened. I like Sparks. We shouldn't have kept him in the dark for so long. For that matter, the rest of the guys from the Night Grove need to know too."

"Former Night Grove."

"Agreed. Not saying anything for so long hasn't set well with me. Sparks is such a good guy and genuinely seemed pleased with your suggestion of starting something new. I won't lie, I'm intrigued too." Dev smiled at his lover, his persistently optimistic, always smiling, gorgeous redheaded lover.

"Good. We should invite him over again next week in order to plan for the holiday. A ritual will take some coordination, lots of phone calls to arrange everything, not to mention getting the rest of the guys on board—not that I think we'll have a problem there. I still think we need to go over to Byron's place and retrieve what belongs to us." Tully's last statement immediately shifted Dev's mood.

"I have no desire to go over there. I don't care if I set foot in that house ever again. I've had my fill of Byron Radcliffe. I never want to see him again."

Tully let out a sigh and gave his boyfriend a slight frown. "Hanging on to all this resentment isn't going to do you any favours. You know, Edmonton isn't all that big, and the supernatural community is a pretty tight-knit group of folks. You're bound to cross paths again."

Dev stared at Tully with a cockeyed sneer. "I know, I know. I need to let go of all this negativity. It just feels like Byron tainted something I'd been chasing all my life. I finally found the Shadow Realm, and you, and magic, and he went and ruined everything."

Tully pushed the door shut to the dishwasher, wiped his hands on the tea towel, and set the rag on the counter, then moseyed over to his boyfriend and wrapped his giant arms around him, snuggling in. "Well, I hope not everything." Tully's grin held a wicked edge. "I know he kind of wrecked a part of the Shadow Realm for you, and I'm sorry about what happened. But I'm trying my best to make up for it. We're not all like Byron." Tully nibbled on Dev's ear.

Dev shivered as Tully's tongue licked his neck.

"Stop it. You're bad."

"The worst."

Tully slid his hand down the back of Dev's shorts and gabbed a handful of furry butt cheek. "I promise I will make it all up to you."

"You already have." Dev nuzzled into Tully's beard.

"I think Sparks would like to make it up to you too." Tully continued to hold tight onto Dev.

Dev pulled away. "What do you mean?"

Tully mimicked Dev's action so he was face to face with Dev. "You mean to tell me you didn't pick up on his—how shall we say—overenthusiastic interest?"

"You're crazy. Or perhaps overly horny?" Dev arched an eyebrow.

"No, seriously. You didn't think so? I mean, the wine, the flowers..." Tully lost the mischievous undertone and seriously questioned Dev.

"I really don't think so."

"Huh, well, maybe I've got it wrong. I don't know, I thought maybe some sexual tension sparked across the dinner table."

"You just want to get him in bed." Dev snickered.

"Well, that wouldn't be horrible."

"Really? Wouldn't sex make the coven a little...uncomfortable?"

"Why?"

"Sleeping with someone who you're also doing magic work with?"

"Ah, my baby witch." Tully laughed.

"What?"

"It's not uncommon, especially in all-male covens. I mean, it's not like sex is rampant, but celebration of sex and sexuality certainly is. And so long as everyone is consenting, in agreement, then where's the harm? I mean, we're all adults, right? And it's only sex."

"I still haven't wrapped my head around the nudity thing, and now you're telling me all-male covens are basically orgies."

"I didn't say orgies. Sex is a natural part of life. I can tell this still makes you uneasy. We need to work on you being more comfortable in your own skin. You are beautiful, Dev. Celebrate your body!"

"So, you want to?"

"What, have sex with Sparks? Ah, have you seen him? Don't you?" Tully teased.

"Well, he's good-looking, sure...but I have you. I don't need good-looking." Dev squirmed, being held fast by Tully.

"Granted, he's smarter than I am. You could have brains and beauty all at once."

"That's not what I mean." Dev glared at Tully. Not mad, but slightly uncomfortable at where the conversation was headed. But with Tully's close proximity and the salacious topic of discussion, Dev wouldn't be able to deny the prospect of all three of them didn't excite him, judging from the stiffening occurring down below. After all, he'd never had a threesome.

"I know. I'm teasing you. And I'm enjoying it thoroughly." Tully chortled. "And I can tell from the tent in your shorts you also think it's kind of naughty. And I know you like naughty!" He reached down and grabbed Dev's erection and squeezed him gently. He gave Dev a kiss.

"You are a monster."

"Nope. Not me. That's your best friend's boyfriend. He's the monster. And as I remember, Cam wished for a monster boyfriend, not me. I've got you, and you're perfect."

"Sparks, huh?" Dev returned the kiss.

"Listen, if the situation presents itself, then sure. I won't say no. But don't think I haven't forgotten our last conversation on this. You have to be comfortable with whatever relationship arrangement we construct. And whatever you decide is okay with me."

"Well, he is kinda cute."

"There's my witchy-poo revelling in sex! Honestly, it's all about having fun and feeling good. Nobody wants friendships to be weird or get complicated."

"I don't know if I'm ever gonna get used to this."

"I told you. The world of the male witch is sexy."

"Yes. You mentioned. I'm starting to see how much of that is true."

"Well, given what happened this year, we missed Beltane. If we have a new coven next year, I promise nothing but flowing wine and sex parties."

"I take it back. You're not a monster, you're a sex fiend."

Tully roared. "I'll take it."

While still firmly gripped in Tully's strong arms, Dev attempted to switch gears. "So, forming a new coven. Sounds like work."

"Not as much work as I'm about to put you through." Clearly, shifting Tully's focus wasn't going to work. The corner of Dev's mouth raised in the beginning of a sly grin. He relaxed into Tully's muscled arms.

"Oh, do tell." The heat from Tully's hand still massaging his crotch had grown Dev's excitement into a rock-hard attention.

"I'd much rather show." And with a thrust, Dev got hoisted off the ground and thrown over his boyfriend's shoulder. Dev giggled as Tully carried him down the hallway toward the bedroom.

The ensuing show lasted a couple of hours and proved to be spectacular.

AS THE LAST rays of daylight beamed through the dense foliage of the Ancestral Lands, the thick overhead canopy shone a magnificent lime green while the shadows beneath the sacred grove grew long. An odd branch on every other tree began to show signs of autumn. The green vegetation had begun its transition from summer brilliance to the tawny colours of fall. The change of seasons had started, if only in its infancy.

Everton Lilch raised his brown wet nose and inhaled the drifting scents in the twilight's breeze. He retracted his lips and exposed a row of dangerous teeth. His tongue lashed out as if tasting the appetizing odours.

The heat of the August sun, descending in the twilight sky, burned. The forest floor, littered with a dusting of shed leaves no longer able to withstand the searing temperatures, crunched and crackled under the weight of his monstrous body. Ev restrained from panting as the noise would give him away.

This deep in the forest, escaping the pungency of the woodland wasn't possible. From the damp moss covering the north side of the gnarled bark of the coniferous trees to the sweet smell of decaying vegetation and the loamy rich fragrance of the earth, the scents almost overwhelmed Ev.

But nestled in among all those calming aromatics one unmistakable trace rose above all others, reminiscent of an afternoon spent in a spring garden. Ev detected fresh cut grass, clean water, crisp leaves, and the rich, heady balm of patchouli and mint. The odour was excitement. The scent was fresh.

It was Cam Habersham.

The newly formed fae brought back memories of carefree weekend afternoons where there were no chores, life relaxed and slowed, and the day held all sorts of lazy pleasurable possibilities. Everton licked his chops again, let his tongue hang loose as he huffed in the air around him, absorbing as much of Cam's scent as possible.

Their initial introduction hadn't been optimal. But after being rescued and freed by the witch boys, Ev was surprised they had helped Cam find his people. Ev had followed them, not wanting to be too far from Cam. He had promised the fae one night in heaven for getting him free from the Coven of the Night Grove's dungeon. Cam and his witches had made good on their vow. And good witches who kept their word meant Ev also needed to re-examine his stance on the magic slingers.

The Coven of the Night Grove had been his pack's sole enemy for so long that when Ev took over the alpha role from the former leader, he'd absorbed all the old traditions and beliefs. The most deeply held tenet stipulated all witches were to be destroyed. And he followed through on that course of action at every chance he got. Now, however, with the Night Grove no longer in existence, and having been assisted by a small group of the human magicians, he had reason to question his motivations and previous teachings.

Dev Khandelwal and Toliver Mack had proven to be the exact opposite of Byron Radcliffe and his goons. Cam's faith in his friends had been accurate. And Ev now needed to make good on his end of the deal. One night in heaven for Cam meant a rollicking good time. A one-night stand. A hook-up.

But despite a silly promise made in the desperate attempt to bargain freedom, Ev had the opportunity and time to study Cam and get to know him.

The young man was brash, ridiculous, and clever as hell. Outlandish and fabulous every waking moment.

He was also the most stunning creature Ev had laid eyes on. Ev had fantasized on how he would position him, grasping his horns, ensuring Cam's tail wrapped around certain furry bits. So many positions. So many fantasies.

But the more time Ev spent with Cam, the more he wanted the horned and winged fae. One night spent in the throes of ecstasy would never be enough to satisfy the desires he harboured.

And yet, despite his yearning for Cam, he hadn't mustered the gumption to follow through.

After one taste of Cam, he'd want more, and more, and more. And given Cam's promiscuous nature and dating history, he concluded Cam would never give him more than a single night of pleasure. And one encounter simply wouldn't satiate Ev's needs.

It was easier to sit here, at a short distance, and torture himself with the deliciousness Cam exuded, than potentially risk being devastated by rejection. Ev believed wholeheartedly Cam would have laughed him out the door should he have asked for more than what had been promised.

So he kept his emotional distance and, to some extent, a physical distance as well.

But desires are funny things. They kept pulling him in closer, wanting to see the fae, needing to touch him and stroke his glorious membranous wings. Ev craved the bony and ridged feel of the strong curve of Cam's great horns.

Tantalizing images that some may have deemed taboo dominated his daydreams. His fascination with the fae wasn't a first-time thing. There'd been others like Cam, and his packmates were less than approving. But nothing compared to Cam.

And it's not like a potential mating would produce baby werewolf-fae. It's not like they had to be worried about offspring, but even still, an alpha in charge of the most well-known witch-exterminating wolf pack in Western Canada connected romantically to one of the fae? Impossible. Unbelievable.

Certainly not respectable.

As the alpha, he'd never be challenged on who he chose as a mate, or even who he selected as a sexual partner, but there would be whispers. And whispers would lead to dissent. And dissent signalled a lack of respect had wormed itself into the pack. And if that happened, he'd lose control of his wolves.

Everton lay his head on his paws and whined while watching Cam and his tutor, Sen, as they practiced fae magic in the sacred grove of the Ancestral Lands.

Cam was everything. The Royal fae made his heart sing, and yet, Ev saw no future with him.

And so, he remained hidden in the dense underbrush. Watching the Eldritch creature with an intensity he normally reserved for prey made him long for Cam even more. Ev's ears twitched as he listened.

"No, Cam. Honestly, did you not study the scrolls I gave you? They were very precise. You should have this perfected by now. You're running out of time."

"Not helping, Sen. Not. Helping." Cam's face portrayed his utter disdain for his manservant.

"Watch. It's simple." Sen's long sinewy body reminded Everton of a thin sapling. His limbs were taut and thin. Even his fingers seemed impossibly long. The tone of his skin reminded Ev of the light bark of an ash tree. "Breathe in, hold your breath, and then imagine disappearing into the shadows. Watch." A lock of Sen's bright-red hair fell in front of his eyes, and he made an exaggerated gesture while filling his lungs. Sen closed his eyes, and before Ev squinted and leaned in closer to study the sinewy creature, the tree sprite melded into the recesses of the twilight's oncoming darkness.

"Easy for you to do!" Cam sneered as he mumbled under his breath.

From within the shadowy alcove of a giant elm, a disembodied voice spoke, "I've melded into the shadows Cam, not transported myself to Japan. I can still hear you."

In a heartbeat, Sen reappeared as gracefully as he had disappeared.

"This is a giant waste of time. I'm never going to get this."

"It is a skill that may save your life one day. What would happen if human hunters found their way here? You can't appear as you do now to them, and you haven't mastered your human illusion yet. This is the next best option."

"I thought you said Lady Aine had ensured this place would never be found by humans? So why would I need to learn this?"

Sen put his long fingers over his face and pulled his hand down. His eyelids stretched, and his lips extended with the yank from his fingers. Cam frustrated the creature. Understandably though. Cam wasn't being cooperative.

Ev snorted. He agreed with Sen—Cam did need to learn these skills. Watching the banter between the two amused Ev. He stretched out a bit, his hindquarters cramped. The confines of the hollow he had found were becoming uncomfortable for his large, furry wolfen limbs.

A branch snapped.

Sen's head twisted toward the noise, and he sniffed the air.

The Japanese tree sprite's face furrowed as he grimaced. His eyes turned red, and his teeth sharpened to points as his lips drew into a snarl. The creature bent into a battle stance, his head bobbed in several directions, and his pointy ears twitched. Sen took a cautious step toward where Ev lay hidden.

Cam, eyes wide, unaware of the present danger, backed up against a tree.

Sen sniffed the air again, then relaxed his stance. He returned to his usual harmless-looking self. He frowned. "Your boyfriend is spying on us."

"What?"

"I give up. If he's here, we're not going to get anything done." And with that, Sen turned and leaped, disappearing into the branches of the trees. A few leaves fluttered down as Sen retreated to the village on his aerial escape.

"Ev? You there?" Cam called out.

There was no point in hiding anymore. Ev dug his paws into the soft soil and pulled himself out from under a fallen log that had created a hollow, hidden by the underbrush. He stood erect on his hind legs, towering seven foot four, muscular and furred. Anyone other than Cam may have shrunk away from the beast.

"What are you doing?" Cam flung his arms out to his side. Ev smelled a mixture of arousal and annoyance. "Interrupting Sen from one of his instructional lessons will have pissed him off to no end. I'm going to hear about this later." Cam rolled his eyes, then glanced up at the immense monster. "Quit trying to be imposing. And you're slobbering. Stop it." He walked a few paces toward the frightful creature.

Ev dropped onto all fours, then vigorously shook his fur out. Twigs and dirt flew in all directions. Cam halted his steps and lifted an arm to protect his face from the assault of dirt and debris.

Maintaining his wolf form now would be silly, and having a human conversation wasn't possible. Wolf tongues do not speak human words. Thinking of his bipedal self, Ev pulled up his memories of humanity, and with bone snapping quickness, the wolf disappeared, and Everton the monster-sized human stood in front of Cam.

"Hey."

"Hey, yourself. You spying on me?"

"No." Although he had been doing exactly that.

"Hmph." Cam gave him a suspicious look. "Sure seems like it." Cam's gaze wandered over Ev's naked body, which produced a feeling of pride. He liked his body. He puffed out his chest and allowed the visual exploration. Transforming from wolf to human didn't involve any clothes, and this deep into the Ancestral Lands, Ev hadn't stashed any, so he stood before Cam exposed. But after having been a werewolf for several decades, one got used to being nude in front of others. Cam's wings bent to a strange angle, which Ev interpreted as him attempting to be coy and flirtatious. "You're looking good."

"Ah, thanks." Despite his comfort with his nudity, the compliment stoked heat which rushed across Ev's collarbones and up into his cheeks. He never understood how others were comfortable with praise. He would have much rather Cam touch him instead.

"So...?" Cam questioned and grew silent, and awkwardly took a step closer to Ev.

"So, I wanted to come out and see you. I'm returning to the city."

"Oh." Cam's entire demeanour changed. Like Ev's statement had sucked the wind out of him.

"Yeah. My packmates keep calling. Apparently, they need me home. Some emergency."

"Nothing bad, I hope?"

"I don't know. They wouldn't say. Just that I am needed."

"Oh." Cam glanced at Ev, then refocused his gaze toward the ground and kicked at a twig on the forest floor. "You gone long?"

"Again, I don't know. But I didn't want to leave without saying goodbye."

"Like, goodbye, so long? Goodbye, I'll see you later? Or goodbye, goodbye?"

"I don't know what all that means." Ev's brain jumbled thoughts and feelings. This whole attraction thing confused his normally logical, reasonable thought processes.

"Are you coming back? Or is this goodbye forever?" There was an edge of panic in Cam's voice.

"Well, I hope not forever."

"Jeez what kind of emergency is this?" Cam put his hands on his hips and furrowed his brows. This wasn't going the way Ev had envisioned.

"I'm sorry, Cam. I honestly don't know."

"You still owe me. Remember? I haven't forgotten your promise, and I *really* want to cash in. Get what I'm saying?"

Ev closed his eyes and bowed his head. "About that."

"Don't you dare renege!" Cam's eyes widened as his lips pursed.

"Look, it's complicated."

"Complicated, how? You're naked, I get naked, and we have fun."

"There's, you know, a little more to it. I—" Ev stopped himself. His heart ached and sank. If he spoke his mind, he risked brutal humiliation. Cam's tongue had delivered many a sharp and pointed retort. He didn't want to think what his pack would say if they ever discovered how deep his infatuation with the fae went. "I'm sorry, Cam. I really am."

Ev's gut twisted with anxious arousal, fear, need, and sorrow.

In the heat of the moment, he grabbed Cam by the shoulders and yanked him closer. Without thinking twice, he kissed Cam on the lips. Not just a peck, but a real kiss.

Cam, obviously shocked, barely had time to register what had happened before Ev let him go.

With a twist away from the fae, and the snap and crack of a few bones, Ev freed his wolf and soared over the bramble of bushes that marked the edge of the sacred grove.

Chapter Four

SPARKS'S SHIFT AT the hospital had kept him running all night long.

It has to be a full moon.

He reached into his back pocket, pulled out his phone, and checked his Moon Cycle app.

"Well, see, that's no surprise." Sure enough, the full moon cycle had begun. Technically, the actual lunar event was a single day, but the three days prior to and after always displayed a higher level of crazy than any other time during the month. "Good Gods, we're only on the first day of this."

And normally, Sparks would have been in sync with the phases of the planetary changes, the waxing and waning of the moon only one of the celestial bodies he *used* to regularly track. But without a coven, there simply hadn't been any need or desire to keep up with it.

Resigning himself to a full-moon-crazed week of busy shifts, he continued down the hall toward the nurse's desk. He'd been paged, so presumably they had a patient transport or some other required task that promised to be distasteful.

As he approached the hub of the floor, with clinical staff swarming around like hummingbirds dive-bombing one of those red, plastic, sugar-water-filled feeders, his phone buzzed. A text had come in.

Sparks ducked into a nearby stairwell to look at his phone. Technically you weren't supposed to be carrying the device on shift, but everyone did anyway.

> WIATT: *How was your visit with Dev and Tully?*

Wiatt, his younger brother and the family necromancer, was a pretty decent guy, despite his penchant for dead things. Wiatt had been a twin. "Had been" as Wiatt's womb sibling had died in utero, but because of complications their mother experienced during the pregnancy, she had to carry both fetuses to term. Once Wiatt's talent had been discerned—at a tender age—the community elders assumed his close proximity to the dead at a point in time when Wiatt's development would have been heavily receptive to supernatural forces created a magical tether to the underworld. Wiatt's abilities stunned others of his kind. His talent enabled him to summon spirits long departed—a difficult task for most—had channelled beloved souls and allowed them to speak through his body, and at least once he'd played host to an unsavoury entity who expressed a great interest in tasting Sparks's flesh. But Wiatt's favourite witchy talent and the one he excelled in was the reanimation of small dead things.

Nothing complex like a human, but there had been a few hamsters in the Gemmell household who had enjoyed a second life.

> SPARKS: *It went really well. What are you doing for Mabon?*

> WIATT: *Same as you. Nothing. Although I have some bones to harvest from a fox corpse I found out*

in the woods. I was going to boil off whatever meat still exists, clean and scrape them, and start the curing process.

SPARKS: *Gross.*

WIATT: *But effective.*

SPARKS: *Dev and Tully were thinking of having the guys over. There's talk of putting something new together.*

WIATT: *Are you ever gonna share with me what the hell happened that night you were called over? All the rest of us ended up with a 'coven has been cancelled indefinitely' text. A message which sent everyone spinning, I might add.*

SPARKS: *Not my story to tell, sorry.*

WIATT: *I'm your brother. Really?*

SPARKS: *Really. Dude, I'm sorry, I can't. Maybe they'll say something at Mabon? You in?*

WIATT: *Well, I've nowhere else to go. Why not?*

SPARKS: *Don't sound too happy about it.*

WIATT: *Maybe the dead will tell me...*

SPARKS: *Wiatt!*

Sparks rolled his eyes. Wiatt also held a university-level degree in being an ass, but he never devolved into being cruel. His sense of humour reflected his magical alignment. Deadpan and a little off. People often steered clear of Wiatt because of the dead's affinity for him, and his brother liked to dress the part and play up the whole Goth, black-witch role. It involved a lot of dark clothes and the occasional swirling cape. Wiatt spent much of his adult time alone and, to some degree, had grown to be comfortable by himself. But if truth be told, he most likely wasn't by himself—it's just his company had more ethereal qualities and were only seen by Wiatt. Sparks had a soft spot for his brother and protected him and squashed any rumours he heard in the community. After all, Sparks, as the older sibling, had a duty to make sure Wiatt was okay.

He'd have to tell Dev and Tully that Wiatt agreed to participate in celebrating Mabon.

The prospect of the coven getting together again had instantly eased Sparks's troubles. After his visit with the guys, he had finally slept a good night's sleep, and his wayward abilities had somewhat settled.

Sparks emerged from the stairwell, sliding his phone into the pocket of his mint-green scrubs, and continued his way to the nursing station.

"Hey, Shammy, you called?"

"Sparks! Yeah, Mrs. Middleton." Shammy—the charge nurse for the Geriatric Medicine ward—had been at the hospital as long as Sparks had worked there. She had a gentle soul, a warm touch, and the patients didn't seem to mind her fondness for tattoos and piercings. Her septum piercing glimmered brightly in the overhead fluorescent lighting.

"Oh no." Sparks had transported Mrs. Middleton for several diagnostic procedures. She had been well into her eighties, and a little cranky, but when you weren't feeling well, being grumpy had to be expected. "When?"

"About twenty minutes ago. Can you take her downstairs?"

"Absolutely." Sparks looked up to Shammy. She personified nursing and Sparks had watched her for years with her patients. She always took extra time to ensure everyone in her care was comfortable. One day soon, Sparks would be a nurse of the same calibre. He only had one more year left of classes to earn his nursing degree. School, hospital work, and being a witch proved to be an exhausting schedule.

"Thanks, Sparks. Hey, don't forget, Sharon's retirement tea is this afternoon in the conference room. The new resident will be there. There'll be cake. I know you like your cake." Shammy referred to Sparks's predilection for a tight ass, not the sugary carb kind of cake. Sparks was a butt man, and Shammy and he would stand back and evaluate the new medical students as they started each rotation.

Sparks smiled and winked. "I wouldn't miss it for the world."

Once in Mrs. Middleton's room, Sparks adjusted the metal gurney so the brakes were off the wheels for her final trip *downstairs*.

That was the code word for the morgue. If people were around, or within earshot, the staff referred to the cold drawers as *downstairs* so other patients and their visitors didn't get upset. After all, he did spend the majority of his shifts in a ward designated for the elderly.

Someone had gone to the trouble to appropriately cover Mrs. Middleton. Wrapped in plastic, with ties around her head, middle, and feet, tagged and bagged, she had been prepped correctly. Dead bodies were treated with health codes in mind. But if the general public had any idea how their last journey would be carried out, Sparks conjectured most would choose to leave this world in other ways.

If Sparks had a choice in the matter, he'd prefer to be lugged off and buried in the woods. No plastic. No metal. No sterile environments. Just him and his connection with nature.

Maybe even pushed away from shore on a rickety raft out into the middle of a huge lake during a summer thunderstorm surrounded by floating lanterns and a cheering crowd on the beach. Now *that* was going out in style!

He glided the bed down the hall and into the service elevator. The uneven floor between the elevator car and the hospital floor made for a bumpy transition. Oddly, a family had found themselves on the wrong elevator, and instead of asking Sparks for assistance, the parents continued their argument about which floor they needed to go to.

The youngster who accompanied them spied the metal box hiding Mrs. Middleton. The child's eyes widened as he snuggled up against one of his parents' legs. Sparks smiled at the kid and surmised he was smarter and more observant than most. But as Sparks continued to try to convey comfort with his friendly grin, the boy's horrified glare became far too familiar.

The glazed-over stare mimicked his brother when Wiatt conversed with the dead. This child was a medium. A seer of the dead. Sparks crouched, resting on his haunches to equal the same level as the boy.

"It's okay. I'm going to take good care of Mrs. Middleton."

The boy didn't look like he believed it.

"She's so angry," he whispered.

"She always kinda was," Sparks chided.

The door opened, and the parents hurried their child away.

The family exited on the main floor. The doors closed and Sparks and Mrs. Middleton had an uninterrupted journey down to the morgue.

Once alone, Sparks cleared his throat and bellowed with authority, "No funny stuff, Mrs. Middleton. I have a necromancer for a brother, and if you get mean, I'll have him transport your soul into a cockroach's body." Wiatt had taught him to convey a sense of power and control; otherwise spirits would run roughshod over anyone present.

After handing off the body to the medical examiner, Sparks took the long way to his usual fourth-floor assignment. But before returning, he passed by the cafeteria to see the lunch special—hot roast beef sandwich—written in fancy script across the chalkboard. He'd had the hot roast beef before. It wasn't special.

Sparks turned a one-eighty to head toward the elevator which would take him to the main floor and the courtyard where food trucks were often stationed in the nearby parking lot. Tiny restaurants on wheels would offer up a better selection of food options. As he turned to head down the hallway, his shin slammed into the corner edge of a footplate on a wheelchair. He damn near toppled over, trying to catch himself and not fall face first into the chair's occupant. Through his flailing, the scrubs entangled even more, catching his pant leg and ripping it.

Dammit. He'd have to go buy a new pair of pants.

As Sparks righted himself, he refocused on the more important part—the patient in the chair. He came face to face with *him*.

Byron Radcliffe sat in the wheelchair, his hands hovering over the wheel's brakes, as if he didn't know whether to bolt or hold still. His laugh lines were deep, and his crow's feet wrinkles expressed more exhaustion than the joviality Sparks had known from Byron. His hipster-styled beard had been trimmed short, and his hair had been buzz cut. Byron had lost his charisma, his larger-than-life presence. He had in a few short months grown old.

"Ah, sorry, Byron. You okay?"

"Sparks." Byron ignored the question.

"What are you doing down here? Aren't you up on three?"

Byron glanced over his shoulder. Sparks followed Byron's lead and stared in the same direction. A large sign above two swinging doors read "Rehab Department."

"Ah. Right. I guess. How's the shoulder?"

"I hear you're the one who brought me in?"

"Yes." Sparks wanted to get away so badly. Nervous energy coursed through his body, making his feet twitch. This was beyond awkward. He had known Byron for years. Byron had assisted him as a teenager trying to get a handle on his ability, which had been a task considering the wildly fluctuating emotions of a gay teenage boy. When Sparks had come of age, Byron had been the one to introduce him to his first coven, the Brethren Elementals, although by the time Sparks turned twenty-three, he had joined the Night Grove. With his birthday this past February, Sparks had turned thirty-one. That made eight years of being in a coven with Byron as its leader. The man had been like an older brother, if not a father figure.

Sparks had been the one to bring Byron to the hospital, but in retrospect, he hadn't visited him a single time since his admission. In fact, he'd gone out of his way to avoid him. He had checked on his health status occasionally with Bryon's nurses but had steered clear of any personal encounters.

Sparks had seen the wounds on Byron's shoulder, and only one creature could create such havoc. A werewolf. And the night he spent cleaning up the splattered remains of Eddie and Gus had also been the work of the violent beast. The claw marks and teeth and size of the wounds made the culprit pointedly clear. Oddly, Sparks had no clue where Addas had been that night or why he was missing from the scene, or even why the mammoth man hadn't shown up the last few months.

Instead, Sparks made some mental leaps of logic.

Any witch would have recognized Addas's infection. The man had literally grown half a foot in the last year.

Grown adult men don't continue to gain height or physical mass regardless of how often they might have gone to the gym. No amount of working out would have ever built up muscles like Addas had gained in such a short time period.

And now that Dev and Tully had clued him in to what Byron had done, the sacrifice of smaller creatures, the imprisonment of Dev's friend who had turned fae... Sparks wanted nothing to do with his ex-high priest.

"So, from the look on your face, I guess the boys told you everything." Byron scrunched his lips together. They were thin and white. He glanced away, his eyes watery. Even Byron's hair had changed. His closely shorn head held far more grey and had thinned. Trauma hit the body hard in many ways.

"I guessed some of it. I only found out recently about the extent of...well...everything." Sparks took a nervous step backward, away from Byron.

Byron turned away and cleared his throat.

Despite everything that had happened, a sharp pain speared Sparks's heart, and his stomach dropped. In all the years he'd known Byron, he had always been a paragon of strength and knowledge. He wanted to give the man, his former High Priest, a hug, and yet...

Byron had been knocked off his proverbial pedestal and the crash landing had been hard.

"You okay?" Sparks knelt beside the chair, but still had a hard time initiating and maintaining eye contact.

Byron sniffled. His head bobbed, attempting to convey as much, but his face scrunched up and turned bright red. An obvious attempt at trying to contain his emotions. He reached up with his arm and went to wipe away the tears that were beginning to form, but his wounded shoulder wouldn't let him.

"Dammit." Byron bit his lip, glanced at Sparks, then shifted his eyes away again while lifting his other arm. Using his sleeve, he wiped his face. "It's definitely not okay, Sparks." An edge of anger and hurt cut sharply in his words. Byron took in a huge breath. As he exhaled, he quivered. "You've always been a kind-hearted man."

Sparks glanced at his watch. Lunch started in a handful of minutes, and his break didn't last long. "Do you need help getting back to your room, or..."

An internal battle warred within Sparks. A man he'd known for so many years, who had committed some grievous crimes against the Shadow Realm and its community, sat unravelling before him. He wanted to be mad at Byron for all the wrong things he had done, yet, he had done horrible things trying to save the love of his life. Sparks had to wonder if the situation had been reversed, would he have done any different.

Byron continued to fight some overwhelming emotions.

Sparks looked around, growing increasingly more uncomfortable with the current situation. Thankfully no one was nearby. "I'm sorry, Byron. Not everyone knows. I only found out recently. I should have come seen you...but..."

"No. I get it." Byron wiped his face again, then dismissed Sparks's comment with a wave of his hand.

"But you've been dealing with this all by yourself. And that's not good. Anyone would have had a hard time."

Another tear rolled down Byron's cheek as he sniffled again. He ignored the teardrop. "I don't know what I'm going to do without him. He was everything to me. Even more important than the Night Grove."

"I know."

"No, I don't think you do. And honestly, I hope you never have to go through any of what I'm feeling right now. I know I did some shitty things..." Byron swallowed hard and managed to pull himself together. So much rage nested in his soul. Sadness too. Two emotions that left unchecked were a bad combination. Especially if a werewolf incubated beneath his skin. "I'm getting out soon. Even though I didn't get any visitors, I didn't exactly communicate to everyone in the group either. So I'm just as much to blame."

"But Byron, you needed time. To heal. To cope."

"Yeah. It's okay. I'll be okay."

"Do you want me to take you back to your room?"

"No. I don't even need to be in this chair, but the hospital has rules, and as long as I'm a patient, I can't walk about unless I'm supervised. Wheel around, sure. Then I won't fall. It's fine." Byron shook his head, his jaw clenched so tight the vein at his temple throbbed.

He swivelled his chair away from Sparks and headed down the hall.

Chapter Five

CAM ROLLED HIS eyes as he studied the giant tome in front of him.

"I have never been so bored in my life," he griped as he glanced over his shoulder. Sen sat in a chair on the opposite side of the room, heavily engrossed in texts and scrolls of his own, making copious notes.

"Quit talking and keep studying. Your test is at the end of this week. You need to master the history of your species," Sen grumbled while jotting something else in his massive moon book.

Apparently, all fae kept a moon book. The tome was the equivalent of a witches' book of shadows. A collection of spells, incantations, herbal concoctions, and other assorted magical things that would help hone Cam's abilities.

"I just don't see the point."

"The point is it's required. The sharper your mind, the better your skill in all things fae. And let's face it, you suck at being fae. Lady Aine is going to tan your hide once she skins your furry body. You'll make a nice throw."

"Ha-ha." Cam scoffed, sending a sneer toward his tutor and manservant. It's not that he didn't appreciate Sen's efforts, but Cam's brain kept refocusing on Everton, worried more about what he had done and why the wolf had run off. However, Lady Aine terrified him. The Queen had made fae societal expectations crystal clear: learn how to be fae. If not, it was entirely possible Cam would be on the receiving end of her ability to inflict enormous amounts of pain and ensure Cam's complete destruction. He needed to learn and master all the fae ways, and those responsibilities should have taken precedence. A certain monster kept interrupting everything.

Clearly, Ev had feelings for him. The wet wolfy kiss planted on Cam before Ev had leaped into the dense forest surrounding the Ancestral Lands had been legendary. The tingles and furry feelings the lip lock had summoned cancelled out any kiss Cam had received from anyone else. And that was saying a lot. Cam had had lots of boyfriends, and he'd tasted his fair share of bearded men. All of them of the bear persuasion. Preferably big, burly, and brawny men. The wider the shoulders, the better. And Ev exemplified his infatuation with beastly boys.

Cam's wings fluttered. He spied Sen out of the corner of his eye. His involuntary wing action had made the tree sprite glance up. Cam received a side-eye stare, with a raised eyebrow. He didn't think the man cared much for him, but then, he hadn't given Sen any reason to like him.

Pursing his lips and feigning studying, Cam stuck his nose back in his book, but instead of reading, he started contemplating his escape. How possible would it be to slip out of the Ancestral Lands and go hunt down his wolf?

He had no car. He had no idea where to find Ev. It's not like he'd ever been to Everton's house.

But if he managed to figure out how to slip in and out of shadows, he would be able to run the Yellowhead highway back to Edmonton at dusk without being seen. The more shadows, the better. After studying Sen's demonstrations—

and yes, he had in fact paid attention to the act of slipping meant bending light and shadow, and time as well. The ability allowed the fae to travel at ultra-fast speeds. He'd be approaching city limits within an hour.

A quick visit to Dev, his bestie, who had been granted from the horned God Cernunnos himself the ability to track down anything, would be in order. Finding Everton's den shouldn't be a problem.

It was a plan.

Maybe a good plan.

He just had to get out of Sen's sight for a moment—

"Cam!" Sen's face popped up directly in front of him. His eyes were saucers. His pupils thin slits, and the toothy beaming smile stretched from pointed ear to pointed ear. Sen's unruly bright-red hair reminded Cam of those ridiculous troll dolls old women would bring to bingo in hopes of bringing them luck. Silly women. Trolls don't bring luck. They eat you.

"What?" Cam shrunk away from the violation of his personal bubble.

"You're doing it!"

"I'm doing what?" Cam furrowed his brows in disgust as he cringed. Spit had flown out of Sen's mouth.

"You're human!"

"What?"

Sen bounced over to the side table where a handheld mirror lay with an assortment of other personal hygiene accessories. In the blink of an eye, Sen had returned and held up the mirror.

Cam, transfixed by the face looking back at him, forgot about everything else around him.

His old face.

Human light-brown eyes and scruffy cheeks. Not the cat-eye green with gold flecks and stretched pupils. His perky ski-lift nose had returned; long gone was the flattened nose with nasal planes and a philtrum.

Cam ran a hand through his thick, long hair. His fingers grazed the bony protrusions of his horns, but the reflection showed no such idiosyncrasies. The image casted back at Cam sent sharp pains through his heart. He studied his previous incarnation, a body he had inhabited a mere six months ago. Beautiful, unshaven, boyfriend material, and most importantly, human.

He bit his lip and a corner of his mouth twitched, gradually turning into a bit of a frown.

"What's the matter? This is a miracle! Cam, you figured out how to maintain the illusion. It's solid! All of you. Your wings are gone." Sen dropped the mirror and rushed around to Cam's back. He lifted the loincloth Cam had finally conceded to wearing. "Yes! The tail is even gone." Sen joyously yanked on his now invisible tail. Cam had impressed his tutor.

Cam swatted Sen away and glared at the sprite. He huffed as he glanced sternly at the floor.

"What's the matter? I don't get it. You should be thrilled! How did you do it? What was the trigger?"

Sen had never been human. He couldn't comprehend Cam's loneliness or understand he'd lost the most important thing in the world. Something Cam would never be again. Something he'd never placed any value on before.

His humanity.

He was the only one in the village who had "turned" fae. Everyone else here had been born that way.

Cam grabbed the mirror Sen had brought over, and as he studied his reflection, he involuntarily stroked the face in the glass looking back at him.

"Oh, this is such a great achievement!" Giddy with excitement, Sen clapped his hands together. "Lady Aine will be pleased, Cam. Trust me. This is a good thing." Sen grabbed the mirror out of Cam's hands. He bopped over to the dresser and replaced the hand mirror to its resting place, all while sporting a toothy grin, as Cam returned a half-hearted smile. Sen hadn't picked up the hurt in Cam's soul or the pain at seeing his former self. "I think it best I go tell her straight away!"

The sprite disappeared.

As soon as Sen had left, Cam retrieved the mirror and continued studying his human visage. How he had missed his old self! Cam's mood withered, and his scheming and plotting morphed into nostalgia and longing. And as his mind shifted to different emotions, so did the vision in the glass. In a heartbeat and a ripple of the air, his fae self returned. The man in the mirror once again reflected an Eldritch fae, complete with horns, wings, and—as he glanced at his backside—a tail.

He let out a sigh.

Looking over to the side table where the mirror had come from, Cam spotted Lady Aine's glass vessel, glinting in the sunbeams that sparkled through his bedroom window. The vessel required his seed, and the container had to be filled and given to the queen before the entire village travelled underground for the winter.

After staring at the vial for a few minutes, and still clutching the handheld mirror, Cam made up his mind. His brows furrowed and lips pursed; his tail twitched to and fro, annoyed, and determined.

He'd find a way out of this hellish study hall. Fuck the spells and the history. He wanted his wolf—and his old life—back. He needed Dev too.

The decision had been made. Cam would flee the Ancestral Lands and to hell with Lady Aine and her expectations.

SPARKS HAD AN incredibly busy afternoon. After stumbling into Byron, he had been summoned for not one but two biological clean-ups, a half-dozen patient transports, and one uncomfortable and awkward security situation where Mr. Patterson had decided hospital bed gowns were the devil's clothing and he would leave the hospital. Nude.

The last situation required an unending supply of patience and carefully chosen words in order to calm Mr. Patterson and convince him some clothing may be a better option than none, and staying in the hospital and getting better was probably smarter than trying to "just rest up" at home, as the old man had put it.

After all, he had already done that after his hip replacement surgery and had been readmitted as he hadn't kept his wound clean, leading to an infection. The man needed antibiotics and to be supervised to ensure the stitches from his surgery stayed intact and his dressing changes happened regularly.

Arriving home, Sparks closed the front door and stripped off his scrubs. Unlike Mr. Patterson, he no longer required clothing, and as much as he loved his job of assisting patients and loved where he worked, the hospital had a certain smell that clung to the scrubs. When his shifts ended, Sparks preferred to not think about it, or smell it, until he had to arrive for his next shift.

He opened his fridge and stood naked in front of it, spying the various containers of leftovers. An old box of Thai food, partially hidden behind an even older bottle of pop someone had left behind from a party long past, caught his eye, but when he flipped open the top flaps of the takeout container, the assaulting foul smell suggested an immediate case of food poisoning.

"Oof. Well, that's not for dinner." He opened the door to the cabinet under the sink, where his garbage can resided, and pitched the outdated food into the bin.

The rest of the fridge didn't hold anything appetizing, unless you counted a jar of mayonnaise and three packets of hot sauce.

"Going out for dinner it is." Except Sparks hated eating alone—especially out in public. He reached for his cell, sitting on the kitchen counter by his keys, and punched a few buttons.

"Hey!" He was genuinely surprised to get an answer.

"Hey, yourself, what's up?" Tully said from the other end of the phone connection. Sparks heard his smile through the cellular technology.

"Well, I'm freshly stripped from my hospital shift, and I'm starved. Anything left in my fridge is inedible. You guys wanna go hit Yousef's?" Yousef's Shawarma was a small, hole-in-the-wall, mom-and-pop-type restaurant near the university that everyone went to. Notoriously busy any given day of the week and their falafel had won yearly awards for being the best in all of Edmonton.

"Dev's out. Work thing. He never gives me too many details, which is fine with me, but he muttered something about a family's house boggle going missing, and he had been 'guided' to go find it. After that, he had an eight o'clock appointment about a child exhibiting unusual behaviour. I imagine he's going to be late tonight. Poor guy will be exhausted when he gets home. I should pick something up for him and stash it in the fridge. He'll be jealous we went without him."

"Late night appointments and house boggles do not sound like fun."

"No, those boggles can be little buggers." Tully snickered.

"Tell me about it. My aunt had one. She couldn't keep anything gold in the house. Damn thing always took the metal and hid the items in a pile like a dragon hoard. She lost a family heirloom to the monster. Why on earth would this family want to go find a boggle? Good riddance I say."

"No idea. Again, I don't get the details. And frankly most days I'd care to not know. Our supernatural community is rather...uh...fucked up."

Sparks laughed. "True dat. Well, you wanna come? I swear I'm so hungry right now I could eat a skunk. Besides, I have gossip."

"Sparks, bad boy. Gossip?" Tully's voice indicated he was more interested than his words let on.

"You know you want it."

"Yes, yes I do."

"Well, yes, actually you do. I inadvertently stumbled overtop of Bryon today. I do mean that literally. I almost fell into his wheelchair while he sat in it."

"Ouch, on several levels." Tully went silent for a minute. "So, how was he?"

"He's a mess, Tully. Honestly, I felt bad."

"This is why I love ya, bro. You have the biggest heart I've ever known. Dev still would like nothing more than to string him up and eviscerate him."

"I get it, but he cried in front of me. When was the last time you remember ever seeing Byron so emotionally distraught, he shed tears in front of you?"

"Ah, never."

"Exactly. I've known the man for half my life, and he's always been a paragon of masculinity, strength, knowledge, and power. Today he was none of that."

"Damn."

"Come with me to dinner. I'll tell you more." Sparks's tummy rumbled.

"You're a tease. You know that, right?"

"Yup. As long as you're getting a boner, then I'm doing it right."

"I'm as hard as lumber right now." Tully laughed loudly. Sparks chuckled. This is what he missed. The banter and play with his male buddies in the coven. Mabon promised to be a reconnection to his community where the remnants of the Guardian of the Night Grove would reassemble and once again be a brotherhood—if only for the night. "I'll come get you. Be there in ten. Gotta put some clothes on and text Dev to let him know we're going out."

"Sure thing. Hurry! I'm starving." As Sparks clicked his phone off, he glanced down at his naked body. "What is with witches and their propensity for nudity?"

Shrugging, he placed his phone on the counter and went to go find some clothes to wear for his dinner date with Tully.

Chapter Six

CAM SLID DOWN a supporting beam from the rooftop he'd been lying on for the last twenty minutes, waiting for the foot traffic below to disperse. As he descended like a spider on a silk thread, his gaze darted back and forth, trying to spy out any other fae creature that might tattle on his whereabouts. Cam needed to ensure his withdrawal from the Ancestral Lands imitated ghosts: deathly quiet and invisible.

He had taken nothing from his room. If there had been any indication Cam had abandoned the village, Sen would have Lady Aine rain down on him with the fury of a late summer prairie thunderstorm. A scolding Cam didn't want to experience.

What he wanted was Everton, and after pining away for less than a day since Ev's departure for the city, every thought Cam had focused on the wolfman, which only made him more intent on getting what he wanted.

A late August evening in the Ancestral Lands village meant the shadows had initiated their nightly stretch. Not like the dim gloom of a September night, where there would be the slightest bite of cold on bare skin. No, not yet. It was still hot, too hot, and Cam's nerves were strung tight rehashing his impromptu escape plan over and over in his mind. Tiny beads of sweat dotted his forehead and spine. Normally, a couple of beats from his wings would have circulated the air around him enough to cool him. But such an action might attract attention.

Down the alley Cam spied the main village's square. A large bench sat beneath one of the mammoth rowan trees where some of the lesser fae made their home. Another location to avoid. As he peered through the lengthening shadows, a massive shape sauntered across the central plaza, its head adorned with horns, similar to his own, but they were much larger, and there were more spurs than the two he sported. This monstrous beast displayed an impressive rack, each protrusion draped in moss and lichen hanging in streamers. Tattered membranous wings jutted out from a solidly muscled back. Cam leaned forward and squinted, trying to discern what he was seeing.

The creature held a familiarity Cam couldn't place. He'd never seen anything like the beast before...

Then he knew.

It was another Royal male fae, much like himself, but this specimen had aged. His gnarled limbs swung with encumbrance, and the beast appeared tired. His nose lay flat across his face, wider than Cam's. His skin was spotted with decorated and etched spirals and fae script and looked like someone had carved the designs out of his hide—a tattoo of sorts—but made in bark. Sharp spines protruded from the base of his jawbone and more bristles continued down his neck, across his shoulders, and down each arm.

This was an elder.

A grim picture of where Cam's future lay.

"Damn, that's ugly," he whispered.

He turned away and slipped past the plaza, hopping over a stack of barrels. He climbed up and over a roof, then scampered toward the edge of the settlement. He had been down this path before. Sen had taken him through here to the clearing, "the only place safe enough to practice fae magic without blowing up the entire Ancestral Land population." A direct quote from Sen, one he had sneered at his manservant for making. Clearly, Sen held no optimism regarding Cam's abilities. The pessimistic outlook may have been warranted, considering Cam's complete lack of dedication to his studies.

As he rounded the next corner, his shoulders firm and flat against a tall fence that kept the stock of animals the fae used for food, he focused on the last bit of his journey out of the village.

If he were to make his way down this road unseen, he'd have conquered his retreat and defied any detection, breaking free from all this fae nonsense and leaving him free to find Everton.

Cam held his breath.

Closing his eyes, he pictured his destination—the clearing. He needed to end up in the clearing.

Without realizing it, Cam silently slipped into the shadows. His flesh cooled as the darkness enveloped him. He shivered but revelled in the joyous sensation. The pull and obscurity of the gloom, huddled in the deepest corners and overhangs called out to him. And he easily and gladly responded to its call.

Cam vanished. Not like when he had been captured by Byron. Invisibility only worked when his anger flooded through him, which in turn made him disappear from view.

This was far different. Cam slipped into the "in-between," a chasm nestled quietly between the dark and the light. A grey zone where few ever went.

He had slipped into the shadows.

"Hmph, maybe I should've paid more attention to Sen. This isn't all that hard," Cam whispered.

Focusing on his mind's image of the clearing where he and Sen had spent many an afternoon, his body whisked along the last road behind a crate tucked under the eaves of a storehouse, then spilled into a narrow crevice amongst two buildings.

Almost there.

Peering out, Cam spied a massive oak which marked the beginning entrance to the village. The east side of the tree darkened with the oncoming dusk.

Calling out to the murkiness, he pushed out with his mind until he found the quiet within the dead zone of the dark and melted into the void, slithering toward—

"Before you leave..." A hand clasped his shoulder and sharp nails dug into his flesh.

The hand jerked him around, obliterating the focus Cam needed to jump the distance.

Cam's instant reaction to the intrusion alarmed his senses. His hackles rose, teeth elongated and sharpened, his lips drew back, and as he turned he crouched into a fighting stance.

Lady Aine stood before him, one eyebrow raised, and with a slight twitch of her mouth, and a snarl, Cam's instinctual reaction to being caught off guard morphed sharply into submission for the queen—lest he lose his head.

"Your Eminence"—Cam bowed—"my apologies."

"Hmm, yes, well. I'm not certain the apology is sincere, considering."

"Lady Aine, please, I just—"

"Cam, ever since you arrived here, you have been nothing but a thorn in my side. I have thousands of fae to look after from varying factions, and many of them are from other places around our world, sent here to learn our ways and traditions. You continually occupy my space with less than pleasant news.

"And now you're attempting to leave, without permission, when I have made myself very clear that without learning the basic minimum of abilities you will put all of us in danger. I can't let that happen. If you leave now, you leave for good.

"However, you *still* have one responsibility to fulfil." From deep within the folds of her gown, the queen extracted the vial that had sat on Cam's dresser. "You need to return this, full."

"But if you cut me off—"

"Yes, well, it has been so for thousands of years. Exiled fae don't generally find a way to survive." She sneered. "Unfortunately, you don't seem to be able to settle here, and so here we are. I need your seed; you don't want to stay. What am I supposed to do? You remain the sole fertile Royal male in this clade until a new Royal fae is born. The only way that is going to happen is for you to father one, or for another human to morph into one of us. And I think you of all people have learned how rarely that occurs."

"I have." Cam's head dropped along with his shoulders. "But Lady Aine, Everton has left. I need to find him. I can't stay here. Every single thought I have returns to him. Studying is impossible. Sen is impossible. This isn't who I am."

"And yet, it is, Cam. This village and all the fae are now exactly who you are. We are your family. There is no going back to a human existence for you, ever. And you will live hundreds of years. We could have protected you, housed you, and loved you as one of our own. We see no difference between you and us, despite your origins. You can't see that now, and I'm not sure why, but you seem unable to find a home here. Which means as much as you failed to apply yourself, we have also failed you."

Lady Aine shook her head and the disappointed look in her eye shamed Cam ever more.

"Perhaps I have been too swift in judgement. Why is this wolfman so important to you? I have heard the tale of your imprisonment and how you met the man. Clearly, I am missing some important piece of information as to why you have developed such a connection to another species—which, I may add, is distasteful considering their propensity for violence. You do know they are baseless hunters intent on destruction?"

"I know very little of them." Cam's chest drew in tight as he pictured Everton. As a human, Ev towered over most men; his muscles bulged with every movement. Tall, furry, muscled, and bald. As a monstrous beast, Ev could rip apart anything that stood in his way, yet something happened while they had been held prisoner by Byron Radcliffe. "I'm not sure I understand why I can't stop thinking of Ev, and I don't really care what he is. I feel better when he's near. And every time I've managed to pull off a fae ability, it's been because of him. Angry someone was hurting him, scheming, and plotting to find a way to be near to him. Even jumping the shadows tonight, a first, was easy to do, as he was my intended destination.

"I don't understand why he left." Cam bit his lip as his head dropped. Why Everton managed to consume so much time within his brain mystified him.

"All right, I've heard enough." Lady Aine rolled her eyes and sighed. "I am nothing, if not patient and forgiving. One last chance. Never let it be said I am not without compassion." She thrust the glass vial toward Cam, its pearlescent sheen glinting in the last rays of sunlight the day would deliver. "You still must fill this. I will not waver on this task. You remain our sole sire, and we are few in number, Cam. Each generation is greatly anticipated and needed. However, I will give you free leave until Groundswell Day."

Cam's eyes went as wide as saucers. They were going to let him leave, and not upon pain of death, or exile, or anything else horrendous.

"But Groundswell isn't a determined date," Cam replied, confused about the issue of returning.

"Exactly, and I will tell you this. It's too hot for this late in the season. Something isn't right. I know you saw Aelfric, though I doubt he has granted an audience with you. His patience isn't as far-reaching as mine. He is concerned, which is why he paces in the main square. There is something unaligned, and we are not sure what. Perhaps it is nothing, but I can't be certain." Lady Aine cocked her eyebrow again, an indication to Cam he had better pay attention. "If there is any sign of danger, I will initiate Groundswell and protect our kin. So, you are taking a risk, Cam. Going underground may happen at any moment. I feel in my bones a sense of urgency to protect our village. But I also appreciate you need to figure out this dalliance of yours, and perhaps this adventure will also fill my vial. So go, but do so knowing you may be locked out. And if I miss my cycle and cannot produce progeny next spring, there will be a whole fresh new hell for you to pay. Do I make myself clear?"

"As bright and shining as the sun." Beetle wings, hummingbirds, and dragonflies swarmed in his stomach. The excitement Cam revelled in at being released almost overtook him, but a good chunk of his midsection was taut with fear. Being locked out of the Ancestral lands equalled death.

Cam could go free but had to return to finalize his only task. Returning a filled vial of his seed from a coupling fuelled by heightened emotions. The time afforded to him to complete his task remained unknown.

Sounded like a plan meant for him to fail.

"I understand." Cam nodded once.

"Good, I also hear from Sen you figured out how to hold your human guise. Let me also remind you that no one beyond the Shadow Realm is ever allowed to see our true form. If I hear of wayward sightings of winged and horned monsters coming from the city, I will know it was you. Be sure to mind your magic, Cam."

"Yes, ma'am." Cam's manners made an abrupt appearance.

"Then off with you." Lady Aine burst into a thousand butterflies which dispersed as thousands of staccato wing beats. Relieved over the lack of her presence, Cam became acutely aware of the terror in being free to go.

The pearlescent vial lay at his feet, shimmering in the waning sunlight.

Cam stooped to pluck it up. As he glared at the glass he sneered.

"Fuck, I swear, I'm cursed."

Chapter Seven

SPARKS HAD DONNED some clothes and waited outside his apartment building for less than ten minutes before Tully showed up in his silver Audi.

"Hop in!" Tully yelled, complete with a silly grin.

The top had been stowed, and as they drove off toward their intended destination, the warm summer breeze ruffled Sparks's long hair. Sparks couldn't remember another summer that had been so hot. The convertible ride proved to be a cool blessing.

"Yousef's?" Tully turned to ask.

"Unless you have a better idea?"

"Nope. Whaddya think about getting our meals to go and then heading down to the Glade?" Tully threw out the suggestion which immediately got Sparks excited.

"I haven't been down there since last summer! Let's do it."

To the rest of the world, the Glade appeared to be nothing more than a cleared-out section of forest scrub within Emily Murphy Park, a popular recreational area on the south banks of the North Saskatchewan River in downtown Edmonton. But if one were part of the Shadow Realm, the Glade was a mystical, sacred, and revered fountain of rejuvenation.

The vast majority of Edmonton's city dwellers didn't realize that the centre of the Glade pinpointed the exact spot where a ley line erupted at the earth's surface. An abundance of magic gushed out from the clearing's middle, contained on all sides by massive elms planted in a perfect Druidic circle. Those bound to the Shadow Realm would gather in small groups, or in solitude to watch the sprays of energy bursting forth in a fountain of liquid gold raw energy, its radiance fantastical to those whose magical abilities allowed them to see the metallic showers of wild spurting eruptions. Creatures that inhabited the area, both magical and otherwise, would venture close, as fascinated with the supernatural feature as humans. It wasn't uncommon to see an ambling porcupine, a wayward coyote, or even a lurking mountain cougar spying on the activities within the dale. Great horned owls dotted the treetops, and the occasional clipped rhythm of pileated woodpeckers echoed through the wood. Once a bear had even been reported.

Guaranteed, if there were humans present in this often overlooked area, they were bound to the Realm.

Sparks surmised that adult humans who were regular folk dismissed what their intuition told them, and so they missed out on the charm and magic life offered all around them. But those who would listen to the whispering of the trees as river valley breezes blew through the leaves or got lost in the iridescence of insect wings were more apt to see the beauty and magic all around.

Nine times out of ten, those people were witches.

To get to the Glade, one had to follow a well concealed footpath through the brush leading away from Emily Murphy Park proper and toward the North Saskatchewan River. But once a foot was placed within the glen, a warm calm welled up inside, spreading through the body like an opioid high. The slow pulse and beat of the wellspring created a distinctly quiet shrine. A safe circle to stop and regroup, a time to set aside the troubles and worries of everyday life, where a witch could ground and recentre. Even a short visit guaranteed the visitor an instant feel-better rush, but for those in the supernatural community, the area's fountain of health and wellness cleansed the negative vibrations from a witch's soul.

The area had also been consecrated. The respected and cherished glen had not been blessed by any Christian devotee, but by the old Gods and their followers. Many of the city's covens had also warded the surroundings to ensure peace, despite whatever philosophical or theological turf wars may have been current.

After the boys had grabbed their delights and said hellos to Yousef himself, a quick drive into the river valley, some clusterfucks in trying to find a parking spot, and then a quick hike had them sitting within the Glade with their food still warm.

Sparks peeled the paper from his falafel pita, stuffed full of crisp shredded lettuce, jalapeños, and black olives and liberally slathered with tzatziki sauce.

"Oh man, so good." Sparks's garbled words fell out while enjoying the tangy and spicy flavours dancing across his tongue. Heat from the peppers sank in after a few bites. Fire erupted as if live coals had been placed in his mouth. His cheeks reddened and the back of his neck ignited. Sensations Sparks thoroughly enjoyed.

Tully eagerly devoured his shawarma.

"So, I was thinking..." Tully gulped down a bite, then glanced at Sparks, who was lifting his soda and taking a sip. "Would you consider going to Byron's place with me and retrieving some of our things?"

"I don't know. It's a little dodgy, don't you think? I mean, after seeing Byron today, I'm torn. Sure, that stuff belongs to us, but he'll be gutted once he finds out. I don't think he can take another disappointment."

"Hmph. Well, Byron's feelings aside, it is sketchy. But there's a treasure trove of witchy things that belong to the Guardians of the Night Grove—well, maybe not *that* coven anymore—but the next coven at least. They certainly do not belong to Byron. If nothing else, my workbooks and robes are still there, and I was halfway through researching a lineage of fire elementals. I would like to get those items back."

"I've been thinking about this since dinner with you and Dev the other night, and especially after my collision with Radcliffe. I don't disagree with you; I have stuff there too. But anything once used by the Night Grove has history attached to the object now. Byron's vibes, actions, and motivations are all collected in those objects. I don't know if I want to carry that forward into anything we start up. Isn't it better to leave negative shit in the past?"

Tully sighed. "Yeah, I guess you're right." He squinted his eyes and tilted his head. "I don't know, but somehow taking the Guardians' relics feels a bit like repayment. What Byron did was so shitty he should pay and I'm not fond of waiting for the law of three to kick in. He left an irreparable scar on Dev's heart."

"Toliver Mack! Are you being petty?"

"Oh honey, gay and petty. I want revenge. Never piss off a fag." Tully winked as he said it. "But if you're gonna make me mad, let me know. I have the perfect outfit for a revenge-rage occasion, and the wig to go with it."

Sparks shook his head while giggling. "I don't doubt your closet contains all kinds of surprises. Probably comes complete with matching spike heels. But I think we're better off without confiscating tools imbued with negative energy. Honestly. A clean start would be best.

"You know, crafting some of our own altar adornments would be a great way to initiate a new tradition with the guys, creating the cornerstone of something new. I think there's merit in starting fresh. All that negativity has physical and metaphysical ramifications. Byron looked twenty years older. He's lost and broken. Frankly, he needs help." Tully rolled his eyes in response to Sparks's statement. "I know, but holding grudges isn't healthy either. You didn't see him. He's a mess. Such a huge fall for someone who we all placed very high up on a pillar of success and power.

"No one has visited him either. He's been in there for months, and he hasn't had a single visitor. The ache in my heart as I stood there listening to Byron talk about Addas almost crippled me. He's in so much pain. I don't want to add to his misery."

Tully leaned close to Sparks and bumped shoulders with him.

"You're such a good person. I'm a total shit for even suggesting it."

"No, you're not. You're one of the most positive people I know. And I think you wanting to get back at Byron is a little bit of protecting Dev. And I think that's awesome of you. I wish I had someone in my life who'd do the same for me. But from what I've seen of Dev, newbie witch or not, the man can protect himself."

"He most definitely can. I swear he's got more ability in his pinkie finger than I do coursing through my whole body."

"That talented, huh?"

"In spades, and not just in magickville either." Tully gave Sparks a knowing side glance. "Well—" Tully shrugged and popped the last bite of his meal into his mouth, chewed and swallowed, then continued. "Maybe a quick stop at the old coven house to pick up only our things is in order. Yeah?"

"I can get on board with that."

"We should go tonight, get our stuff, and be done with Byron. But I must stop at the house first and check on Uncle

Bart. There are no home health services past eight. I need to make sure he's taken his meds, leave him his glass of scotch, and switch the channel on the TV so he can watch reruns of *The Golden Girls*. You should come say 'Hi.' He loves when cute men come to visit."

"I'd love to! I haven't seen him in ages. He's always got stories."

Tully nodded. "That he does."

Sparks crumpled the empty sandwich wrapper into a ball, intent on taking the trash with him, when a thick rumble of a growl crept across the grass like an angry swarm of ants.

"What the fuck?" Tully's perpetual grin vanished, his eyes going wide.

Sparks motioned for Tully to be quiet.

"I thought this area was sacred?"

Sparks glared at Tully.

The Glade, despite its protection, still attracted all kinds of beasts, both virtuous and unsavoury, to its power. And the Shadow Realm held equal amounts of light and dark creatures. Nature always maintained a balance. A witch needed to be on constant guard in case something untoward slithered nearby. Technically, they should be safe within the arms of the ancient elms encircling the dale.

The growl materialized again, seemingly from all about them.

Both Sparks and Tully gazed around the clearing, attempting to source the nightmare snarl's origin.

"Tully, I think we should head to the car."

"Good idea."

As the two gathered the leftovers from their dinner, they cautiously retreated.

Tully grabbed Sparks by the crook of the arm and whispered, "What is that?" He pointed at the ground toward the edge beyond the elms where the dense vegetation obscured the river.

Sparks squinted as he craned his neck to look. "A pair of shoes?"

Darting glances by both men attempted to spy any foul beast lying in wait, making them potential prey. The two cautiously approached their discovery.

Tully pulled aside a few branches, only to gag and look away.

"Holy shit." Sparks motioned Tully to step aside. Being in the healthcare industry, he'd seen how magnificent and disgusting the human body could be. Festering wounds, bone poking through skin, blood gushing from lacerations, but none of those compared to what lay before them now.

The shoes weren't empty. Poorly hidden in the shrubbery lay a desiccated corpse. Its skin blackened and taut against its bones resembling the ancient mummies Sparks had seen in the British Museum in the Egyptian room on a trip to London several years ago. The eyes had sunk into the skull, and the lips were stretched and pulled back, exposing white teeth as if the dead were baring its fangs in warning.

And whatever this had been, the beast had had fangs.

"Tully, look at its teeth."

"Do I have to?"

"It's a Shadow Realm beast."

"How many monsters do you know wear running shoes?" Tully turned his head away to glance behind them. The light in the Glade had receded, casting a yellowish pall over the area. "The sun is going down. We need to get the hell out of here."

"We do, but I need to—" Sparks yanked a few branches out of the way and examined the remains. "Tully, look! It's got tufts of fur and the hands are...dammit, this is a werewolf. Well, *was* a werewolf? What the fuck can do this to a goddamned werewolf?"

"I don't know, and I don't care. We need to get the hell out and call the Magistrates. They'll clean this up."

"As much as I hate dealing with them, I agree."

"Okay, now we really need to see Uncle Bart. He might have answers too."

Sparks and Tully beat a hasty retreat to the silver Audi parked close by, but given the current circumstances, Sparks wished the car had been closer. Its current position, however, maintained a safe distance from the shrivelled werewolf remains. Unfortunately, the parking spot also lay beyond the sanctuary of the Glade.

The minute the two sat within the confines of the vehicle, both let out deep breaths as Tully pushed the button to enclose the roof. He didn't want to sit in a convertible exposed to whatever may or may not be still out there.

Jolts of electricity lit and danced along the surface of Sparks's skin.

"It'll be okay." Tully followed the electrical blue snaps of electricity as they ascended Sparks's arm. He placed a hand on Sparks's thigh, giving him a pat of comfort, while his other hand punched in the Magistrates' number.

Six-six-six.

The Magistrates were the governing body of the Shadow Realm. They settled magical disputes, sometimes took the law into their own hands, and most importantly, kept the supernatural community safe from the darkest elements of both the magical and mundane world. Some would say the Magistrates protected the mundane world from the Shadow Realm. Regardless, they were known for swift justice and expedient cleanups.

Their word was law.

Behind closed doors and away from potential snitches, stories were told in hushed whispers of cases the Magistrates took where things went wrong. Innocent folks who had disappeared and evil beasts never caught were regular late-night topics of gossip around the cauldron fire.

In general, you wanted to stay as far away as possible from any involvement with them.

The phone only rang once when an automated call system launched. Tully pressed the button on his cell for speakerphone, which played the phone's audio through the Audi's speaker system.

You have reached the Magistrates. Please punch in your identity code followed by the number sign.

Tully punched his number in. All members of the Shadow Realm had one.

The phone went silent for several long seconds.

Thank you. Your number has been confirmed. Please listen carefully to the menu as our options have changed. If this is in regard to a supernatural dispute, coven boundary disagreement, or clarification of magical lineage, please press one. If this is a call to report a suspected presence of a tier four entity, please press two. If this call requires an immediate presence from a representative of the Magistrate Council, please press three. If you would like to leave a message and have someone contact you at a later date, please press four. To hear the menu options again, please press zero.

The presence of an unusual werewolf corpse didn't warrant a tier four entity emergency, but what may have caused the body to look like a dehydrated rotted prune absolutely caused concern. Sparks hoped Tully wouldn't press a number to invoke an immediate presence from the Magistrates.

Reporting the incident, then having nothing to do with any of the representatives from the Magistrates would be the best possible outcome.

"What do you think?" Tully glanced over at Sparks.

"I don't know. Two, I guess. Nobody wants them to show up."

Tully pressed number two.

> *Please stay on the line. The location of your call is being triangulated.*

The message went deathly silent, stirring panic in Sparks.

> *Thank you for your call. A representative will be at your location shortly. Please remain calm, and if possible, place yourself within a protective circle with appropriate defensive wards.*

The line went dead.

"Shit." Tully locked his phone and slipped his cell into his pocket.

Sparks stared at Tully. "Let's get the hell out of here."

"We're supposed to stay here until someone arrives."

"Seriously?

"I punched in my code, so they're going to be able to identify me, and if I abandon the area now..."

"Ugh. This is not how I intended on spending my night." Sparks groaned.

"Me neither, bud. Me neither."

The two fell silent for several minutes, waiting for the imminent arrival.

Shadows were growing long as autumn twilight settled in; the sun dipped lower than the canopy line of the wooded city park. The sky blazed with streaks of orange and red. To the east, the horizon darkened.

"Man, what's taking them?" Tully tapped his fingers on the steering wheel.

"Shh...what was that?"

"What?" Tully asked.

"Shh." Sparks leaned closer to the car's window.

In the blink of an eye, whatever daylight remained evaporated as the car plunged into a void of inky nothingness.

"That is not good." Sparks's saucer-wide eyes stared at Tully. In all the years Sparks had been part of the Shadow Realm, he had never found himself in danger. Tonight, he could no longer make such a claim.

From outside the Audi, a phlegm-filled exhale slithered across the top of the car.

The temperature dropped several degrees as ice crystals formed in the corners of the windows, and Tully and Sparks's breath hung in the air before them.

Sparks's eyes widened as his usually pale skin whitened even more. "That is really not good. Fuck!"

Black mist wafted and swirled around them, writhing and twisting, growing so dense nothing beyond a couple of feet outside the windows was visible.

A skeletal hand lashed out from the vapour and grabbed the edge of the hood, followed shortly by another. Their contact with the car's metal hood banging an ominous *thunk, thunk.*

"Oh my Gods, Tully, it's a wraith. Who cares about the Magistrates? Get the fuck out of here!"

A skull emerged as the two hands clinging to the metal lip of the car's hood, where metal met the glass of the windshield, twisted and pulled the spirit entity from the haze.

The blackened skull resembled the corpse they had found in the woods. Bits of rotted flesh stuck to the bone in random spots. Its jaw opened as another breathy hiss escaped the creature's maw. The clothes this body had once worn were blackened, as if the evil of its being had stained them. Ripped and shredded, they hung from the torso like the spectre had donned a flowing cape and veil. The ragged ends disappeared into the mist, and discerning where the vapour began and the creature's flowing cloth remnants ended became impossible.

"This is most definitely a tier four entity. Wraiths were all supposed to have been banished."

"Tell that to him!" Sparks pointed at the ghostly visitor, its jaw snapping in jerky movements as it clawed at the windshield trying to get to the living occupants within.

Bone-like talons scratched down the length of the windshield.

From inside the car, a bright-white flash erupted as a ward sigil ignited, beaming with such intensity both Tully and Sparks had to cover their eyes.

"What the hell is going on?" Sparks cried out.

"An Uncle Bart feature. Did you see the rune in the middle of the sigil?" Tully peered between his fingers to see what was happening. The glare still beamed with blinding intensity.

"Bitch, I can't see shit right now."

The wraith retreated. It hovered a safe distance from the car, but gyrating and swiping in their direction all the same.

As the initial explosive glow subsided, the boys stared out the windows of the car. Each of the glass panes were etched in the same combination of witch marks. A pattern of runes meant to ward off anything attempting to do its occupants any harm. A circle of triangles pointed outwards, the symbol for *Thurisaz,* representing physical harm. Inside the circle, an upside-down *U* shape was *Uraz*, symbolizing spiritual power, and the rune *Algiz* which appeared similar to a stickman with his arms outstretched, a mark of protection.

"I think we should leave," Tully suggested.

"You don't say." Sparks's sarcastic retort was out of nature for him, but he had never been in this deep of a shit show.

Tully pushed the key fob button as the car revved to life. The extra electrical current running through the vehicle's body juiced the magically enchanted windows.

They shone brighter, crisper, clearer.

The wraith outside retreated further.

Tully threw the car into reverse and slammed on the gas pedal. The car flew out of the parking lot and, in a hot second, left Emily Murphy Park to the wraith and the yet-to-show Magistrates.

Chapter Eight

CAM HAD NOT adequately prepared for, nor had he antici-pated the dangers in his impromptu exodus from the Ances-tral Lands. Travelling Highway 16, also known as the Yel-lowhead, at dusk created a perilous adventure.

Jumping the shadows and weaving through the in-be-tween only applied when the distance between hops stayed within the realm of visually available landmarks. In other words, Cam had to see where the intended destination lay in order to advance his journey. As the sky tinted to purple, the shadows became more frequent, and it grew less easy to dis-cern one location from another. Although, there were more locations to choose from as the day receded and lost out to the night.

Halfway through his journey, he emerged from the dusk right beside a deer. Stumbling across crepuscular creatures shouldn't have been surprising, but both Cam and the leggy beast jolted in surprise. The doe, terror registering in its wide brown eyes, bounded off, gliding across the field at breakneck speeds. Cam clutched his chest, bent over on the spot where he'd been assaulted, and waited for his heart rate to return to a normal pulse.

The increased number of semi-trucks rumbling down the highway during the waning daylight hours also meant crossing the road carried a different sort of risk. Squashed by a B-Train wasn't high on his list of things to do either, so Cam kept to one side of the highway.

A couple of hours short of midnight, Cam emerged for the last time, melting out from the inky black behind the heritage burr oak planted in front of Uncle Bart's house. Regardless of who owned the house, Cam needed to see Dev and use his friend's God-granted tracking skills to hunt down Everton's werewolf den. Cam had to get into the second-floor apartment, where he and Ev had spent a night after being rescued from Radcliff's dungeon.

Cam knocked on their door.

And waited.

"Hmph." He walked out into the yard and studied the dark house. There wasn't a single light on. "Well, shit." It had never dawned on Cam the guys wouldn't be home. "I wonder…"

Fae are nimble creatures. Agile and crafty to boot. Cam discovered sliding his fingers into the roughness of the house's stucco allowed him to scale the side and check a few windows. As luck would have it, the bedroom window had been left open.

After slicing the bug screen covering with his sharp nails, Cam squeezed in through the tear. The ancient house showed signs of age and the window frame's wood crumbled and splintered during Cam's entrance. Cam pulled a fair-sized wooden spike out of his thigh and grimaced while he did so. He imagined the lecture he would get from Dev for destroying the mesh barrier and wood casing, but waiting in the yard all night for Dev or Tully to come home wasn't an option either. After all, keeping up a human guise and waiting on Dev's front stoop would have been impossibly boring. His journey had left him drained and fae magic did require a marginal amount of gas in the tank. After his trek, all his energy had bottomed out. At least here in Dev's house Cam's glamour didn't need to be held. Relaxing, a shimmer of air rippled over his body as his horned, winged, and swishing tail body returned.

Cam sighed. The mental exhaustion from maintaining the fae magic had taken more out of him than he cared to admit. But his first stop before finding somewhere to curl up and patiently wait for the boys was the refrigerator. His stomach twisted and cried out for attention at the mere thought of a juicy slab of flesh.

And thankfully, someone had taken out meat and thawed it. Two good-sized steaks had been left on a plate in the fridge where the freezer ice had melted, leaving a viscous juicy puddle of pink beef juice.

Teeth elongated and sharpened in Cam's mouth. His eyes narrowed as his jaw extended. Lifting each chunk of flesh up and over his waiting maw, he gorged himself, savouring the salty taste and sinewy texture. He licked the plate clean of any indication of its previous contents, then set it back in the fridge. After all, leaving a dirty plate on the counter would be rude.

Cam's belly protruded with a food baby bump. He rubbed his midsection as he forced up steak-flavoured burps.

He sat on the couch for a bit. His tail kept getting in the way and the cushions had been made of some fabric his furry wings stuck to. Cam pried his wings away—like pulling apart Velcro tabs—twice before giving up on the piece of furniture. Instead, he paced the hallway looking at the various photos hanging there in a decorative pattern. Some were art; others were mass-produced prints. An odd one here and there was a framed snap of Dev and his redheaded Tully.

"This is boring as shit."

Cam found his way into the extra room the boys used as

an office. Poking around, he picked up a stack of papers that included investment statements, a couple of bills, and some junk mail.

Directly under the monitor, a small stack of business cards lay in a rectangular plastic holder meant for them. A stylized picture of Dev had been created as part of the business logo on the card. Cam picked one up and scrutinized the cartoon-like doppelganger.

"Community Sociologist. What the fuck does that even mean? Gods, Dev. I leave you for a few short months and you go do something like this? Ugh. You so need an image consultant." Cam shook his head. His tail switched back and forth, clearly annoyed with Dev's choices.

Under the job description an address and phone number were listed.

No landline existed in this apartment. The guys relied on their cell phones. The address wasn't too far away, and in fact, Cam had walked down Whyte Avenue so many times the neighbourhood had been seared into his memory. He recalled the historic brownstones which had seen multiple renos over the course of the building's lifetime that would match up to the address listed on Dev's business card.

If that's where his best friend worked, Cam needed to head over there. Working late on a weekday is exactly the kind of thing he'd expect from his lifetime pal.

Cam would be there in minutes.

It was worth a look. What else was he gonna do? Stick around the apartment and pace the halls?

He stepped over to the window and peered out into the yard. Cam spied the monster heritage oak tree in front of the house. The tree had officially been designated as such, proudly displaying a brass plaque indicating its protected status.

Cam slid the window open, and this time, removed the screen instead of slicing through it. One reprimand on a torn window screen would be sufficient.

Clutching the card closely and thinking about his best friend in the entire world, Cam breathed in deeply, focused on the darkest side of the tree, and like butter set on a burning element, dissolved into the night.

EVERTON LILCH GRUMBLED as he turned the kitchen faucet off. He picked up the dish towel in one hand while selecting a plate balancing on the top of a mountain of now clean dishes, containers, bowls, and assorted other kitchen weapons.

Franco sat at the raised countertop bar, directly across from Ev, as he shovelled in the last of the leftovers in the fridge.

"Glad you're home." Franco's mangled words fell out as gravy slopped from his fork onto his monstrous beard.

Everton grimaced at the sight.

"You know, for a house full of grown-ass men, I would have expected the pack den to be kept up to a reasonable adultlike living standard. This place looks like a Gods-damned frat house." Ev squinted at his second in command.

Franco was a good guy—a beast of a man, almost as big as Ev, but then, all werewolves, male or female, were massive.

Franco peered at Ev with a glint of "I told you so" in his light-brown eyes. He refocused his attention to his meal and continued to shovel the slop from the bowl into his face.

"Seriously, Franco, this place is a dump. What the hell?"

"The guys don't listen to me like they listen to you. I mean, you are the alpha. Yeah? Orders come from you. Best I can do is tell them Daddy's gonna be mad when he gets home. And here you are, at home, and mad. So I didn't lie."

"Yes, but as my second, you're not commanding respect

or keeping them in line. I need you to hold this all together for me when I'm not here."

Franco shrugged. "Then be here. I don't want to complain or bitch but this isn't my job—this honour belongs to you. I kept this lot together for a whole year. We even had a plan to bust you out of the witches' dungeon. We were close to executing it, too, and then bam, you show up. And then poof, you're gone again."

A counterpoint to that train of logic didn't exist. Yelling at Franco for speaking his mind would be detrimental to their relationship. Besides, the man had summarized the situation rather neatly, and Franco's observations left Ev second-guessing his abilities as the alpha.

At least the house still stood, though its cleanliness remained questionable as Ev studied the main floor. With five men, each the size of a Mack truck, living in the renovated two-story, the domicile lacked enough open space to be comfortable. Once a month, though, the residence emptied, giving the walls a break, a chance to breathe, and an escape from the infected bloodline curse the inhabitants all endured.

The house, located right along Edmonton's River Valley, allowed the men to run free and stay relatively out of sight from the city's inhabitants during those full moon periods. The pack had a quick escape to a large tract of wooded valley. Any hunting within city limits was strictly forbidden, and kills were only allowed outside the boundary of the city.

Everton never questioned what got killed, only where the werewolf carnage took place. The last thing they needed were the city cops banging down their door on the regular, or worse, the Magistrates.

The Darkmoon Prairie Walkers had been around almost as long as the Guardians of the Night Grove, their sworn enemies. In fact, Ev couldn't remember which came first. Not that he'd been around for either group's inception, but he'd been the alpha of this pack for the last fifty years or so.

"Where is everyone?" Ev gave up, throwing the tea towel on the counter. He leaned against the bank of drawers behind him and crossed his arms over his chest. Muscles along his forearm rippled as he clenched his fists.

"Josip is visiting his ex-wife and the kids—" Franco picked up the bowl and scraped the bottom with his spoon, attempting to get each drop and morsel of stew. "—and Serge is out trying to find Lars."

"What do you mean 'trying to find'?" Ev cocked an eyebrow.

"Well, if you'd use the cell phone you have, you'll have seen the dozen or so texts I sent about a week ago when Lars didn't come home from the last boundary run." A regular scamper near the pack's territory edge was performed on a rotating basis. Like doing house chores. Except the run allowed them to shift, and any werewolf loved a good run.

Ev dropped his head forward in disbelief, dug his phone out of his back pocket, and stared at a black screen.

"You probably have to turn it on." Franco growled as he pushed the empty bowl aside. Ev glanced up briefly from his phone to eyeball Franco. The pout on his bearded face indicated his disdain, but Ev was unsure if the frown had been meant for him and his clueless abilities with technology, or for a now-empty food dish.

Ev held the side button and turned the device on. After a quiet couple of minutes, Franco stood up, walked around the kitchen island, and stood beside his alpha. He grabbed the phone and punched a few buttons. Everton gaped in awe at the rapid movements of Franco's fingers.

"There. I set up your notifications which you had turned off."

"Maybe because I didn't want to be disturbed."

"That's nice when you're on vacation, but when you're the leader of a pack of misfit wolfen beasts who are generally self-destructive, make bad decisions, and run hot and angry most of the day, you might want to stay in communication with me so I can update you on everything going on."

"Hey! Not fair. I came back to the city because you called and told me there was an emergency."

"I had been calling you for two weeks! And yes, there had been an emergency. We still have an emergency and now a missing wolf."

"Okay, well, Lars has been known to get his ass thrown in jail for bar fights. Has anyone bothered to check them out first?"

"Of course I did. I also called the hospitals and a handful of funeral homes. Nothing. He's flat out missing. But that's not the worst of it."

"Do tell, what other scenario would prove to be worse than Lars missing?"

"There's another alpha in town. And he's been down in our River Valley in front of the house. His scent is all over the place."

"You sure it's an alpha? Wouldn't be the first time we've had a drifter wolf come through town."

"Oh, quite sure. It's the same heady scent you give off that gives us all an erection whether we want one or not. And I've snuffled out the pheromones down by the riverbanks right outside our front door. Whoever the culprit is, he's been watching us."

"No shit."

Ev grit his teeth over this catastrophic information. A drifter wolf passing through town, no problem. Hell, even another pack moving close by was fine, so long as they kept their distance. Edmonton's city limits stretched far enough in all directions to handle two clans of werewolves. But shapeshifters weren't exactly common. You can't breed a wolf. Only make them, and most don't survive the bite because a werewolf who is lashing out and biting is seeing nothing but red. And in the confusion, anger, and bloodlust, there isn't enough common sense running through the wolf's brain to say, "Whoa buddy, just a nip is all you need." Nope, it's rip them to shreds.

But an alpha wolf who's encroaching on pack territory and spying out Ev's pack house? That's problematic. Another alpha infringing this close usually meant there'd be a challenge for dominion close at hand.

"I'm too old for this shit." Ev shook his head.

"That's why I call—"

The door exploded open as Serge came loping in. Still wolfen—sort of. Tufts of fur had sprouted out in patches, limbs were gangly, stretched, and half human. Serge's face was misshaped, giving him a goofy comical look rather than the terrifying maw of a predator. His haunches backpedalled as he tried to catch himself on the hardwood floor. The beast panted and slobbered everywhere, vainly attempting to get a foothold on the slippery floors.

"For fuck's sake, Serge, pull it together. You're ruining the fucking floors! You will fix every scratch you make." Everton's hackles went up despite only having a short-cropped fringe of hair around his lower scalp. His shiny dome had been a source of amusement for the rest of the pack. Some werewolf. Bald.

Everton glared at Franco. "What the fuck is this?"

"Serge has figured out a half-assed way to morph directly before the full moon."

"What in hell's name?"

"This is yet another reason we need you here. New wolves need guidance. Otherwise, they figure shit out on their own."

"This is not good." Ev slapped his mitt of a paw over his face, struggling to comprehend how a shift had gone so wrong.

Everton's dominant presence needed to be consistent.

His heart ached momentarily as memories of Cam and quiet afternoons spent in the Ancestral Lands clearing came to mind. Sun beating down, a light breeze coming off the nearby mountains. Those afternoons had been heaven.

The pack house held nothing but stress and ulcer-inducing emergency situations.

With a few snaps and bone cracks, and a small puddle of drool and blood soaking into the claw marks he'd made in the floorboards, Serge stood naked in the entryway, chest heaving, and a sheen of sweat covering his body. His dirty-blond hair and fur, soaked and matted, stuck to his skin. Smears of mud, grass, and twigs dotted his body.

"What the hell?" Everton crossed his arms for the second time in minutes.

"I found Lars at Emily Murphy Park. He's dead. The Night Grove witches did it! I saw them there, hovering over his body. You should see what those bastards did."

Chapter Nine

TULLY BURST INTO Uncle Bart's bedroom. Sparks got dragged along, his arm nearly wrenched out from its socket by Tully's bearish grip.

"You're late." Uncle Bart stared at them as they exploded into the bedroom. He tapped his index finger on the surface of his smart watch then waved his finger at Tully. "If I tell your mother, she'll be pissed."

"You wouldn't." Tully stopped with a lurch. Sparks careened into his back, almost tipping them both over, but the sheer volume of muscled expanse making up Tully's shoulders made for an effective block.

At least Sparks didn't tumble over.

"Try me," Uncle Bart said as Sparks pulled away and found himself in the middle of the two men currently locked in a staring contest. Uncle Bart matched Tully's steely gaze. The two stared at each other in a death match of wills. An uncomfortable silence settled in the room. Sparks fidgeted as he moved to the side.

Uncle Bart broke out in hysterical laughter. "What, and get my favourite great-nephew in trouble? Bitch, please."

"Jesus, old man…" Tully's shoulders slumped in relief as he swatted his great uncle's feet which were neatly tucked under the crocheted bedspread.

"You're my only source of fun."

"Oh, I highly doubt that." Tully bent and picked up Uncle Bart's tablet which had been discarded to the floor beside the bed. The unmistakable grunts and groans coming from the device overshadowed the TV which nattered on from the corner of the room. From over Tully's shoulder, Sparks blushed as naked bodies in adult positions flashed across the tablet's screen, also explaining the suggestive soundtrack. The tablet streamed a live porn session. Tully flipped the screen cover over the porn and reprimanded his uncle. "You are terrible."

"If you think this is bad, you should have seen me at your age. Dates galore and an orgy every Saturday night. Okay, boys, you are late, not that I care, but I can smell bad juju on you too. Where have you been? Sit. Tell Auntie Bart everything."

Sparks snickered.

"Sparks, come sit next to me. You haven't visited in such a long time, and I missed seeing those flowing locks of hair."

"You, sir, are one pervy old man." Sparks chuckled as he walked around the other side of the bed and took a seat. "And I love it, Auntie, don't ever stop." He smiled from ear to ear which evidently made the old man happy as he returned the grin and gripped Sparks's hand.

Tully pulled up a side chair and sat while grabbing Uncle Bart's other hand and giving it a squeeze. "So, what did you do to the Audi's windows?"

"Ah, so, I'm not wrong. You boys are too young to have experienced all the glory of both the light and the dark the Shadow Realm has to offer. I knew those sigils would come in handy one day. It's a compound circle rune of protection against negative and evil energy." Uncle Bart peered into Tully's eyes.

Uncle Bart was in his eighties. A definite rarity in the world of male witches. Most tended to peter out in their sixties, having used up all their life force casting spells.

Magic was not free.

Uncle Bart had progressed his way through the ranks of the witch world, journeying through the Shadow Realm, and had aptly and honourably earned the title of Elder. Sparks had heard him referred to as "one spooky-ass bitch" by many people.

With an alarming quickness, the old man's hands shifted. He grabbed both Sparks and Tully by their wrists and clamped down tightly.

His eyes milked over, like he'd been plagued with cataracts. His head jerked backward.

Tully had told Sparks on numerous occasions how he'd been subjected to Uncle Bart's visions his entire life. He had several unique talents. He was a witch of the black robe, like Dev, an Aurologist. His source of magic drew from his emotional state, which consumed energy from his soul, or from others. But his primary gift concerned all things within the prophetic arena, like clairvoyance and clairaudience. Not only did he see the future, he also relived the memories of others as well as being able to dig into the past. He had occasionally even recounted people's past lives.

The man's abilities were exceptional, but he'd had years to sharpen them.

And Sparks had never had a visit with dear old Uncle Bart where he hadn't blushed at least once. Uncle Bart did not suffer from any form of shyness. If anything, he epitomized the characteristics of a "dirty old man." But everyone humoured him, and he never harmed anyone, or did anything without consent. Push people's boundaries? Absolutely.

He didn't get out of his first-floor apartment much anymore and spent most of his days online talking with friends who were still around, and astral projecting.

Sparks had heard Tully tell stories of the man using his abilities with wild abandon, which of course made Tully give him shit numerous times for using energy to do magical things. But Auntie Bart was formidable, and Tully regularly told of his unceremonious dismissal. *"At my age I'll do whatever the hell I want!"* A constant reprimand for suggesting he should calm down and pack the magic away.

With a shake of his head, Uncle Bart's eyes cleared, and he released his death grip.

"Wraiths, huh? They were banished. How are they even crossing the veil to get here? Coalescing into our realm takes energy from the ley lines, and they were denied access, and for good reasons. Those fuckers can't be argued with. They'll leave a trail of desiccated dead bodies behind them. If they absorb enough energy and become corporeal, you'll have a wight on your hands. Once that happens, they'll start summoning more of their own kind. You'll end up with an infestation faster than you can recite a canticle."

"Well, there's been some developments over the past few months." Tully grimaced as he pried his gaze away from his great-uncle and instead studied the old shag carpet in the bedroom. Evidently no one had informed Uncle Bart of *the incident*.

"What happened to Byron?" Uncle Bart cocked an eyebrow.

"How do you know this shit?"

"I'm a witch. I know things."

"Don't use that line on me, old man." Tully shook his head as he stood and went over to the dresser and counted out the pills Uncle Bart needed to take before bedtime.

"It's true, though, isn't it? So what the hell happened to Byron? If there are wraiths, that means the wards on the leys are broken. And if you have wraiths, then demons aren't far behind. Next thing you know we'll have nests of vampires too. I never liked Byron. Shady as hell. Arrogant and overconfident. But he knew his shit and he kept the worst of the

Shadow Realm at bay. So, if the wraiths have returned...I repeat, what has happened?"

Sparks grimaced. They weren't leaving without a detailed account of the night he'd cleaned up a blood-soaked basement. Uncle Bart missed nothing and picked up on the subtlest of clues.

"Out with it, boys. What the hell is going on?"

"It's complicated," Tully stammered.

"Well, I have nothing but time, so best you spill the beans."

Tully and Sparks spent the next hour telling Uncle Bart all the particulars. How Dev used a summoning board which catapulted him into the Shadow Realm, and into Tully's life, the ongoing feud with the werewolves that led to Addas's infection, which turned into a cause for Byron—who stopped at nothing trying to fix his lover.

Next, he told of the sacrificing of fae for their life essence, and how the boys discovered Byron had tricked everyone into ingesting the fae's bodily fluids—

"And once you're fae touched, you're never quite human again," Uncle Bart finished. "Well, shit. Byron got himself into one hell of a pickle this time, didn't he?"

"I think he feels really bad about everything though. When I saw him at the hospital, he sobbed in front of me. He's always been the quintessential embodiment of witchy strength and power. That day, he was a broken mess," Sparks added.

"Damn right. He should be. What a clusterfuck. Well, that settles it then."

"Settles what?" Tully gave Uncle Bart the side-eye.

"You boys have to take over. If the ley lines aren't throttled, Edmonton will turn into a death pit, just like New York did in the 70s and stayed that way until the early 90s."

"Come on, Auntie Bart. New York was a mess back in the day, true, but everyone knows the change in policing turned the city around." Sparks prided himself on the volume of useless facts and trivia he had tucked away in his brain.

Uncle Bart cocked an eyebrow and smirked. "Youngsters." He harrumphed. "No, you fools. Same thing happened there. Central Park is one of the largest eruptions of ley energy on the continent. The Carousel was built overtop of the fountain of energy. The circular ride is a clever device. It's one massive ward. Each one of those carved horses is marked with sigils to ward off negative energy. And every person who rides the carousel is stripped, just a smidgeon, of their life force, which is turned into a continual source of energy to power up the wards.

"Emily Murphy Park here in Edmonton is the same damn thing, except no one's bothered to build a ward at the source of the eruption. Instead, the Guardians of the Night Grove placed wards on the ley lines leading up to the fountain, keeping a wider berth of evil free space that acts as a dome of protection over the entire city. Byron showed me once...he has a globe channelling the energy from the line running under the coven house. In turn, the sphere powers the wards. The contraption's a clever design, but I know he stole the specs from the coven in Montreal that did the same thing. Their botanical garden? Another eruption site."

"See, I told you, the old man has stories." Sparks raised an eyebrow.

"But the Guardians are no longer. Eddie and Gus are...well...gone. Addas is missing, or dead, and Byron's infection is incubating. He's only got a handful of months left before his first transition, and witch werewolves never survive," Tully stated.

"Yeah, but he's witch, werewolf, and fae. Who the hell knows what that combination is going to produce? And for that matter, Addas had the fae in him too. We all do, thanks to Byron. For all we know, Addas is alive and well."

"I never liked Byron Radcliffe or his goons—but he did a job for this city. A thankless one few know about. You boys need to take over, and quick. Or we'll all suffer."

"Well, Sparks, Dev, and I have already talked about forming a new coven. In fact, we were going to bring the guys together for Mabon."

"Good. Do it. And fix this mess." Uncle Bart stared at each of them again. Sparks squinted and studied the old man as his glassy eyes peered right through him. "Hmph."

"What? Whenever you grumble, it's never good."

Uncle Bart kept staring. "You, and Sparks, and Dev. A good mix of energy to start something new. Threes are good. Maiden, Mother, Crone. Son, Father, Sage. You'll need each other."

Sparks cocked his head to one side. Uncle Bart sometimes got a bit mystical.

"Sure, it's not as if we haven't already contemplated the idea of a new coven, but we'd be building it from scratch," Tully said. "We don't have the resources Byron had access to. I don't have a globe of ley line enchantment to throttle ley line energy."

"Byron led the old coven. He doesn't own its books, scrolls, tools, or magic. If there are things you need, you go to the house and get them. Boys"—Uncle Bart continued to stare at each of them in turn—"this is a serious problem that needs to be dealt with. Wraiths are bad. Demons are worse, and there are other things lurking in the darkness of the Shadow Realm we don't want here in our home. Fix this. I'll help you get what you need to start things up. But you need to control the ley lines. That's all there is to it."

"Oh, that's all." Tully rolled his eyes.

At that moment Sparks had an inkling, a pull in his gut, suggesting his bottle of wine spelled with *Laguz* was coming to fruition. Like most things when magic got involved, the end result wouldn't be as one would have hoped or intended.

THE CLOCK'S ARMS were perilously close to midnight, and Uncle Bart's eyes drooped with sleep. Too tired. This getting old business wasn't for the faint of heart. Everything hurt: joints, knees, back. But seeing Tully always lifted his spirits. He enjoyed the company of his great-nephew. The addition of Sparks had been a welcome surprise. The flowing locks and tight body made the man a delectable morsel of meat. He'd have to get the tissues and lotion out later.

But despite any old man crushes, he had made the boys a promise, and one he meant to keep. Exhaustion from a day of doing nothing weighed heavily on his bones and his bed was warm and cozy. But this estate and this city had always been his domain. Uncle Bart had witnessed the cold hand of the reaper collect several of his friends. His time on the physical plane had nearly played itself out, but he had no intentions of leaving his corner of the world in this disastrous state.

There were a few things Uncle Bart needed to do before he would make the transition to the Eternal Grasslands and Wild Forests to be with his Gods and Goddesses.

"Ester? Where are you at, girl?" Bart called out and if anyone had seen him do it, they'd have considered him ready for the nursing home.

A book fell off the shelf.

"Oh, come on. Now's not the time to play coy. I need you."

The TV in the corner, which had been muted while playing the nightly news, flickered.

"Goddamn ghosts. Ester, I'm not playing tonight. I need your help."

The crocheted bedspread pulled itself off the bed.

Uncle Bart rolled his eyes.

"Fine. Be that way. I will give you what you want, but you have to do something for me first."

The lights in the room went off. The TV died.

"Finally."

In the darkness, an ethereal mist poured into the centre of the room, coming from all over. In a twirl of shimmering diamond dust, Ester coalesced and formed at the front of Bart's bed. She was dressed in clothes from a long-forgotten era. The bodice pulled tight and buttoned from the navel to the throat. The collar enclosed the neck and from the way Ester held her head rigid and upright, as Bart stroked his own neck, the garment looked distinctly uncomfortable. The flare at her hips, though, spoke of voluminous and heavy fabric as the skirt puddled onto the floor. Her long hair, silver in the darkness, was tightly braided and twirled into a bun pinned to the back of her head—a severe and stunningly handsome look.

She stretched out a vaporous hand and placed her dead fingers on Bart's leg.

The appendage emanated ice-like temperatures, but she meant no harm. She wanted to help. Bart sensed it, a warm calming sensation easing his heart and mind.

Of course, there was a price. Nothing from the Shadow Realm came without cost.

"The boys need our help. The library downstairs, you know of it. You've been there before, right?" Bart asked.

She nodded once.

"Take others if you need help, but all the items belonging to the Guardians—take them to the library downstairs. We shall relocate everything they'll need to reincarnate the old coven into something new. The items the Guardians housed? Bring them here. My Tully and his mates need to take over."

Again, she closed her eyes and nodded once.

"Good. As I promised, you'll get payment. I'll let you have my body for a day, but only one day. Understand? One twenty-four-hour period. Acceptable?"

Another nod.

She evaporated.

The light flickered until it shone bright, and the TV stuttered briefly before blaring out the nightly news.

"She never did learn how to adjust the volume." Uncle Bart grumbled as he threw back the covers and swung his legs out of bed. He had on an old stained white T-shirt that hung loose on his skinny frame, and only boxers covering his bottom. Scrawny pale legs told the truth of his age. The skin, paper thin, showed spider veins and blotches. The markings of age everyone inevitably obtains. A sign we have lived life.

On an unsteady gait, he ambled across the room, grabbed the remote, and pressed the Volume Down button. The TV fell silent.

"Now, where did I put you...?" Uncle Bart, still in his skivvies, scoured the bookshelves lining the wall. He thumbed a few spines, the contents of the shelves conjuring up snippets of his life. Spells cast, monsters conquered, loves come and gone, friends and bonds created through magic—all were documented and kept here on one shelf or another. He'd had an extraordinary life. One he was thankful for.

"There you are."

He pulled out a scroll and ran a finger over the wax seal. The paraffin contained concentric swirls of brown and black. Brown for Earth and home, black for protection and binding. The shape within the stamp was of the great antlers of the horned God.

"I had hoped we'd never have to use you again, but I'm afraid we need you now."

Calling forth his energy, Bart closed his eyes, and in the dimness of his bedroom, he glowed with a blue-tinged phosphorescence.

With his finger, he wrote three runes: an off-centred cross, a harsh jagged letter *B*, and a diamond with legs.

"*Nauthiz, Berkano, Othala,*" he whispered. The lines thickened and turned black.

The wax seal cracked and split. The scroll unravelled.

The paper revealed an architectural diagram of his house and yard showing the measurements of each room, its walled structures, and the multiple stories as well as the garden out back. This document consecrated and protected the boundaries of his property. In the witch world, the scroll acted as the deed of ownership to a magical entity—and the old house had loads of magic. Not only was it a collection of lumber and bricks, this structure had sentience. The house reacted and thought on its own and operated as a host to several other beings.

As the runes burned into the paper, the diagram shifted and changed. A room appeared in the lower level which hadn't been there before, and in the garden, an additional plot of land jutted out.

Out in the backyard, a hedge grew, tall and thick. One opening appeared; where the branches of the boxwood grew in the archway, the leaves did not. The wooden frame twisted upon itself in an intricate weave, a braid of sorts, creating a portal into a clearing. On the far side of this hidden grove, a massive gnarled and heavily leafed Higan Cherry stood guard. The branches had seen many a winter, a hundred years of summers, a thousand prairie thunderstorms.

It was tall and strong.

Its roots also housed an Earth elemental. The guardian of this witch wood who had been put to rest many years ago.

"It's time to wake up," Uncle Bart whispered.

Chapter Ten

STANDING AS STILL as possible, like a cat eyeing potential prey, Cam studied the lobby of the small office. A couch against the far wall didn't look too comfortable. A coffee table held several coasters but still had water rings on its surface while a few magazines were scattered here and there. A bad artificial plant stood in the corner of the room. Cam would have sworn he had stumbled into a doctor's office.

The door on the far wall had frosted glass panels, and lettering across the centre of the windowpane read, "Dev Khandelwal—Community Sociologist."

Cam shook his head. *What the hell?*

A crash ripped Cam's attention away from the title, as the tinkling of broken glass filled the air.

A woman screamed.

Muffled voices were followed by an ominous growl. His wings vibrated with nerves.

"What the hell?" he repeated, but this time in a hoarse whisper.

He approached the door and cautiously opened it a crack to peer inside.

Dev sat behind a desk. A woman slumped in her seat opposite to Dev. Her long hair hung listlessly on each side of her head, and from the sobs and the movement of her shoulders, he knew she was crying.

"I don't know what to do."

"Well, I promise I will try to help you. This, however, is beyond my abilities. I'm going to have to call in some additional support. Can you tell me again how you got my contact information?"

She sobbed, sniffled, and continued. Cam jerked his head toward a shadowy motion that caught his attention.

A child, maybe seven or eight years old, crawled on tippy toes backward up the wall.

"I posted a video of Noah on a parenting forum. We are at our wits' end and don't know what to do. The church hasn't been of any help. This isn't normal!" The woman gestured to the boy who had crouched up into the corner of the ceiling. "Normal children don't do this."

The boy hissed.

Dev put his head in his hands. "It's all right, Mrs. Andersen; we will figure this out, but I may have some rather unconventional ways of dealing with Noah. I'm afraid I won't be able to do anything tonight. Do you feel like you can wait a few days? Are you okay to take him home?"

"As long as you promise to help. He's not violent. But look at him!"

The boy's head darted in Cam's direction, his eyes glowing red. He hissed.

Dev shot a glance toward the cracked open door and furrowed his brows.

Oh shit.

Cam's memories shifted to Everton, and their time spent together stuck in the witch's dungeon. Byron had just finished torturing him, jabbing long needles into his spinal column. Anger erupted in his belly, while the vengeance he wanted bubbled to the surface of his skin, making him hot and itchy all over.

In that instant, Cam disappeared.

"Mrs. Anderson, do you think you could come see me on Thursday, around one in the afternoon?" Dev clicked away on his laptop.

"It will have to be after sunset. Noah won't come out of his room until the sun has gone down. He's up all night." She sucked in a desperate breath, her inhale hitching several times. This woman was on the edge of a breakdown.

"All right. Shall we say eight in the evening on Thursday? I'll see what I can do to have someone here who knows more about this sort of thing."

"What is this thing?"

"Well, I have some suspicions, but I don't want to say anything until I'm completely sure. But regardless of what I think, I want you to know I will help you. Okay?"

"Okay."

Dev stood. He glanced toward the door.

"Thursday evening it is." Dev extended his hand toward the office door, right where Cam stood.

"Yes, fine. Noah, come on, baby, we're gonna go home and come back to see this nice man in a couple of days, okay?" Noah scampered down from his resting spot up near the ceiling. His body actions were jerky, and his head twisted the wrong way as he climbed down on all fours, inverted. He mimicked a spider to perfection.

As the woman left the office and exited the lobby, Dev closed the door behind her and turned the bolt sideways, locking himself in the office. He put his back to the door and slid down a few inches, letting out a massive sigh of relief.

"You can come out now, Cam," he yelled.

"How'd you know it was me?" Cam's tail switched to and fro as he stopped thinking about the torture session induced by Byron Radcliffe and instantly revealed himself.

"Really? Like I wouldn't know when my best friend was standing in the room with me?" Dev grinned like a devil. "What the hell are you doing here? I thought newbie fae weren't supposed to leave the Ancestral Lands." Dev's dishevelled clothes and the black circles under his eyes told Cam he'd been working too hard.

"Jeez, you look bagged. And hi, it's so good to see you after so many months." Cam coyly smiled at his friend.

"Come here." Dev opened his arms and pulled the Eldritch fae who had been his longest and most cherish bestie in for a hug. But the embrace turned out to be awkward, what with Cam's horns and wings.

Still, Cam melted into his friend. He'd never been without Dev for so long.

"I have so much to tell you," he mumbled into Dev's shoulder. "I hate the Ancestral Village. Lady Aine is a heartless and scary bitch. Everton dumped me."

"Wait. What?" Dev pulled away.

"How come you look so beat? Everything okay?" Cam changed the subject.

"Work has been slightly insane."

"That's it? Everything is okay at home?"

"Oh my Gods, yes. No, Tully and I are fantastic. Don't give us another thought. Seriously, I've been pulling twelve-to-fourteen-hour days. It's ridiculous."

"What the hell is a Community Sociologist?"

"It's just a name. Basically, word got out I'm a social worker/healer/fixer of things for residents of the Shadow Realm. I handle individuals with issues and groups with problems. I deal with their magical difficulties. When the

Horned One made me a tracker, and the Goddess made me her emissary, shit got busy. And now apparently, I have cases coming in from outside the Shadow Realm because the little boy who scaled my office walls—they are not a magical family." Dev yawned and stretched.

"The kid looked like he was possessed. Like head-spinning Linda Blair pea-soup-puking possessed."

"That's exactly what I think too—except we're not supposed to have any demons in Edmonton."

"Why not?"

"Something Tully told me. The Realm holds both light and dark creatures, but for the longest time, Edmonton has been devoid of anything truly dark. He didn't get into it. But I haven't got the foggiest how to treat someone who's possessed if that's what is really going on. I need to figure out what's wrong with the boy. I might know who to talk to, but I need time to make a few phone calls.

"Now, tell me, what the hell are you doing in the city and not with your nose stuck in a book learning how to do all the fae stuff? Although it would seem you have invisibility nailed. Nice! When we left you, Lady Aine said you'd be there awhile. A couple of months doesn't equal 'awhile.' What gives?" Dev hadn't taken a breath through his ramblings. Cam gawked in amazement. His best pal since forever had always been the quiet one. Cam, on the other hand, was the gregarious, talkative troublemaker.

"Too long, didn't read version?" Cam raised an eyebrow.

"Please, I'm exhausted and need to get home. You can give me all the gory details tomorrow, but out with it. What's up?"

Cam fished out the glass vial Lady Aine had given him from the drawstring bag hanging at his hip. He placed the vessel on Dev's desk.

"I need to fill that."

"What is it?"

"A vial that needs to contain my seed."

"What? Eww, Cam, get it off my desk."

"It hasn't been filled yet. Well, at least, not that I know of." Cam picked up the glass container, brought it close to his face, and peered into it.

"Gross."

"Completely." Cam shoved the vessel into its bag. "Basically, Everton has been with me all summer, and we've spent a load of time together, but not *together* together. If you get my drift. And as the only fertile Royal fae in the Ancestral Lands, it's up to me to get Lady Aine preggers, but we all know *that's* never happening. Your homie don't play those games. So, I have to fill the vial and make sure Lady Aine has it in her hot little 'gotta have babies' hands before Groundswell."

"Wow. What the hell is Groundswell? And filling the vial shouldn't be much of a problem. Grab an internet connection, stream some porn, and—"

"Yeah, that's not gonna work. It can't be filled by my own doing. The seed must be the result of a coupling, preferably one where I'm emotionally attached to the other person." Cam spoke the last words as if he'd chomped down on the most bitter of leaves.

"Oh." Dev grimaced as he nodded his head in understanding.

"Right. Your horned, tailed, and winged best friend doesn't make 'emotional connections.' They're too...complicated. Except I kinda already made one with Everton. Dammit. And the fucker left."

"Left the Ancestral Lands?"

"Yeah."

"And went?"

"Here to the city. Which is where you come in. I need to find him, get the vial filled"—Cam tapped his hip where the bag hung—"and then get the damn thing back to Lady Aine before the village goes underground for winter. *That* is Groundswell."

"Ah, gotcha. So we need to go see Everton." Dev shrugged.

"I don't know where he lives. We never went to his place."

"Oh, red flag, red flag!" Dev snickered.

"Shut up." Cam punched Dev in the shoulder. Not hard, just enough.

"Ow. Fine. So, you need me to witch-find my way to Ev's place so you can get jiggy with him?"

"All right, when you put it like that, you make me sound desperate."

"Well, you are, aren't you?"

"Okay, sort of. Would you?"

"For you"—one side of Dev's mouth twitched up in a wry smirk—"of course."

"You're the best. Thanks."

Dev reached up and ran his fingers over Cam's bony horns.

"I'm never going to get used to those."

"They're kinda cool, but a bitch to sleep with at night."

"I can't imagine."

"Oh, but wait. Watch this!" Cam once again summoned an image of Everton, which triggered so many of his abilities and delved into the scheming part of his brain. Trying to figure out the right thing to say when he showed up on the doorstep, what Ev might say back to him, and how he would worm his way into Ev's big wolfy heart...and with a ripple of air caused by his fae magic, the Eldritch Cam dissipated, and human Cam stood before Dev.

"Holy shit! Dude. That's amazing. You're getting a handle on your abilities! So, are they gone?" Dev put his arm up toward Cam's head again.

Cam slapped his hand away, "Of course, they're still there. It's just an illusion."

"Damn good one."

And with a constant banter back and forth, Dev and Cam left Dev's workplace and headed to his parked car.

"WAIT A MINUTE. What do you mean the Guardian witches did it? I can assure you that is certainly not the case." Everton remained still, maintaining his pack leader stoniness, and squinted at Serge.

The man had a tendency toward the dramatic.

"I'm telling you, two of their witches were poking and prodding Lars's dead body. They did it!"

"Yeah, I find that hard to believe." Everton shook his head. "Did you think maybe to bring the body home so we can deal with it? Or did you leave him lying on the ground for the cops to find?"

"I...ah...well." Serge bit his bottom lip.

"I'll go get him." Franco volunteered.

"I...I'll help. I'll go too." Serge's gaze darted toward Everton.

Everton loved all his guys. They were good men. Most of them stumbled into lycanthropy by being in the wrong spot at the wrong time. A shifted wolf retains some human thought and reason, but instinct and the wild call get in the way. An encounter with a werewolf always wound up in two scenarios. Dead or turned.

All of them had scars, physical and mental, from their infections—but despite their affliction, they were decent folk at heart. Apparently, none of them were capable of doing housework.

"No, Serge, let Franco retrieve the body. You can help do some bloody housework. I might be pack leader, but I'm no fucking den mother. Jesus, this place is a mess. I can't leave any of you. And before you go"—Ev gestured to Franco, then to the empty bowl and dirty spoon sitting on the raised eating bar of the kitchen island—"clean this up."

With a shake of his head, and a run of his hand over his scalp, Everton had had enough for the day. Halfway up the stairs the back door slammed, which indicated Franco's departure, followed by a knock at the front door. Ev halted his step toward his second-floor bedroom.

"What the fuck now?"

Before Ev had turned around and walked down the stairs that led to the front door foyer, Serge opened the door completely naked.

From behind Serge, Ev spotted Cam.

Cam nervously beat his wings and stroked his horns. His tail flicked back and forth as he gawked at the nude werewolf pup. He stood on Ev's front porch in nothing but a loincloth.

Serge immediately went defensive. A growl rumbled from the young wolf's chest.

"Settle, Serge. That's enough. And go put some goddamn clothes on." Ev's voice boomed. "Cam, what the hell?"

Ev shoved Serge out of the way, then grabbed the fae and dragged him into the house's entryway. He poked his head outside, surveying the front yard, making sure none of his neighbours were out to potentially spot a nearly naked Cam. Instead, Ev spied Dev in his car, driving away.

"Cam, what the hell are you doing here? You aren't supposed to be off the Ancestral Lands. You won't survive yet. You're too...immature. Didn't Lady Aine have you locked in the village?"

"Yeah, so about that. We need to talk."

Cam gave Ev a nervous half grin as an inquisitive Serge's nose sniffed the air in front of him, trying to get a whiff of the unusual guest.

Chapter Eleven

SPARKS AND TULLY had retreated upstairs after their visit with Uncle Bart. Midnight loomed. Sparks had already contemplated heading home, as his evening shift at the hospital tomorrow would come quickly enough and reporting for duty without a good night's rest would mean a non-productive and scatterbrained stint. Instead, he sat at a bar stool on the edge of the kitchen counter, deflated, still alarmed over the wraith incident, and his mind racing from visiting Uncle Bart. He craned his neck to one side, stretching out the tightening muscles.

"You want a beer?" Tully asked.

"Ugh, I should go, but if I'm being honest, that wraith thing scared the shit out of me. I'll take the beer."

Tully opened the fridge and pulled out a couple. He handed one to Sparks but also brought an empty plate out. He scrunched his face into a ball of confusion as he placed the dish on the counter. He wiped his fingers on his shorts.

"Dev told me he had taken out a couple of steaks for tomorrow night's dinner. So, this is weird." Tully shook his head and dismissed the oddity. He had other things to worry about right now. "You know, I should text him. It's not like him to be this late." Tully glanced at the clock on the microwave, then opened a drawer and rummaged through its contents. Finally, he passed Sparks a bottle opener. Craft beers rarely came with a twist-off top. "And stay here tonight. You don't have to go home. We got lots of room. I wouldn't want you to wander the streets alone knowing a wraith is out there."

As if on cue, the *clickety tinkle* of a key jostled in the front door's lock and the deadbolt slid open, breaking their conversation.

"And that will be Dev." Tully turned, opened the fridge, and pulled out a bottle of wine.

"Oh, my Gods, you're so sweet." Sparks grinned, impressed with Tully's attentiveness.

"If it's this late, and he's just getting home, he'll need a drink." Tully winked at Sparks while pouring his boyfriend a glass.

"Hey, honey, I'm home," Dev yelled from the foyer. There was some rustling as shoes were removed, and then the pad of socks walking down the short hallway thudded until their owner appeared in the kitchen where they sat. "Oh, hey, Sparks!"

Tully met Dev halfway, grabbed him around the waist, and planted a kiss on his man.

"Here, you might want this."

"Oh yes, I do. You will not believe the night I had."

"Same! But you go first. What happened? Why working so late?" Tully pulled away and stood at the end of the kitchen counter where Sparks sat. He grabbed his beer. Sparks spun around and waved a nonchalant hello to Dev.

"Well, which first? You won't believe who dropped by for a visit." Dev took a sip of his wine, gently placed the glass on a nearby ledge, slipped off his satchel, and dumped the bag in the corner of the dining room.

"Okay, nope, no idea. Who?"

"Cam."

"Wait, I thought—"

"Mm-hmm, me too. He's managed to escape Lady Aine's control and needed to go see Everton but didn't know where the wolfman lived so I had to use my God-given tracking ability to find the man. Apparently, they broke up and Cam is finding out why, or what's going on, or...I don't know. It's Cam, therefore it's complicated. But I hope he sorts his mess out."

"That doesn't sound like fun."

"No, and frankly witch-finding is mentally exhausting. But Cam is at the pack house. I'm sure he'll be over tomorrow. Now, believe it or not, that wasn't even the oddest bit to my night, and Sparks, I'm glad you're here. I think I'm gonna need your brother's help."

"Wiatt?"

"He's a necromancer, yeah?"

"He is."

"Well, my late-night appointment turned out to be a mother from society at large. In other words, not a member of the Shadow Realm. She brought in her youngest son, who proceeded to climb the walls."

"Oh, did stuff get broken? Hyperactive kid?"

"No, I mean literally climb the walls. He crouched in the corner up by the ceiling, spider walking his way up and down, eyes glowing red, hissing at all of us. If I didn't know any better, I'd swear the kid has a demon in him. But I don't know anything about demons or possession, and I hoped your brother might?" Dev turned and gave a pleading look at Sparks.

"I can text him and ask? He plays with dead things, but demons might be altogether a different bucket of magic."

"I'd appreciate it. Give him my number and ask him if he'll get in touch with me?"

"Well, wraiths and demons in one night. This is not a good sign." Tully grimaced as he shared a knowing glance with Sparks.

"What do you mean, wraiths?" Dev's eyes went wide.

"You might want to drink the wine." Tully pointed to the drink still being cradled by his boyfriend. Dev lifted the glass and took another hearty sip, but his focus never veered from Tully as his boyfriend explained, "So, Sparks and I went and had dinner down at Emily Murphy Park—down by the Glade? We found a dead body. Desiccated. Dried up like a mummy. Then a growl, which wasn't particularly welcoming, rumbled across the clearing. We beelined it for the Audi. Called the Magistrates to deal with the corpse when we were attacked by a wraith.

"Turns out, Uncle Bart had spelled the car, so we were safe. But if he hadn't, we'd both be shrunken dried-up mummies, and you would be very single."

"Holy shit, are you guys okay?"

"I'm freaked out, to be honest. Never seen a wraith before," Sparks admitted. Dev sidled over, wrapped his arm around Sparks, and gave him a gentle squeeze.

"Well, you can stay here tonight," Dev said.

"That's exactly what I told him."

"This is freaky—what the hell is going on?" Dev plopped himself down on the stool next to Sparks.

"Uncle Bart has an idea," Sparks added.

"No surprise there. He has all kinds of ideas." Dev snickered.

"I told him about Byron," Tully confessed.

"You didn't! We agreed to spare the old man from the gory details."

"Well, he pulled the memory-reading trick. We went to visit him right after the wraith incident, and you know how he is, smelling bad juju." Tully mimicked a dog sniffing the air, kind of what Uncle Bart had done. The words were a trademark phrase Uncle Bart used often.

"He always smells something, but he's never pulled the sight on me."

"Count yourself lucky. He's used that crap on me my entire life. I didn't have to come out to him, he smelled 'bad juju' picking out the various dates I'd had. Honestly, such a consecutive string of bad dates." Tully shook his head. He did love Uncle Bart though. Everyone did. "Anyway, this time, he grabbed us both, dove into Sparks's and my memories, and dug around in there until he found the attack." As Tully relayed the spooky Uncle Bart story, he tapped the side of his head. "Now here's the fun part."

Sparks confirmed, "Happened just as the man said."

"I'm not sure I'm ready for this."

"He never liked Byron, but apparently the Guardians of the Night Grove provided an essential service to the Shadow Realm residents in Edmonton by throttling the energy coming into the city from various ley lines. They were denying access to the more dangerous creatures. So, if the Guardians are no more, Uncle Bart says we have to take over."

Dev stared blankly at Tully, and then at Sparks.

"How exactly is one supposed to harness and slow the energy from a ley line?"

Tully and Sparks both shrugged.

"Apparently with some magic globe or sphere harnessing the energy," Sparks offered.

"Tully, we've seen that globe. I bet you anything the orb in Byron's study, the one shooting sparks across the miniature map of the world's ley lines, is your energy harnessing device."

"Oh, there's a thought. Uncle Bart also said Byron had borrowed or stole the idea from the Montreal Coven—they had done something similar."

"So, there's one answer. We contact Montreal and ask for help."

"See, I knew there was a reason I keep you around. Isn't he the best?" Tully winked at Sparks.

"Sure is."

"Oh Gods, you two. Enough. That makes me think though…"

"About what?" Sparks emptied his bottle of beer. The brew had gone down way too easy and before he had the empty bottle set on the counter, Tully had opened another bottle and placed the chilled beverage in front of him. Giving in proved easier than arguing. He hoisted the bottle in a "cheers" motion and took a swig.

"I know what you're thinking," Sparks started but stopped to take another sip of his drink. "Wraith attack and a child possessed by a demon. The ley lines have already been pumping out raw energy for a few months. Byron's globe has obviously gone out of commission along with the old coven."

"Yup. That's exactly what I was thinking. So, we need to get on this fast."

"And we will, but not tonight. I've had enough for one night. Sparks is staying over, right?" Tully glanced at his friend.

"I guess so. You keep feeding me alcohol. Can't leave behind a half-finished beer and be a rude guest."

"Okay, well, I for one have had enough Shadow Realm for the night. Let's go soak in the tub."

"Oh hey, we haven't had a soak since last week. Hot water would feel amazing. I'm in!" Dev stood from the chair and walked into the dining room. At the back of the room, adjacent to the kitchen, sat a small dining area for four. An intricately carved armoire brimmed with various kitchen accoutrements, dishes, and ornaments, but on the other wall, a large set of French doors led out to an upper story deck.

Sparks had been out on the deck before but didn't realize a hot tub existed.

"When did you guys get a hot tub?"

"We didn't. Uncle Bart had it installed a few weeks ago. Claimed his doctor told him the hot water would soothe his bursitis. As far as I know, he's never even stuck a toe in his soup pot."

"I didn't bring a swimsuit." Sparks frowned. Plunging his tense muscles and frayed nerves into a tub of roiling and boiling water would have taken the edge off the frightening assault and wacky visit with Uncle Bart, not to mention ease the tension from his crazy hospital shifts.

"Really? You need a bathing suit? Sparks, we've all been naked together. It's no big deal. Besides, the guy from the Spa Spot told me bathing suits retain laundry soap from the wash and would leave residue in the tub, so either you picked a suit that only ever got washed in hot water, or you don't wear a suit. Frankly, so long as Uncle Bart isn't in the tub at the same time, I'll leave the suit off." Tully stripped off his shirt, walked down the hall, opened a linen closet, and grabbed a bunch of towels.

Sparks couldn't help but notice the way the kitchen light caught the metallic highlights in Tully's red chest hair, making the fur gleam like fine copper filaments.

Before Sparks balked any further, Dev and Tully were bare-assed, towel in one hand, drink in the other, and heading down to the hot tub.

"Well, fuck it." Sparks ripped his clothes off, tossed them on the bar stool, grabbed his beer and a fresh towel that smelled like fabric softener, and headed outside.

As Sparks descended the stairwell, he discovered both his Shadow Realm brothers gaping at a massive hedge behind the tub. In the centre of the wall of leaves, an archway had been meticulously grown, its sides a complex weave of the boxwood's branches. The knotted curve reminded Sparks of fae construction. Intricate, beautiful, and alive.

"Wow, that's something!" Sparks pointed toward the archway.

"No shit. It wasn't there this morning." Tully gawked at the detail of the arch, walked over, and ran a finger over the beautiful knotwork.

"This is crazy!" Sparks replied, coming in close to Tully and studying the lattice over Tully's shoulder.

"I came down here this morning to adjust the chemicals. Uncle Bart has asked me to look after this beast. He got the toy; I have to look after it." Tully turned to look in Dev and Sparks's direction. "It's not that I don't mind. I mean, we live here nearly rent free. I can't complain. But this?" Tully pointed to the looming hedge and stylish gateway. "I think I would have noticed something so spectacular."

"I've never seen it. But I don't come down here as often as you do," Dev said.

"Well, okay. Let's go take a peek."

"I'm naked!" Sparks gestured to his exposed bottom half.

"This hedge is so tall, no one is going to see you. Stop being so self-conscious. Besides, you look great." Tully waggled his eyebrows, turned, and walked through the archway.

"It's true, you do. I wish I had a nice little treasure trail like you." Dev pointed to the thin line of hair running from the bottom of Sparks's pecs to below his belly button.

"You two are incorrigible, but thank you."

"Listen," Dev confessed to Sparks, "Tully will be the first to tell you, I am not generally comfortable walking around like this, but you're my Shadow Brother. If I can't be comfy with you, I'm a lost cause." He spoke loud enough for Tully to hear him, as his boyfriend had already gone beyond the hedge and out of sight. Dev turned to Sparks and whispered, "Honestly, I'm so self-conscious right now, but it's something I'm working on. It's just a body, right? Tully's been taking me to the nude beach all summer. He's hoping I get used to showing it all off so when I work skyclad my self-consciousness isn't mucking up my magic."

Sparks chuckled.

"Right." Sparks threw his arm around his fellow Brother's shoulders. "Okay, let's be comfortable together. Now, where did your boyfriend go?"

"I believe he went through the magical doorway to Narnia." Dev pointed and smiled at Sparks.

Sparks snorted at the horrible fantasy reference.

Dev leaned into him, and Sparks took that as a sign of acceptance.

The night air of late August should have held a titch of cool to it, but Sparks didn't feel cold at all. In fact, being out exposed to the starlight freed his mind and grounded him.

Until they passed through the archway.

Tully motioned for them to stop.

"Don't move."

The boys had passed through the gate to discover a whole new section of the garden. The entire circumference was surrounded by the boxwood hedge, tall enough to block out any nosy neighbours or noise from the surrounding city. Above them, the night sky put on a show of dotted and sparkling stars. The perimeter of the witch wood was heavily planted with flowering shrubs and herbs, many of which Sparks recognized as common ingredients needed for herbal magic remedies.

Knee-sized silver mounds of wormwood were sprinkled throughout the garden. Foxglove spikes in full bloom in varying tones ranging from white to deepest purple jutted up above fern fronds, while wild chamomile covered the soil.

But the season for foxgloves had already passed for the year, and one didn't expect blooming ginger plants to be grown in an Alberta backyard, yet there were several heliconia sporting their hanging, waxy bright-red and yellow bracts and florets. At the end of the grove, a massive Higan cherry swayed in the gentle night breeze.

But beside the wood, an angry swarm of roots writhed and tossed, vines lashing out and snapping in the air. Leaves burst out from the centre, raining down around the mass of squiggling plant parts.

"What the fuck?" Sparks whispered.

"I have no idea—"

Tendrils shot out from the mass, bouncing their way across the Glade, kicking up sod and dirt as they hurtled toward the boys.

Sparks sucked in a single breath.

The entire world stopped. Everything around him moved in slow motion as he attempted to turn away and retreat through the archway.

He never made it.

Chapter Twelve

"OW, OW, OW. What the hell?" Cam glared at Everton who dragged him up the stairs and into a spacious, well-decorated bedroom. A monstrous king-sized bed dominated the room. Its four black posts lacquered to a high gloss stood like overlord wardens, the sharp points crowning each spire as a dire warning. Fitting sleeping quarters for a werewolf.

A black pillowed duvet covered the mattress. Sunbeams shone through a bay window complete with plantation style shutters. The wallpaper's pattern of fleur-de-lis crisscrossed the walls in stark white with raised black velvet.

The bedroom furniture consisted of a chest of drawers, a desk, and what appeared to be a jewellery stand. A solitary black leather recliner sat nestled away in a corner, paired with a rivet-adorned ottoman. A side table housed a reading lamp.

The room boasted the touch of an interior designer, not what Cam had expected at all. Cam's irritation at being man-handled evaporated as he studied the room, taking in the luxuriousness.

"Damn, Ev. Nice taste. I like."

"Thank you." The response came short and curt, and judging from the scowl residing on Ev's face, Cam's compliment hadn't landed well. "What are you doing here? You are supposed to be in the Ancestral Lands learning how to be fae."

"Yeah, that wasn't working out so well."

"Cam, dammit, if you don't learn what you need to know to survive being outside of the fae lands, your ignorance could mean your life. There are weird rules with your kind about who gets to live out in the wide world and who doesn't. Last I can recall, you hadn't been granted freedom."

"Exactly. No freedom. But you're partially wrong. Lady Aine has given me time to come and figure things out."

"She kicked you out, didn't she?"

"Not exactly."

"For fuck's sake, Cam. I'm taking you back to Lady Aine right now." Ev's shoulder width filled the entire doorway to his bedroom, and as he turned to go downstairs, with the intention of Cam following him, Cam made him halt in his steps.

"Ev, I came here to see you." The statement wasn't the whole truth. The confession didn't have all the emotions summing up the nervous and anxious tingles Cam had floating in his belly when contemplating adult fun time with Ev. Explaining his needs and being truthful with Ev was proving to be a difficult task.

"Cam, I know I promised you some fun—"

"A promise you haven't kept, I might add." Cam shot Ev a dirty look.

Ev huffed. Had he been a dragon, Cam imagined a curled puff of smoke billowing out.

"It's complicated."

"Not really."

"You cannot stay here. It isn't safe."

"Isn't safe? Do you know how many semi-trucks, reckless drivers, and unmentionable amounts of wildlife I dodged in order to get here? Travelling the Yellowhead at dusk isn't exactly safe. And yet I made it. I think I can take care of myself."

"I don't know how you did it—"

"Shadow jumping. It's actually rather easy."

"Would you let me finish a single sentence?" Ev crossed his arms, his face turning red.

Cam chewed the inside of his lip. He had a special talent for being a wiseass and excelled at annoying the hell out of people. Pushing buttons brought an unending amount of joy, but from the frustrated and disturbed look on Everton's face, he reconsidered and sat on the edge of the bed. After all, he hadn't come here to destroy his relationship with Ev. He wanted to solidify their connection.

Turns out Ev had invested in a decent mattress and luxurious bedding, as Cam's nearly bare ass wriggled on the comforter, enjoying the silky touch of the bedspread. Cam refocused on Ev, and the fae in him read his werewolf in a heartbeat. Cam's face flushed a celery green.

"I'm sorry."

"Jeez, Cam." Everton uncrossed his arms and ran a palm over his bald head. "It's not that I don't want you here. I'm happy to see you, but your timing is shit."

"Why, what's going on?" Becoming fae had never been a "to-do" list item for Cam. Up until recently he thought fairies equated to Tinker Bell from Disney. So being thrust into the body of a high-ranking member of the Eldritch clan of fae species left him with different senses than what he'd had when human. Wings and horns aside, knowing the emotional state of the people around him unnerved Cam, and right now the volatile mix of emotions from Ev confused the situation.

The attraction flowing out of Ev gave Cam some hope.

But under the desire, Cam sensed fear, anger, violence, and a lack of trust. The messy, thrashing nerves muddled the current situation, and Cam started to second-guess his reasons for coming.

"Well, Serge found one of my wolves murdered. I need to figure out who did it, how they did it, and take appropriate action. There aren't too many things in this world that can fell a werewolf. But whatever killed Lars is stronger than either you or I. That means there's something out there I can't protect you from. I don't want you in a situation I can't guard you against." Ev took a seat on the other corner of the bed, his gaze shifting to the floor.

"Look, I know I've been a real shit, and I caused nothing but issues for Sen and Lady Aine, but Ev, I did conquer some of my abilities. Look." If Cam made the mental trek to the place in his head where plots and schemes were conceived, his human guise would shimmer into existence. In order to prove to Ev he had done at least some of his homework, he conjured up the next steps in his master plan to get Lady Aine's vial filled, sending his thought patterns into over-drive.

In a shimmer of air, Cam the human appeared, staring at Ev with dark-brown eyes, and natural highlighted, wavy hair resembling a model's. His shaggy beard, which had highlights of green grass, had reverted to Cam's typical scruff. The long, pointed horns were no longer prominently on display, only curvy tangles of hair.

The guise, however, didn't come with any clothes other than the loincloth Sen had eventually got him into. Cam hadn't planned on bringing any additional humanlike attire, so he had morphed himself into nakedness in front of Ev, but getting naked with Ev had been the reason why he came for a visit.

"Congratulations on figuring out your illusion spell. Maybe I can take you out for dinner." Ev had a partial grin. It wasn't hard to also notice Ev's gaze giving him the once-over. "Perhaps if we go out, you could put on some clothes? You know, though, as cute as the human Cam is, I like the fae version too. Maybe even more."

"What? Really?"

"Really. I kinda have a thing for the fae. Not all of them, but your kind, the Eldritch. I don't know...maybe it's the horns..."

"You kinky motherfucker. I never would have guessed you liked monster fucking."

"I told you before not to put me into a box or label me."

"You did say that. Okay, so be it." Cam mentally wandered away from the place where machinations took form and let his mind roam to more erotic zones. And with the ripple of hot summer air, human Cam evaporated.

"That's better." Ev leered. "Ugh. You know how cute you are, right? Either way."

"No, I don't. You keep telling me, but I wish you'd show me." Cam's wings fluttered. His tail jumped, too, but he currently sat on the appendage so instead of a flick, the furry extension twitched, making the fuzzy tip hanging between his legs stretch toward Ev.

Ev's gaze caught the movement.

"I want to play with your tail," he whispered.

"Look, wolfman, you are more than welcome to play with my tail, my wings, stroke my horns, or anything else for that matter."

"Cam, I...I know I promised you a roll in the hay," Ev stammered but stopped. His skin flushed as he glanced away.

Cam had never seen the top of someone's head turn red.

It was kind of cute.

He shuffled over and sat closer to Ev.

"I have kept you at an arm's length the entire summer. I know how cruel you must think I am for doing that. I haven't been fair to you."

"No, you have not. But your insistence in keeping your distance has kept me horny as hell. Look." Cam pointed at his loincloth which sported a prominent point, making the garment tent. "This is the effect you have on me. You have kept me hopelessly distracted and hard. This is why I'm here, you oaf. I can't concentrate long enough to study, or master anything about fae business because you keep getting up in my business. In fact, all my magical abilities have hinged around you.

"I want to be invisible? I think back to when you and I were held in the witches' dungeon and that asshole Byron tortured you. I get so angry. The images of Byron cutting you open, the blood spilling out, you groaning in pain enrage me still. I go instant no-see-em when I go there. I want to look like my old self? I think about how I'm gonna get you naked and have my way with you. Or any other master plan I have to ponder through—for whatever reason, scheming brings about the human guise.

"Shadow jumping I can initiate when I'm wanting to be next to you." Cam leaned into Ev and tipped his head so that one horn lay on the beast of a man's shoulder.

Ev put his paw on Cam's thigh and gave him a squeeze.

"Higher," Cam whispered.

Ev chuckled. "You are terrible."

"I know."

Ev inched his hand up.

Cam shivered. "Higher." He egged Ev on.

Ev shifted his hand high enough he grazed Cam's balls.

"Now we're talking. You know you don't need permission, right? Like, it's all there for you."

"How come you're so sweet on me?"

"Have you seen yourself in the mirror?"

"I'm a bald-headed beast with tufts of hair sprouting in places where most men don't have any. And I have a hunting, moon-crazed monster hiding inside of me."

"Mm-hmm, I like all of that." Cam placed his hand on top of Ev's and guided the giant palm to wrap around his rock-hard cock. "You're not the only one into monsters. I like you. I want the fur, muscle, bald head, and wolfy bits. All of it." Cam leaned into Ev for a kiss.

Ev didn't pull away. Instead, he rubbed the length of Cam's erection and met the kiss with eagerness. The whiskers from Ev were rough against Cam's lips, but the wolf pack leader's dominant size cranked Cam up. Ev pulled him down onto the bed and rolled over so his massive frame hovered overtop.

Cam wrapped his legs around Ev's waist, while his arms tugged at Ev's shirt, pulling the edge out from its tucked position in his jeans.

"You are all bad." Ev lifted his torso and arms, so Cam had easier access to pull off Ev's shirt.

Once Ev's bare skin became exposed, Cam ran his hands over his beast. Ev was furry. Everywhere. Front, back, sides, like he had said, tufts where most men don't have any. Cam's fingers stroked all of it, like mauling a life-sized teddy bear. His own teddy bear.

Cam tweaked a nipple.

Ev growled.

"Don't start something you can't finish."

"Oh, I can finish. In fact, I desperately want to finish."

With a tug on his loincloth, the garment fell off. Cam tossed it over the side of the bed. As much as they had flirted with each other all summer, being alone with Ev had been a rare moment. Certainly never enough time to be *alone and naked* with him.

This was the first time he'd ever been hard and exposed in front of him.

Ev smiled, but the devil glimmered in his eye, and for a brief moment, Cam caught a flash of yellow. The wolf inside had stirred.

Ev wrapped his meaty paw around Cam's cock, stroking his upward curved rod slowly, then stopped at the base and gave the shaft a good squeeze.

"Pants off. Now." Cam dictated orders.

Ev slid down Cam's body, backward off the bed, which put his erection right in front of Ev's mouth. His tongue lashed out, lapping up the precome running down the side of his rod.

"Clothes," Cam demanded.

Ev stood, undid his belt buckle, unzipped, and let his pants drop.

"Ah, see, that's all mine. Come here." Cam motioned for Ev to climb on top again.

Ev did as instructed.

Cam delighted in the skin-on-skin contact. A thousand tiny jolts of electricity hummed and sang through his body as he finally got to feel the warmth and fur of his wolfman against his own skin.

Ev straddled Cam's chest, putting a knee in each armpit, and positioned the tip of his large helmet cockhead a whisper away from Cam's lips.

"I see everything is as big as you are. Lucky me."

Cam opened wide, salivating at the tasty treat grazing his mouth.

He wrapped his lips around Ev's head, letting his tongue lick the underside, delighting in the velvety skin. Ev grabbed Cam's horns and thrust himself deeper into Cam's mouth. Cam's lips stretched, trying to accommodate the girth, when the door to the bedroom slammed open, and one of Ev's wolves came barging in.

"Oh, dude! What the hell? Shit, fuck." Serge did an about-face and turned away. "I can't believe I just saw that. Oh my Gods."

"Fuck, Serge, you ever heard of knocking?" Ev pulled out, his erection dying a thousand deaths as Serge continued to bemoan the sight he had witnessed.

Cam closed his eyes and swore a million curses onto the subordinate wolf.

Ev jumped off the bed, grabbed his pants, and pulled them on. He hopped on one foot as he attempted to cover himself as fast as possible.

Cam rolled over and buried his face into the duvet.

At this rate, Lady Aine's vial would never get filled.

Chapter Thirteen

TREE ROOTS AS thick as a man's thigh wrapped themselves around Sparks's leg, locking him in place. Lightning arcs danced across the surface of his skin. As a tree root burst from the soil beneath him, Sparks drew two runes in the air. *Inguz* and *Algiz*. A diamond and a pitchfork. The two together when combined with his electricity would send a protective burst of electrical energy.

As he completed the runes, he forced his energy into them. The symbols shimmered, turned silver, then exploded.

Beside him, Tully had conjured a wall of steel from the metal in the earth, while Dev attempted to syphon energy from the attacking plant.

No one was having any success.

"What the hell is this thing?" Tully yelled.

Dev turned, his face painted in panic as he yanked a tree root off one arm. Another erupted from beneath the soil near his foot, writhing around until the vine found his leg and constricted around his calf.

Tully had no better luck, as tendrils dove under his barrier and came up beside him, ensnaring him. The more the three men fought, the tighter the roots pulled and the faster they appeared. From one thick tendril, several smaller ones grew, just as strong, but sinewy.

Within moments all three of the boys were mummified in plant growth.

A numbing sense of dread overcame Sparks. His stomach dropped; a pit of despair blossomed and spread.

This is how I die.

The branches bound his chest tight, to the point where taking a breath was difficult. He tried to call on his magic, but clarity of mind is required to initiate a spark of magical energy, and a free hand to draw a rune would have helped. With panic overtaking his brain, he couldn't concentrate long enough to manifest any electrical flashes.

Muffled screaming emanated from where Dev had stood, now a sarcophagus of thrashing vines.

When Sparks spelled the wine, he had no idea the magic would lead them here, united in death.

This promised to be the end of his journey on earth.

He took one more breath, the roots pulling in even further.

A vine wrapped around his neck, under his Adam's apple, and squeezed.

He wheezed out a breath.

"Phineas, what have you done?" A voice rumbled across the witch wood.

Sparks sucked in a gulp of air as the living plant noose loosened, hesitated.

"What have you done to my boys? Let them go. I assure you they mean no harm."

Like a pile of snakes scared off by the sight of a flying hawk, the tree roots slithered away and disappeared into the ground until only a small roiling mound of vines remained at the base of the giant Higan cherry.

Sparks's skin had indentations all over from where the plant had tried to squeeze him to death. He rubbed his wrists, trying to get the blood to flow, willing the circulation to return to his extremities. His skin tingled and prickled.

"You guys okay?" Tully yelled out.

"Yes, what the hell?" Dev glared at Tully.

"I don't know," Sparks hissed, doubled over, trying to catch his breath.

With his head between his knees, Sparks became acutely aware of his lack of clothing. As he stood at the far edge of the glen, closest to the archway, sucking in air, and hyperventilating, a warm hand at the base of his spine comforted him.

"Buddy, you okay?" Sparks glanced up to see both Dev and Tully. He released a huge breath, clarity returning to his head. He shook off the last few minutes, his skin slick with cold sweat, the kind that happens when you're afraid. As he stood, with the assistance of his Realm brothers, he had the chance to take in his surroundings.

As much danger as he had been in, the Glade's beauty astounded him. Deadly beauty, apparently, but stunning in the bright light of near full moon. The obviously curated plants around the perimeter gleamed, even at night, but the centre of this witch wood held the biggest surprise.

Four massive granite boulders sat at the cardinal points, each rock a slightly different hue, and embedded with semiprecious stones representing the elements associated with each direction. Jade for Earth and the North compass point, topaz for Air in the East, amber representing Fire in the South, and aquamarine for Water in the West. A slate stone walking path connected each of the massive boulders.

"You like?" the disembodied voice called out.

"I know that voice… Why do I know that voice?" Dev's head swivelled, surveying the area.

"Dev, have you forgotten me already?" The voice suggested mischief, teasing Dev.

"Oh!" Dev dropped to one knee and bowed his head. Tully glanced over at Sparks, repeating his shrug.

"It's the Horned One," Dev whispered.

And on cue, the hedge at the end of the witch wood parted, a giant of a man stepped through, and as He passed, the boxwood knit together again.

He stood tall, a rack of stag horns jutting out from His temples. He took a few steps toward them onto the northernmost edge of the stone circle. The *clop-clop* of His hooves reverberated within the wood. From the waist down, He was goat, standing on ungulate legs. But the full girth and length of His manhood was prominently displayed between His legs. The God wore no breeches, no covering. Like all animals in nature, He bared His body.

"Dev, no need for formality, it is I who visit you, and with impeccable timing I might add." The Horned One glanced toward the writhing ball of tendrils, which slithered behind the massive birch. The God stepped forward again. He stood within a few feet of the three witches. He gestured toward the earth, and the ground shook. The soil birthed another smaller boulder. He took a seat on the smooth stone which resembled a throne. He leaned forward, resting His elbows on His knees, clenching His hands together in front of Him, as His face took on a serious, pondering visage.

Gone were the goat legs. Feet had replaced the hooves.

His stoic stance broke as he smirked at Dev.

"She wants me to tell you She's impressed. You've done well by Her. Well done. Not a feat easily accomplished." The Horned One winked at Dev. His eyes shining an emerald green. "Now boys, we have work to do. I guess I should have seen the consequences of introducing Dev into the

Guardians, but I am not Her. She is far more perceptive and proactive than I'll ever be, and so, I need your help cleaning up this mess."

The sense of dread and impending death which had moments ago overwhelmed Sparks disappeared. Now a mix of outright panic, adulation, and abject fear washed over him in wave after wave of nauseating fear. The Horned One, the ancient God of the hunt, addressed him.

"Sparks, I feel your unease. Please, be at peace, and come forward." The God gestured by waving him closer.

He wanted to comply, but his feet wouldn't move.

"Am I that frightening? It's the horns, isn't it?" With a shake of the God's head, the pointed rack disappeared.

The man before them epitomized beauty. Wild unruly chestnut hair with chaotic twirls crowned His head, dancing in the night breeze. His muscular body rippled with taut muscles, even still the bulk belied his true strength. He had lived for many lifetimes, had watched over generations of men, and His strength had been sung in praises for centuries. He carried the weight of troubles His witch men endured, and that surpassed even the heft of carrying a full-grown stag across his shoulders, which He could do with ease.

His beard, thick and long, grew unruly; as wild as He.

Wildflowers rapidly sprouted close to His feet, tiny bell-shaped white blossoms popping open despite the fact no sun shone. His aroma enticed Sparks, even from where he stood.

"Come, I need you close."

Sparks's breath hitched in his throat. It took every ounce of willpower to place one foot in front of the other. But he managed.

"There you go." The God's gentle eyes and open arms conveyed warmth and friendship. Cernunnos beckoned him forth.

Each step forward became easier and easier, until he stood before the seated man.

The God rose from his throne. He towered over Sparks. He raised His arms and placed a gentle palm on the tops of Sparks's shoulders.

"You, my young man, long for unity, connection. You require a tether to others in order to feel whole. And I know you are aware of these feelings. I am happy you chose these two as your Shadow Realm brothers. Your wine spell rippled through the realm and settled in my lap. I feel the yearning within you, and no man of mine should be left alone unless that is what they desire. This is not what you desire, and so you shall be alone no more."

"Your wine spell?" Tully stared at Sparks as he spoke but silenced himself as the God raised a single eyebrow and glared in his direction.

"I'm sorry." Sparks grimaced as he glanced over his shoulder, scrunching up his face, a worm of regret burrowing into his guts.

"Nonsense." The God pulled him forward and locked him into an embrace. He kissed Sparks's forehead. "You did exactly as I wanted. Did you not succumb to the overwhelming need to magick the wine? Even though you understood Dev and Tully had not consented to being enthralled, you proceeded anyway. That push, the desire to call your lightning forth and complete the spell, that, my son, was me."

Sparks's brain exploded into a myriad of images all of which should have filled him with terror. He stood chest to chest with a God, but across the surface of his skin a warm breeze blew, caressing him, comforting him. He sniffed the air and savoured aromas of autumn apples, cinnamon, and the damp moss that clings to the northern side of trees in a dense forest. With one arm still wrapped around Sparks's waist, the Horned One turned him to face his brothers. "Tully and Dev, Sparks did not act alone. I had a hand in what he did. I need you three to be bound together, for the task at hand will require the combined strengths between all of you."

Dev shook his head. "Oh, dear God."

"Deer, elk, sometimes goat," the God replied. "Bear when needed, occasionally bull if you ask Her."

Dev covered his face with one hand.

The God boomed with laughter.

The witch wood shook.

The God turned to the man still clutched in his one arm. "Sparks, you call upon the element of electricity. The very thoughts in our brains are electrical impulses. Our muscles move with instructions sent forth in waves of energy through our bodies. Thoughts therefore have tangibility if directed; they can also be sent across distances. Tonight, I give you another talent, that of telepathy—an extension of what you already wield—but only between you and your brothers. You will be able to communicate with them wher-ever they are." The God's gaze fell on both Tully and Dev one after another. "You will be able to hear Sparks's words, and he yours, when you desire to know one another's words."

The Horned One turned Sparks around again so He was face to face with him. He leaned in and kissed Sparks on the lips.

Sparks melted at the touch, treasured the connection, and savoured the taste of the God's tongue as it pressed past his lips, demanding entrance and running itself overtop his own. The kiss lingered. The smell of ancient forest groves, apples and spices, moss, and leather enshrouded him as the God explored his mouth.

He returned the motions on instinct.

The God held his face in each of His hands, and the kiss continued.

Warm, wet, and forceful, with the brush of whiskers across his lips.

Sparks became aroused. Blood rushed from his head and into his loins. And before he had a chance to think of playful puppies or housework chores to douse his desire, the God had his manhood in His hands and stroked him. Sparks's knees shook as a shiver ran down his spine.

The God broke away from the kiss but brought Sparks in tight and held him nestled close to His side.

Sparks stared at his Shadow Realm brothers, embarrassed by his current state, and his cheeks flushed, disbelief running rampant as his brain whirled.

"Tully, come."

Tully strode forward without hesitation.

The God wrapped His other arm around Tully's shoulders and brought him in close on His other side.

"Tully, the metallurgist, capable of taking the steel of the Earth and bending metal to your will. You embody strength, the core of stability. You create a shield impervious to all others, and you will need thick skin in the years to come. Barriers to protect yourself, and your brothers here. But I give you one more gift."

Releasing Sparks, the God turned to him. "Don't go anywhere, my son, I need you close and hanging on to me." He leered at Sparks, a hint of mischief glimmering in His sparking green eyes.

The Horned One took Tully and mimicked His previous stance with Sparks, placing a hand on each side of Tully's head. "Now listen carefully, boy, and look into my eyes. I will get you through this next part. Do you understand? This will hurt only momentarily, and I'll be here with you to get you through this."

Tully nodded, but his eyes were wide.

"I give you Phineas. He is primeval, and a protector. But he is now yours to command. Be good to him, and he will guard you and those you love with a ferocity few can conquer. Sparks and Dev will need you to stand by them. Will you accept this?"

"Yes?" Tully stammered out. It sounded more like a question than an affirmation.

The horned God raised one hand and snapped His fingers.

Phineas, the writhing mass of roots, hadn't left his position by the ancient and gnarled tree. But upon the God's command, the creature slithered toward them.

Tiny sprigs of new spring plants grew around Tully's feet.

Phineas burrowed into the ground, disappearing from sight.

Then, a single tendril wriggled forth from in between the God and Tully. The vine lashed out like a nematode seeking a host. Snapping at the air, writhing wildly. The snake-like creeper found Tully's dangling arm.

Tully glanced down. His eyes grew wide.

Phineas wrapped around Tully's wrist several times, then halted as the God spoke, "Tully, stay with me. Relax into me." The God leaned in and planted an animalistic kiss on the muscled red bear of a man.

Sparks licked his lips, wishing it was he receiving the attention. Not as aroused as he had been, his manhood thickened again as he voyeuristically enjoyed seeing the God make out with Tully. The vine from Phineas crawled up Tully's arm, and as its leading tip reached Tully's thick bicep, the plant pulled up and reared back like a cobra about to strike.

Tully's body jolted when the shoot invaded him, and he let out a short gasp, but the God held him tight and allowed Phineas to continue.

Phineas dug its way in, burrowing into Tully's bicep, snaking around his arm. Sparks watched as the skin on Tully's arm wriggled and shifted as the root burrowed under it. Once Phineas settled, the skin darkened, and an image bled and ran across the dermis, almost as if Tully had been tattooed.

The Horned One broke the kiss and pulled Tully in close, wrapping His arms around his shoulders, a gesture most men couldn't accomplish due to Tully's width. Pulling Tully into a full bear hug, He squeezed as the vine settled into him, becoming a symbiotic part of Tully's being. He ran His hands up and down Tully's back, comforting him, until Tully relaxed, slumping into the God's arms.

"There. You now are one. He is yours and in a small way, you are part of him. You'll have Phineas's knowledge of the world. The biosphere of green life sees things we do not. You'll also be able to call on Phineas whenever you need him." The God reached between Tully's legs and cupped his balls, giving them a gentle tug. "It'll take some stones to wrangle him, for he is wild, an Earth elemental, but you are strong, both in body and mind. Do not fear him."

Tully stared into his God's eyes. He ran his hands over the man's massive chest, then lay his head down on His shoulder and whispered, "Thank you."

The God chuckled.

"Dev, come, please."

Dev approached until he stood in front of his God. He attempted to kneel, but the Horned One stopped him.

"No. Not tonight. Tonight we celebrate. Dev, you need no other talents. You are complete as you are, with one small exception. As much joy as Tully brings you, I know you have enough love inside of you for one more." The God glanced at Sparks. "Tully, I know you, too, can make room in your heart for another, and to share your love of Dev." He turned to Sparks. "You will never need to long for unity or a sense of belonging ever again."

The God stepped nearer to Dev so their toes were touching, as were other parts. He brought all four of them together, close, in a furry muscled huddle.

"Will you three accept one other?" The God cocked an eyebrow. He leaned forward and kissed Dev on the lips, and Dev responded, "I do."

The Horned One turned to Tully and kissed him.

Tully responded, "I do."

He shifted to Sparks and did the same, and Sparks replied, "I do."

"Then, my men, I consecrate this union of three. You will lead the way for others and take the place of the Guardians who came before you. We have much work to do. But before the work begins, we shall have some fun."

The God grabbed Dev's manhood and fondled him until his cock stood ramrod hard, and with His other hand, He gently guided Sparks down.

Understanding the request and glancing up at Tully to ask permission, Tully raised his eyebrows as a wicked smile blossomed. He nodded. Sparks glanced to Dev and asked a silent question.

Are you okay with this?

The words ricocheted in Sparks's head, and from Dev's widened eyes, Sparks guessed he had heard them too.

I think I am. Dev's voice echoed in Sparks's mind.

The God laughed as He grabbed Tully's hand and guided the bear paw to His own massive cock, which stood straight out and leaked.

"Oh my Gods, we're about to have sex with a God." Tully sucked in air as he tentatively grasped the girth of Cernunnos.

The God laughed again. "Do not be shy. I take pleasure in your touch. We shall enjoy the delights of one another. Besides, how else to expect me to seal the God-given talents I bestow upon you? I promise you, we shall have a grand time."

In the middle of the witch wood that hadn't been there the day before, Sparks, Tully, Dev, and the Horned One did exactly what the God had expressed. Hands explored muscles and fur. Wet mouths tasted bare skin. Shudders of delight were relished as uncovered flesh became sticky and wet. No body part escaped a caress. Sparks revelled in the taut muscles of Dev's lithe body, so different than Tully's bearish mass. Dev's member was hooded and long, whereas Tully had heft and thickness. Sparks's lips barely engulfed Tully's rod, the corners of his mouth straining.

But he gave his damned best effort and ignored his body's insistence the girth would be too much. After tasting his Shadow Brother, he grasped Dev and attempted to swallow the lengthy shaft.

The God positioned Himself behind Tully, slathered His fingers with His own excretions, wet Tully's hole, and entered him, slow and gentle, as Godly endowments are fiercely large. Tully sucked in a breath while grasping for his lovers. Dev cradled his red bear and stroked his thick cock. Sparks kissed him while petting his chest. The God continued His gyrations, grunting and thrusting like a wild animal until He spent Himself.

Tully's eyes had rolled to the back of his head as he became lost in the pleasure.

A God's seed endowed the recipient with the bestowed gift.

And then it was Sparks's turn. The men lay Sparks across the smooth flat boulder as Cernunnos filled Sparks with his beastly meat. Sparks whimpered until the momentary pain of taking in the Ancient One subsided, losing himself instead in the rocking motion as the divine creature buried himself deep within him. His enormous nut sack slapped against Sparks's butt cheeks, but Sparks became distracted from the rough hands the God had placed on his hips as Dev straddled him and took Sparks inside him, riding his length as he stroked himself. Tully stood above him and offered up his thickness, which Sparks eagerly consumed. And when the God set his seed the second time and roared with delight, all three men came at the same time.

The witch wood shook as the God thrust one last time. He pulled out, still thick, but spent, running His rough hands down Sparks's legs. The God's caress ceased as He disappeared into the darkness of the evening.

An image coalesced in Sparks's mind: three threads, one silver, one black, and one grey, weaving together in knotwork akin to the lattice arch that led into this witch wood. The threads writhed into the shape of a stag's head with a magnificent rack of horns. The three colours represented each of the men. Not only did they call themselves Shadow Brothers, but now, they were lovers.

The night grew still, and the three collapsed into one another, sleep overtaking them.

Chapter Fourteen

STOMPING DOWN THE stairs, Everton wrestled with a T-shirt, attempting to get dressed as he descended to the first floor of the pack house. He wanted a full report from Franco, and considering how far things had gone in his bedroom with Cam, a small part of his rational brain was grateful for Serge's interruption.

Serge had already scuttled away, yelling about his bleeding eyeballs.

Those brief moments with Cam, staring into his fae cat-like green eyes, grasping those horns—the fire burning in his groin indicated Everton the human and Everton the wolf wanted Cam for the long haul. Not only for a tawdry, sweat-covered, juice-flowing, fur-covered, hot moment. He wanted more of everything Cam had to offer. Daily. And Cam wanted the tussle as well, but would he keep Ev around for good?

Ev shook his head. Time to focus. He needed to see the body Franco should have arrived toting. Studying the remains might give him some clues as to what had happened to Lars, and perhaps even indicate what kind of creature took him out.

Whatever manner of Shadow Realm beast killed Lars, the monster had to be insidiously powerful.

Stupid Lars. If there were two paths of action to travel, guaranteed Lars would choose the road to destruction, putting himself and his packmates in harm's way.

Franco stood in the kitchen, pouring a cup of coffee. If Ev started drinking coffee this late at night, he'd never sleep.

"Hey, what did you find out? Did you put Lars in the shed?"

"Yeah, so, about that." Franco dumped a few teaspoons of sugar into the brown liquid and stirred.

"Oh. My. Gods. Is that coffee?" Cam gasped, from behind Everton.

"Who the fuck?" Franco's body position changed from "relaxing at home" to "on guard."

"Chill." Ev raised a hand. An indication to stop any aggression. "Franco, this is Cam. Cam, this is my second, Franco."

Cam's tail flicked back and forth, and his furred wings fluttered.

"Nice to meet you, Franco." Cam extended his hand in greeting. Franco took the fae's elongated fingers, squinting and eyeing Cam carefully. "Ev, you never told me you had a second, or that you left the best-looking wolf in charge!"

"Cam." Ev glared at him.

"What? It's true. Look at him! He's almost as beastly as you. And judging from his beard—" Ev shoved a hand overtop of Cam's mouth and shook his head.

Franco chuckled to himself.

"There's something you need to know, Cam. Not everyone in this pack house will be friendly or accepting of your gregarious and flirtatious nature. They are werewolves.

They have a tendency to go off. Unchecked anger issues. Yeah?"

Cam cocked an eyebrow and moved his head to stare at Franco.

Ev followed his gaze.

Franco had a huge shit-eating grin plastered on his face. He winked at Cam.

"Okay, you"—Ev wagged a finger at Franco—"do not encourage him. Please. I have enough of a bleeding ulcer from leading you monsters. Let's try to not aggravate my wounds any further."

"Well, Cam, nice to meet you. Eldritch? Yes?" Franco's grin turned into a bit of a leer.

"Apparently. It's complicated." Cam made a goofy face, leaned over to Ev, and whispered, not nearly quietly enough, "You can bring him to bed with us if you want." He waggled his eyebrows. "Can I have some coffee? I haven't had real coffee in forever!"

Franco burst a gut laughing. "Sure. You want milk, cream, and sugar or...we might have artificial sweetener here somewhere?"

"Black, but with sugar is fine, thanks."

"We're gonna get along just fine." Franco opened a cupboard, pulled out a mug, and made a coffee for Cam. He leaned over to Ev and whispered too loudly, "I would probably join in."

"You two will be the death of me." Everton's cheeks and scalp glowed a deep beet red. Considering Serge had interrupted what promised to be a spectacular blowjob, the idea of returning to his bedroom and ripping Cam's clothes off got him all hot and bothered. Sharing him with Franco... just...no.

Well, maybe?

No. Never.

"Nicely done." Cam grinned a sharp-toothed smile toward Franco.

"Okay, enough out of both of you. Franco, what did you find out?"

"Well, nothing you're going to be happy about."

Serge entered the kitchen, wiping his eyes. "I can't get the image out of my head."

"Shut up. You'll be fine," Ev said. "Maybe next time, you'll knock."

"What the hell are you?" Serge glared at Cam.

"Oh my Gods, this isn't school time. Serge, sit and shut up." Everton scolded the young pup.

"Hmph." He slumped onto a kitchen bar stool on the opposite side of the counter from where Cam sat. He leered at the fae, studying him, and kept glancing at Cam's horns and wings.

Cam stretched his membranous wings outward, making a show of them.

Everton grew more and more frustrated.

"Franco, what do you mean?"

"I mean by the time I got to Emily Murphy Park, where Serge insisted the witches had killed Lars, the Magistrates were already there, and they had confiscated the body."

"Shit."

"Yeah. That means we can expect a visit from them soon."

"They don't control us," Serge piped up.

"No, they ensure Witch Law is carried out. But I don't need them snooping in our business, which they will do now that they have possession of a dead werewolf. They have the potential to make our lives difficult. And I don't need any more difficult situations. Lars being dead is quite enough."

"None of you seem too broken up about this Lars," Cam offered.

"He was a total asshole, and guaranteed, his attitude did him in." Franco rolled his eyes.

"Franco, he was still pack!" Ev hated how his day had transpired.

"Didn't make him less of an asshole, Ev," Franco retorted, then turned to Cam. "He was a pig. You should see how he kept his bedroom. I constantly had to clean up after him. He left dead bodies lying around the city—not that he ever told Daddy here." Franco jutted a thumb in Ev's direction. "I cleaned those up, for the pack, and you're welcome. Lars never did dishes, mowed the lawn, or went grocery shopping, even on his scheduled days." Franco nodded toward a calendar hanging on the side of the fridge. The grid had names written on each day. "I bet Cam would be a better packmate than Lars." He grinned at his new buddy.

Cam beamed as his wings slanted sideways. A sure sign he was playing coy.

"Okay, I can't. You two are not going to be besties." Ev tried to pull the coffee mug away from Cam, but Cam's grip tightened around the cup while he glared at Ev and snarled at him.

"You leave my coffee alone. Besides, I'm allowed to flirt with whoever I want. And if we're gonna all get together later, I want to know him better." Cam winked at Franco, who did everything possible to not laugh out loud.

Serge, on the other hand, sat on the end of the eat-up bar, shell-shocked. His mouth hung open as his stare rotated between Ev, Franco, and Cam.

The door opened and Josip walked in.

Ev put a hand up to his forehead and rubbed.

"Josip, weren't you visiting with the ex?" Ev barked out.

"She's a bitch, and all the reasons why I left her were on full display. Had to leave. Couldn't be in the same room. Who's the fairy?"

"Hi, I'm Cam." Cam bounced out of his chair and extended his hand for a second time.

Josip, as tall as the others, did a double-take at Cam. He pulled away, squinting at the fae with suspicion.

Cam stood there, hand extended, left hanging.

"Yeah. Okay." He ran a hand through his salt-and-pepper hair, scratched the nape of his neck, then turned to Everton and tossed him a cell phone. "Check out the pictures. I picked up his alpha scent when I had to go for a walk around the block. The ex wasn't playing nice, and before I lost my cool around her and the kids, I walked out. Needed some space. You'll be surprised who I stumbled upon. We battled him last year."

Ev tapped the phone to wake it up. No security existed on Josip's phone, no password or face recognition. Ev would have to chat about safeguarding pack business with Josip, but the forty-four-year-old divorcé didn't do well with tech devices. Or his anger management skills, hence the divorce.

Josip also wasn't particularly happy about being the only straight male in the pack, but no other pack existed within Edmonton's city limits, and the Night Stalkers in central Alberta had a notoriously savage reputation. Despite his anger issues, Josip at least stayed in his kids' lives and tried to be a decent father. Being associated with such a violent group wouldn't have helped his custody arrangement.

When Josip did get the kids every second week for an overnighter on Saturdays, the entire pack house devolved into utter chaos.

He opened the photo app. The first few photos he glanced at were taken at such a distance it remained impossible to accurately identify Addas. In the third photo, however, the dominating frame of the man made recognition easy. From the deep tan of his Middle Eastern skin to the four days of heavy scruff, the beast-sized male was Addas. Byron Radcliff's lover had managed to survive his first shift.

The renegade mutant wolf had been the reason for Everton's captivity and torture for over a year.

"That's the one you bit, yeah? Looks like revenge didn't work out in your favour," Josip sneered.

"Jesus Christ, he's huge. I didn't think he'd survive the gnawing you gave him. Looks like the witch survived the bite and his first transition!" Franco peered over Ev's shoulder. "Shouldn't have. Everyone knows witch-werewolf combo doesn't work. But..." Ev closed his eyes and pursed his lips. Anger stirred in his gut. The all-male coven had caused him and his packmates nothing but problems for decades. The ambush they were led into, the ensuing fight where Everton witnessed his packmates being destroyed by witch magic still caused him nightmares. The subsequent abduction and torture for a year compounded his rage.

Then Cam had shown up.

"Except, Addas isn't only a witch-werewolf. He has a little bit of me in him."

Franco screwed up his eyebrows and twisted a glance toward Cam. "What do you mean?"

"I told you about the fae in the dungeon."

"Oh my Gods! You're *that* fae?" Franco slapped Ev's shoulder blade. "You should have said something." Franco walked around to sit beside Cam who had retaken his seat at the kitchen eat-up bar. Franco leaned into Cam. "I need details. He won't talk about his time there." Franco stared at Cam, who in return delivered a wicked smile and a raised eyebrow, nodding.

"Gurl, you know I'm going to give you all the deets." Cam tried to suppress a huge cat-caught-the-canary grin. "Oh yeah, we're gonna be good friends." He giggled.

"Fuck me dead," Ev muttered. "Josip—" Ev tossed his phone back to him. "—send me the address. I'm going to go talk to Addas. Maybe we can resolve this and get him to move away."

"You seriously think he's going to leave the city where his lover still lives?" Cam piped up.

"What do you mean?" Serge, who from the perpetual confused look on his face hadn't followed much of the conversation, tried to join in with the rest of the adults in the room.

Cam raised an eyebrow. "Well, look at the lengths Byron went to in order to save Addas from what everyone believed to be a death sentence. In the end, all of Byron's efforts were for nothing, and not only did Byron fail spectacularly, he also got himself infected. If I were in Addas's shoes and turned out I survived my first transformation into a werewolf—when everyone said I shouldn't, or wouldn't, but did, and then infected my lover—don't you think I'd stick around to make sure my lover also survived their first transformation? If Byron doesn't, I bet Addas will leave. He'd have nothing left to stay here for.

"But if Byron does survive, I would imagine Addas would attempt a reconciliation. A make up for, 'Sorry I bit you, but I had mad werewolf rage. Can you ever forgive me? I love you forever and ever' kind of bullshit. Right? And then they would be witch-fae-werewolves together and continue with the Guardians of the Night Grove. Wouldn't that be fucking special?"

"Your boyfriend has a point." Franco squinted and pulled his mouth to one side, remaining quiet as he concentrated.

"He's not my boyfriend," Ev blurted.

Franco glared at Ev. "Funny, your scent is all over him, and I don't mean your cheap aftershave." He cocked an eyebrow while sneering at his pack lead.

"You're awfully close to being insubordinate," Ev growled.

Franco shrugged.

Cam bit his lip, trying not to laugh.

"I think Ev has issues with dating someone with horns and wings, and he also doesn't follow through on promises," Cam explained to Franco, ignoring everyone else in the room.

Serge shifted uncomfortably in his seat.

"I'm out. Here..." Josip walked over to the side counter where the landline resided at a small desk, jotted down the address, ripped the sheet off the pad of sticky notes, and thrust the yellow piece of paper toward Ev. "I'm not sitting around for this shit show. If you want help, you know where to find me." Josip opened the door to the basement and disappeared.

Ev grumbled, as the basement door closed. "Great, thanks." Sarcasm and ire dripped from his wolf tongue. Ignoring his wolves' disobedience, he continued, "Okay, I'm going to go talk to Addas and tell him to keep his distance. He can't be anywhere near here on the cycle. Which is in two nights."

"Huh?" Cam furrowed his eyebrows. They had grown longer as his body had settled into becoming fae. The ends twirled up, giving him a distinctly lynx-like appearance. The pointy furry ears added to the illusion.

"During the full moon, wolves get a little cray-cray," Franco added. "We retain most of our consciousness and memories when we shift outside of a full moon, but only mature wolves can shift beyond the pull of the cycle. Immature ones have to learn control over their inner beasts. Isn't that right, Serge? The babies only shift during the moon cycle's apex. Serge here figured out some fucked-up, in-between state. Looks fucking goofy."

"Franco, don't egg him on," Ev warned.

"Fuck you, Franco." Serge stood and lunged at his superior. His chair nearly toppled.

"Serge, second time today. Settle." Ev glared at him. "Why don't you go upstairs and chill out?"

"Fuckers," Serge spat out, then listened to his pack leader and left the room.

Ev sighed. "I don't have the energy for this."

"Relax." Franco tortured him further. He continued his explanation to Cam, "Addas is still immature as a wolf, so he won't be able to control his shift. A young wolf during a full moon is usually a disaster. Guaranteed. He's also likely to suffer from bloodlust and he'll hunt. If he's in city limits, he'll kill anything he can stalk. People included. He'd be better off vacating the city and going hiking in the mountains for a few days."

"Which is exactly what I'm going to suggest. I don't care if he wants to stick around to find out whether or not Byron survives, but he needs to keep his damn distance." Ev shoved the sticky note with the address of Addas's last known location into his pocket.

"Plus, alpha werewolves emit a pheromone that attracts wolves who are not alphas. And the stronger the odour, the less resistance there is to the chemical aphrodisiac. Having more than one alpha in an area means there's constant competition for pack members."

"You do know there's no such thing as alpha wolves, right? It's total bullshit. There's a dominant couple in every group who leads the wolf pack, and those wolves tend to be the parents of a family group." Cam challenged Franco. He'd learned about this in his university biodiversity course years ago during one of his "I'm finding myself" semesters.

"True. I'm impressed. Doesn't work the same for werewolves, though. Whether I like it or not, Everton smells amazing. The scent is sex on a stick, and one my wolf wants to be around. So, two alphas in a small geographic area is problematic. The competition for a leader creates chaos, and subordinate wolves will choose the stronger odour or the wolf who wins a battle challenge for the territory.

"And as much as I hate to say this, we tend to fare better as part of a group. Lone wolves end up going loopy."

"Oh, so Ev smells good? I mean, I agree, but clearly I'm missing out on something tasty." Cam gave Ev a lascivious stare. "So, what you're telling me is Ev smells sexually amazing?" He questioned Franco, putting his arm around his new friend and leaned in as close as his horns would allow. "So, both of you at the same time isn't too far of a stretch!"

Franco, not able to hold in his amusement any longer, bellowed out in laugher.

Ev wanted to die; he had never been so embarrassed.

"Sure, I'll come along for the ride." Franco grinned.

"I hate both of you right now. I'm going to go find Addas."

"It's almost midnight!" Franco appeared shocked.

"I need some alone time—away from you two. At least I can survey this address and make a plan. Cam, can I drop you off at Dev's?"

"Why? Can't I stay here?"

"I don't think that would be smart."

"He'll be fine, Ev. I'll look after him. Go do what you need to do. The other two won't dare challenge me to get to him. Won't listen to me for shit when it comes to chores, but I can take them both. Cam will be fine."

"All right, whatever." Ev didn't have any more fight in him. "Behave."

Ev shot the two a warning look, grabbed his keys, and left.

Chapter Fifteen

EVERTON ARRIVED AT the address Josip had given him. His destination landed him in the southeast end of Edmonton, an industrial area littered with old strip malls and mid-ranged warehouses. His Jeep Wrangler rumbled to a slow stop as he pressed on the brake pedal. Everton glanced out of his driver's side. The window, rolled down as it always was, allowed him to hang his head out the window, tracking the scents of the city.

Everton sniffed a few times.

A flicker of rage ignited within his puffed-out chest. Wolf pheromones were present. Nothing fresh though.

He threw the rugged-terrain puddle-jumper into park and turned the engine off. He sat quietly, eyeing the run-down mechanics shop from across the street. Made sense. Addas was a technomage. Not one of those fancy computer programmer types, but a witch who had a thing for mechanics. Still fell into the technomage realm. And most people, when faced with absurdity or uncertainty in their lives, fell back on the things they were good at. Relying on what they're comfortable doing helped ground a person. Finding the small elements in life that made sense gave way to comfort. Once they find themselves on solid ground, it becomes easier to rebuild.

Everton suspected Addas had returned to his regular skill set: a lonesome witch, good with his hands and mechanics, who had been tricked by his own lover into consuming fae mojo juice. He'd also survived a werewolf infection. Most likely, Addas was the first witch-fae-werewolf the world had ever known. A crazy-ass situation anyone would be reeling from. So, finding Addas working in a garage fixing cars made complete sense. Mutant creature or not, the man needed to ground himself in familiarity.

And being the only one of a kind will make someone feel all kinds of isolation.

Everton had spent years by himself, a few decades wasted in hiding and separating himself from society. He didn't want to hurt anyone. He also had no intention of reliving his past nightmares.

A LONG TIME ago, in the same city, but several generations past, a young man of German descent had left behind the mother country and come to the wilds of Canada to be free.

To be away.

Gone from his family's expectations, absent from a girl he was expected to marry, and a family he should have raised, Everton had run. No, that wasn't quite right. He hadn't run from anything. He had turned his back on his family, flatly refusing to do anything tradition dictated and, instead, secured the means to make his own way in the world.

And Canada had offered him a chance to recreate himself in a land offering opportunity—if he didn't freeze to death making his dreams come true.

And so, after a few years working odd jobs, labour jobs, and a few morally questionable night jobs, Ev earned enough coin to purchase a one-way ticket on a boat to come to the New West.

Once he landed on the eastern shores of an already booming Canada, more months passed by with the likes of late-night bar fighting, hard, muscle-cramping, and dangerous work in mines, and then securing a long stint for an entire season as a farm hand. In short order, he had saved up enough money to make his way out to Alberta. Everton learned from the Smiths—the family farm he had worked on in 1926—that land near Edmonton was rumoured to be decent. More importantly, Everton had scraped together enough coin to purchase his own farmstead. And a twenty-year-old didn't have a lot of resources. But he did have big dreams.

And so, Everton made a plan.

He took the train out to Edmonton.

He found a small swatch of land within a day's ride to the province's capital.

And the first year proved difficult, but he got by.

The second year yielded better crops and more livestock birthed in his stable. He managed to stash money away in an empty coffee can.

And then the 1930 dustbowl hit.

Everything went to shit.

Ev lost everything.

So, one night, after leaving his little farm behind, he found himself down to his last few coins, in a bar, drained of hope, and desperately needing to drink enough to forget his name.

Until a monster of a man sat down at his table.

"I'm sorry, friend, but tonight I am nobody's version of good company." Everton didn't even raise his head to look at the stranger, hoping his harsh German accent and curt words were enough to dissuade anyone. He took a chance at glancing across the table, his eyesight already swimming from one too many beers.

"I can see your attempt to drown yourself, which is why I chose to sit here. You look like you need a friend, and I do as well. A good friend. The name is Jensen. Jensen Bishop. And you, my new friend, look like a decent meal is required before the brew takes over."

"I have no money for a meal," Everton replied. "In fact"—he lifted his head and squinted at Jensen—"I barely have enough to pay for what I have already drunk." He hic-cupped.

Jensen chortled deeply. He reached across the table and placed a beastly paw on Everton's shoulder. "My friend, you are fortunate I have arrived. In the nick of time, I might add."

Everton studied the brute who grasped him. He wore a flat cap and sported a long beard. He had age weathered into his face, evident too by the patches of silver and grey in his hair and beard fighting for space. But the man's grey eyes, encircled with a gold-yellow ring around the pupil, drew Everton in.

Jensen's mouth ticked up in a wry smile, and he winked once at Everton.

The fire in Ev's belly rekindled as he tried to fight the demon of his attraction. Longings for other men were in part the reason for his departure from the old country. He couldn't very well marry a woman and give her children when he had no attraction for them. This man with his age and silver whiskers made his loins burn.

"Come. I have a room down the street at the hotel run by the railroad. I can feed you much better there. The food is shit here." The giant rose from the table, turned, and walked out of the bar.

Everton's gaze followed the colossus out the door.

He hoisted the stein and drained the last of his drink, left his last coins on the table at the seedy bar with flat, stale beer, and followed Jensen out into the night.

Little did Everton know that one decision would forever change his life.

GETTING OUT OF the truck, Everton stretched. Vertebrae popped and his shoulder snapped into place. Sitting for too long when you were this old had detrimental effects on his skeleton. Despite the wolf beneath his skin preserving him for many more years than would be considered natural, parts of him still aged. And shifting as often as he had tended to make the bone structure inside him prone to falling out of place.

Inhaling deeply, Everton picked up traces of Addas's pheromones and followed his nose to the back of the building, behind the mechanic's shop. The sour, old, and decayed smell of an alpha meant Addas hadn't been here in a couple of days. But underneath the alpha scent an undercurrent of rot tainted the morning air.

A sweet stench only produced by one thing.

Snooping around a werewolf's den wasn't a smart plan. Wandering into the cavern of an alpha was liable to get you ambushed. But Everton needed to know what he was up against. Besides, taking out a newly shifted pup would be an easy accomplishment—alpha or not.

There had to be a reason Addas made random visits to his pack house and not knock on the door. Everton had to assume Addas was spying him out, checking on the competition. Trying to determine how easy it would be to take the old man out. So Everton needed to do the same.

What was the expression?

Know thy enemy?

Addas's history and past connections assured Ev of his enemy status. A witch first, and one of the assholes who had worked with Byron Radcliffe to take Ev and his boys down. Byron had only partially succeeded the fateful night he lost three of his packmates. Everton got his revenge.

Inflicting Byron Radcliff's lover with a werewolf infection had been the best kind of retaliation possible—turn Byron's lover into the thing Byron hated the most.

But everyone knew a witch-werewolf combo wasn't possible, so the men would have a year of torment knowing an inevitable death neared. And nothing reverted a werewolf infection.

Didn't matter Byron had taken Everton hostage, or that he'd tortured him endlessly over the course of Addas's infection. Everton lived knowing Addas's fate would kill Byron just as much as the infection would kill Addas.

It was the perfect revenge for the murder of three of Everton's packmates.

And then Cam had shown up, and Everton's world turned upside down.

Or at least held a glimmer of hope.

Over the short period of Cam and Ev's incarceration together, Everton discovered another reason to live—and to escape.

A compact tank of a furry, winged, and horned fairy.

Memories of Cam made Ev relax and reminisce of sunny, lazy, summer afternoons stretched out in the tall prairie grass.

Those niceties evaporated as the stench of rot grew thicker in the back of the garage and refocused Everton's mind.

A fly buzzed around Ev's head. Everton frowned.

Prying open the rear door to the garage, after busting the lock, an obtrusive wall of stench knocked Everton over. He covered his nose and turned his head away.

As the sun rose and beamed across his shoulders, the rays of a new day spilled in through the busted doorway, shedding light on blood-soaked carnage.

Body parts were everywhere.

Addas had successfully made his transition to wolf. But without the guidance of a senior pack member, he'd succumbed to the bloodlust.

Ev studied the bloodied mess coating the inside of the mechanical shop and reconfirmed why new wolves were sent to *the shed* in Ev's pack. They stayed there during the full moon until they'd learned control.

Addas had killed.

And the wolf would continue to kill now that the beast had a taste for death.

THE SUN SHONE through the large round window. Sparks's eyes fluttered open. As he regained consciousness from a good night's sleep, his brain slowly ticked into full gear. Warmth, comfort, and silky sheets made him want to snuggle deeper into the bed. The soft pillow and human touch of skin and fur pressed up against his back made his body involuntarily wriggle into the cozy embrace.

His arm found another body in front of him, and in his half-asleep state of consciousness, he pulled the solid mound of muscle in closer to him.

Sparks's eyes popped open.

The unmistakable red of Tully's hair meant his Shadow Brother lay in front of him. He swivelled his head to his side. Dev big spooned him from behind. He lifted the covers and peeked. There wasn't a stitch of clothing anywhere.

Memories from the night before flooded into his brain.

The light dusting of hair on Sparks's chest lay matted and sticky in spots.

A momentary rush of embarrassment caught him off guard.

What the hell did we do?

Glancing over at Tully's arm, he noticed a new tattoo had appeared. A tree graced his upper shoulder, its branches wide, gnarled, and twisted. The tips were covered in leaves of green. Roots wound down his arm, creating an intricate Celtic knot pattern that stopped at his wrist.

Phineas.

Sparks glanced around the room. He recognized the upstairs apartment Dev had once briefly called home. He laid his head on the pillow but became keenly aware of another sensation.

As per usual, he was rock hard. His morning male alarm clock.

Tully shifted so Sparks's erection fit neatly into the crack of Tully's furry ass cheeks.

Dev reached around Sparks's front and cupped his balls.

What the hell is going on?

"Good morning." Dev kissed the back of Sparks's shoulder. "I believe the three of us had incredible sex last night with the Horned One and one another. You were amazing!" Dev gently kneaded Sparks's nut sack.

"Good morning?" Sparks replied. His cock throbbed and twitched up against Tully's ass while he let out a moan from Dev's actions, vaguely aware Dev had vocally answered the internal question he'd asked himself.

Tully rolled over to face them. His own hardness now rubbed up against Sparks.

"Definitely a good morning." But Tully stopped and cocked his head to one side, peering quizzically at Sparks. "You okay?"

"I think so?" Sparks replied.

"Do you want me to stop?" Dev said, a touch of alarm in his voice. Sparks shifted so he lay flat against the pillow, looking at his two friends.

No, not really, you two feel so fucking amazing. I just can't believe I'm here right now, and the last thing I want is to be somewhere I'm not wanted.

Dev and Tully grinned.

Sparks's words had obviously been received.

"Oh, I think it's safe to say you're wanted." Tully beamed.

"You guys are awesome, but that's not what I meant. You two are fantastic together, not with me thrown into the mix. But you heard the God last night. He said, *the three of us*. He basically wed us out in the witch grove." Sparks's mind recalled the damn bottle of wine he'd spelled, and internally he berated himself. This is not what he had intended.

Dev shook his head but sported a cockeyed grin.

"Tully, what did you say to me after we had Sparks over for dinner?" Dev asked.

"Well, I do believe I predicted this exact moment."

"And what did we both agree to?" Dev asked again.

"As long as everyone was comfortable and agreeable, we would never say no, because damn, Sparks is one handsome son of a bitch."

"Guys." Sparks flushed in embarrassment, moaning as Tully grabbed his still hard and leaking cock, stroking him while Dev continued to gently tug on his nuts. "As good as this feels, and despite the fact I really like both of you, I don't want to come in between you or be the third wheel. I don't want one night of sex to ruin our friendship."

"Sparks, buddy, do you think we'd be here if we thought that might happen?" Tully propped himself up on one elbow but continued to indulge in his stroking.

"I don't know. Weird things can happen after...you know?" Sparks stammered.

"Then we don't let our relationship get weird." Dev placed his hand on Sparks's chest, running his fingers over his fine chest hair. "Look, if anyone is going to be hesitant about any of this, it should be me. I'm still new to this whole boyfriend thing, never mind the witch thing. Tully keeps telling me how sexy the world of male witches is, and right now, I totally see why. Besides, I don't think this will be a simple one-night affair. I got the very distinct sense from Cernunnos that He wants the three of us together."

"Yup. I heard the same thing." Tully nodded.

Sparks bobbed his head awkwardly.

"Fair enough, but I can't help think my magic influenced this in some way. And I cast the spell and used rune magic on you without your permission. I feel a little guilty."

"Okay so, how about this, we take this one step at a time, we enjoy ourselves in the process, but we all agree to talk about anything and everything and ensure the three of us are always in a good headspace. Besides..." Dev squinted, initiating an internal conversation. *I don't think our thoughts are our own anymore.*

"Holy shit. I think you're right." Sparks's eyes went wide.

"Oh, damn. I heard that too. Cool." Tully flipped the covers back, exposing the three of them. He lifted his fingers away from his stroking action and displayed them for Dev and Sparks to see. Sparks had leaked so much, honey dripped from Tully's fingers.

"I'm thinking you might like this," Dev whispered loud enough for all to hear. "And for last night being my first threesome, I gotta say, I'm digging the fun of an additional man in my bed. My two boyfriends are fucking hot!" Dev leaned over and kissed Sparks and then Tully, then grabbed one of Tully's dripping fingers and sucked the precome off.

Sparks was in heaven.

"Well, I didn't get to do this last night, and I'm a sucker for a morning protein shake, so, Dev, if you don't mind, perhaps we'll give our new addition the morning welcome?"

"You lucky bastard," Dev whispered into Sparks's ear. "He does this thing with his tongue—"

Sparks gasped as his eyes went wide.

"Yeah, that thing. Awesome, isn't it?"

"Oh, I'm not gonna last long if he keeps up the licking. How does he do that?"

"This is how we get up every morning. Think you can handle it?"

Tully garbled out some words, but his meaning got muffled by Sparks's morning erection.

"I think so." Sparks turned to Dev. "Can I kiss you right now?"

"Hells, yes." Dev ground his bone into Sparks's side as he placed a warm wet kiss on Sparks's lips.

Sparks became lost in the sensation of Dev's tongue and Tully's warm mouth as he moaned loudly.

He broke away from Dev and his kiss. "Tully, I'm gonna come."

Tully clamped down on Sparks's dick and sucked even harder.

The three didn't get out of bed until almost noon.

Chapter Sixteen

CAM AND FRANCO sat together, chatting at the wolf pack's kitchen eat-up bar.

Cam tipped up his mug and polished off another cup of coffee. His tail flicked back and forth at a rapid rate, and his wings were gyrating.

"I think I've had too much caffeine." His brain hummed with activity. Thoughts were foggy, and he couldn't decide if the inability to focus stemmed from a lack of sleep or from too much hot brown water.

Franco chuckled. "You are too funny. More?"

"Fuck yes. The fae have no idea what good coffee is. Tea? That shit is everywhere, but no one appreciates the velvety goodness of a good roasted bean."

Franco slid off the bar stool, intent on making another pot. "So, tell me about you and Everton. I've known him for a long time, Cam, and I've never seen him so—what's the word I'm looking for—conflicted? I mean, it's not like he's been home a lot. A year penned up with witches, and then he spent most of the summer with you. But when I have seen him, or talked to him, he's fighting with his own thoughts."

"Yeah. He hasn't been an open book with the mushy feelings and all. Frankly, I'm starting to wonder if he likes me or not."

"Oh, he quite likes you. Of that I am certain. He wouldn't escape from a yearlong captivity only to scamper off again unless his heart is entranced. And that would be because of you. He's smitten. He should have stayed here and reorganized the pack. The guys won't listen to me as well as they do Everton. They're all going off and doing their own things, which would be okay normally, if Daddy is supervising and comes around every now and then to guide and protect. He's been an absent father, and so the angry teenagers have been running amok doing stupid things."

"Like getting killed." Cam grimaced. "Yeesh."

"Exactly like getting killed. Lars never thought of consequences. He made village idiots look calculating and intelligent. And then there's Serge. He needs help, he's still young, and he has problems transitioning, which isn't unusual for a new pup. But he's not new anymore. He's been relegated to *the shed* for each full moon for the past year and a half. Usually, the coaching process to learn control is a two- or three-month thing. That boy is in desperate need of Everton."

"What's this shed you keep talking about?"

"Oh, I'll show you later. We have an underground bunker with these massive chains and manacles. Sometimes werewolves need to be restrained."

"Ah." An image of an enraged werewolf lunging, snarling, and snapping, restrained only by a thick chain, sent a shiver down Cam's spine. He shrank into himself when he grasped the fact he'd spent the night talking with a feral beast capable of death and destruction.

"Don't worry. I'm all trained up." Franco winked.

The coffee maker gurgled and sputtered, indicating a fresh pot waited to be savoured and enjoyed.

Franco grabbed the glass carafe and poured Cam another steaming hot cup.

Cam's eyes widened and he grinned from ear to ear, pointed teeth extending beyond his lips as he dumped the required sugar into his mug.

"Whoa, I thought I had sharp teeth."

"Sorry. I'm still getting used to this fae business." Cam reined in his meat-eating fangs. "Guess I'm not much better than Serge."

"Oh, trust me, I think you have better control than Serge. I spent two days fixing the shed after the last full moon. What a fucking disaster."

Again, Cam pulled away if only a tad, trying to picture exactly how off the hook a beast had to be for another werewolf to call the event a "fucking disaster."

Cam contemplated this in detail and took a sip of his fresh coffee when Everton walked in through the back door. A thundercloud of doom and despair hung around him, which made both men stop their banter and stare at the pack leader.

"That's not good." Franco cocked an eyebrow.

"No, it's not. Cam, you are not safe here. I need to return you to the Ancestral Lands."

"I'm not going back there." The hackles on Cam's neck rose in defiance.

"Dammit, Cam, this isn't an option."

"What did you find?" Franco stared at his alpha through furrowed brows.

"A pile of bodies in amongst his lingering scent."

"Oh, yeah, not a good sign at all." Franco glanced at Cam and grimaced.

"All right, as much as Franco has taught me about werewolves over the course of the evening, you're gonna have to spell this one out for me."

"Oooh, and I've learned so much about the Eldritch!" Franco and Cam shared a side-eyed glance and then, while directing their focus back at Everton and in precise synchronicity, managed a perfect high-five clap between them without ever looking at each other.

Everton ran a flat palm over his scalp.

"Fuck me, I can't deal with you two. Cam, I need you to do what you're told." Everton sighed.

"If I did that, you would still be a plaything for a psycho witch." Cam folded his arms across his chest and sneered. "Besides, you're not my pack leader, so...that's a no from me."

Franco clamped down on his lips, physically attempting to bite back a laugh. "Okay, we can argue about where Cam is safest later. What did you see?"

"Fine." Ev glared at Cam. "Addas has successfully shifted into a werewolf. We were fairly certain before, but I had no real proof. I'm sure Franco has told you new wolves go through a kind of mentorship or have a pack to guide them?"

Cam nodded. His tail swayed.

"Lone wolves on their first shift can go a little...off."

Franco turned to Cam. "See, anger issues."

"Knock it off, Franco. I'm worried. There were at least a dozen bodies in his den and not full ones, which means he's eaten them."

"Oh, gross." Franco shuddered.

"What's the big deal? Isn't that kinda what werewolves do?" Cam flung his arms up.

"A new wolf, if not guided, loses control, succumbs to bloodlust, and does what any predatory animal wants to do: hunt, kill, and eat its prey. Problem is in a city centre like Edmonton most of the prey are human. Missing humans tend to draw attention if they aren't forgotten sections of society, like the homeless. Bodies ripped apart and left lying around attract the attention of human law enforcement, or worse, the Magistrates."

"I get maybe half of this. Murder, bad. Gotcha."

"All of this has the potential to attract attention to the Shadow Realm, with obvious pointers to something non-human who committed the crimes. There's the odd mundane individual who knows about the Realm, mostly individuals who come from magical families who didn't end up expressing any ability themselves, and they usually try to hide us or reduce the exposure. Think of them as allies."

"Okay, following along so far. Murder, bad, exposing Shadow Realm, also bad."

"If the Magistrates suspect one of us beasties is the culprit, they will get involved. They are the keepers of Witch Law, and although they have no dominion over all the creatures in the Realm, they tend to exert their influence anyway. Historically, the entire Realm regards them as the peacekeepers, or at the very least, the witches who keep the Realm as concealed as possible. The community gives them leeway because all of us remain protected from humans. Humans have been known to do some pretty horrible things to anything non-human. So, the Magistrates get carte blanche to ensure the Realm remains concealed. And they have been known to take things to the extreme to safeguard our secrets."

"Oh. Murder bad, exposing Shadow Realm, really bad, the Magistrates super-bad. Okay, now I understand. But I still don't get why you want me to go back to the Ancestral Lands. What's that gonna do?"

"Get you out of harm's way. Cam, if Addas comes knocking, he'll show up as a werewolf, and his visit won't be to stop by to make new friends."

"Okay." Cam glanced at Franco. "Two alphas in close proximity, apocalyptic bad."

Franco smiled.

"What the hell have you been telling him?"

"All the things you should have." Franco glared at Everton. "We'll talk about your relationship skills later."

Cam's eyes nearly popped out of his head, and his stomach dropped.

Franco chuckled as Cam shifted in his seat, uneasy with the confessions to Everton.

"Believe me, I'll be painting you in as good a light as possible. I want you to stick around." Franco turned to Ev. "He's fun. You need to seal the deal here. He's a small amount of sanity in this crazy house."

"Oh my Gods." Ev's cheeks were flaming red.

"So, Cam, you have a friend who lives in the city, yes?" Franco asked.

"Yeah, Dev and his boyfriend Tully. Why?"

"Well"—Franco glanced between the two of them—"Ev, how about if Cam went and stayed with Dev at least until after the full moon, which is the day after tomorrow. After that, he should be okay to be here at the pack house. No?"

Ev shook his head and closed his eyes.

"I like this plan!" Cam enthusiastically gulped down the last of his coffee. "It'll give me a chance to get caught up with Dev."

"See, all settled then."

"Fine." Ev grumbled. He grabbed his car keys from where he had laid them on the counter. "Let's go."

"What? Now?"

"Yes. Now."

SPARKS FELL BACKWARD into the bed, and as his head hit the pile of pillows, they enveloped him. There were sticky spots and wet pools of goo all over. Far more than when he had awoken. The boys spent the better part of the morning getting sweaty and leaving no square inch of skin undiscovered. Sparks closed his eyes and relished the euphoric high thrumming under his skin. He had never had sex like this.

Dev and Tully were simply magnificent. Hot. Sexy. And stunning.

"I can't move." Tully laughed.

"Me neither. I'm done. Every muscle aches, but in a good way," Sparks replied from within the nest of blankets and pillows. They were still all tangled up together.

"Well, I don't know about the two of you, but I need a shower, a coffee, and some breakfast. I don't think I've burned that many calories in weeks." Dev extricated himself from the limb pretzel the three had formed and slid out of the bed. Sparks listened to the pad of feet as Dev headed toward the bathroom down the hall.

Tully nuzzled up beside Sparks. "Hey, handsome."

"Hi, yourself." Sparks beamed as he looked toward the voice, only to see the predictable ear-to-ear grin his Shadow Realm brother always wore. Except now, his happiness shone even brighter.

"Any regrets?"

"It's still weird. I mean, wow. I don't think I can ever recall a marathon sex session like last night and this morning, nor do I think I have the energy to repeat this daily, or even weekly. And I think this is gonna take me some time to adjust to, you know?"

"I do. I think I like it though."

"Me too. You guys are comfy. You've always made me feel at ease, with a sense of belonging, and the minute I met Dev, I knew he was special. I didn't know why though."

"Ah, guys..." Dev yelled from the bathroom.

"What's up?" Tully shouted.

"I think you want to come and see this."

Sparks and Tully shared a glance between them, Tully's face contorted into a goofy confused look.

Flipping the covers off, the two bounced from the mattress of the extra-king-sized bed and followed in Dev's footsteps but stopped as soon as they got to the end of the hall.

"What the fuck?" Tully's mouth hung agape.

"So, this didn't exist yesterday?" Sparks questioned.

"Nope. Sure as hell did not."

What had been Dev's apartment bathroom, with a tidy one-man shower stall, toilet, and single vanity had expanded.

The bathroom had an echo—it had grown so monstrous. A stretched-out vanity with three sinks, an electrical plug at each station, and a light above every basin had formed along the far side of the room. One end of the bathroom had a massive, tiled shower, with rainwater heads and massaging jets situated at each end, and in the middle. A pane of glass blocked the bathing area with a sliding glass door, barn style, to prevent water from spraying all over the room. On the other end of the room, a massive claw-foot bathtub sat, but instead of being the typical oval shape, this was triangular. Three grown men would easily fit into the vessel.

There were two urinals attached to the wall, and a water closet with a toilet.

"Wait. Check this out." Dev opened a door near the tub that Sparks had assumed was a linen closet. The darkened room lit up automatically as Dev walked through the doorway. He took a few steps down a concealed hall and disappeared.

Tully and Sparks glanced at each other, shrugged in unison, and followed.

A sprawling walk-in closet awaited them. The room had been neatly partitioned into three obvious sections, each containing rod space, a bank of drawers, a shoe rack, and a tower of shelves.

"I don't have enough clothes to fill my section." Tully chuckled.

"Phht. I do." Dev laughed. "You can give me some of your space."

"Not likely!" The two teased, but then got quiet as they turned to stare at Sparks.

"Wow. Ah, this is...making some assumptions." Sparks ran a finger along the empty shelves. "Tully, does the house often remodel itself?"

"Not that I've ever known about. But I'll be asking Uncle Bart later!"

"Sparks, you okay? You look...pale." Tully walked over and put a hand on his lover's shoulder.

"There's no hurry, or even expectations on my part that you move in here. You're certainly more than welcome, but yeah. This is fast." Dev raised his eyebrows.

"We're happy to have you live here, Sparks. But you get to make that decision. Fuck what the house thinks." Tully moved in behind Sparks and wrapped his bearish arms around Sparks's middle.

Sparks leaned his head back and rested on Tully's shoulder. "You guys are the best. Ah, well, I think the Horned One has some expectations, which are being manifested in the house's layout. Can I take some time to think about moving in?"

"Absolutely." Dev replied in a heartbeat. "You can stay here, or you can go home. You can do whatever you want. This house is now as much yours as it is ours. Right?" Dev glanced at Tully.

"Yup. All for one, one for all," Tully announced.

"How very Alexandre Dumas of you." Sparks giggled. "Okay, enough mental gymnastics for one day. Give me twenty-four hours to sort shit through my own head?"

"Deal." Dev winked.

"Now, you said something about breakfast. I'm starving!" Sparks licked his lips.

"I think our resident chef should whip us up something." Dev gave Tully an obvious hint and a half grin.

"On it. Maybe we should—" Tully stopped and craned his head to one side. "Do you hear something?"

"I swear he has the hearing of a dog." Dev rolled his eyes.

"Shh. Seriously."

The three remained perfectly still and deathly silent.

There were some faint noises coming from downstairs.

"It sounds like someone is opening up the refrigerator and freezer." Sparks pinched his eyebrows together. Tully harrumphed. "Okay, what the fuck?"

The three men made their way toward the bedroom, found their clothes, donned them, and went to the staircase leading down to the second-floor apartment Dev and Tully had called home.

Except the old staircase had disappeared. A circular, wrought iron set of stairs had taken its place.

"This house is fucked up." Dev shook his head.

The three descended, and the stairwell wound up landing in an expanded foyer, near the front door to the main floor of the condo.

Peering down the short hallway, Sparks witnessed a tail flicker, and some furry-looking membranous wings flutter.

"Ah, I think your friend is here, Dev." Tully stared down the hallway.

Dev, being the shortest of the three, craned his neck around Sparks and peered into the kitchen.

"Yup. That's Cam."

"Oh, thank Gods, I thought I was gonna have to go all

bear man and save you two from an intruder." The muscled, redheaded witch puffed his chest out.

Dev and Sparks glared at Tully.

"Are you fucking kidding me?" Dev snarked back.

"Relax, I'm joking. I know all too well you can look after yourself. You got more magic mojo than I'll ever have."

"And remember that." Dev chuckled. He gave Tully's cheek a quick peck and continued to saunter down the hall to go see his friend.

Sparks glanced at Tully and raised an eyebrow. "I don't know if I can handle both of you at once." He bit his lip trying to suppress a laugh, but a small bit of doubt sprouted inside him that wondered how this threesome was going to work. Relationships were hard enough between two people. Three would prove to be a challenge.

Tully nodded, understanding Sparks. "I hear you, brother. I hear you. We'll figure the dynamics out together. Now, brace yourself. Cam is a whirlwind."

Sparks walked down the hallway and entered the kitchen to find Dev holding his head in his hands.

"What's the matter?" Sparks was confused. Dev appeared out of sorts.

He ate everything.

The fridge and freezer were wide open.

"What do you mean, everything?" Tully growled.

"He ate all the protein. Fae thing, remember?"

"I was hungry! I left you the eggs. Those are nasty." Cam lowered a monster-sized uncooked pork chop, which still had ice crystals clinging to the surface of the flesh, into his toothy maw.

"You know I could cook if you'd like." Tully placed his hands on his hips.

"Oh no, it would take too much time and be such a hassle. No, no worries. It's fine and delicious just like this. So…" Cam's pointed tongue lashed out, cleaning off his moustache and beard. "You want to explain how you managed to remodel the entire house in the few days I've been over at Everton's? What's with the three offices?" He cocked an eyebrow and squinted, glaring at the three men.

"The three what now?" Tully asked.

"Down the hall." Cam's wings pointed the way.

Past the kitchen, the hallway continued and at the end had been the bedroom Tully and Dev had used. The extra room had held a day bed and a desk Dev often used if he worked from home.

"What the hell…" Tully stormed off, then a laugh bellowed through to the kitchen. "Oh, you gotta see this."

Everyone piled down the hallway and confirmed what Cam had stated. The bedroom Dev and Tully had slept in up until last night no longer existed. In its place, the bedroom and office had split into three. Each room an equal size, housing a chair, a desk, and bookcases lining the walls with a window allowing the bright summer sun to illuminate the workspaces.

"I will be having *long* conversations with Uncle Bart. This is utterly precocious."

Above each doorway, a symbol had been engraved into the top frame of the door jamb. At the end of the hall where the bedroom had been, an inverted triangle with a horizontal line had been etched into the wood. The symbol for Earth. To the left, the symbol scratched into the wood frame formed a circle, the symbol for Spirit or Soul, and to the right, a single wavy line, representing Energy.

"Me." Tully pointed to the triangle. "Dev." He turned to the door with the circle, "And Sparks." Tully glanced up at the energy line and cocked a wry grin. Rounding about, he waved his hands like Vanna White in front of the door marked for Energy.

"I mean, I could be offended, or I might be warm and fuzzy inside. The house obviously wants me to feel welcomed, regardless of how fast this is all happening."

"What's fast? Who's fast?" Cam sputtered, his wings barely fitting in the hallway, his tail lashing from side to side. "Oh!" His eyes got wide as he glanced at each of the men. "Wait. Dev. You bastard. You got yourself another one and I still don't even have one boyfriend? Oh my Gods. Rude."

"Now wait—" Dev started but a rap at the door to the condo interrupted him.

"What in all the Gods' names..." Tully muscled his way down the hall. Cam had no recourse but to make a hasty retreat into the kitchen to allow Tully to move toward the front door.

Sparks positioned himself at the dining table which sat to the side of the kitchen with a clear view of the front entry.

Tully yanked the front door open to reveal a gorgeous young woman decked out in a red and gold sari.

"Dev!" Amna yelled out.

"In here," Dev replied from behind the kitchen counter, where Cam had taken roost.

"Dev, what in seven hells' name is—" Amna halted, studying the boys. She glared at Dev briefly, then swung around and stared at Sparks. Her face immediately changed into a mask of confusion. She whirled around and glared at Tully who had taken up space right behind her.

"Hello, sister-in-law." Tully returned the look.

"What is going on here?" Amna waved a finger at all three of the men, then spied Cam in all his fae glory. "And what the hell happened to you?"

"It's a long story," Cam spouted off while his tail swayed.

"Well, I have all afternoon, and my sisters from the coven have a message. So, Dev, make the tea; screw the coffee. We need to chat."

"It's so nice to see you, Amna." Dev clapped his hands together, but his face didn't match the words.

Sparks shook his head. This was an absolute clusterfuck.

Is this going to be my life from now on?

Dev and Tully glanced at him, and both grimaced.

"What is this?" Amna immediately picked up on the obvious private dialogue. "Oh, my Goddess, you three have bonded together. Nope, you're on your own. Father will freak the hell out. I'm not explaining this business to him. Have a good time defending your relationship status."

"Nothing a little charm can't handle!" Tully offered as he held up both thumbs and moved them in a circular motion.

Amna waved her finger at him. "Not again. It took me a week to put them right!"

"So, are we eating breakfast? I'm starving," Cam asked.

The three men all gaped at him.

Chapter Seventeen

CAM SAT AND drank coffee watching everyone else eat toast with preserves, eggs with melted jalapeno cheese, and vegetarian sausage links. He used all his powers of self-control to not throw up. He swallowed several times as bile rose in his throat. Human food had lost all appeal.

Now, raw flesh...bring it on.

Eggs didn't count.

Blech.

His tummy demanded more sustenance.

Tully hadn't been able to whip anything up for his specialized palate as he had cleaned them out of anything meat related. So, Cam settled for coffee instead.

The buzzing in his head and constant pounding in his chest determined he didn't need any more. His wings were on a permanent buzz mode from all the caffeine he'd ingested in the last twelve hours.

"Tully, this is delicious, thank you." Amna nibbled away at her plate of sautéed veggies, toasted artisan bread, and a raspberry anise jam. Amna was vegan. Even the eggs were off limits. "But, Dev, you still haven't told me what the hell has happened. You've ignored my texts for the last week, and you haven't been to see Mom and Dad. They are furious, and I continue to have to wear these outfits to appease Mother. I want one day in jeans. Just one day!

"So, care to share with me why it is I sense a darkness looming over this city? My sisters have all encountered some unusual shadow activity. And as much as a hellhound might be fun to play fetch with for a brief bit, it's not a creature you want around for the long haul."

"Hellhound, that's nothing. Tully and I were attacked by a wraith." Sparks countered Amna's polite conversation.

Amna's eyebrows shot up.

"See." She waved a finger at Sparks. "This is what I'm talking about. For a very long time, Edmonton has not had to put up with such creatures. What has happened to the Guardians?"

"Okay, so...let me get this straight. You didn't like me associating with Byron Radcliffe and his coven, but now that they are no longer around you want to know what happened?" Dev flushed. Cam had seen the response before when Dev's sister taunted him. Typical sibling rivalry. But then Amna had grown up with Dev and understood which buttons to push to achieve the highest level of annoyance.

"Dev, oh my God. What do you mean they are no longer around? I didn't want you getting mixed up with him and his weirdly loyal—what did he call them...Knights? Byron Radcliffe was an arrogant and cocky asshole who did some rather morally questionable things. But the Guardians of the Night Grove have long held the tradition of ensuring the deepest of the darkness stays buried. For that, we were all grateful. Not everything in the Shadow Realm should see the light of day.

"So, I repeat, what happened?"

"Girl, how long can you sit there and eat fake protein? 'Cause this story is twisty and complicated." Cam clicked his tongue to add emphasis to his statement. His wings folded together as he stared at Amna and mustered up a most serious glare.

"You haven't changed a single bit, Cam. One would have hoped such a physical transformation would have changed a few other qualities." Amna jeered.

"Rude," Cam replied as his tail twitched. He turned to Dev and mouthed, "I never liked her," as he pointed in Amna's direction.

Dev rolled his eyes.

"Cam's right, the situation is sordid, but basically, the Guardians of the Night Grove are no longer. Eddie and Gus, his Knights, are dead. Byron got mauled by his lover, Addas, after he turned into a werewolf, and Byron has spent the last few months in hospital recovering." Sparks nodded at Dev's commentary. "We don't know what happened to Addas, but it's possible he's dead."

"Nope, not dead. Very much alive." Cam stated matter of factly, although he drew out the "very" for dramatic affect. He took a sip from his mug.

'Wait, what? How would you know this?" Tully glared at Cam.

"Ah, hello, sleeping with the Edmonton Alpha?"

"No, you're not—but you want to." Dev corrected.

"Also rude," Cam replied, shifting his focus between Amna, Sparks, and Tully, but refused to look at Dev. "So, I came to the city to smooth things over with Everton—we're going through a little bumpy spot—and while I hung out at the pack house, things happened. Everton got all alpha on me, or tried to, saying it wasn't safe for me to be at his place because of another alpha wolf in the city...which is why I am here—" Cam returned his focus to Dev, glaring. Hard. "—hiding for my very life."

"Oh my Gods." Dev shook his head.

"What? Another alpha? And Addas is alive...how? Wait. Are you saying Addas is the other alpha?" Tully's face contorted as he strung together the information.

"Ding, ding, ding! We have a winner." Cam's sharp pointy teeth presented themselves as he grinned, looking like a serial-killer version of the Cheshire Cat.

"How did this all come about?" Dev squinted at Cam.

"The guys had seen another wolf in the vicinity, and there were these pheromones floating around that were apparently from another alpha—I think—I don't know, there were a lot of werewolf words. Anyway, Josip inadvertently came across the scent again in another part of the city and snapped pictures of Addas. At first the other wolves weren't sure but the size alone of the beast. I mean, my Everton is just as big, if not bigger, but, well, after spending some time in your ex-high priest's dungeon, I think I know Addas when I see him."

"So, Addas is alive."

"Oh yeah, and bloodlusted right out. Dead bodies everywhere. No one's safe. And the full moon is in a couple of days. Danger. Beware. All that stuff," Cam added while finishing the last sip of his coffee. He looked forlornly at the bottom of the mug.

"Do you want more, Cam?" Tully asked.

"Don't you think you've had enough?" Dev shot Cam a disgruntled look.

"No! How dare you?" Cam gave Dev the side-eye, then grinned and nodded vigorously at Tully. But the twitchy smile garnered a shocked grimace from Tully, as Cam brought a hand up and covered his sharp jack-o'-lantern-like teeth. Admittedly, the teeth were disconcerting. He concentrated on a plot he had contrived to get Everton naked and glamoured his teeth, reverting them to a human form. Remembering Dev had been nasty to him, he turned and scowled at Dev, again.

"You two are friends, right?" Sparks asked, looking concerned. Cam couldn't blame him, what with being slightly strung out, and a flesh-eating Eldritch fae. If you weren't used to fairies, the sight of one might be unsettling.

"The best. He's like my brother." Dev smiled. "Getting each other's goat, though, we live for that shit. Don't we, Cam."

Cam affirmed Dev's statement with another round of vigorous head bobbing.

"I'd never have guessed." Sparks raised his eyebrows.

"Well, this makes for an interesting turn of events. Addas is alive, Byron doesn't know it, there are dark things creeping into our once-protected city, and we've been tasked to take over and ensure Edmonton's safety," Dev said.

"I'm sorry, who tasked you? I mean, that's kind of the reason I'm here." Amna wiped her mouth with her napkin, set the cloth down, then glared at her brother. "I knew you had connections to Byron, so I thought I would come over and see if you'd ask the Guardians what has happened. But I see there's more to the story, and you've managed to get yourself neck-deep into all of this. So, who exactly stipulated you take over?"

"Everybody," Sparks, Tully, and Dev uttered in unison. The three exchanged glances between themselves, then laughed.

"I don't know if I'll get used to three of you." Amna's brows furrowed while Dev snickered. "It's not funny, Dev. This is dangerous. I can sense creepy-crawly energy, and the shadows are moving. I've had gooseflesh for over a week. I'm so nervous and high-strung I haven't slept in three nights. The nightmares are horrific. Something is going to happen, and soon, if whatever the Guardians did to protect this city isn't put back in place."

"Well, that's probably not going to happen anytime soon either." Cam cocked an eyebrow at Amna. "The big orb Byron used to store the throttled energy from the ley lines went kaboom. Byron made Addas connect the globe directly to the ley line so he'd have enough energy to use in casting the healing spell to cure Addas's werewolf infection. Shit went sideways and everything blew up."

"We need a new globe?" Dev's eyes were wide.

"Uncle Bart said Byron had stolen the idea from the coven in Montreal who utilized something similar," Tully explained. "So that tells me we need to go to Byron's house and search through the Guardian's stuff to find contacts to the coven in Montreal. And maybe there's documentation on how to build a new globe. While we're over there, we might as well retrieve our personal things."

"Byron's discharge is slated to happen soon," Sparks added.

"Maybe we should go right after breakfast?" Tully suggested. "Can you guys come?"

"I can't. I have some calls to make about a case for work. Which reminds me..." Dev turned to Sparks. "Do you know if your brother is around today? I need to chat with him."

"Should be. He rarely leaves his basement with all his dead things."

"Lovely image."

"He likes bones. He keeps them down in the cellar where the temperatures are cooler, and he has a lovely layer of graveyard dirt to lie them on. He's an unusual one."

"I hope he has some answers for me." Dev frowned.

"Well"—Tully put his mitt on Dev's shoulder—"Sparks, can you come with me?"

"I can. We'll have to be quick. I have a night shift I'm covering at the hospital tonight, and I need time to sleep before." Sparks threw Tully a wink.

Cam groaned and rolled his eyes.

He smelled sex on them. Sparks wore bags under his eyes, as did Tully and Dev. But they all sported afterglow grins too. Cam cocked an eyebrow at all three of the guys, knowing full well what had transpired last night.

"I DON'T KNOW, Sparks, I remember there being more stuff here."

Sparks scanned one end of the room, standing in front of a wall full of scrolls while Tully picked through a bookshelf in Byron's study—the exact room where he'd been locked in with Dev while Dev had attempted to find the trigger to release his power.

Sparks had listened to Tully tell the tale on the ride over. All the details including the blowjob leading up to the magic siphoning incident. Given what Sparks had been treated to earlier that morning, Tully's story tracked. His new lover had an unusually dexterous tongue.

Between the two of them, there were a couple of boxes they had filled with ceremonial robes, workbooks belonging to the guys, and the odd tome or scroll referencing energy tapping, redirecting of ley lines, and harvesting supernatural power. There wasn't nearly as much material as Sparks had hoped, but enough to perhaps get them started.

Tully moved over to Byron's desk and rifled through drawers. "Byron had to have had a journal, or phone book—something about the Montreal coven."

"Don't you think his contacts are all stored on his cell like everyone else? Or his laptop? And I don't know about you, but the only phone book I've ever seen had been stashed in a drawer at my parents' place. I don't think I've ever seen anyone use one."

"Yeah, I guess you're right. I wonder...maybe Uncle Bart has connections to the coven. I'll have to go ask him. I have other things to talk to him about. Namely, the house and its mysterious ability to renovate itself."

"Oh yeah. Weird," Sparks replied quietly as his tummy dropped. The last couple of days had been a bit tumultuous.

"Okay, speak. You've been off, and you never get *that* quiet." Tully stopped perusing papers he'd found and put his hands on his hips, the muscles in his forearms rippling as his grip tightened.

"It's so fast, Tully, and I feel guilty."

"Why?" Tully's jaw dropped.

"You guys are so perfect for each other, and then I'm feeling all lonely and dumb by myself, so I go cast a stupid spell and land up between you two. That's why. Both of you have been awesome but come on...you're still getting used to your own relationship. I go rogue with the hocus pocus and the Horned One decrees us a throuple. I mean...really?" Sparks flushed as he spoke, but the rising doubt bubbled over as the words fell out of his mouth.

"Look, I get it. Dev and I haven't had a chance to talk yet, but we will. I can guarantee you if there is any issue, Dev will voice his concerns, and in a nice way. He's a good man." Tully moved in front of the desk toward Sparks.

"You are two of the most incredible guys I know. I don't think I measure up in that equation. And I am seriously worried about doing anything that might compromise our friendship. Don't get me wrong, last night was bloody amazing, but—" Tully took two steps and closed the distance between him and Sparks.

Tully grabbed him by the shoulders and pulled him in, squeezing the air right out of him.

"Not another word."

Sparks struggled to breathe.

"You are more than worthy, firstly. And secondly, I have reservations too."

"What?" Sparks pulled away.

"I do. Why wouldn't I? You're right—one night having some sexy fun with a friend, not a big deal...but Cernunnos basically wed us out in the witch grove. He clearly wants all of us together. And the house? Like, what the fuck? I'm worried this instant melding of the minds thing is going to cause problems down the road. But..." Tully pulled away and stared Sparks in the eyes. "I'm willing to let go of my concerns and insecurities and try. There's obviously a reason, and truthfully, out of all the other guys, I can't think of a single one I'd rather have join us."

Sparks broke the gaze and stared at his feet.

"You're too good to me. You always have been. Dev barely knows me."

"But he will, give him a chance. I know he'll come to love you as much as he does me and vice versa. You and I already have coven history together. We get along great; I don't think taking our connection to a more intimate level is going to change how we feel about each other. If anything, we might cement our bond more. I mean, we did get pretty sticky."

They both chuckled.

"I'm overthinking this, aren't I?" Sparks bit the inside of his cheek, feeling foolish, and as insecure as a teenager. He should grow up, take the decree from the Horned One, and play it through.

"No more than I am."

"Really?" Sparks's mouth twitched upward in a half grin.

"Really." Tully leaned forward and gave Sparks a peck on the lips.

Sparks relaxed. Tully had a more sensible way of looking at life.

"I did have a lot of fun last night. And I'd be lying if I didn't admit to replaying some of our antics throughout breakfast. Especially the thing you do with your tongue."

Tully laughed.

"You want me to do it again?"

"Right here?"

Tully laughed. "Maybe later. Right now, we need to find anything else we possibly can so we can take over the Guardians' ley line throttling. I think we've managed to collect anything personal, and the guys' robes and workbooks."

"You're awesome; you know that, right?"

"As are you." Tully winked at Sparks, then released him. "I wonder if there's anything here on alpha werewolves. I have to admit I know shit about them, other than Byron always said how horrible they were."

"Yeah, I don't understand the animosity. Everton seems like a nice guy."

"A nice guy who'll rip you apart if given the chance."

"Fair, but I don't think he would."

"Can you believe Addas is still alive? I mean, who would have imagined the triple combo of witch, werewolf, and fae would have saved him." Sparks continued his scan of the wall in front of him.

"I know. And I'm surprised there's so little written about hybrids. I mean, I have fae in me—we know my ancestors are the result of a dalliance with the fae. That's how I'm able to charm people so well."

"Oh my Gods, I completely forgot about your additional talent. Have you been charming me all this time?"

Tully laughed again. "No, I wouldn't charm you unless you agreed to it, or in an emergency. But just so you know..." Tully grabbed Sparks's hand and rubbed the back with his thumb.

Sparks melted into Tully's magical touch. His fingers pressed into the plump meat of Sparks's palm, his thumb rubbing circles into the back, and Sparks relaxed.

"See?" Tully cocked an eyebrow, then immediately stopped.

Sparks shook his head. "That's insanely awesome. But if you wouldn't mind moving your thumbs to my shoulders and releasing some of the tension there, I'd be eternally grateful."

Tully burst out laughing, slapping Sparks on the back. "Tonight, after your shift, if you want, you come over to the house... I mean...our house...and I'll get the massage oils out. I'll fix you up."

"Sounds amazing."

"So..." A familiar voice startled them from behind. Sparks and Tully flipped around to find Byron standing at the entrance to his study. "Addas is alive? And you two are doing what, exactly? Stealing?"

"Oh, shit," Sparks whispered.

"Hey, Byron. Not stealing. Taking things that belong to us, and any coven documentation related to the ley line stuff you used to do. We've been given a mandate."

"I see." Byron tossed a large, fist-sized, amber rock into the air, then caught it. "How exactly do you know about Addas?"

"That is complicated, but the werewolf pack you had us all hunting down are not a bad bunch of guys. They've passed along info to us, indirectly, and we know Addas is, in fact, alive. He's also an alpha."

"Good. You can take me to him."

"Ah, I don't know. We're, what? Two days away from the full moon? Besides, his exact location is a mystery to me, but the pack knows." Sparks said.

"You have two choices. One, you can take me to Addas— I don't care how you get the information on his whereabouts—or two, you can stay right here in my study until you agree to do the first option." Byron tossed the rock into the air again.

"Crap." Tully eyed the amber as Byron juggled it.

"What?" Sparks glanced over at Tully with alarm and panic.

"I recognize the rock—Dev played with the stone the last time we were in here."

"That's right. You always were a clever boy." The rock flipped up into the air again.

"Byron, we don't know where Addas is—and with the full moon so close, do you think tracking Addas down is smart? Why don't we wait until after the moon cycle?"

"I haven't seen my lover in several months, and I need him. So, again, take me to him or you'll stay here."

"But Byron—" Tully lifted a hand up in defiance.

Tully's uncooperative response set Byron off. Sparks saw months of pain, guilt, and anger ripple across their ex-high priest's face and morph into rage. It made him feel bad for the man.

Until the amber rock came hurtling toward them.

"It's a soul trap. Sparks, jump!" Tully threw himself in the opposite direction from where Bryon had aimed the amber stone. Sparks attempted to follow Tully's lead, but neither of them was fast enough.

As the amber hit the wooden floorboards, it shattered into several pieces, releasing a yellow glow saturating the space around Sparks and Tully.

SUSPENDED IN MID-AIR, the boys floated and bobbed in the dense buttery glow. The shocked expression frozen on their faces made Byron's heart happier. But nothing would make him feel right about anything until he wrapped his arms around Addas, then dropped to the man's feet and begged for his forgiveness.

He only hoped Addas would still have him.

Reaching into his coat's pocket, Byron pulled out his cell phone, found the phone number he wanted, and punched the Call button.

Addas and he would be together again soon enough.

Chapter Eighteen

CAM HAD PERCHED on a stool at the eat-up bar in Dev's kitchen and continued to sip coffee as his best buddy cleaned up the remains of the impromptu brunch. He fidgeted constantly, fingers tapping, feet stomping, and tail jerking. They were actions more likely for Dev, and his friend usually twitched like a madman whenever he got nervous. Cam wasn't nervous, he was strung out.

Dev's sister, Amna, had left, emphasizing as she departed how her sensate ability had shifted and her sense of doom had lessened. She had confidence in Dev, Tully, and Sparks. The boys had promised they would do *something* about the ley lines. However, what the boys' plan might involve to curtail the potential onslaught of darkness, no one had any guesses. Tully and Sparks disappeared after breakfast to go to the old coven house and see if there were any resources related to storing ley line energy.

Dev had confided in Cam his worries on their lack of knowledge for tapping and storing ley line energy. Dev, Tully, and Sparks agreed they should have been aware of the Guardians of the Night Grove's community service. Keeping everyone safe while suppressing the worst of the Shadow Realm weighed heavily on Dev. What a formidable task.

Cam continued to vibrate, trying his damnedest to focus on the conversation. He hadn't slept the night before, and he'd consumed more coffee than any human, or fae, should have ever attempted. His heart thumped, but he still gripped a cold cup of joe in his clawed hands.

His wings were shaking at a furious rate.

Dev finally stopped talking long enough to notice. "Okay, you know what, I think it's time for water. Gimme that." Dev wrenched the coffee mug away from Cam's feral clutches and replaced the coffee-stained mug with a tall ice-cold glass of water. "You need to flush some of the caffeine from your body. You look like you're stoned."

"I kinda feel stoned." Cam glared at Dev, but concentrating on any one thing for more than a second or two proved impossible. The world had fogged over while his head thumped. Even his skin crawled.

"Jesus, your eyeballs are dancing."

"That explains my vision."

"Wow, okay, well, when you put your mind to something, you go all in. Exactly how many cups of coffee have you had?"

"No idea. The party started last night at Everton's. Franco and I drank coffee all night waiting for Ev to come home while he scouted out the address Josip gave him to find Addas. I think we went through four or five pots. Caffeine doesn't affect Franco though. He kept up with me cup for cup. He likes coffee." Cam blinked several times rapidly as Dev studied him intently.

"And you have had at least a pot and a half to yourself here. Okay, no more…for a while. A *long* while." Cam had been scolded by Dev for years, but not since he had turned fae. And now Cam found himself hissing at his friend. "What's your expression? Rude." Dev snorted. "Jeez, dude,

I'm only trying to make sure your ticker doesn't explode. Do what you want. I am not your momma."

"I know. I know. I'm sorry. It's just the Ancestral Lands don't exactly have a Starbucks, you know? And they drink nothing but *tea!* Ugh. Gross."

"Okay, so, fairies drink tea. Noted. Now that we're alone, tell me *everything else!* What are the Ancestral Lands like? Is Lady Aine as terrifying as she looks? And what's the deal with you and Everton?"

Despite their bickering at breakfast, the teasing had long been forgotten. It's what they did with each other. Push buttons until someone snaps, laugh like hell at the other person, then forget about it, and continue to be besties. Cam didn't know where to start with the whole Everton mess so chose to talk about the fae stuff.

"Lady Aine is a monster. She's all light and grace one moment and then pointy teeth and razor-sharp nails the next. She's ripped into more than one belligerent or unlawful fae and eaten them. In the Royal court, no less, and in front of everyone. She scares the living crap out of me. And as much as I know I should have been paying more attention to my studies, Everton dominated every minute of my day. Too much went down in too short a period. This"—Cam waved his hands across and down his body—"was the beginning of it all. You and your summoning board! Although, the tail comes in handy." Cam glanced over his shoulder at his appendage as the furry tail flicked back and forth.

"I can only imagine. I have to admit the tail is awesome. You look cool!"

"Yeah, so cool." Cam threw Dev a sarcastic stare, complete with a set of daggers. "Dev, I would give anything to have my old body back. This fae business is bizarre. I mean, sure, I can move through the shadows at breakneck speeds, and I can climb anything, but I look like a freak. Going out in public is impossible unless I use magic to disguise myself, and contrary to what other fae will tell you, using magic all the time is exhausting." Cam huffed out an exaggerated breath. "I just want to be me again." He slouched, sinking further into his chair as he placed his head in his hands, glancing at the surface of his drink where the ice cubes floated in the water.

Dev put his hand on Cam's furry and clawed fist.

"I'm sorry I got you mixed up in all of this. I wish I could reverse the spell for you."

Cam sighed. "Thanks. I know you didn't do it on purpose, and I wrote down my own wish—you didn't do that to me. Writing 'make me the fairy I truly am' wasn't perhaps the smartest thing I've ever done. And everyone keeps telling me there's no going back—what's done is done, and Djinn magic can't be broken. So, here I am. Wings, horns, tail, and all. But I'm glad Everton likes it. Kinky motherfucker."

"Really? All of it?" Dev asked with a touch of the devil in his tone.

"Oh yeah. Says he wants to hold on to my horns while—"

"Too much!" Dev held his hand up, palm out. "TMI, dude. TMI."

Cam chuckled. Dev always acted like he wanted the details but continually displayed his prudish attitudes.

"Seriously, though, what's the deal? You're not one to hold out on the bump and grind."

"I know! I get the sense he's retreating, and I have no idea why. Dev, I really like him. I didn't jump into his pants like I usually do with other guys. Instead, I spent time with him and got to know him. He's a sweetie. A monster of a man with a raging beast inside him. He has the biggest heart and always wants to protect me...and, well, damn, he's a good guy. I want to see more of him. I like being around him. But he keeps distancing himself, and yet, the emotions wafting off him are driving me crazy. The blue balls I have suffered because of his reluctance to get jiggy should be considered a hate crime. And now Lady Aine has introduced *the complication*." Cam rummaged around in the sac hanging from his waist. He fished out Lady Aine's vessel and plonked the sculpted glass on the countertop.

"It's a pretty little thing, but I wish you'd stop putting it on surfaces where I eat. I don't know where Lady Aine's seed vessel has been, or the last time someone supplied contents, or when the lovely vial got thoroughly washed."

"Ha-ha." Cam rolled his eyes.

"Have you told Everton any of this? You've never talked about anyone with this much angst. Oh, except Andy. Do you remember Andy? Gurl, you were kookoo for cocoa puffs over that guy."

"I was young and stupid."

"And he broke your heart, too, if I remember. But there's been so many others since then. It's hard to keep them all straight with you."

"You're a riot." Cam teetered slightly in his chair as a wave rolled over him, instantly cranking up his temperature and making him burst out in tiny beads of sweat. He flapped his hand like a fan. "Damn, is it hot in here?"

"No, it's not."

Cam continued to fan himself. Then he sneered at Dev. "Of course I remember Andy. Andy gave me my first kiss and my first blowjob. He crushed my heart, dumping me for an older man. If you recall I also swore I'd never let another dude hurt me. But I'm desperate here. I need to get this thingy filled and delivered to the queen before she puts my head on a pike at the entrance to the Ancestral Lands." He glanced at the pearlescent vessel. "And I wouldn't put impalement past her. She also warned me to get this to her before Groundswell. And with the weather being as weird as it has been, the village might migrate underground at a second's notice. I seriously thought I'd have this thing filled already and placed into her grubby 'gotta be pregnant' paws."

"So, then go get Everton and fix it."

"We got so close the other night, but then one of his damn wolves barged in. There I lay on Ev's bed pinned down on the mattress with a mouthful of—"

"Okay. Oh my Gods, okay. Please stop describing your sex life in gory detail. I love you, but please spare me, otherwise I'll have to go get the bleach bottle and pour some into my eyes."

Cam's toothy grin stretched from ear to ear. He did enjoy making Dev uncomfortable.

"His frankfurter was tasty; I'll tell you that much. Frankly, I'm surprised we even got naked. He has a thing for the horns though. Pervy bastard. But I kinda like it. He's a monster."

"I seem to remember your second wish had a reference to a monster boyfriend, did it not?"

"Shut up. I hereby declare talking about the day of using the summoning board to be forever forbidden." Cam squinted and glared at Dev. "So, speaking of someone else's sex life, what's this third thing you got going on? I'm super jealous. They both hawt! And this is totally not you."

"Yeah, well, it's all very new and rather sudden."

"You're not happy? I mean three's not always a crowd. Sometimes it's a party!"

"No, it's not that I'm unhappy. But you're right—this is not me. This is not how I envisioned my life. Don't get me wrong, Sparks is an incredible guy. Super nice. Really attractive. Gorgeous cock." Dev glanced at Cam to see if the forthright statement would rattle his friend, but instead, Cam leaned in closer to Dev. "Ugh, you're impossible."

"Tell me more! Is it fat? Like, did you try both at once?"

"Oh. My. Gods. No, we are not doing this."

Cam laughed.

"I hate you."

"No, you don't. You love me."

"Yes, I do, though why, I still don't know."

"Okay, tell your bestie in the whole world—what's the problem?"

"That's just it, there isn't a problem. I like Sparks, but the whole thing happened so fast and Cernunnos sort of tied us together out in the witch wood." Dev jerked a thumb over his shoulder.

"All right, back up the bus. Who did what, where? And to whom?"

It was Dev's turn to laugh.

"Sparks and Tully had gone out to dinner together. I worked late. And as I remember, you were skulking about in my lobby—which reminds me I must call Wiatt about a possessed boy.

"I came home after dropping you off at the pack house and found the two of them here chatting away. They had news of their own after being attacked by a wraith and then visiting with and confiding in Uncle Bart about what had happened with the Guardians. I had you, and demon boy...the three of us had all had enough of life's trials and tribulations, so Tully suggested we soak in the hot tub Uncle Bart had ordered a few weeks ago. That's when we discovered a new section of the yard we had never seen before."

"A new section of the yard? Seriously? How the fuck does that happen?"

"Yeah, well, kind of like the house's sudden ability for magical expansion, remodelling, and decorating. Apparently, the yard does re-landscaping as well. Anyhoo, while out in this new area we got attacked by an Earth elemental, almost died, until the Horned One showed up and called off His beastie. He then gave us the mandate to take over from the Guardians, gave Sparks and Tully additional gifts, and pretty much wed us on the spot."

"What? A God descended from on high, granted you an audience, bestowed gifts to your lovers, and then wed all three of you together?"

Dev nodded, tilted his head to one side and raised a single eyebrow. "You won't believe how He bestows His blessings."

Cam's eyebrows raised up into his wavy hair. "Shut up!"

"Yup."

"You mean to tell me the three of you got it on with a God?"

"Yeah."

"Holy fuck, Dev, you horndog. Here I always pegged you as the prude. I'm going to have to revisit. You don't behave like this. I'm the orgy slut! My life is all kinds of fucked up."

"I'm reeling a bit, to be honest, but I don't want to show that to Sparks. What the fuck are we supposed to do? A goddamn God wants us to be together. Apparently the three of us have work we need to do, together. He has plans for us. And Sparks is such a great guy. Do I mind we've been conscripted to be together? Hell no. He's gorgeous. More importantly, he's smart and kind. But I don't know him that well. Tully does, and he spoke fondly of him, often. Sparks is my Shadow Realm Brother. He stepped up during my binding ritual to the Realm and offered himself up. I suppose we should have guessed this might be an outcome."

"So, a throuple. I hate you a little." Cam squinted at Dev, trying to look all fierce and pissed off.

"Ha! No, you're—"

Dev's eyes iced over, like frost creeping across a frozen windowpane. Horror sunk into Cam's veins as the crystals multiplied, covering his friend's eyes. In the time it took to gulp a mouthful of air, Dev had turned into a zombie.

Dev jerked ramrod straight, stiffened up, and stood motionless for several seconds. Cam hoped this wasn't some type of magical seizure.

Cam lurched off his seat as his buddy went cadaver stiff but halted as Dev began to sway. Was this a normal thing for his witchy friend? What did Cam know about witch things?

He was still breathing, and that had to be a good sign.

There wasn't any blood anywhere, no visual wound, no unwanted intruders.

And then Dev's muscles all gave out and he crumpled to the floor. His head made a sickening *smack* as he hit the tile.

Chapter Nineteen

EVERTON BUSIED HIMSELF around the house. The boys had made sure to leave him with a lengthy list of chores. But if he kept busy, he found the tasks freed his mind to contemplate his current predicament.

And he needed to think. At least Cam had been tucked out of harm's way, for now, and his absence gave Everton a clearer headspace in which to think. Relocating the furry fae to his friend's place had been a solid decision by Franco. Kudos to him.

As much as Ev didn't want a confrontation with another alpha, after seeing Addas's den there wasn't much doubt he'd be dealing with an unwanted caller. Cam had to be far away from the packhouse. The fae wouldn't stand a chance against a bloodlust-crazed werewolf. The full moon was in two days, too close for comfort.

Werewolves had to master the wolf within before being able to call upon the beast beyond the cycle of the moon. Ev figured he had a couple more days before all hell would break loose.

Had Addas learned how to shift outside of the full moon? Hard to say. Some wolves come upon the skill easily. Others never learn. Safety first, right?

So, with Cam's wellbeing in mind, dumping him at his best friend's house was the smart and secure thing to do. But now Everton had Cam on the brain. He was disappointed in himself for letting Cam enchant him with that sexy fae body of his. Those horns, and wings, and fur. Oh man, the fur. Everton had been extremely careful to rein in his desires all summer and all that went out the window with one visit to his bedroom. As much as his recent naked tumble with Cam had embarrassed Serge, Ev had thanked the Gods above the young pup had barged in and interrupted the one thing Everton had sworn he wasn't going to do.

If Everton dwelled on the ridges of Cam's horns, or the way his wings fluttered every time he stroked the bristles that lined them, he would abandon any control he had and give in to Cam's pattern of one-night stands. And as glorious as sex with Cam promised to be, he wanted so much more than a single night of splendour.

Everton needed to focus. Ensuring *the shed* got prepped and ready for Serge had to take priority, not Cam's round butt and silky tail.

If Addas didn't show up, Everton would finally get the opportunity to teach the fledgling werewolf how to gain control and not succumb to the bloodlust. Thankfully, Franco had been responsible enough to get Serge chained each month to prevent him from heading toward a lifelong mental health battle.

Everton had put down more than one werewolf who had lost themselves to the blood rage. He didn't want to have to kill Serge. The young man still had a long life ahead of him if he learned control.

At least this time Ev would be around to guide Serge's inner wolf to lean into the change, accepting the beast inside. Making a pact with the hellhound residing under the skin would save him from the hurt and mental anguish. Dancing with the devil always led to a disastrous end, but sometimes taking on the demon you know is safer than any other option. Fighting the change enraged the wolf and would initiate a toxic relationship between the human side and the feral beast. By cementing a tenet of peace, a werewolf's chances at a life without the constant rage was possible. Hopefully, the extended period the pup had endured without the coaching hadn't done any damage to the wolf's psyche.

A year and a half of chained captivity. Ev shook his head, disgusted in himself for letting Serge suffer.

Everton shouldn't have gone to the Ancestral Lands.

It had been a poorly made decision to watch over Cam.

A summer he continually thought about.

"Dammit, focus," Ev mumbled.

"You know—" Franco grabbed the plank of wood roughly nailed to the wall that acted as a railing. The stairs were rough and uneven, and steep. As Franco descended and ended up on the stable, flat dirt floor of the root cellar, he continued, "You could just tell him how you feel."

"What are you talking about?"

"Come on, Ev, how long have we known each other? At least the fifty years you've been leading this pack? You think I can't tell when my alpha has gone moon-eyed over someone, or something? And let's face it, he's completely your type. You like them small, cocky, and attitudinal. The horns too. I don't know what it is with you and horns."

"Gives me something to hold on to."

"You kinky mother—"

"Shut up. And I don't really want to talk about this." Ev's gaze darted in Franco's direction, then shifted away in embarrassment.

"Why not talk about it? You're clearly struggling."

"I have other things to think about right now. There's a raging new alpha in town, and it's part werewolf, part witch, and somehow fae too. I'm concerned—especially after the violent and bloody scene I stumbled into earlier—who the hell knows what to expect with some mutant beast on our hands?

"And then there's Serge. The kid has been cuffed and collared for a year. The imprisonment isn't fair to him. I need to get him broken this cycle. We can't keep locking him up."

"All it takes is one shift with you. You're brilliant at guiding people through it. You taught me in one cycle. Serge will take to it, don't worry. And he understands. When he's calm and sits still long enough, we've had some great conversations about pack, learning control, getting the best out of life despite the beast inside. He's a good kid. Give him some credit."

"I hope so. The alternate isn't appealing."

"You won't have to put him down. He'll learn."

"I can't kill another kid again. I won't do that to Serge. I've pulled the trigger on too many others."

Franco put a mitt-sized paw on Ev's shoulders. "I know. We'll get him through this. But you'll have more success when you can focus all your attention on Serge, and right now you're being divided between Cam and Serge. You need to deal with Cam. I don't understand what the problem is. Grab his horns and get it done. Get him out of your system."

"That's the problem, Franco." Everton's gaze dropped toward the roughly hewn floor. "I don't think I want him gone from my system. Not this time. He's different." Everton turned around to face his second in command, his cheeks hot and flushed. "I like the little bugger. I want him around. He makes the wolf feel relaxed, and I smile when he's being goofy. I don't get to feel calm and peaceful being your alpha. There are too many responsibilities. Cam is freeing. He enjoys the moment and forces me to do the same." Ev frowned and clenched his teeth. "But he's not werewolf. I can't be there to keep him safe all the time. He's fae, and they are...well...small and fragile. Our lives are violent and deadly. Besides, I doubt he wants to keep me around. He likes to play the field. He has more notches in his bedpost than I ever will, and I've lived three times longer than him."

"Four times. You are old. And you also worry far too much. Have you told him how you feel?"

"Gods, no. Why would I want to subject myself to his rejection? Or humiliation? His tongue is sharp enough to deliver some staggering blows."

Franco gave Everton a dirty look. "What is wrong with you? You want him around, but refuse to tell him how you feel, so you push him away; meanwhile, he's chasing after you. You're damaged."

"We all are. We're werewolves."

"Yeah, okay. Look, you are not doing anyone any favours trying to suppress this. You're miserable right now, and you need to be 100 percent in control for Serge. So, I think you need to go over to Cam's friend's place and have the conversation. You need to figure this out. I can't be alpha. I don't have the pheromones. That's all on you, buddy. Go wolf-up and do the right thing. Mmm-kay?"

Everton glared at Franco, his wolfen eyes shining through.

"Stop that. You know I'm right."

Everton gave up on the staring, rolled his head, and shook it, trying to loosen the sticky cobwebs of uncomfortable feelings.

"I hate it when you're right."

"I'm always right. And I like Cam. He's a good guy. I wouldn't tell you to go lay your heart bare if I thought for a second being truthful with Cam would get you hurt. Tell him. It's the right thing to do. I would never set you up for failure."

"What did Cam tell you? You two were together for too long."

"Cam told me what I need to know. Now you need to go find out for yourself."

CAM DRAGGED DEV over to the couch, hoisted him onto it, then propped his feet up and shoved a few pillows under them. He positioned Dev's head so he'd be comfortable. Then he took his arms and laid them across his chest. Cam stood back and studied him.

The position he had put Dev into resembled a corpse in a coffin.

The arms made it weird. Cam moved them to Dev's side.

After further inspection, and an up-close listen to make sure Dev was still breathing, he resigned himself to waiting until Dev woke up.

After several minutes of tapping his foot and staring at Dev, expecting his eyes to spring open, Cam grunted in disapproval. He needed to get Dev to come around. But slapping him was out of the question, and gentle shaking had produced no results. The goose-egg on the side of Dev's head would be there for a couple of days. Cam poked at the bump and grimaced as the fleshy swelling gave slightly under his finger. Cam left his buddy's side, went to the freezer, and grabbed a frozen bag of peas. When he returned to his passed-out witchy friend he laid the chilled veggies over the bump, hoping to reduce the inflammation. If the bulge didn't subside, Cam would bear the brunt of Dev's boyfriend's anger. And Tully's bearish size gave Cam pause.

Dev's head lolled to one side as he mumbled something.

"Oh, thank Gods, you're alive." Cam leaned in close to Dev.

Dev's eyelids fluttered as he mumbled some indecipherable words, then drool slipped past his lips and ran down the side of his cheek.

"Nasty." Cam scowled. His wings sputtered. "Shit, what the hell am I going to do with you?" He pressed the bag of peas firmly onto Dev's head.

Dev's phone rang.

The ringtone's muffled warble continued, which meant...

Leaning in close and putting the side of his head near Dev's crotch, Cam scrunched his face up. He had located the phone.

"Great. I have to go pocket diving on my best friend." Cam glared up at Dev. "You'd better be wearing underwear."

Reaching into Dev's jeans, he discovered with delight the pants were stretchy denim, worn for a comfortable and relaxed fit, which also meant the flexible fabric made pulling the cell out a breeze. Bonus, Cam didn't have to touch anything that didn't require touching.

The phone continued to ring. Looking at the caller ID, the name "Byron Radcliffe" displayed in glowing digital green letters. The asshole witch who had held Cam hostage and tortured him with steel needles poked into his spinal column. Anger swelled in Cam. This was one call he'd answer on behalf of Dev and unleash all the fury of the fae.

He swiped the Accept button, then held the phone up to his pointy and furred ear.

"What the fuck do you want?"

"Who is this?"

"It's your favourite fairy, asshole. I repeat, what the fuck do you want?"

"Put Dev on the phone. I have important things he needs to know."

"I'm sure you do. Unfortunately, Dev can't come to the phone right now. Would you care to leave a message?" The evil intent Cam laced into every word dripped from his tongue.

"Put him on the Gods-damned phone."

"Look, you freak, do you seriously think Dev would let me answer his phone if he was available? Or maybe your dumbass name displayed on his phone, and he wanted nothing to do with you. Either way, stuff it, ya bitch. You're stuck dealing with me, and if left up to me, and we were in the same room, I'd be elbow-deep in your guts. So, your choices right now are tell me what you think is so important for Dev, or fuck off. I'd prefer the latter."

Silence echoed on the phone for a heartbeat.

"Well? What's your fucking message? Maybe I might tell Dev. Maybe I won't. You're not my favourite person in the world so I don't feel like being particularly reliable for you."

"Well, Cam, you can tell your best buddy if he ever wants to see Tully and Sparks again he'll want to come down to the coven house."

"What the fuck? Like I'm going to believe you could hold those two strapping young men? And since when did they let your old, scrawny ass out of the hospital?"

"I got out today and interrupted these two strapping young men, as you put it, trying to steal from me. I don't have to be young and buff, Cam. I have mastery over many spells and lots of objects I can use to keep someone under my thumb. You should know. I kept you long enough."

"You're such a…if I ever cross paths with you, I swear, I will go all fae on you."

"Sure. Like you did the last time?"

"Your healing spell to cure Addas went sideways, didn't it? There's some theories on how that happened."

"Hmph. Yes, well, you didn't have the ability to control much of your inherent fae talents, so I seriously doubt you had anything to do with how the evening played out. Rest assured, I'm here at my house, and I caught Tully and Sparks robbing me, so I have them all wrapped up. If Dev wants his boyfriends in one piece, he'd better come see me. Make sure you tell him soon, Cam. The longer I have them contained the less likely they are to come back normal. Soul traps are ugly contraptions. They make people go a little loopy in the head."

A click indicated Byron had ended the call.

"Shit. I hate that motherfucker." Cam glanced at Dev.

He was still out cold. Cam snapped his fingers a couple of times in Dev's face.

Nothing.

"Ugh. What the hell am I going to do—" Then Cam recalled holding Everton on the cold dungeon floor, his guts spilling out of the gash Byron Radcliffe had sawed open.

The fae have several magical abilities. Invisibility, illusions, agility, chance distortion, and healing. Of course, being Eldritch and of Royal position allotted Cam more abilities than most other fae, but if he conjured up the healing spell, he'd fix the bump on Dev's head and wake him up.

Everton had sworn he'd been healed by Cam that fateful night in the witches' dungeon. Surely Cam could find the trigger to summon the fae mojo and heal his buddy.

Cam pitched the phone onto the coffee table and looked up too fast. The room spun for a second, and he had to steady himself.

"What the hell." He gripped the edge of the table. "I gotta quit drinking so much coffee."

Cam closed his eyes, hoping the sensation would subside. No such luck.

The spinning increased, pitching Cam off balance. Bracing himself by gripping the edge of the coffee table and the arm of the couch, he steadied himself until his vision stopped rolling and the world came to a stop.

Cam sat down on the end of the sofa next to Dev's feet and contemplated what had happened the last night he'd spent in the coven house, and how Everton ended up magically healed.

Chapter Twenty

HOURS HAD GONE by.

Cam dripped perspiration. The fur across his chest and back lay matted to his skin. Even his usually perky wings drooped in exhaustion.

He straddled Dev's chest, trying anything and everything to initiate the fae healing abilities.

Nothing. No spark, no fairy light, no eruptions of glittering sequins.

"I don't get it!"

"Get off of me," Dev mumbled, his head half buried in the sofa's cushions.

"Oh my Gods!" Cam yelled.

"Shh! Fuck me, what the hell happened?" Dev's head rolled forward, as his eyelids peeled open. He tried to lift his arms, but Cam's body prevented the motion. "Could you get off, please?"

"Oh, yeah, sorry."

"Why am I all wet?"

"Oh, ah, I might have sweated a little trying to heal you."

"Gross." Dev's voice was a crackly whisper. "Gods, my head..."

As Cam climbed off, thankful he didn't have to try to initiate any healing fae hoodoo anymore, Dev pulled his hand up to his head and immediately found the large bump.

"What the fuck?"

"You fell down. Hard."

Dev's eyes went wide.

"Shit! Shit, shit, shit!"

"What?" Cam glanced around, wondering if there was something in the room causing Dev's stress.

"It would have been nice if you caught me." Dev glared at Cam, giving him an evil eye. Dev pulled himself up off the couch, his movements calculated and slow.

"Dude, you went down so fast! Your eyes went all icy and white; then you stiffened and went ramrod straight. You were like that for, I dunno, a minute. So, I thought maybe you were okay. When the ice disappeared, you went limp like a noodle. Then *smack*." Cam clapped his hands together for emphasis.

"How long have I been out?"

"I don't know, like...three hours maybe?"

"Shit."

"Quit saying that."

"The sight took over. I've had the vision happen before, but only once. Uncle Bart gets them too."

"Who the hell is Uncle Bart?" Cam tilted his head to one side.

"Tully's uncle, great-uncle...relative. He owns the house. Tully is his favourite nephew, and Tully helps him out with mowing the lawn, taking care of the house, giving him his meds. He's like me...kind of. Same sect of magic. Cam, we have to go to the coven house. Byron has Tully and Sparks."

"How the hell do you know?"

"I just told you—vision."

"Right, so I should probably tell you, Byron called your phone. So I answered it."

"For fuck's sake. What did he say?"

"Blah blah blah, where's Dev? Blah blah blah, I have Tully and Sparks...man, that guy is an asshole." Cam rolled his eyes.

"Cam"—Dev's lips disappeared—"what exactly did he say?"

Cam stared at Dev for the briefest of moments, trying to recall the conversation, but from the scowl on Dev's face, he needed to say something before his best buddy lost it on him.

"Ah, well, he wanted to talk to you, but I said you were unavailable—which you were—you know, nappy time." Cam grimaced. "So, when he figured out who he was talking to, the fairy he'd tortured, we had some words. Fun. He rambled on about Tully and Sparks, something about being imprisoned and that you should get to the coven house as quick as possible because people who are caught in soul traps for long periods of time come out brain-dead. I'm paraphrasing, but yeah. I think that was it."

"Oh my Gods. Okay, we need to go. Like right now."

"But your head, dude!"

"It's gonna have to wait. If Tully and Sparks are in trouble, we need to go help."

"Shit."

"Believe me, the last thing I want to do is step foot in that house or have to look at Byron Radcliffe. But we gotta go rescue Tully and Sparks. Come on, let's go."

BYRON AND ADDAS'S coven house resided in the same neighbourhood as Uncle Bart's sprawling heritage mansion. Old Strathcona was one of the oldest neighbourhoods in the city, and a central location in Edmonton. Very popular with the university crowd, which made sense as the university anchored the area. The community also happened to house the largest hospital in the province, which is where Sparks worked. Cam had spent the vast majority of his early adult life either at the campus taking a variety of courses that never seemed to lead him anywhere or trolling for dates up and down Whyte Avenue.

It didn't take long for Dev and Cam to walk over to the old coven house. Cam, of course, had to conjure up his human guise for the short journey. Evening had arrived, and with the streetlamps on, the shadows crouched in dark corners. Cam wanted to make the entire trip by jumping the shadows, but he would have arrived long before his friend, and then he would have to wait for Dev to show up. Given Byron would be in close proximity, Cam didn't trust himself to not barge into the house and kill the ex-high priest. No, it was easier to walk alongside Dev and continue to concentrate hard on maintaining his illusion.

By the time they arrived at Byron's house, Cam's head weighed heavy, mentally drained from spellworking.

"This fae magic is hard." Cam shook his head as a shiver ran down his spine. As the sensation crept down his back, he shed his old human self. In a fairy shimmer, the Eldritch fae flexed, and his wings popped out on each side. Cam stretched his arms toward the sky. A few bones snapped into place. "Better."

They stood on the stoop.

"So, do we knock, or just enter?" Cam questioned Dev.

"I should be polite and knock, but fuck all of this." Dev put his hand on the doorknob, twisted the handle, and pushed the door. To their surprise, it swung open.

"Come on. I know where they are."

"How?"

"I'm a witch. I know things."

Cam didn't like the response. It made him uneasy, but he followed his friend faithfully.

They passed through a minimalist living room, what appeared to be a well-stocked kitchen, and when they came to the back door of the house, which had sustained severe damage, they hung a sharp left and descended a steep stairwell.

"This is creepy. I barely remember anything but the dungeon, but I'll never forget what happened there and the amount of pain Byron put me through. Let's get this over with, and quick. I don't like being here."

"Agreed." Dev continued down the stairwell.

"Does this go on forever?"

"No. Here." Dev stopped at a small landing and turned to face a room off the steps. A door hung crooked, only attached by the top hinge.

Inside the room, faintly lit, Byron Radcliffe sat in the same chair Tully had perched in while waiting for Dev to figure out how to tap into his abilities.

"Took you long enough." Byron sneered. "Not sure how well they'll fare." His head canted in the direction where Tully and Sparks bathed in a light amber glow. Their bodies hung in the air as if they were floating in viscous liquid.

Reading the emotional state of the room was something innate in all fae. Cam hadn't spent a large amount of time in the company of non-fae folk since he had transformed. At least, not until his recent trip to the city. At first, the extrasensory perceptions took him aback with the empathic sensations. They weren't exactly subtle, and they stormed through him like a thunderous stampede, directly affecting his own mood.

Right now, Byron Radcliffe wore a suit of stoicism, but under the cold exterior the man was anything but calm. Frenetic energy made his insides twitch, all while a deep-seated river of anger greased the lining of every muscle. Byron, though stoked with a palpable ire, struggled to keep his eyes open as exhaustion and pain made his thoughts thick with fog. Cam had to wonder if his recent discharge from the hospital had been too soon.

This man had tortured Everton for over a year and had damn near killed him. The same man who had strapped Cam to a wooden cross and stabbed him repeatedly with monster-sized needles. Cam had spent many a night fantasizing on the reciprocation of pain he had promised himself he would inflict if ever he'd gotten a chance.

And now here he was, face to face with the asshole.

Except now, knowing what the witch was feeling, Cam bit his bottom lip and grasped his midsection as the pangs of guilt washed over him for contemplating his revenge-fuelled scenarios.

Byron's love for Addas consumed him, hence his reprehensible actions in attempting to cure his boyfriend—the one person in the world who meant anything to him and the man he had seen himself growing old with. Cam shook his head. An undercurrent of need ran through Byron with his love of power and authority as well. But Byron had been well adept at being able to juggle both as priorities. Right now, though, Addas remained the sole concern.

Dev's lower lip twitched and the anguish in him met similar levels to Byron's emotive state as Dev glanced toward Tully and Sparks.

"What the fuck did you do to them?" The words flew out in a fit of rage.

Cam focused in on the guys trapped in the warm glow of amber. "They're okay, Dev. They're scared as shit, but they are okay." There were frozen in time, like in science fiction films where astronauts were placed into animated suspension chambers.

Cam peered closer as an unusual flicker within the light made him take note.

There were two of Tully, and Sparks, but the second ones were faint, almost ghostlike, barely even there.

"Get them out of there." Dev made a move toward Byron.

"Ah, careful, newbie witch. I've been at this a while longer." Byron stumbled as he stood but corrected himself. Holding his hand out, he summoned a ball of flame that sat in the palm of his hand.

"Fuck off, Byron. I might be new at this, but my swooning over you ended a long time ago. Get. Them. Out. Now. Or I'll bring my own magic to the table. Trust me, in your state right now, I'll blow you over." Dev's face had turned dark, with brows furrowed together and squinted eyes, his expression completed with a deadly sneer. Cam had never seen his lifelong pal look so ominous. He would have never believed Dev capable of hurting anyone—until now.

"They won't go anywhere until you agree to help me."

"Ah, let's see. You knew I was destined for the Shadow Realm for years, and never told me. You had me tailed by Tully. You kidnapped and tortured my best friend and tainted the entire Shadow Realm for me all within the course of a couple of weeks. Tell me, Byron, why the fuck would I want to help you with anything?"

"If you don't, those two boys will stay in the soul trap until they die. And given how long they've been in there, I'd say they only have a couple more hours left. It's hard to breathe submerged in amber. They will eventually become oxygen deprived."

"Why are there two of them?" Cam asked.

"What do you—" Dev glanced toward Cam, puzzlement plastered all over his face.

"There are two of each of them in there." Cam pointed at Sparks and Tully. "The second is so faint I almost didn't see it."

"Perceptive little fairy. Yes, that's the trap at work. The hex ensnares the occupant, and leisurely rips their soul out of the corporeal body. So, I don't see where you have a choice, Dev. Help me find Addas, and I let them go with their souls intact. You don't help me, and well..." Bryon gestured toward the guys. "Apparently, you know my Addas is alive."

"We *heard* he was alive." Dev gestured toward Cam.

"Thank you for confirming. Now"—Byron turned to Cam—"lead me to him, or everyone dies." The flames in Byron's hand went higher.

Cam flinched away from the heat and crackle of the blaze as it flickered in Byron's palm and threatened to leap toward him.

"Dev, can't you use your hoodoo tracking ability to find Addas?" Cam muttered as he put up a hand to block the fire which he swore grew bigger and brighter.

"Jeez, Cam." Dev glared at him.

"Ah, so your abilities are growing. Witchy tracking now? That's handy. So, what's it going to be, Dev?"

Dev's face contorted as he glanced from Cam to Tully and Sparks.

"I hate you so much. I swear to all the Gods, the minute I get the chance to end you, I will finish you off. Release them. I'll help you find your monstrosity of a boyfriend." The anger rolled off Dev, leaving shimmers in the air around him. Cam took another step away.

Byron raised his other arm—the one without the fireball—and uttered a single word.

"*Annuler.*" With the snap of his fingers, the yellowish radiance dissipated into shimmering sparkles and evaporated, leaving two full-sized, muscular men levitating in mid-air. Their partially wrenched souls became far more apparent.

"*Piéger.*" Byron blurted out the French word and snapped his fingers a second time. The second copies of

Sparks and Tully morphed into white strings of light and descended into two chunks remaining from the original amber stone. Byron bent over and snatched up the egg-sized shards and shoved them into his pocket.

"Insurance. You'll get these back once I have Addas."

"You're a fucking piece of work." Dev snarled.

Tully and Sparks dropped with a *thud*.

"Ow." Tully groaned.

Dev rushed over and checked on Tully.

"I'm okay. I feel weird, but I'm okay. What about Sparks?"

Shifting direction, Dev put a hand on Sparks's chest, checking his new boyfriend. "I think he's okay." He made a slight frown.

"He'll be fine. Give him a few minutes," Byron piped up from where he had sat down.

"You, on the other hand..." Tully stood and made his way over to Byron.

Dev, who had been kneeling over Sparks, stood up straight. "Tully, no."

Cam took another couple of steps away, evaluating the scene before him. At one point Byron had been so large, so intimidating, but seated on the chair, with his head cradled in his hands, Cam succumbed to the waves of exhaustion flowing off him.

"Tully, he's done. There's no gas in the fuel tank. The get up and go has got up and went." Cam found a chair and took a seat, his own weariness and Byron's fatigue getting the best of him.

"I don't care. I'm going to snap his fuckin' neck."

"Tully." Dev laid a hand on his lover's arm, but his tone remained sharp. "I made a deal. We honour that. When this is done, I promise you he'll get his due. Until then, we follow through."

Tully snarled at Byron, "You're lucky he's a decent human being." As he pointed toward Dev, spit flew out of his mouth. Tully's usual optimistic demeanour had vanished. "I wouldn't have been so nice."

"Yeah, sure," Byron mumbled. "Remember, at one point you answered to me."

"Those days are done." Tully pulled away from his ex-high priest. "What did you agree to?" He glanced over at Dev.

"He wants us to find Addas."

"And then what?"

Dev didn't reveal Tully's missing soul.

"I don't know, nor do I care. I'll help him find Addas, and then we're done with this asshole. Are you sure you're okay?"

They embraced. "I'm okay. I promise. Let's make sure Sparks is too."

"Absolutely."

Dev and Tully hoisted Sparks up and settled him down on a settee in the corner of the study, propping him so he'd be comfortable.

"Ah guys…" Cam's gaze shifted toward Byron. The boys followed his stare.

"So what?" Tully growled. "Would be easier to take him out right now."

Dev shot Tully a warning glance.

Tully frowned but backed down.

Byron slept on the chair, drained and exhausted from the day's events. Clearly not fully recuperated from his werewolf wounds and stint in the hospital.

Chapter Twenty-One

EVERTON PULLED HIMSELF out of bed the next morning, drained and still sluggish. He hadn't had a restful sleep. His brain twisted and turned with images of Cam, colliding and interspersed with scolding sneers from Franco.

His second in command had held his position for decades and often dropped hints and doled out varying perspectives he hadn't considered. But every time Ev contemplated telling Cam about his need to be more than a roll in the hay, the imaginary conversations running through his head on how that would play out made his tummy roll and heave.

He couldn't face Cam and bare his soul. And yet, he had to. Damn Franco.

After pulling on his sweats and glancing at his phone, discovering he'd awoken before seven in the morning, he resigned himself to making breakfast.

He whipped up some eggs, burnt some toast, remade the toast, and kept everything warm in the oven, waiting for the rest of the pack to crawl out of their dens. Serge emerged first from the basement he shared with Josip.

He scratched himself, yawned, then made his way over to the coffee pot and poured himself a cup.

"You want some breakfast?" Ev asked.

"Yeah, sure, man."

"So, we gotta talk about tomorrow night."

"Yeah." Serge's voice softened, resigned to his fate.

"It's a precaution. If Addas shows up causing issues, I don't want you flipping out. I promise you, if I can't guide you through this cycle, I will be here for the next one."

"I know. Franco and I talked about *the shed*. It's only twenty-four hours of complete insanity." That statement gutted Ev. He never wanted any of his wolves to suffer, and here the kid had gone through an entire year and a half of full moon cycles chained like a dog to a cement wall. He'd failed as an alpha. "To be honest, afterward, I don't remember too much. There's a lingering sense of 'what the fuck happened,' but the twitchiness I get after being bound goes away in a couple of days."

"Serge, you shouldn't have had to go through anything more than a single cycle. I am so sorry. I will do everything I can to be there for you tomorrow night. And if Addas doesn't show up, you're golden. If he does, I want you tucked away and safe. Okay? This is about safety. And as long as you don't make a first kill, I can wrangle you. You'll be okay. But I owe you. You should never have had to wait this long."

"It's okay, boss."

"I am not your boss."

"Daddy?"

"I am also not your daddy."

"Yes, you are," Franco declared as he waltzed into the kitchen. "Oh, you made breakfast. About time. I'm tired of getting up early and fixing food for these ungrateful bastards." He shovelled some eggs onto his plate and grabbed a piece of toast, then sat next to Serge, leaned over, and bumped shoulders with him. Ev was grateful he had Franco around. He played the role of big brother to every member of the pack.

Serge smiled. He picked up his plate and coffee and went into the living room. The TV came to life as voices rumbled from a gardening show.

"He'll be okay." Franco's nonchalant answer came as he scooped a forkful of eggs into his mouth.

"I hope so."

"So, you gonna call Cam today?"

"You're right, you know. It's the last conversation I want to have."

"Because feelings are complicated and yucky." Franco chuckled.

Everton growled, "Yes."

"Trust me, you need to do this. You've been off since you've been home, and I don't mean since you returned from the Ancestral Lands. Since the witches' dungeon you've been angry and testy. I know that's sort of to be expected after what you went through"—Franco held up his hand to stop Ev from chiming in—"but this is more than leftover trauma. Obviously, the two of you have connected on some level. He's goo-goo for you. I promise. I know you'll never believe me, but I see those lovey-dovey feelings when you look at each other."

"He told you he's goo-goo for me?"

"No. Don't be absurd. I don't think Cam is aware enough of his own feelings. The fae is clever, but he's got some growing to do. He's young. Don't you remember what you were like at his age?"

"That's exactly what scares me. I don't want to put a bunch of emotional effort or energy into anyone who—"

"Everton Lilch, are you telling me, after your one hundred and twenty-some years on this rock, you're still worried about laying your heart bare and potentially getting hurt?"

"Aren't you?"

"Sure, but that's part of the game, dude. If you're not willing to risk anything, then the relationship isn't worth the effort. If you can't be emotionally invested, how do you expect him to be? Come on, you should know this. Feelings are complicated. They're tricky too. But if you don't put yourself all out there, how can you ever expect him to do the same?"

"You're right." Ev placed both hands on the kitchen countertop, leaned forward while his head hung. He let out a long breath. "I hate this."

"Uh-huh. But the sex will be stellar when you finally get some. I promise. Especially after you waited this long. Think of those horns." Franco winked at Ev.

"Excuse me?"

"Relax. Cam told me everything. I cannot believe you held out on him for the entire summer. That's just cruel to both of you."

Ev had had enough of being emotionally pummelled. "Fine."

"Fine. Then you'll call him? I think you need to have this conversation today, figure out how you two are going to move forward, and get your head in the game for later when the big bad witchy-fae-alpha-werewolf comes knocking on our door. 'Cause I think we all know that's happening, and it ain't going to be a good thing. That boy needs your help." Franco angled his head to the living room. "And all this in two days. You're a busy man."

"I hate you when you're right."

"Which is always." Franco shrugged, got up, and joined Serge in the living room, leaving Everton alone with his thoughts.

He really had to do this.

He would call Cam after cleaning up from breakfast.

CAM, DEV, AND Tully had taken turns throughout the night getting some shut-eye, but always ensured one person remained awake.

No one trusted Byron, who had slept through the night. Sparks had as well. Cam detected an overwhelming tidal wave of concern from Tully and Dev. With Sparks not regaining consciousness from his entombment in the soul trap, they all wondered if the imprisonment would have lasting implications.

Byron had passed out, and as much as everyone in the room hated him, Cam had whispered to both Dev and Tully what he had sensed from the ex-high priest.

"It's sad. He's utterly drained, and he's lost all hope but clings to the notion that finding Addas will make everything better. There's this stinking undercurrent of rot which I can't figure out, but the stain taints and clouds everything about him. Mainly, he's lost without Addas."

"I know what the rot is about. It's his werewolf infection. The impending doom he thinks is a death sentence. If he follows in Addas's footsteps, he'll be fine. But if he believes Addas is some bizarre anomaly, the first to shift and survive...then who knows? Maybe he still thinks he's gonna die. But I guarantee the rot is his incubating werewolf," Dev mused.

"I don't care what the problem is. He's a total asshole for everything he's done." Tully shook his head.

"I understand, Tully. I do. Believe me, I feel the same way, and the last thing I want is to help him in any way. But I made a deal, and unlike him, I will stick to my word and complete my tasks with honour. There's a small part of my brain saying I should feel bad for him, and logically I guess I kind of do, but in reality? I'd sooner see him dead."

"He trapped us in a potentially lethal situation. I'd like nothing better than to do the same thing to him." Tully, who usually retained a positive and optimistic attitude, brandished his anger and violence like a weapon.

"He is at his wit's end. Tell me something, guys, if the roles were reversed, and you had only one option left in order to save each other, or Sparks, what would you do?" Cam tilted his head as he questioned them. Seeing both sides of the situation might have been distasteful, but he sympathized.

Tully fell silent for a moment. His head dropped, a sign he agreed.

"Oh, hey, guys, Sparks is waking up." Cam's wings fluttered.

"It's about fucking time." Tully flipped his phone over and checked the time. It was damn near eight in the morning. "Hey, buddy, you okay?" Tully put one of his meaty hands on Sparks's shoulder and gently shook him.

"Oh Gods, what the hell happened?" Sparks grumbled as he rolled onto his side and pushed himself up. Propped on an elbow, Sparks didn't last long in the position as his face paled and he slumped back into the couch again.

"Just take your time. Byron's not up yet." Dev sat on the floor next to the couch.

"How long have I been out? Last I remember is hitting the floor."

"All night. We were worried. I think we all needed some rest." Tully stretched out as he spoke. Bones snapped into place as he reached for the ceiling.

"Okay, eww," Cam chimed in after hearing the bones pop. The crackle reminded him too much of Everton. Cam had managed a few hours of rest, but after having consumed so much coffee the day before, his sleep had been fitful and disjointed. Residual caffeine coursed through his veins even now, making him jittery.

Sparks hoisted himself up again. This time, he managed to maintain a sitting position.

"Gods, I feel weird. Someone gonna fill me in?" Sparks's face conveyed an obvious confused state.

"We're gonna help Byron."

"Say what?" Sparks furrowed his brows.

"Yeah, man, I don't like it either." Tully glanced toward Sparks.

"Okay, look, here's the thing." Dev's eyes narrowed as he spoke methodically. "I get here, and Byron has you two trapped in a thick amber light and tells me you'll slowly suffocate to death if I don't agree to help him find Addas. What was I supposed to do? Two of the most important men in my life are being held hostage by the one person we all hate." Dev threw his hands out to the side.

"Ahem." Cam cleared his throat and threw a nasty look toward Dev. "Two of the most important?"

"Sorry, two out of three," Dev corrected.

"You did what you thought best, but now we gotta track down Addas?" Sparks glared at Dev. "You do remember how big he is, yes?"

"And a bloodlust-crazed, alpha werewolf!" Cam added. He perused a collection of stones, crystals, and gems Byron had accumulated and laid out in a glass cabinet.

"Like, is that even safe?" Sparks questioned. *I'm not sure I signed up for this.*

"Yeah, safe? Probably not, but what choice do we have? And none of us signed up for this shit. We find Addas, and then we leave. I'm so done with all of this. I want to wash my hands of him." Dev jerked his head over his shoulder to indicate where Byron lay asleep in a chair. "We'll start our own group, and I'm going to forget he was ever part of my life. I think concentrating on you two for a while would be nice. I'd want this to become...okay." Dev chewed the inside of his cheeks.

Sparks glanced at him with concern. "Are you having second thoughts about this?" His finger made a quick triangle between him, Dev, and Tully.

"I'd be lying if I didn't say so."

"Then I'm out. I'm not coming in the middle—"

"Stop." Dev threw his hand up, palm out toward Sparks. "Look, this triad didn't exactly happen organically. A God appeared and the next thing we know, 'Do you take your husband' got tossed around. That's bound to throw anyone off. All of this is happening way too fast. I want some time and breathing room to figure this all out. I need to get my head right about this. None of my issues are because of either of you."

"Oh God, I'm glad you said it. Me too!" Tully stared at the floor. "I know we'll get there, and if the God put us together, He's going to keep us together for His own purposes. I'd like to enjoy the ride instead of fighting my feelings all the way. Whaddya guys say?" Tully peeked up from behind arched eyebrows.

Cam pretended to be engrossed in the crystal collection but was captivated by the guys' conversation. The teensiest smirk formed on his face. The situation surpassed weird, and he would have never seen Dev in the middle of a conversation like this. Was he jealous? One hundred percent. But Dev was his brother from another mother, and after growing up together and sharing their hopes and dreams, Cam wanted nothing but the best for him.

"This isn't the time or space for this conversation. Maybe we can circle back later, but I want us to try. I mean, Cernunnos himself has basically tied us together, right? So, when we get this finished with Byron, I'm gonna need a long nap. After that, we can discuss how we move forward. Deal?" Dev laid down the law.

Cam was so proud.

"Deal." Tully puffed his chest out, displaying his pride too.

"Okay. Nicely stated, Dev." Sparks acquiesced. "You're right, this isn't the time and place, but I have reservations. I so do not want this to end up wrong. I like you guys too much."

"Nothing's gonna go wrong." Tully's lips twitched, and his ever-present optimistic grin returned.

"Now, we have to wait for this asshole to wake up."

"I've been awake for the last ten minutes. Have you three come to resolutions on your complicated feelings? Are we all good? Or can we go?" Byron pulled himself up off the chair he sat on, turned, and glanced at the three men.

Dev pursed his lips as the muscles in his jaw clenched tight.

Sparks narrowed his eyes as he stared at Byron. "Aren't you in a fucking hurry? Fine, let's get this shit show over with," he spit out, then hoisted himself off the couch.

FIVE MEN IN Tully's Audi TT RS was a feat. Cam couldn't help thinking about a clown car at the circus. Tully's broad shoulders prohibited him from sitting in the back seat of the car; thankfully, seeing as it was his car, he drove. Both Sparks and Dev were slighter but were still full-grown men. Cam had always been stocky, and his transition to fae hadn't changed his body frame, but at least his shorter stature helped him sit in the middle. Except for the horns on his head which poked the interior's lining on the retractable roof. His prehensile tail and massive wings didn't help much either. Byron, a couple of months ago, had been similar in size to Tully, but since his werewolf infection, he had grown larger—just as Addas had grown. The car, stuffed to capacity, crammed the occupants together, and no one wanted to exist that close to Byron.

Cam sat in the middle of the back seat, the least comfortable spot.

He had two sets of elbows digging into his ribs and he was forced to lean forward as his wings created a real space issue despite the fact he had them folded together and twisted to one side. He sat on his tail, crimping the appendage, which hurt like hell, and he'd been made to sit on the console, a spot not meant for a fifth person. The faster they all got out of the vehicle, the better.

Byron shifted as he dug in his pockets, which caused the tight quarters to be even more cramped.

Cam glanced over his shoulder at Byron and gave him a dirty look, but Byron's eyes were closed, as he mumbled words over and over. So instead, Cam shifted his wings which thwapped Byron in the head.

Byron scowled at him.

Cam threw him a dirty look, then turned to face the front of the car.

Dev sat in the passenger seat, beside Tully.

"No, turn left here."

"How do you know where to go?" Sparks leaned forward and asked Dev.

"I don't know, exactly. A gut feeling. Think of a compass swinging toward true north. The needle points in the right direction. All I have to do is think about who, or what I'm trying to find," Dev explained.

"Can someone roll down the window? It's hot in here," Cam begged. Dev glanced at his friend; concern plastered all over his face.

"Is the witch finding always accurate?" Sparks asked.

"No."

"Great," Byron retorted.

Dev turned his head to face Byron as he glared at the man.

"No one asked you. Actually, a thank you would proba-bly be in order."

Byron glared, narrowing his eyes.

"Seriously, someone needs to roll down the window. I think I'm gonna be sick."

Tully slammed on the brakes.

"No one is throwing up in my car." He slammed the vehicle into park. "Everyone out."

Cam tore over Sparks to exit the car before he hurled into some bushes on the boulevard.

"Oh man, that's nasty." Sparks turned away.

"You okay?" Dev asked from behind Cam as he knelt in the bushes.

"Yeah." Cam coughed the word out; then threw up again.

"Hey, guys, look." Sparks pointed to the trunk of an elm tree on the edge of the boulevard.

"That's a territory mark." Byron ran his fingers over the gashes in the tree.

"Seems like we're on the right trail at least." Tully sneered at Byron.

Three hours later, and after visiting several of Edmonton's southeastern and central neighbourhoods, finding various remnants of Addas's wardrobe, and at least two dumpster bins marked with urine, they still hadn't found Addas.

Chapter Twenty-Two

EVERTON HAD MANAGED to delay his phone call until almost mid-afternoon, finding multiple projects to prevent him from picking up the cell phone and punching in numbers.

After cleaning up the kitchen from lunch and having prepared dinners for a couple of nights and portioning out leftovers to be frozen, Ev glanced around the open space of the main floor and spied crumbs, wolf hair, and dirt everywhere. The place needed a good vacuuming. Walking toward the broom closet, he stopped short when Franco appeared between him and the vacuum.

"What the hell do you think you're doing?"

"Cleaning the house! None of you deem housekeeping necessary, despite the chore roster."

"Wrong answer. Oh my Gods, what are you, fourteen? Call him. Now."

"I will when I'm done."

"Do I need to remind you that Addas may show up at our doorstep at any moment? And there's a young wolf pup who desperately needs your attention? Or did you conveniently forget about him? Deal with your shit so we can deal with life."

Franco reached around Everton, dug in his back pocket—

"Hey." Everton attempted to protest and grabbed Franco's hand, but his second in command demonstrated his agility and managed to snag the phone away from Ev.

Franco thrust the cell in front of Ev. "Do it."

"I will."

"Now."

"Later."

"Now while I'm watching."

"I hate you."

"I know."

Ev rolled his eyes and harrumphed, which came out as a resonating growl.

Franco cocked an eyebrow, crossed his arms over his chest, and tapped his foot.

Shaking his head, Ev punched in his security code to open the cell and all its apps and functions, called up Dev's number, then pressed the Call button.

"It's ringing." He had called Dev's phone as Cam's cell had had a terrible accident shortly after he'd arrived at the Ancestral Lands. Cam took a while to adjust without having a way of staying connected with the modern world. Cam and his phone were tied closely together. Glued to the device painted a more accurate picture as his phone had rarely left his hand. Everton had promised to help Cam get a new cell, but with everything that had transpired, the opportunity had never come to pass.

Oddly enough, Cam had learned to live without the technology.

Ev waited for several rings, and when no one picked up, he discontinued the call and shoved the technology into his pocket.

"No answer. Now will you leave me—" The phone started to ring.

A *woop, woop, woop* peal of a siren rang from Ev's pocket. Everton stood there until the phone had chimed three times.

"Well, are you going to answer it? Or will I?"

"Grrr." Ev pulled his phone out and glanced at the caller ID to see "Dev Witch" displayed. He tapped the answer button. "Hello?"

"Hey, it's Dev. You called? Sorry I couldn't get to the phone on time. We're out and about."

"Yeah, no worries. I need to talk to Cam, but if you're out with Tully, I'll drive over to your place."

"Oh, ah...Cam's with us."

"Out in public?"

"Yeah. Surprisingly, he's maintaining his illusion magic rather well."

"Out shopping for clothes for him? He'll need some."

"Long story, but no. I'm glad I've got you on the phone. I need an expert in werewolf behaviour."

"Why?" Ev spat out and furrowed his brows. Whenever he frowned, his forehead wrinkled up as well. Again, those magical werewolf bits and parts didn't keep everything from getting old.

"Ah, well, we've found some claw marks, and a couple spots where we're pretty sure Addas has peed on objects to mark his territory. But we've been searching now for several hours. Everyone's tired, but we just want to find him."

"Find Addas? What in hell's name for?" Everton almost yelled into the phone.

"That is part of a very long story, but basically, we're returning Byron."

"And Cam is with you?"

"Yeah, you wanna talk to him?"

"Where the hell are you?"

"We're down by the Kinsmen Centre. I'm trying to use my tracking ability to find Addas, but we're not having much success. He must be on the move. Every time we get to the destination where he should be, there's no sign of him, only claw marks and pee spots. This is frustrating."

Everton's eyebrows, which were blond, meaning they weren't a prominent feature on his face, shot up as high as he had ever raised them.

"What's the matter?" Franco demanded.

"They're chasing down Addas."

"What?" Franco opened his mouth to add more to his last statement when Ev put a massive paw overtop of his lips.

"Okay, listen close." Everton flipped his phone to look at the time. It was almost four in the afternoon. Where the hell had the day gone? "Addas is one day away from a full moon, and he's already killed humans, which means he's gone into bloodlust mode. He should be okay if he's human, but if he happens to wolf out, you'll all be dead. Do you understand me? You need to call off this search until I get there."

"Ah, I don't know if I can do that, Ev. I have Byron here with me, and we kind of made a deal to get him and Addas reunited."

"I don't care. Being torn apart is the result if this goes sideways. You're not far from me, literally fifteen to twenty minutes away by foot. I'll be there in ten. Stay out in a sunny area and preferably around other people."

"Um, well, I'll see what I can do, but you'd better hurry. Byron's not a happy man, and the closer we get to Addas the more agitated he's getting."

"That'll be the call of his sire working on him."

"Sorry, the what?"

"I'll explain when I get there. Keep Cam safe. Don't let him do anything to put himself in harm's way."

Everton clicked End to finish the call, slipped his phone into his pocket, and stared at Franco. "Lock up Serge. I have to go. They're down by the Kinsmen Centre and on Addas's trail, which means he's close by."

"Oh, shit."

"Exactly."

CAM PROPPED HIMSELF on a nearby car with one hand. His illusion magic wavered, leaving the air around him rippling and granting the occasional peek at a furry tipped ear, or a fluttering membranous wing. Nausea overwhelmed him and a slick sheen of cold sweat had broken out across his skin. A dull thud drummed out a persistent beat in his head. He swallowed hard, attempting to quell a rise of bile in his throat. The car ride had been too long, too hot, and too cramped.

It wasn't like Cam to get motion sickness. He'd never had it before, and even now, out of the car, the symptoms had subsided and were marginally better, but he felt like hot garbage.

"You okay?" Dev came over to him. "You're paler and greener than normal."

"If I currently am attempting to be human, I shouldn't look green at all."

"Fair." Dev grimaced.

"No, truthfully, I feel like crap."

"Everton said he'd be here shortly. You gonna last?"

"Yeah, I'll be okay. Thanks, Dev." Dev gave Cam a pat on the shoulder and went to stand with Tully and Sparks. Byron wandered several feet away, scouring the area for his lost lover.

Cam leaned against the vehicle and closed his eyes, intent on resting for a moment.

EVERTON RAN OUT through the front door of the pack house, crossed the street in front of the house without looking for traffic, and took off into the woods lining the river valley.

Edmonton was split in two with the North Saskatchewan River running a snaky and winding trail dissecting the city. Each side of the river had been left heavily wooded and the two sides were interconnected with running trails and hiking paths and numerous footbridges. In total, the area encompassed more land than the famous Central Park of New York City, and the park provided a perfect place for a werewolf to run at night without getting caught or seen by humans.

A werewolf who had control over their faculties who wouldn't tear into the first encountered human.

As soon as he entered the wooded riverbank, Ev stripped and shifted. After decades of practice, the snap and pop of a few bones didn't even register anymore, and as his paws hit the loamy earth covered in patchy weeds and the odd fallen leaf, he pushed off with his hind feet and launched into a breakneck run toward Cam's location.

As the underbrush sped by, Ev picked up on various scents. The late summer heat had forced some plants into their fall shed earlier than normal, and the typical undercurrent of rotting vegetation, so common in the fall, already tickled the back of Ev's nose. Sweat from a nearby jogger left yellowish odour wisps meandering their way through the air currents, while the sunshine and rushing river water conjured a fresh ambience, teasing him with lazy days of lounging in tall grasses. Instead of being calmed by his surroundings, his mind summoned up all manner of frightful scenes with Addas tearing Cam into bloody fae parts.

Faster, need to go faster.

Late afternoon on a weekend in the city's downtown core meant the trails would be busy. He would have to do his best to remain hidden, as a lanky werewolf pulling itself through the woods with a furred humanlike torso and limbs but sporting a canine head with clawed hands and feet would surely cause any normal person to lose their mind. After all, the Shadow Realm still had to remain hidden, despite whatever calamity might be about to take place.

CAM YELPED AS a cold, wet nose brushed the backside of his leg.

Glancing down, he saw Everton's wolf lay as flat as possible to the concrete of the parking lot of the Kinsmen fitness centre.

"Oh my Gods, Ev, you scared the shit out of me."

Ev growled back a response.

Cam stared, horrified, as Ev's wolf initiated the transformation to human. The shifting imbedded nightmare fuel into Cam's brain, unsettling in the way the bones reshaped themselves. Limbs were not supposed to snap or bend the way Everton put himself into human form. The noises during the transformation weren't benefitting his mental health either. Within seconds, Ev stood in front of Cam, naked and gorgeous, and even though Cam didn't feel particularly well, the sight of Everton unclothed in broad daylight with the sun highlighting all his furry bits got Cam's libido stirred into hyperactivity.

"I can't stay like this out in the open. Nor can I be in wolf form, but I got here as quick as my paws carried me. Where's Dev?" Ev asked.

"Dev," Cam called out.

The guys had seated themselves at a picnic table left near one of the soccer fields. They had given up on keeping track of Byron, who had strayed toward the riverbank attempting to find Addas. Dev kept him within eyesight.

"Hey, Ev." Tully waved as the three got up and walked over. He gave Ev the once-over. "So, anybody got any clothes that will fit him?"

"You got any in your car?" Dev asked.

"Nope."

"Naked it is." Ev frowned. His current state of bare-assedness in public wasn't the issue concerning him the most. "I can't stay out here like this, but you cannot be hunting down Addas. I found his den—I believe it's where he was working. The shop used to be a garage."

"Used to be? How did the garage go to a 'used to be' if he is working there?"

"The garage bay is now his den where he's storing his kills as food for later. There are human parts scattered everywhere. Everything is saturated in blood."

"Oh Gods."

"Yeah. That means one thing. His first transformation, although successful, didn't go well, and he gave in to his killer instinct and attacked a human. Once a werewolf makes a first kill, he'll suffer a bloodlust that will never be satiated, and they'll always go after the same type of animal. This close to the full moon means there's potential for him to wolf out. His animal instinct will kick in and there's no reasoning with an enraged supernatural creature intent on the hunt. He's lost to us, and there's no getting him back."

"We should probably corral Byron." Sparks glanced around, a touch of concern in his voice.

"I'd say leave him. Byron's gonna get what he's got coming to him. The asshole deserves to be ripped apart." Everton snarled.

"Do not disagree with you there," Dev said.

Cam's eyes darted between the participants of the conversation, which left him woozy, so he leaned into Everton for support. "Okay, why don't you take me home?"

He smiled up at his big furry wolfman.

"Tomorrow is the full moon, Cam. Addas will shift for sure, and he will be in bloodlust mode. We've already caught scent of his presence, so we know he's been sniffing around the pack house. We suspect he's going to show up tomorrow, or sooner. I don't want you at the house because you'll end up in the middle of a pack of werewolves fighting a crazed alpha. I don't want anything to happen to you, and I'd never forgive myself if something did happen and I couldn't protect you."

Cam's chest constricted as if his heart didn't have enough space. Ev's words warmed him. His big wolfman had expressed concern for his well-being.

"Well then why don't we leave Byron here and—" Dev started but never got to finish.

A howl came from the riverbank. Several people who were walking to their cars, or up to the sports complex, stopped and surveyed the area. Wolves were not expected to be within city limits. The occasional coyote, sure, but they generally didn't make an appearance until after dark and when there were no humans nearby. Wolves in the city would have been a newsworthy event. The beast's announcement had more of an anguished shriek imbedded within a wolf's cry. Anyone within hearing distance would have recognized the animal from its baying but might have guessed the animal had sustained injuries. The unusual cry sent shivers down Cam's spine.

One woman whose eyes went as round as saucers snatched her small child into her arms and beat a hasty retreat to the doors of the building.

The area went dead silent.

No birds chirped. No humans talked. Even the traffic noise had come to an abrupt halt.

As a calm settled over the area, Cam's hackles raised, sensing a dark foreboding.

"Fuck!" Everton clenched his jaw and balled his fists as he transitioned into a battle stance.

A ripple of fear coursed its way through Cam's body. He lost control of his illusion magic, and in a shimmer, Cam's fae stood with his tail hanging dead still. His wings folded downward in fear.

Dev, Tully, and Sparks shared worried glances between them.

"Okay, we gotta get out of this open area. He's close. Addas will scent us even at this distance. Where the hell is Byron?"

"Over there. Near the tree line of the riverbank." Sparks pointed.

"Can you tell what that howl meant?" Dev asked, a pained look of worry on his face.

"Sort of. Wolf language is more conceptual, images mixed with emotions. His howl meant an announcement of territory. But we have a bigger issue to think about. Your stink is going to be all over Byron, and if Addas takes exception, you'll be first on his list to track down and destroy. Part of his cry was 'this is my territory,' and that might include Byron. He's staking his claim. So, he'll attempt to eliminate any others who he thinks are infringing on what he believes is his. And we do not want a confrontation in the parking lot of a goddamn city recreation facility."

"Where the hell do we go?"

"Back to your car and get the fuck out of here."

"Shit." Tully pointed.

Cam stared in the direction Tully indicated. Emerging from the brush, what had been Addas appeared. Bits of werewolf, part human, and weirdly fae, snarled and snapped at the air, looking 100 percent crazed.

Patches of dark fur grew in the centre line of his chest. He sported a tail, but it was longer than a wolf's and resembled Cam's prehensile appendage. His face had stretched into a muzzle, with a dog's nose, and sharp pointed canines extended beyond his lips. Long strings of saliva ran from his mouth, and the eyes were bloodshot. Blood dripped from his muzzle. Two black horns protruded from his temples.

The beast had a Frankenstein-ish appearance as if the worst parts of the three species had been smashed together by a maniacal lab technician.

Addas raised his snout and sniffed.

Byron stood a few feet away. The look on his face conveyed all the hurt, pain, and sorrow Cam had sensed within the man.

Addas flipped his head from side to side, crouching into an attack stance as soon as he spotted Byron. His snout continued to twitch as his eyes narrowed. His head veered away from Byron and locked onto Cam and crew.

His lips retracted as saliva ran, dripping from a mouthful of pointy flesh-eating fae teeth.

Screams of people fleeing the parking lot erupted as Addas snarled, roared, and took a few cantered steps toward them.

The safety of the silver Audi TT lay between them and Addas, but there was no way they would reach the car, nor would they all fit inside the vehicle with its warded windows.

Chapter Twenty-Three

FOR AS LONG as Sparks had been a part of the magical community, he'd never seen a werewolf. He'd seen werewolf wounds—working at a hospital, you got to see all kinds of things—but what crawled out from the underbrush wasn't an accurate depiction of the selenophilic beasts. The fiend lumbered forward on limbs too long, the gait irregular for a bipedal animal. It consisted of a hodgepodge of bizarre parts.

The combination of witch, werewolf, and fae had united to create something even more terrifying. Blood-red cat's-eye pupils glared at them while the beast's lips pulled away, revealing several rows of razor teeth. Pointed inky-black horns protruded from its skull but were almost concealed by thick dark fur.

Its muzzle continued to extend, evident the shift to wolf hadn't completed. But the creature only had a passing resemblance to Ev's werewolf.

Regardless, the monster had morphed into its version of a werewolf in full daylight. Despite the fact the dinner hour drew near, the sun wouldn't be setting until after nine at night in late August. So how the creature had shifted into its beast mode a full day before the full moon, and in the middle of the day, created another mystery. The worst part was there were human eyes everywhere. The Shadow Realm had been exposed.

"We have to get him away from these people," Tully shouted.

"Let's try to lure him onto the hiking trails. At least there'll be fewer folks than an open parking lot at a city rec centre, along a major road going into downtown," Everton bellowed with authority. Despite Everton's nudity, he commanded respect and authority by merely being present, and as he turned toward the wooded park, the rest of them followed his lead.

As he headed toward cover, Addas roared. Sparks gambled on glancing back only to see Byron cowering before the creature on his knees.

"Oh shit, guys..." Sparks stopped and turned to watch.

They had crossed the parking lot toward a line of trees planted to demarcate the sports fields from the concrete pad. From here, they would slip through the empty fields to lure Addas into the hiking paths affording a semblance of cover.

But Byron had screwed up everything.

Supplicated on the ground in front of the wolfed-out Addas, he spread his arms wide and lay before his lover, but Addas rejected the plea. With long talon claws, Addas swiped at Byron, raking his back.

The scream of agony pierced Sparks's ears, making him look away. But the continued shrieking forced him to peek. Like a bad accident, or a horror movie, the scene before him burned itself into his brain. He would never forget this day.

Addas grasped Byron by the scruff of the neck, sharp nails piercing his skin, and dragged him across the cement, scraping his face along the blacktop. Byron flailed and attempted to protect himself, but Addas's brute strength bested him. The beast's snout lifted, and its nose twitched as the monster scented the air. Red eyes squinted as he zeroed in on Sparks and crew, then hoisted Byron and came charging toward them.

"Book it. He's seen us and caught our scent." Ev turned and wound his way through the trees to get deeper into the wooded area.

The rest of them followed.

Trees crashed behind them, as howls of anger announced Addas's advancement.

The late summer season maintained an adequate coverage of foliage on the plant life, even though they were starting to yellow with the advancement of the fall season. The leafy camouflage would, at the very least, shield the Shadow Realm atrocity from the humans.

As Sparks burst through a particularly dense row of bushes and emerged into a clearing, the others joined and flanked him. Standing in knee-deep prairie grasses, already browned with seed heads swaying in the gentle summer breeze, the terror of their situation contrasted oddly to the idyllic setting of a field covered in creamy-white yarrow flowers.

The Glade wasn't large, perhaps thirty feet across. In the background, the gigantic white arches of the Walterdale Bridge gleamed in the late afternoon sun, and beyond that the towering skyscrapers of Edmonton's downtown core rose like sentinels along the steep cliff of the northern riverbank.

They huddled as a group on the far side of the Glade. Sparks crouched close to the ground. He peered down a steep embankment, where the rushing water of the river gurgled. Sliding down this slope would be hazardous. But, if necessary, a hasty retreat down the hill and into the water provided one escape route. But the North Saskatchewan currents were notoriously violent. The waterway had claimed many souls to careless daredevils. Rip currents made the river deadly. This route would be a last-ditch resort to use as a getaway plan.

"Now what?" Dev asked. Sweat glistened on his forehead.

"He'll find us. This is going to end in a battle. A standoff. I will do what I can to stop him, but given his size, and the fact he's not all wolf, I don't know how long I can hold him. I suggest as soon as I engage with Addas, you all take that as your cue to leave." Everton surveyed the brush on the other side, his gaze darting back and forth.

"I am not leaving you to be ripped apart by that asshole." Cam crossed his arms over his chest while his wings beat in defiance. He hovered slightly above the ground.

"Cam, I don't want you to die. Please just do as you're told."

"I know you're attempting to be all chivalrous and shit, but your manliness is not going over well. We fight this thing together. Got it?" Cam shifted position so he floated near Everton.

"Please, Cam!"

"I'm not listening to this garbage. Besides, I've got a few tricks up my sleeve. I'm not as puny and weak as you seem to think." Cam jerked his head, and as he made the motion, a ripple of magic flickered over his body. His wings grew points, sharp, bone-like spears, and they were deadly looking. His mouth filled with rows of teeth, similar to Addas's. His eyes grew red, and his nails on both hands and feet thickened and elongated into spikes.

Addas appeared across the clearing.

"Boys, please?"

"Nope, we're with Cam on this one. We all fight together. Besides, we got some tricks of our own." Dev slapped a hand on Ev's back. "We got you covered on this."

"Why won't anyone ever listen to me?" Everton shook his head, then morphed into his werewolf.

Sparks called upon his magic.

And found nothing.

No spark, no bolt of electricity, no response.

A wave of panic washed over him.

I'm dead. There's nothing there.

Tully and Dev glanced at Sparks, confused looks on their faces.

I've got nothing! There's no current in me!

"Oh shit." Dev's eyes went large and round.

Ev growled as he glanced back to glare at Dev.

Addas took a step forward, bellowing out a challenge.

He still had Byron grasped in his one hand. Glancing down at his captive, he threw Byron to the side like a discarded toy. Byron's body tumbled and rolled, limbs flailing as if he'd been thrown down the stairs.

Sparks continued to flick his hands, trying to ignite anything, when movement across the field caught his eye. Byron hoisted himself up. Being raked and punctured by wolfen fae claws hadn't killed him.

"Sparks can't access his magic," Dev shouted to the group, then glanced over his shoulder toward him and asked, "Is it because of the chaos?" He gestured toward the howling werewolf.

"No! There's nothing there!"

"Tully?" Dev turned and asked.

Tully shook his head, then closed his eyes and placed his hands palms down to the earth.

Nothing.

Tully's eyes popped open. "Holy fuck, what the hell is going on?"

"I think I know—when you were in the soul trap, there were two of you. One version floated behind you much like a shadow. Byron kept those. He has them in his pocket. He called the stones his *insurance* to ensure I'd help him. How much you wanna bet your magic is in there?"

But you can still hear me?

"Yeah, I can hear Sparks!"

"Incoming!" Cam yelled as Ev howled.

Everyone's attention focused on Addas. He raised his snout, releasing a cry as he balled his clawed fists.

He disappeared.

"Oh my Gods. He's using fae magic," Cam whispered.

"Shit! Everyone in a circle, backs together," Tully commanded. Everyone huddled together, eyes searching the immediate vicinity.

Dev gasped first, Addas reappearing in front of him.

Tully and Sparks pulled on each of Dev's shoulders, lurching him backward as Ev loped over the boys and swung a paw.

His fist connected with the side of Addas's muzzle.

Addas's reaction to the punch was lightning fast as he snatched the hand delivering Ev's blow. The mutant werewolf twisted the limb, forcing Ev into a tumble and landing them tangled on the ground.

As the two rolled, Ev kicked with his massive hind legs, knocking the wind out of Addas. The dark wolf rolled to one side, pulled himself up onto all fours, glared menacingly at Ev, and spat out a mouthful of blood while heaving in air.

Ev took the slight delay to get himself right, then went on the offensive.

Claws swiped and blood spray flew. Tufts of fur were ripped out as the werewolves battled each other in a fierce combat, intent on each other's destruction.

Everyone fixated on the two monster werewolves as snapping jaws ripped hides. Wounds bled, fists pummelled, bones snapped, but Addas, using fae magic and dominating Ev in size, gained ground.

Addas launched himself toward Ev. He latched on to his midsection, then wrestled and tussled until he had Ev pinned. Addas opened his maw, exposing several rows of pointed teeth. Saliva dripped off their dagger-like ends.

Sparks caught movement out of the corner of his eye, but this time, not from Byron, who stared transfixed on the fisticuffs like everyone else. No, black mist snaked its way through the underbrush creating a circle around them.

The atmosphere in the Glade thickened and weighed heavy.

Sparks recognized the fog from the other night in the Glade with Tully.

Addas lunged downward, snapping teeth as he went. Ev pulled to one side, narrowly missing a nasty bite. But that gave him a chance to fling a fist into Addas's midsection.

The mist thickened and expanded as a deep well of terror surged through Sparks's guts.

Darkness descended.

Snarls and teeth clamped, growls and grunts echoed as the deadening thud of punches and kicks rumbled through the clearing.

At the diminishing daylight, far too early for sunset, Sparks tapped Tully on the shoulder and pointed in the opposite direction to the monster mêlée.

"Tully. Look!" Sparks pointed toward the edge of the Glade.

Tully tore himself away from the beast fight and squinted. "Is that what I think it is? Oh Gods, it can't be, not now."

"What is going on?" Dev asked, fear written all over his face.

"Remember Tully and I had a brush with a wraith?" Sparks grimaced as he pointed in the mist's direction.

"Fuck off. Now?"

"Okay, I'll go tell it to come back later." Sparks shot Dev a dagger-filled look.

Around the circumference of the wooded area, the mist thickened into a wall, and towered upward until the darkness formed a dome, blacking out the sun's rays. As a false night descended, the whispers of ghostly voices scampered across the clearing.

"Those two fools haven't even registered there's a wraith here." Dev grabbed Cam. "Can you do something to maybe get them to take notice?"

"Like what?"

"I don't know, but we better act fast. Look!" Dev pointed near to where Addas and Ev were still tangled around each other, desperately trying to rip each other's throats out.

From beneath the ground the wraith emerged like a zombie hauling itself out of a grave. Ghostly vapours ascended from the earth, twisting and swirling until they coalesced, forming its skeletal body.

As one of the darkest creatures within the Shadow Realm pulled its torso out of the ground, Ev rolled within swiping distance of the wraith. Brief physical contact would allow the spectre to absorb life energy, granting it additional strength.

Cam shot forward as fast as his wings would carry him, flipping head over tail so he hurtled feet first toward Addas, landing dead centre on his chest. The unexpected aerial assault caught the creature off guard as Addas plummeted backward. Cam launched toward the sky and shouted to Ev.

"Unexpected guest to your right!" Cam yelled.

With a moment's reprieve, Ev glanced in the direction Cam alerted him to, only to find himself face to face with the decaying entity.

"Tully, can you call on Phineas? Maybe he can help. If I can still think thoughts, and you guys can hear them…maybe the God-gifted talents are still ours to control?" Sparks suggested. "If we don't do something, Ev's about to be turned into a desiccated corpse."

The wraith floated above Ev, hissing and lashing out. Vapours and wisps unfurled, the smoke swirling around, steadily increasing in size. An audible wheezing intake of air had everyone holding their breath as the spectre gathered strength.

"I don't even know how to—" From the crook of Tully's arm, a vine lashed out. The tendril spun around a few times before diving toward the earth.

The thick tendril burrowed into the soil and as Phineas extricated itself from Tully's arm, Tully grabbed his wrist and screamed as blood flowed down his hand and pooled on the grass beneath his feet.

Sparks gasped as Phineas erupted from the soil all around Everton, creating a thick tree-root shield as the wraith descended, clawing with its bony fingers. The gaping maw of the skull opened, releasing a shriek as it met the Earth elemental's wooden resistance.

Recognizing the prey under the solid wood defence was no longer viable, a skull with no eyeballs scanned the vicinity to find Byron a close victim. Shifting direction, the wraith pulled itself toward the ex-high priest.

From across the field a fireball shot forward.

The ball of flame blew through the centre of the wraith. Another shriek pierced through the darkness. The death ghost refocused its sights on a different victim. It spun toward Addas, who was still shaking off Cam's kick to the chest.

The flame torpedo hadn't destroyed the undead creature. Instead, it arched across the Glade. Dev jumped to the side, pulling Sparks down with him. As the two tumbled, the fireball singed the back of Sparks's head.

The aroma of burnt hair choked everyone in the area. Sparks's hair continued to ignite and burn.

"Goddamn it!" Tully pulled his shirt off and wrapped the cotton material around Sparks's head, trying to suffocate the burn.

Sparks yowled in pain as the flames created embers from melted hair. Strands of his long flowing locks fell out around him. The unbearable odour resembled the reek of sulphur.

"Is it out? Is it still burning? Are you okay?" Tully cried out.

Dev rushed over and swiped any live embers away from Sparks's shoulders.

"Fuck me! It burns!" Sparks screeched.

Tully removed his shirt from Sparks's head. There were several burn holes in the material. He discarded it on the ground, then spun Sparks around. "You're sure you're okay?"

Sparks reached to his scalp and vigorously rubbed his head. He regretted that action, cringing as he hit the flesh burnt the worst. "I...I think so," he stammered, but the skin had formed a multitude of bumps. Sparks pulled his fingers away, wet with fluid. The heat from the fire had produced blisters. "I'll live, but my fucking hair!"

Dev turned him and inspected the damage. "You're not gonna be happy; there's a lot missing. And the skin is still bubbling. You might have scars."

Everton howled.

Cam floated several feet in the air as the wraith encircled him.

Everton jumped up and clawed at the trailing wisps of the spectre, but the creature hovered beyond his grasp.

The dark ghostly syphon had one skeletal hand grasped around Cam's neck. Cam closed his eyes and remained dead still. The wraith had subdued him with a single clenched fist.

Leaning in close, the phantom inhaled as its skull came within inches of Cam's forehead. Trickles of energy, sparkle fairy lights, wafted off Cam and disappeared up the empty nostril holes.

The darkness within the Glade coagulated. The deepest dark of night soaked the area in nothingness, and as Sparks glanced across the clearing, the blond fur of Everton's wolf flashed in and out of sight. Addas, as dark as his beast's fur, had disappeared.

But a single shining light pierced through the black and everyone glanced up to see Cam radiating light.

It got brighter.

And brighter.

Until the glow turned nuclear, blinding so bright all heads turned away from the searing luminescence.

The wraith screeched, caught in the direct impact of Cam's fairy light.

Sizzling and hissing, the spectre dissipated. As fast as the deadly apparition had appeared, the light banished the creature.

Cam dropped like a lead weight to the ground.

Ev waited directly below him and caught his falling fae, preventing a collision with the hard ground.

A rumbling growl bellowed out from the edge of the clearing. Addas wasn't done.

He charged forward, claws raised, teeth brandished. Sparks cringed as Addas advanced, a wildness lurking in the wolf's eyes—crazed, irrational bloodlust intent on death.

Unless Phineas pulled out a miracle and stopped Addas, or Dev charged and threw out a rune spell in a few short seconds, Everton and Cam were goners.

Addas launched himself forward, knives for nails directed forward, maw open, teeth exposed.

From the edges of the woods, several black-robed, hooded figures appeared.

Sparks spun, and everywhere he paused to stare, more hooded figures emerged from the bushes and trees.

One stepped forward, raising its hand, as a strong-willed but feminine voice cried out, "*Somnus!*"

Chapter Twenty-Four

SPARKS SAT UP at an alarming rate, gasped, then steadied himself as his head pounded and his vision spun. He took in his current whereabouts when the room stopped tilting and spinning. At the exact same time Dev and Tully mimicked the identical actions in waking up.

Sparks didn't feel right, like a hole existed inside him. A part was missing.

The three of them stared blankly at one another, registering the fact they were all still alive, and not in a small forest clearing battling a wraith and an abomination werewolf. But Everton and Cam were missing.

What the hell? Where are we? Sparks glanced around as he projected the words.

There were thick stone walls on three sides and cots attached to the wall on two of the three sides. A sink with a tap and a toilet lay against the last wall.

"For fuck's sake," Tully whispered.

"We're in jail." Dev walked over to the bars and grasped them, craning his head to see down the dimly lit hall.

Soft red light barely illuminated the room. The cell smelled dank and Sparks rubbed his hands together for warmth, finding the dungeon a tad chilly.

Sparks took a seat on the one cot hanging from the wall by itself. The other wall had a bunk bed version. He held his head in his hands. Absentmindedly, he fondled his burnt scalp, and as his fingers grazed the sheared hair, he also ruptured a couple of blisters. He hissed. When he pulled his fingers away, they were greasy from a salve that had been smeared on his burn. He frowned, feeling the short bristles all around the nape of his neck. The lower section of his head had been shaved, but the crown still had long hair.

"Well, I guess I'm going to have to grow this out again."

Tully glanced in his direction. "I don't know. I kind of like it. I mean, you know, once the burn heals."

"Well, this is just grand. The hooded figures, those were the Magistrates, right? We've been thrown in witch jail, haven't we?" Dev asked the other two, while still trying to see down the hallway.

"I'd say that's a fair assessment," Sparks mumbled.

"How much shit do you think we're in?" Dev turned to the others, his face showing panic.

"What's the matter?" Tully asked. "You've gone pale as a ghost."

"I don't like being locked up."

"Are you claustrophobic?" Sparks thumped the thin cushion on the cot, indicating to Dev to take a seat. Dev walked over and sat.

"Maybe a little."

Sparks threw an arm around his shoulders. "Don't worry. We're fine, and safe, and probably in huge amounts of trouble, but for right now we're good."

Tully took a seat on the other side and snuggled into Dev, winding his arm around his middle. "Yup. We got you."

Sparks and Tully shared a quick glance between themselves and acknowledged Dev's current need for comfort.

Dev exhaled, and shook.

"We'll be okay, Dev. Promise." Tully squeezed him.

"Ah, we're in jail," Dev replied.

"Yeah, but we didn't do anything," Sparks replied.

"Except put the Shadow Realm on full display?" Dev corrected.

"Tully and I didn't have any magic to cast, and I don't think you conjured up any hocus pocus. As far as the Magistrates know, we're normal humans," Sparks reasoned, but at the same time he acknowledged the gnawing hole on his insides. The spot where his magic should have been.

I can't believe it's gone.

"Yeah, so…how does that work? How is our magic gone? Our God-bestowed gifts are okay, but our naturally born talents were ripped away from us?" Tully's eyebrows furrowed.

"I don't know what else to tell you, other than Byron took a part of you as his safekeeping. Blackmail material to ensure we would take him to Addas. He promised to give me the pieces of the amber stone that absorbed your other selves. To be honest, I don't know how we merge your spirit bit back with the rest of you, or if the soul absorbs into the body and melds together on its own?" Dev sighed. "This is a fine fucking mess."

"Don't worry. We'll figure it out." Tully squeezed Dev again.

Sparks drew his hand in to himself, noticing Tully's attempt to comfort Dev.

"You guys are good for each other."

"Tully's been a rock for me as I've ambled down my path through the Shadow Realm. I doubt I would have made it as far as I have without him."

"And watching Dev explore this world as a newbie has been exciting for me and has rekindled some of my own joy. He gets excited over the tiniest things," Tully added.

"Right, see, you two have this comfortable fit." Sparks stood and walked over to the bars, turned, and leaned against them so Dev and Tully were in front of him. "I like you guys. A lot. But I'm still failing to see how this is supposed to work as a threesome." He shook his head.

Dev and Tully shared a knowing glance between the two of them.

"That's not entirely fair, Sparks." Dev put his hand on Tully's thigh. "Sure, Tully and I have been together for a few months, but we're still new to each other. We have a bond, yes, but everything in our relationship happened really fast. I mean, I met Tully and within a couple of days I had moved into the upstairs apartment at the house. Within a month of living there, I spent every single moment with him downstairs in his space and moving all my stuff down into his condo made the most sense. With everything that has happened, let's say it's been a whirlwind of activity the last half year. Between me finding the Shadow Realm, the whole Byron episode, graduating from university, setting up my own business, Tully, and now all this—there hasn't been a lot of downtime. I don't see adding you into the mix much of a big deal. More like sprinkling in another dash of crazy. Hell, it's welcome."

Sparks chuckled. "Life has been crazy. But that's just it. You guys don't need any additional messes, or more to add to the mix. Haven't you got enough to deal with?"

"The past few months have been utterly insane, but I kind of like the rapid pace. Keeps me on my toes." Tully smiled.

"I don't know if I can keep running this fast throughout life. I need downtime. And I still don't feel comfortable or okay with coming in between you two."

"I don't understand this 'in between' thing. Can I ask a question?" Dev tilted his head to one side.

"Sure."

"What makes you think you're disrupting what we have? What if you're the icing on the cake? Or the perfect accoutrement to accompany our meal?" Dev pointed to the empty spot beside him, inviting Sparks to sit. "Tully and I have talked about what our relationship means: Are we monogamous? Are we open? If so, what are the rules should something extra come along? Granted, I think we were talking more about a trick or a plaything. But who cares? So, the *extra* happens to be our best friend, who is going to graduate to the next level with us.

"Despite this being sudden and moving at a fast clip, so did Tully and I. I have my own reservations. You're not alone in wrestling with this. But I bet if we give it a chance the weird will disappear and the comfort will settle in. Between Tully's job and mine, where we both keep odd hours, sometimes we go a couple of days without seeing each other. You work wild shifts at the hospital, and so adding another person into the house—when you're ready—means we might get to spend time with someone. Knowing someone's around is comforting.

"Can I ask you another question?" Dev again gestured to the seat next to him, convincing Sparks to occupy the space.

"Okay." Sparks gave in and crossed the musty cell, sat, and resumed his position next to Dev, but his shoulders drooped.

"Why did you stand up for me at my initiation into the Shadow Realm?"

"Huh?" Sparks paused, taken aback by Dev's question. He took a moment to think. "Ah, well, this might seem silly, but the night Tully brought you to the coven, the moment I saw the two of you interacting with each other the energy between you told me you belonged together. You were comfortable, in step, and the vibe you put out into the room had all the guys talking. I guess I wanted to be nearer to you. Selfishly, I wanted to have a part in the interactions I saw between you and Tully. Saying it out loud now makes me feel self-centred. There's something about you, Dev. You're a truly unique individual, and I wanted you to be an important part of my life. You're destined for bigger things, and I think part of me wanted to be included. Plus, Tully's been my coven mate for years. We always got paired together. I don't know—if I'm being 100 percent honest, I also hate being alone."

"Okay." Tully beamed. "So, how about this? You take all the time you need to figure out when you want to be part of this, and how you want to be part of this. I think I can safely say for both of us—" Tully glanced at Dev, waiting for agreement. "—whatever form that takes, Dev and I are good."

"However long?"

"Yup." Dev nodded.

"And this might end up as friends, or occasional friends with benefits, or full-on throuple status—you guys would be okay with any of it?"

"Why wouldn't we?" Tully beamed at him. "Sparks, you've been my best coven brother for years. The sexy fun we had the other night was a first, sure, but nothing about what we did bothered me. If anything, our intimacy brought about a nice progression to our friendship, like taking our trust to the next level. But I don't ever have to go there again if the sex makes you uncomfortable. Want to? Sure. Have to? No."

"You're right. Actually, being with you two was more than nice." A mischievous grin danced across Sparks's face. "But you guys feel the same way, right? It's all fast and a little creepy that the God deemed it all necessary."

"Completely." Dev put a hand on Sparks's thigh. "But, as long as we're being honest, I'll tell you this. Waking up in bed the other morning with both of you was the most comfortable and safe I think I've ever been." Dev glanced at

Tully and smiled, then turned slightly to Sparks. "However, or whatever makes you the most comfortable for this to work out as Cernunnos needs, I'm okay with. But I would be lying if I didn't tell you I am hoping I get to wake up in bed again with both of you."

"I agree. Besides, I wanna practice my tongue thing on you again. I don't think I've ever had anyone squirm so much. Or come as hard."

"Oh my Gods." In the darkness of the cell, the shadows hid the blush creeping into Sparks's cheeks, but the guys had settled his anxiety. Regardless of some God's mandate, they wanted him around. "Okay, now you've given me a chubbie. I'll confess, I wouldn't mind waking up to you two, doing those things...often."

"It's settled," Tully stated. "When we get out, you're moving in."

"Tully!" Dev snapped at him and slapped his thigh. He turned to Sparks. "You take your time. Make whatever decision you want. We're here for you. Period."

"Okay. I'm glad we talked. This whole thing's been bugging me."

"I think we have some adventures left to deal with. We got to get your soul bits reassembled into both of you, and then we have to start up our own coven. The crazy you spoke about, Sparks? That ain't going away any time soon." Dev gave Sparks one of those *know what I mean* looks.

Sparks rolled his eyes.

"All right." Tully stood up and turned to face both his guys with his arms out. "Bring it in. Weird or not, complicated or not, we got one another's backs. Right?"

Dev and Sparks stood up and walked into Tully's arms.

"Three amigos it is."

"Hey, Tully?" Sparks canted his head to one side as he stared at Tully's shoulder. He grabbed his arm and pushed his T-shirt sleeve up to expose more of his flesh.

"Where the hell is Phineas?"

The tattoo had disappeared.

CAM RUBBED HIS neck. There were raised welts hot to the touch from where the wraith had grasped him, and a lump in his throat made it hard to swallow. In addition, the skin on his neck and scalp burned, and Cam didn't know if the heat was a residual effect from the wraith or if he was running a touch of a fever. Maybe after all the adventure and running on empty this indicated the onset of a cold or flu? Did fae get colds?

Everton, on the other hand, hadn't woken yet, had reverted to his human self, and had several spots where bandages wrapped bleeding wounds. The white gauze showed blood had seeped to its surface, but whoever administered the first aid had stopped the bleeding as the bloodstains hadn't spread.

Cam sat close to Ev, waiting for him to wake up. The evening had been intense, and now he understood the danger Everton had tried to warn him against.

Addas's weird fae werewolf beast remained locked in his memory like a thing of nightmares. The twisted images would haunt him for some time to come.

A hand ran up Cam's side, and he jumped.

"Fuck me!" Cam, his internal musings forgotten, jerked his head toward the source of the touch. Of course it was only Ev, who stirred from his sleep. After the events of the night before, Cam was jittery.

"Where are we?" Ev rubbed his face and tried to sit up.

"Don't know. Can't say, but it's got bars and a really shitty view." Cam's tail twitched between his legs. Sitting meant he forever sat on his tail.

"Ah, right, the Magistrates. We'll be in their cells until they come collect us and interview each of us."

"I didn't apply for a job." Cam sneered. "Sounds like you've been here before."

"A time or two. Werewolves aren't the Realm's favourite creatures." Ev shook his head. "Come here."

Ev grabbed Cam, careful of his wings, and pulled him down to lie with him.

"This is nice." Cam snuggled in.

"You never listen to me. I thought for sure I would lose you."

Cam stiffened. Did Everton express emotions?

They shifted around so Cam lay face to face with Ev. Cam got coy, canting his head to one side as he gazed with longing into the hazel and gold eyes. Except his horns got in the way so he nearly ended up gouging Ev's face instead.

"You're a monster with these things." Ev put his hand to Cam's head and gently ran a finger over the tip of his horn. The ghostlike touch sent a shiver down Cam's spine.

"I can't believe you like those things."

"I love them." Ev stroked the horns again. "You okay? The wraith had you in its grasp pretty tight, but I gotta say, I won't ever underestimate you ever again. Your illumination magic is deadly bright! How did you know the light would kill it?"

"I didn't. I figured the wraith lived in the darkness, so I needed to shine. Total gamble."

"It paid off."

"Yup. Like I said, I'm not some puny weakling."

"No, you certainly are not. Cam..." Ev let out a gruff harrumph.

"Out with it. I can tell you've wanted to say something for weeks but haven't. I know you promised me a night in heaven if I got you out of the witches' dungeon. I won't hold you to the promise if you're not into it." Cam frowned. Reading Ev's emotional state, even as a fae, left him swimming in confusion. Ev had kissed him like tomorrow would never arrive. He'd managed to get the guy naked and hard and was about to get Lady Aine's vial filled when they were unceremoniously interrupted. Even now, Ev had pulled him into his arms. All the signs pointed toward Everton having feelings for Cam.

And yet, he kept tearing himself away, confusing everything.

"I've been a bit of an ass, and I'm sorry." Ev frowned.

This wasn't what Cam had expected to hear. "Go on."

"Franco had mentioned you two talked. And then he gave me a good solid scolding."

"I like Franco; he's a good guy." Cam grinned, imagining Franco lecturing Ev.

"He's the best. And he knows me really well, and he's a good judge of character. He demanded I come clean with you. And, well…I think we're gonna be in this cell for a while, so I might as well get this off my chest."

"I'm listening." Cam braced himself to hear the inevitable. Would Ev tell him he wanted to be around? Or despite the current cuddle situation would Everton blow him off? Fae or not, being able to read emotions or not, the rolling intensity of conflicting vibes confused the hell out of Cam.

"I really like you."

Cam cocked an eyebrow. "Okay."

"No, like *really* like you." Ev sighed, glanced away, and continued. "I don't know how to say this."

"Just say it. You don't want to be with me. It's okay. I get it." Cam started to push away from Ev, and the beast of a man tensed, holding Cam so he couldn't escape.

"What? No. What gave you that idea? Gods, if anything, it's the exact opposite."

"Say again?"

"Cam, I want us to be together," Ev blurted out. "There, I said it."

Cam lifted a finger and waved it a couple of times, trying to figure out what those words meant.

"So, when you say together, you mean...what exactly? Like sexy fun times together? You want to ride the fairy, or *together* as in friends who go to the movies, or...what?"

"Sure, all of that. Together, as in—I hope—you'll come live with me when you don't have to be in the Ancestral Lands. As in, I want to date you. Like, be my boyfriend."

"Oh my Gods."

"I know I'm a total loser. I know you like to play the field and have lots of dates. If I had the ability to not be so jealous, then maybe this would work. But my wolf and I—we're a one fae, one wolf kind of guy. I would let you run and have fun, but I don't trust myself to be okay with an open relationship. I want you all to myself. I want us to go see movies, to go run through woods, to hang out with Dev and Tully."

"Dev, Tully, and Sparks."

"What?"

"Yeah, that's a thing now."

"All three of them?"

"Yup. I think they're still figuring themselves out."

"Wow. Cool."

"It is." Cam leaned forward and kissed Ev with a quick peck.

"I like those."

"Why didn't you tell me this before?"

"I couldn't. I wanted you so bad, but I also know you like to date. You're so young, and I'm an old guy. I didn't want to stifle you or disrupt your groove. You need to go out and—"

"Everton Lilch, stop right there. Not another word." Cam shook his head, carefully, cognizant of his horns. "I liked dating guys because of the fun I had in meeting new people, but I was also searching for the one guy who would be my everything. I hadn't found him."

"So...a boyfriend isn't out of the question?"

"Gods, hell no. It's what I've wanted for as long as I can remember. But there's not too many men out there who can handle my crazy."

"I love your crazy. You make me feel young, hopeful, and you make me laugh. I like who I am when you're around. And your horns are hella fun." Ev stroked the bony, ridged protrusions.

"You know, you wouldn't think I could feel you stroking my horns, but I totally do, and it's insanely hot."

"I can tell." Ev ground a thigh into Cam's groin, rubbing the stiffening bone.

"Everton, are you saying what I think you're saying? You want to be my monster boyfriend?"

"Can we try?"

"Well, I guess my last wish from Dev's damn summoning board has finally come true. I thought you would *never* ask! Yes, you dumbass wolf." Cam snuggled in closer and this time planted a lingering kiss on Ev.

Ev wrapped his big arms around Cam under his wings and held him close.

Cam ventured forth into Ev's mouth with his tongue, and Ev let him explore. Cam delighted in Ev's gruffness, and the wiry whiskers, and the furry bits his werewolf sported. Cam's hands ran over Ev's monster pectorals, and through the fur covering them. Giving in to ecstasy, and forgetting about Ev's bandages, he broke the sensual kiss and said, "You might like the horns, but wait until you see what I can make my tail do."

"Show me?" Ev grinned.

"Here? What if someone comes?"

"It's late at night. No one is coming. They will interview us all tomorrow."

"But you're all wounded, and I don't want to hurt you."

"Cam, I've waited an entire summer for this. Show me what your tail can do."

Cam bit his lower lip and grinned at the same time, staring deep into Ev's hazel eyes with the yellow-gold ring around the pupils. Tugging at the ties that held his loincloth in place, Cam let his only piece of clothing fall, exposing his excitement.

Raising his tail, Cam snaked the appendage forward as he shifted away slightly from Ev's torso, granting him access to Ev's body. The long appendage, covered in soft fur, and much like the horns, registered all the sensations of touch when he used his tail as an extra hand. Grazing his tail along Ev's muscles sent pleasurable ripples through him.

Creeping up Ev's thigh, he wound the tail around Ev's thick engorged cock. He was cut, so no foreskin hooded the glans. Cam didn't mind. Either way Ev's manhood made him salivate. He used his tail to squeeze Ev's wolfy bits and stroked him using his appendage while his hands tweaked Ev's nipples. Ev had enjoyed some nipple action when the two of them had been in Ev's bedroom. Cam licked the side of Ev's neck and nibbled his ear.

Ev groaned.

"Oh my Gods, yes."

Ev's gaze descended to Cam's groin, spying the up-curved throbbing bone he sported. Ev wrapped his rough and calloused wolf paws around the shaft and caressed him. He shivered with delight. Ev's meaty and hot palms ignited the roaring fire of desire in the pit of Cam's belly. He thrust into Ev's hands.

They played with each other, enjoying the sensual touches. Cam begged Ev to shift different parts of his body.

He licked Ev's fangs, played with dense patches of fur, and stroked his wolf tail.

Ev took his time discovering how Cam's wings sprouted from in between his shoulder blades and then running his hands over the fur along the base of each wing.

Mouths tasted flesh and fingers gripped muscle. There wasn't a spot that didn't get a tongue bath. And between furious bouts of rubbing and kissing, they slowed and snuggled.

"Ev, I do have something I need to tell you. I mean, if we're a thing—then there's something you should know."

"Okay." Ev drew the word out, cautious at what Cam might drop on him.

"It's a fae thing."

"All right." Ev shot him a side-eye glance.

"So, here's the deal. Lady Aine needs to get pregnant." Cam grimaced.

"And? Why are you telling me this?"

"I have to be the one to get her in the family way."

"Ah..." Ev's face scrunched up in disbelief.

"See! I made my stance quite clear. The boy parts work for other boys only. She got kinda rude after I came out to her, but she gave me a jar, and as long as I fill it, she'll do the rest. But I have to get a filled vessel to her before Groundswell. And she warned me the descent under for the winter might happen early."

"Okay, so you're gonna be a dad!"

"Hell, no. I'm not suitable to be any kind of parent. At best, I'll be a donor. But I'm the only living fertile male fae. Apparently, that's fae tradition at work. Only the youngest Royal male in the village can be dad worthy. I don't know; it's a fae thing." Cam shrugged.

"So then...fill the jar?"

"I can't...you know...by my own hand. The stuff needs to be obtained through an emotional attachment with someone else." Cam raised an eyebrow and stared at Ev. "You're someone else."

"Oh! So you want me to..." Ev reached down and grabbed Cam who remained rock hard, and he stroked Cam a few times.

"I was hoping you would...maybe while you fucked me. I've been waiting all summer."

Ev waggled his eyebrows. "I think we should try right now. Go get your jar."

"Now?"

"Why not?"

"Hot damn." Cam stooped over to where his discarded loincloth had fallen off the bed onto the floor and discovered the hip sack he carried had been confiscated. "Oh shit, it's gone."

"I bet you anything the Magistrates took it. They remove all items from anyone they put into lockup. You know. Magical beings and creatures have various ways to escape. So I'm usually left in here naked."

"You're naked a lot. Not that I mind."

"Comes with being a werewolf. Can't shift in clothes."

"Well, damn. Here I thought I was going to satisfy Lady Aine's ridiculous expectations. Truth be told, I feel obligated to get the task done. Can you imagine me back in the Ancestral Lands and everyone pointing and sniggering at me? I would be the laughingstock of the fae for not getting the queen pregnant."

"You know, we could practice now. Wouldn't want to do anything wrong once we have the vessel. Too important to Lady Aine. Right?" Ev hadn't let go of Cam and continued to feel all the fun parts.

"You don't say?" Cam arched an eyebrow and beamed at his new boyfriend with a pointy grin.

AN HOUR LATER, Cam and Ev had fucked themselves into a delirium. Hot and sweaty, Ev held on tight to Cam's horns as he thrust deeply. Ev was thick, not long, but his cock had girth. The sting at first from being stretched hurt like a mother, but after a few minutes Cam relaxed, and now he enjoyed the fullness and the sensation of Ev's wide mushroom-capped cockhead running over his prostrate.

As he gave into the sensations, Cam's want and need for Ev grew, and the lustful frenetic energy peaked. Cam would do anything for his wolf if feeling this good happened on the regular. The growling from Ev was nothing short of monstrous, as he held on tight to Cam's horns, using them for leverage. Ev bucked from behind. His wolfen fur rubbed up against Cam's back and wings.

Ev stopped and flipped him over, raised Cam's legs, then spread them.

"I want to see you when I come." Ev panted.

Continuing the assault on Cam's ass, Ev pounded and the slap of flesh against flesh echoed throughout the stone cell. Anyone within earshot would have known exactly what the wolf and fae were up to.

Ev picked up the pace, and Cam clenched tighter, hoping to bring his wolf to a rousing climax.

Cam rode his own wave of desire, which heightened his fae magic, making him glow, and even though he hadn't touched himself, his orgasm threatened to arrive far too soon.

Ev dropped Cam's legs and grabbed his buttocks. He scooped Cam up and held him against his body. As he continued to thrust, he slid a hand around to hold the back of Cam's head, guiding him to his mouth.

Ev's wet kisses sent Cam into overdrive. As Ev thrust up, Cam met the action as they set themselves in motion together. Their hot bodies glistened with sweat, tongues tasting each other's mouths, until Ev growled a deep throaty rumble, held Cam extra tight, and pushed his cock in as far as his member would go.

Ev howled as he erupted, clinging to Cam.

Cam returned in kind, pushing himself down on Ev as hard as possible until the unmistakable tipping point of pleasure signalled his own climax was at hand. He exploded in synch with Ev, producing a shower of fairy lights that erupted all around them, cascading down like their own private fireworks.

The fucking slowed, and Ev lowered Cam to the cot. The sudden void as Ev let himself slip out disappointed Cam. He wanted his monster boyfriend to be inside him all night long. Ev kissed Cam's lips, his chin, and the base of his neck, licked a nipple, nibbled on the fleshy parts of his belly, then tongued Cam's throbbing erection.

He pulled off and glanced up at Cam with a befuddled stare. "Didn't you come?"

"Everywhere."

"There's no...um... I wanted to taste you."

"What do you mean? I shot all over."

"Cam, there's nothing here."

"What?" Cam pulled his head up and looked. Running his hands over his torso, and the material covering the cot, he found sure enough, he wasn't sticky, and his fingers did not encounter a single wet spot.

Chapter Twenty-Five

AFTER BEING ESCORTED into a large amphitheatre made entirely of stone, Sparks, Tully, and Dev were situated as spectators in the first row seated at the farthest right in the theatre. The roughly hewn granite bench made for an uncomfortable and cold seat. Cam and Everton were separated from the witches by a couple of sections but sat in the same row. Byron and Addas were nowhere to be seen. Everyone wore restraints, which given the circumstances, made sense. Without the use of hands, most magical creatures would be prevented from casting complicated spells, and having a werewolf bound on the day of the full moon was just smart.

Sparks studied the room before him. The amphitheatre had the same smell and ambience as the jail cells they had been left in overnight. They had to be underground given the musty odour. The room glowed, bathed in identical lighting to their overnight accommodations—an eerie red casted ruddiness. On the walls, ceiling, and floor various sigils had been carefully crafted. Hex script accompanied them, too, and although Sparks's skill with various languages proved adequate for his level of witchery, he readily admitted to not being able to identify all the various styles.

He did recognize the Theban alphabet, Norse runes, Enochian symbols, and even Grimm which was disconcerting as Grimm seals meant dire business.

A guard stood sentinel before them and two were stationed on each side of the long table laid out across a raised dais on the floor of the amphitheatre. A line of Magistrates entered the auditorium, one after another, seven in total, all wearing deeply hooded black robes which puddled and swished on the floor as they moved. The hoods also concealed their faces.

In perfect unison they glided over to the table and took up a position behind the chairs. Again, with alarming synchronicity, they sat. From under the table a variety of items were laid on the surface, which had been draped in a black tablecloth. Cell phones, several crystal shards, a hip sack, a glass bottle, several wallets, loose change, an amulet, and some vials filled with a curious green liquid formed a perfect row displayed out in front of the Magistrates.

Recognizing the black cell phone cover with a single red rose emblazoned on its back, Sparks hoped at the end of all of this they would get their personal effects. Replacing a cell phone right now would be prohibitively expensive. Money he didn't have, and his contract on the cell still had over a year left.

The night before had been long and left him chilled to the bone with nothing but a simple cot to sleep on, and no blanket to keep himself warm. In the early morning, everyone had been removed at the same time and berated at length, barraged with questions and demanding intricate details of the day's events leading up to the wraith attack. Sparks hadn't had much sleep and second-guessed his recollection of the previous days' events. He had hoped his memory of the facts proved precise enough for the Magistrates and he had tried to omit anything that might land anyone in hot water. Sparks worried if his story matched Dev and Tully's.

And despite the conversation and numerous assurances from the guys, he still waxed and waned over their new arrangement. He needed time to himself to think about where he wanted and needed to be.

The hooded figures seated at the large table before them remained anonymous—maintaining an air of mystery—as they had during the interrogations. They took their time getting organized, bringing out case files, pens, and several laptops. The lengthy time they took to get organized also had the effect of maintaining authority over the prisoners. Being a Magistrate within the magical community wasn't a sought-after position and carrying out punishments and sentences required a certain amount of ruthlessness. No one wanted to know their neighbour, or worse, coven mate had been conscripted into being a law enforcer for the Shadow Realm.

Sparks understood the need for hiding identities.

"Witches, come forward." A woman spoke. One whose tone didn't leave any room to question her authority.

Dev, Tully, and Sparks presented themselves before the Council.

"We have reviewed each of your statements. Your stories have all corroborated the others closely enough. However, you are still guilty of being present with a group of individuals who exposed the Shadow Realm to humans. The situation required a massive containment and cleanup. The penalty for such a crime is usually a binding for a year and a day. No access to magic whatsoever. But we have also learned you three are responsible for taking over the role the Guardians of the Night Grove have performed for many, many years.

"Because of this, we are willing to forgo said binding so the throttling of the ley lines can be re-initiated. Make no mistake, you are on a timeline to get this done. We have too many reports of banned and exiled dark creatures returning to our neutral zone. We expect safety to return to our city in short order. You have one month. On or before the next full moon, the ley line issue needs to be resolved.

"Please take a seat." With a wave of her hand, a guard appeared to the left, and escorted the boys to their assigned stations.

"Cameron Habersham and Everton Lilch, please approach." This time a different hooded figure spoke. A masculine voice. A different guard ensured the werewolf and the fae approached the Council but maintained an appropriate distance.

"Cameron, although the destruction of a wraith would normally be considered a commendable action, the way in which you accomplished the feat led to multiple reported sightings. You have saved this city from a serious threat, but in the same breath you exposed the Shadow Realm. As we cannot weigh in on matters of the fae, we have asked Lady Aine to be present. Lady, the floor is yours." The hooded figure gestured toward the top of the theatre which remained covered in shadows.

A series of steep stone steps led from the floor up to the darkness in the rafters. From this concealed place, an ethereal white glow descended until Lady Aine stood in the centre of the dais close to the front table.

Lady Aine's face left no expectations for Cam's judgement to be anything less than severe.

"Cam, what do our traditions and customs say about formal settings such as these? What are you to do when someone who outranks you enters the room?"

"Shit." Cam immediately took a knee.

Everton, not familiar enough with the inner workings of fae court, only wanted to support his new boyfriend, and he, too, kneeled before the fae queen.

"Everton, it is noted that you are attempting to be polite, but you are not one of mine, and therefore I do not expect you to maintain our customs. However, your efforts are appreciated. Cam, take note. This is an example of respect."

"Yes, ma'am."

"What did I tell you on the day you attempted to flee the Ancestral Lands?"

"That I wasn't to get caught."

Lady Aine cocked an eyebrow, clearly surprised Cam remembered. "Correct. And yet, here I am. I am extremely disappointed in you. You continue to abuse my graciousness. I had so hoped with a little free rein you would have come to understand what we are, and why our traditions and customs are so important to follow. You have failed, once again, spectacularly.

"It hurts me to do this, but you are exiled, Cam Habersham. Your presence is a threat to fae and as such, I cannot risk the safety of my people over the insolence of a single human turned fae. You have not accepted the responsibility to uphold our laws and customs. You refuse to assimilate yourself into our fold. Therefore, you are no longer welcome in the Ancestral Lands. You shall not return. You are no longer a part of us."

"But your highness—" Cam started, but Ev interrupted.

"Your ladyship," Everton spoke. "Please, may I?"

Lady Aine eyed Everton carefully, then said, "Very well."

"I apologize for Cam. I know he can be rash, careless, and thoughtless at times."

"Not helping!" Cam glared, but Everton waved him to be quiet.

"I know what it's like to be lost, to feel like you're the only one of your kind. And to some extent, Cam truly is unique—at least here in these parts. He is very young and still learning who he is. In my rebellious youth I sacrificed everything, including my own humanity, over rash decisions and needing to do things on my own terms."

"Go on." Lady Aine's jaw tensed as Ev continued.

"I beg of you to give Cam a one-year grace period. He will stay with me, in my pack. When I deliver him to you next fall, he will be a different man. I promise."

"Well." Lady Aine raised an eyebrow. She stood silent for several moments. "Let me make something clear to you, Everton Lilch, werewolf. We generally do not allow your kind within the limits of our village. For many reasons. Unchecked anger issues being top of the list. I am impressed you have control of yours, especially on the day of a full moon. That speaks to your level of mastery over your bestial side." The queen turned to look at Cam.

From where Sparks sat, his gaze followed Cam's tail flicking to and fro like a metronome. The motion accelerated which Sparks took to be his nerves. Cam's skin glistened from beads of sweat.

"My decision is final. Cam has already been granted more than enough chances. He is to be left on his own. However, I will grant you an audience in one year's time, near Groundswell. Present your case to me, and I will evaluate whether Cam has evolved. If I cannot measure a suitable change, your exile will be permanent. Regardless, Cam will never be able to live in the Ancestral Lands. Your only option now is whether I will entertain the notion of you being a welcomed visitor. But know this. Even a single year cut off from his own kind, Cam's odds are not good. Even now I can sense the separation sickness which will eventually overtake him. We will not be available for assistance. This sickness will kill him if left unattended. You are on your own to figure out your salvation." She turned to Cam. "If you can show a marked change, and endure until this time next year, I will reconsider whether or not you will be able to be counted among our kind." She paused. Her words created a tension that lay heavy in the space between her and Cam. She turned toward Everton. "I will send word through a messenger of where and when to find me. I expect you to show with or without him. Understood?"

"Yes." Everton stretched out and grabbed Cam's hand.

"Very well." Lady Aine burst into a cloud of butterflies, beetles, and dragonflies, and in seconds every insect had fluttered or skittered away, leaving no trace the fae had ever been present.

"Shit!" Cam stood, approached the long table where the Magistrates all sat, and attempted to grab the pearlescent vessel Lady Aine had given him.

The guard unleashed a whip, and in a graceful stroke of his arm, the sinewy rope lashed out, encircling Cam and holding him tight to where he stood.

"You will return to your spot immediately."

Cam's head hung. He backed up and repositioned himself beside Everton. This time Cam grabbed Everton.

"I believe sufficient punishment has been carried out for the fae. Everton Lilch, you are charged with shifting in front of humans, thus exposing the Shadow Realm. We have no ability to strip your body's lycanthropy away from you. You are, and shall always be, werewolf. However, we can prevent you from shifting for a period of time.

"It is this council's decision to halt your shifting. But to remain human seems too easy. You will shift and once in wolf form we will bind you for twelve moon cycles."

"No." Everton's eyes went wide.

"You can't!" Cam shouted.

"How can I help Cam if I'm—"

"Guards," the Magistrate called out and the man with the whip came and forcibly escorted Cam and Everton to their seats.

"Bring in the last party."

More Magistrate guardsmen appeared from a side entrance. A contingent of them, each holding a weapon. There were staves, war hammers, a mace, and a particularly sharp-looking set of khopesh swords.

In the centre of the guardsmen a heavily shackled and chained Byron and Addas—who was thankfully human— were escorted. They were led to the centre of the room and made to kneel before the Council.

"Byron Radcliffe and Addas Khoury, two highly respected members of our community, are now brought before us with a roster of committed crimes. Sacrificing fae for power. Exposing the Shadow Realm to humans. Interfering with the natural development of a witch. Illegal entrapment of community members, extortion, murder, and use of banned substances to name the most heinous infractions." The hooded figure shook their head. "I am at a loss. Needless to say, your abuse of power has been rumoured for quite some time, but we never had any proof. Now, here the evidence is all laid out before us. Do you have anything to say for yourselves?"

"I did everything to save Addas, and I would go through every effort to spare him all over again."

"As much as I understand the need to protect the ones we love, there are boundaries. You should have sought out help. But instead, you deviated into treacherous territory, and look where that has landed you."

"But he's still alive."

"Yes, but he's an abomination. Addas, your place of employment was searched on the advice of Mr. Lilch. Do you have anything to say?"

"I couldn't help myself." Addas's face had been stoic. Not any longer. He broke down. "I need help. I don't want to be this."

Chains rattled as Byron attempted to reach out for his lover, but Addas flinched and moved away from him.

"Addas Khoury, you are as far as we know, one of a kind. You will be kept here, in Sanctuary for the time being, but kept in a magically induced coma. Your abilities are unknown, as is your strength, and given the werewolf nature and bloodlust, you are also a dangerous creature with a penchant for killing. You will be studied. I do not know the outcome—if you can be saved or not—but we cannot release you into the world. Do you understand?"

Addas hung his head.

"Do you have any last words?"

"I'm sorry." Tears rolled down Addas's face, but the salty drops ran red streaks down his cheeks. His eyes filled with blood.

"Guards, Magistrate Eighty-Six, please proceed."

A guard pushed a gurney out from behind the curtains which concealed the side entrance to the dais. Another guard escorted Addas to where a silver-lined table awaited. The guard gestured for Addas to lie on the table. He hesitated but complied.

The silver made Addas's flesh sear, and although his face clearly registered pain, he accepted his fate. Every muscle in his enormous body seized, awaiting his final sentence. Addas sobbed and kept whispering over and over, "I'm sorry."

A Magistrate appeared from the side wearing a robe of blood red. They approached the gurney.

Black salt was poured around the edge of the gurney. The rock crystals would help ensure nothing magical would get in, or creep beyond the boundary.

The robed figure poured a single glass of liquid overtop of Addas. His clothes dissolved, leaving him naked and shivering. But the oddest thing happened. The only fluid poured over Addas had come from the glass, and yet the water continued to expand, filling the bottom of the table, pooling in the corners, and forming puddles. The searing of Addas's flesh stopped, and wisps of smoke left wiry trails as they snaked their way skyward, dissipating into nothing.

The fluid continued to rise, with the black salt acting as a demarcation line. Addas struggled as the liquid submerged him. The salt crystals formed the base of a cube and the water rose straight up. The effect mimicked an invisible aquarium, but the fluid was far more viscous. As the magically contained cube filled up, submerging Addas's face and nose, he struggled, fists fighting to break free, legs kicking. But the containment held fast. The water congealed, becoming thick like someone had added gelatin into the mix. The box took on a decided pink hue, but Sparks's scrutiny failed to discern if the inherent nature of the magical liquid reflected the rose colour, or if the ambient light in the room caused the unusual pigmentation. Addas's chest rose spasmodically as he gulped in the substance. He jerked a few times, then stilled, his panicked eyes closing.

Addas floated in the thickness surrounding him, and although he had been drowned while in human form, his body was forced into a magical state of relaxation. The body shifted and changed. The transformation to his werewolf-fae state wavered back and forth. His ears would elongate, then reshape to human. His muzzle formed and retracted. Fur erupted in patches, and as randomly retreated into the skin.

"This man is suffering. The containment field is meant to induce a state of paralysis and neutrality. His body is at war with itself. The corporeal form doesn't even know what state is a baseline. He must have been constantly fighting to maintain any semblance of control." The Magistrate's head dropped slightly. Sparks didn't know if the action indicated a silent prayer, or resignation to a creature meeting such a horrific fate.

"Byron Radcliffe, your fate lies before you. You have months left before your own werewolf infection comes to fruition. Your end will be similar to Addas's. Until such time, you will remain incarcerated. However, given your abilities and knowledge, you will be stripped of your power."

The Magistrate nodded once toward the red-robed figure.

"No!" Byron cried out, struggling in his chains. "No!"

Several guards surrounded him to ensure compliance. As the figure in red approached, they motioned to Byron's right arm. Three men were required to hold the struggling witch still.

Magistrate Eighty-Six pulled a crystal-tipped wand out from within a fold of the robe and, with deft movements, a slice ripped through Byron's arm. The flesh was pried apart by two more guards wearing latex gloves. Byron screamed in pain as his shadow onyx, wrapped in red silk thread, was extracted from in between his arm bones.

It didn't come willingly. After having been situated in there for years, the stone had become part of the body. No single stone would inhibit a witch's ability, but without the shadow onyx, the tether to the Shadow Realm would be weakened.

The red-robed enforcer took the stone and placed it on the table, then returned to Byron and motioned toward his chest.

The guards ripped Byron's shirt open, exposing his skin.

From another fold within the red robe, the Magistrate removed an athame.

"Byron Radcliffe, I carve *Kena* inverted into your skin. A symbol normally meant to open you up to the craft when drawn in a reversed position you become closed off from the supernatural." The blade cut deep, and the blood flowed freely. "I also invoke *Hagalaz*, the rune for radical change and catastrophe, for without your abilities you are embarking on a new journey."

Magistrate Eighty-Six raised his arm with the blade pointed high. A glimmer appeared in the air as if the currents in the massive room blew toward Byron where he kneeled.

"The Magistrate is like me, normally wearing black robes—a witch of the soul. He's absorbing energy in the room, a syphon," Dev explained quietly.

"Finally, I invoke *Isa*, the rune of stagnation, stasis, and stillness. You will be forever held in this blank state. No powers, no abilities. You are now stripped of your witch powers." The last statement echoed through the chamber; resonating vibes rippled through the room with energy the witch had gathered. The robed figure pointed the athame at the three runes carved into Byron's chest, transferring the collected power into the runes with intention.

A stillness enshrouded the stone room, which struck Sparks as odd as an amphitheatre's construction is meant to enhance any noise coming from the stage area.

One could have heard a pin drop.

And then...

A single bass note reverberated like someone had hit a massive drum. A ripple emanated in a shock wave out from Byron.

The stilling had ended.

Magistrate Eighty-Six took a few steps away. The guards picked up Byron, who didn't fight. He hung as limp as a rag doll in their arms.

"Well, he won't be causing any more problems for anyone," Tully said, but a hint of fear trembled in his voice.

"May that never happen to any of us." Dev grimaced.

Sparks's wide eyes absorbed the horror he had witnessed. Living without his magic would be worse than death. The brief amount of time Byron had ripped his naturally born abilities away from him left a lasting impression. Sparks focused on watching Byron being hauled away, trying to forget the rest of what he'd already seen.

"Tully, Sparks, please come forward."

Sparks glanced at Tully, and Tully nodded his head in the direction they were meant to go.

"Go, for Gods' sakes don't make them wait," Dev whispered.

Sparks and Tully made their way to where they had stood before.

"These amber shards were determined to be, in fact, as Dev stated, part of a soul trap. Your essences are captured within. Another abuse of Byron's power." The Magistrate stood, picked up both pieces, examined them, and held each one close to Tully and Sparks. "Tully, this is yours. Sparks, this one belongs to you. Smash them at your feet, please."

Doing as told, the boys hoisted the rocks above their heads and threw them at the ground near their shoes.

The impact shattered the stone, and the captured essence within swirled up and, sensing their respective owners, twirled around their bodies, until they were absorbed.

Tully breathed in deep, while the hole within Sparks filled, making him whole again.

"Better?" they were asked. Tully bowed in acknowledgement. Sparks mimicked his lover in order to maintain a good standing with the enforcers. "Good. Tully." The Magistrate nodded to one of the guards, who disappeared beyond the curtain, then returned with a large glass jar containing a swirling mass of vines. "I believe this is yours."

"Phineas!" Tully beamed.

The guard lifted the lid on the jar only to have Phineas torpedo itself out and scamper across the floor toward Tully. As he outstretched his arm, Phineas leaped, tendrils snapping like whips until they lashed around Tully's wrist. As the Earth elemental burrowed its way into Tully's arm, he winced, but smiled knowing the creature had returned.

"Please return to your seats, but take your cell phones with you. Dev, please?"

Dev climbed down and presented himself. "Do you know what this is?" The Magistrate held up an amulet.

"No, I do not."

"This has your name engraved on it. There are a number of runes also burned onto the object. However, our inspection also revealed the amulet has been cursed. Byron would have planted this on you if he had had the opportunity. Never wear it, but I give it over to you to do with as you wish."

"May I ask, what is the curse?"

"Solitude."

Dev shivered, glancing at both Sparks and Tully. Reluctantly he took the item, pinching the leather strap that had been strung through an eyelet, careful not to come into contact with the object.

"It won't do you any harm unless you wear it. The curse is fresh and has been recently laid overtop of what had been created as a talisman of welcoming. The runes nestled into the goat's head symbol were used often by the Guardians of the Night Grove. By chance were you thinking of joining the Guardians at some point?"

"I had been asked. That never came to fruition."

"I see. Well, I believe the intent had been to give the talisman to you upon your agreement to join the Guardians. Regardless, this belongs to you. Please take your cell device as well."

Dev returned to his seat, still carefully keeping the amulet as far away from himself as possible. Tully took it from Dev and slid the cursed thing into his pocket.

"Cameron and Everton, please." The Magistrate gestured to the spot where she wanted them.

The red-robed figure appeared once more.

"No. Please, not yet," Cam cried out.

"Punishments are exacted the day the sentence is delivered. There are no exceptions."

Ev and Cam made their way down to where the Magistrate had wanted them, but before anything happened, Ev grabbed Cam, hugged and kissed him.

"It's only a year. I won't be able to talk to you, but I'll never leave your side. I promise."

As Cam clung to Ev, he shifted into his wolf form. With all the snaps and morphing body parts, Cam ended up on the floor hugging the thickly furred scruff around Ev's wolfen neck. Ev licked his lips, and with his snout, nuzzled Cam's ear.

Cam's next breath hitched as he clung tight to his man.

The enforcer removed a talisman in the shape of a wolf's head from around his neck and placed the necklace over Ev's head. The minute the carved wolf made contact with Ev's fur, it melted into his body.

"The amulet will keep you bound like this for a year and one day from now. Perhaps you will take the time to contemplate appropriate places to release your wolf. As with all werewolves, your wolf form is not a true measure of the canine species, and therefore, your presence anywhere will be in question. You must remain hidden for the duration of your sentence."

Cam sneered at the Magistrate.

"I'm sorry, young man, but there are consequences to actions taken. No one creature within the Shadow Realm is exempt. Magic is not free. There are costs to everything. I have no electronic device for you, but Ev's is here, as is your satchel and this vial, which originally had been collected empty, and now the vial appears to be filled. With what, I am not certain, but this is yours nonetheless."

Cam grabbed the items, shoved the cell and the bottle into his hip sack, tied the strings around his waist, and retreated to his seat. Ev padded behind him.

"You are free to go, but Dev, Tully, and Sparks—remember—one month from now your task must be completed."

The guardsmen and the Magistrates left the amphitheatre.

Chapter Twenty-Six

IN ORDER TO maintain a level of secrecy, the Council had hooded Cam and Everton, Tully, Dev, and Sparks, kept them cuffed, and deposited them where they had been picked up, near the Kinsmen Sports Complex.

Discarded in the parking lot, they were left to their own devices. The boys split up with Cam and Ev going one way and the witch men going their own.

It became a dodgy business getting Everton back to the pack house without half of Edmonton seeing its first werewolf. But they made their way home by slinking through the river valley and keeping to the dense brush. Thank all the Gods the last throes of summer had left the majority of the leaf canopy intact and the annual defoliation hadn't started in earnest.

Upon arrival, Franco greeted them at the back door. They only had an hour or so until sunset, then moonrise would happen shortly after. Franco had a litany of never-ending questions about why Everton had shifted. Cam spilled the beans and explained the punishments. With Ev being in a perpetual state of werewolf-hood for the next year, the first evening of a full moon promised to be filled with surprises. Either Ev would continue with his regular wolfen state, or his werewolfisms would ramp up. To be on the safe side, Franco took Everton to *the shed*, where the wolf would be chained and shackled alongside Serge. This way the motion-activated cameras would pick up the night's activities and Franco would be able to review the footage the next day. As soon as Cam turned to leave, Ev whined.

The whimper sent a spike through Cam's heart.

"I'll be back tomorrow. I promise." Cam went into the cage, wrapped his arms around Everton's massive wolf head, and scratched his guy behind the ears.

Everton nuzzled into the scritches, his tail thumping a steady beat of happiness. Cam closed his eyes and contemplated the next year of his life. His boyfriend would be a wolf, enjoying pets. This would take some getting used to.

Franco would be shifting soon as well and would have to assume pack lead for a while longer.

"You know, Josip and I are probably okay to be around, but you'd most likely be safer staying with your friend if that's possible. I mean, I don't want to kick you out, I'm just trying to think of what Ev would do."

"You're right. Can I use your phone? I'll call Dev and ask."

After a brief conversation with an exhausted Dev, Tully, and Sparks they were glad to welcome Cam for the night.

"Do you have time to drive me over?" Cam asked Franco.

"As long as we make it quick. Let's go." Franco palmed Cam's shoulder as they headed out of the back door.

Cam swore the entire ride over to Dev's as his tummy lurched and heaved. He didn't feel right, and now he questioned this whole "sickness" thing Lady Aine had mentioned.

SPARKS, TULLY, AND Dev had been rudely tossed to the curb, unshackled and unhooded. The van which had transported them screeched away. Ev and Cam took off through the river valley to get Everton home as fast as possible. Tully's car had had a sleepover in the rec centre's parking lot, only now the windshield sported a lovely parking ticket.

"Damn it." Tully ripped the infraction out from underneath the windshield wiper blade. "Two hundred and fifty dollars!" His eyes bugged out as he scanned the paper.

"I'll help cover the costs," Sparks offered.

"As will I." Dev leaned into his boyfriend. "I'm exhausted. Let's get home."

"Guys, do you mind if you drop me off at my apartment?"

"Of course not!" Tully shot a questioning glance toward Dev.

Sparks frowned as he took note of the disheartened tone left hanging between him and the guys.

"I need some time. I think we all do. I mean, how can you argue with a God, or a house with shifting walls? Honestly, I've never heard of a building spelled to remodelling itself to accommodate more people. As magically delicious as that would be to live in…I need some time to piece everything together and figure out how I see myself in all of this."

"Sure thing." Dev put a hand on Sparks's shoulder, but a ripple of disappointment flashed across his face.

"Don't worry. I need some "me" time to get my head on straight. It's all good." Sparks attempted to ease the tension.

Instead, the drive to Sparks's place deepened the stress between the three. Sparks had hoped his words would de-escalate the strain, not ramp up everyone to a tipping point. His words were meant to allay any unrest. Sparks needed to take a step back, evaluate, and figure out how to move forward for himself.

Dev's phone rang, which helped to break the silence, and when Cam had asked if the guys would mind putting him up for the night—away from the werewolves—the anxiety and nerves stirring up Sparks tapered off. He needed a night to himself and his thoughts; besides, the guys would be busy with Cam.

CAM ENDED UP arriving at Dev's place about the same time they did. Franco didn't even get out of the car. Time ticked away closing in on the full moon, so Cam exited as quickly as possible with his bulky wings and let Franco go. As he drove off, he threw his hand out of the window and waved goodbye.

"Was it something we said?" Tully asked Cam as Franco left.

"No. It's a full moon and Franco's got limited time to get home before...well, you know."

"Ah, right." Dev nodded. "Okay, let's get you inside before the neighbours think they're seeing things." Dev glanced at Cam's wings, which sputtered. "Please don't tell me you're hungry, because we haven't had time to replenish anything since your last visit."

"No, actually, I feel like crap. I think all I want to do is lay down and sleep for a while."

"Well, I think we can accommodate your request."

They headed up to their second-floor condo when Tully stopped. "I should go check in on Uncle Bart. He's been left alone for almost two days. I'll be up in a bit. Besides, I need to ask him if he has any contact with the Montreal group. We need to get on this ley line business."

Dev leaned over and gave Tully a peck. "Don't be too long."

Dev and Cam continued upstairs. Once in the apartment, Dev took Cam to his office where there had been a small love seat. That would have to suffice for now as a bed for Cam. But upon them entering the room, the small couch had been replaced with a murphy bed tucked up against the wall.

"Well, seems the house was expecting you." Dev gave Cam a "whatever" gesture, throwing his hands out to his sides. "This house is beyond weird."

From Dev's office which now also doubled as a guest bedroom, Tully announced his arrival. "Hey, honey, I'm homo!"

Dev rolled his eyes and Cam snickered. "We're in here," Dev responded.

Tully found them both and appeared as surprised as everyone else with the recent furniture addition. "When did we get a murphy bed?"

"Tonight, apparently. You can thank the house."

"So weird. I wish I had asked Uncle Bart about his auto-renovating home, but there's a note on his door that says to leave him be for twenty-four hours. Problem is, I don't know when that note went up, and so when is twenty-four hours up? I knocked, but Uncle Bart didn't answer."

Cam flopped down onto the pulled-out bed and sighed. The mattress had bounce to it, and after sitting on the comfy memory foam top, he had to admit he was bushed.

"Well, give him the night. We can check in on him to-morrow." A corner of Dev's mouth tipped up in a gentle half smile.

Tully pointed at their house guest. "I think he's done."

Cam had passed out.

SPARKS DROPPED HIS keys on the kitchen counter, add-ing to the hodgepodge mess of items. He stripped as he made his way toward his bedroom. He studied his tiny apartment. Piles of books and papers littered most flat surfaces. The shelving units desperately needing dusting, and the kitchen sink had a mountain of dishes begging to be washed. He never spent much time here, either pulling extra shifts at the hospital or going out with friends, and that made him wonder why.

Why did his home not provide comfort?

Regardless of the stacks of books, his plants, knick-knacks, and photos that evoked memories, without someone to share them with, Sparks wallowed in loneliness. And for him, being alone exaggerated the emptiness of the apartment, despite all the things contained within it. Hearing Byron had cursed an amulet meant for Dev with solitude sent shivers down his spine. Sparks relished conversations with other people, having someone else's energy in the same room, enjoying a movie together or even sitting quietly and reading. Knowing someone else shared the house had huge appeal. Didn't matter if any interaction occurred or not. Physically being present around others helped to ground Sparks.

If Sparks didn't want to be alone, then wasn't the prospect of having two people around him at any time even better?

A solid reason explaining why the concept of three together in a relationship unnerved him didn't surface. Was his apprehension the fear of something different, or going against societal norms? If that was the case being gay should have bothered him more. But being different than the perceived norm didn't flummox Sparks, and the opinions of others had never been important to him. Perhaps the nagging realization that relationships in general were hard enough between two people, never mind three, bothered him? The last thing he'd ever want would be to ruin the friendships he currently had with Dev and Tully, and introducing intimacy added another layer of complexity to an existing relationship.

Sparks ran his fingers through his hair and grimaced as his fingers grazed over the shaved part of his head. The tender skin complained at the touch and would do so for a while. He walked to the bathroom and attempted to look at the back of his head by using two mirrors.

The reddened skin still had blisters, and the hair had been buzzed right short if not burnt off altogether. Sparks said a silent prayer to the Gods that the burns wouldn't disrupt the growth or density of his hair.

He frowned. Everyone knew Sparks by his long hair. An investment of three years had been required, coupled with an assortment of hair products and routine care in order to keep his locks in good condition. Maybe change would be good.

With the top still long, the varying lengths didn't match. He'd have to visit a barber shop tomorrow and get a professional to fix the mess.

In the meantime, his mind wandered back to Dev and Tully.

Sparks's apartment overflowed, stuffed to the brim with witchy things. He rarely threw anything out and had amassed quite a collection of books and occult things, and that didn't even include all the workbooks, robes, and assorted projects he kept with the coven. Would the guys want all this stuff in their house? Did he come as an entire package? When they asked him to move in, did they take into account the numerous boxes coming with him?

Sparks sauntered into the living room and perused his living quarters, his eyes stopping on the terrarium in the corner that held not only a small handful of plants, but also his mating pair of crested geckos. Would they be welcome too?

There were too many questions, all overwhelming Sparks with the speed at which his brain tussled and warred with the varying pros and cons. So there was only one thing to do—a long hot bath with some lit candles, a stick of incense, and a prayer to the Gods.

Hopefully, he'd find some answers.

CAM TOSSED AND turned all night long.

Feverish and sweating, he conceded to being ill.

Normally, a night's sleep left him refreshed the next morning. The dull ache in his muscles and the thudding in his head, and the wild swings between sweats and chills guaranteed a fitful night devoid of sleep. If he did happen to doze off, his brain entertained him with horrifying images of Addas's wolf-like fae creature who prowled after him, only to catch him and rip off his wings. In the next dream Cam had gone feral and his blood-red eyes pierced through the darkness while his elongated teeth sunk into a ripped-off leg from some human.

The disturbing images became more and more grotesque, and the blur of emotions teetered on rage mixed with fear. Eventually he woke up with a terrifying start, drenched in cold sweat, and having soaked through the bedsheets.

Cam glanced at the clock on the wall. It was still early. The first sunrays of morning lightened the room he occupied. The sky's colours melted from black to dark purple, pinks, and oranges. He figured a nice hot soak would do him good, and despite being wrapped up in a blanket he shivered. He needed a bath. Or better yet, a hot tub!

He left his bedroom, crept down the hallway, opened the back door, and slinked his way down to Uncle Bart's soup pot.

He pried open the lid. A rush of stream greeted him as he propped the canopy open, and climbed in.

The hot water settled in his bones as the enveloping steam obscured his vision evaporating the stress of the last few days. At ease and toasty, Cam closed his eyes, finally comfortable.

SPARKS AWOKE THE next day having meditated half the night. He had come to a conclusion.

He had to put trust and faith in his Gods and follow through on what they had asked of him, otherwise he didn't feel right in calling himself a witch. There would have to be some ground rules set out with Dev and Tully, requiring a lengthy conversation, but one Sparks grew confident in having, knowing the results would be fair and most likely agreeable.

Regardless of figuring out how he needed to move forward, he still harboured some anxiety over the change in relationship status.

But conviction had won over anxiety and lack of self-confidence. With grit and determination, Sparks had a lengthy to-do list for the day and he set out early enough to get everything done.

First stop would be to grab coffee at the local Tim Hortons, where he also picked up his favourite breakfast sandwich. Then he made one additional side trip to Spirited.

"Well, look at what the cat dragged in!" Naggy sat behind the counter propped up on a stool that elevated him high enough he could survey his shop, and its customers. He greedily eyed up Sparks, then took note in the change of hairstyle. "What the hell happened to your gorgeous hair?"

"Thanks, Naggy, good to see you too. Ah, an accident."

"Boy, some accident! Damn, those burns look painful."

"Yeah, they don't feel great either."

"Wait, I've got something for the blisters." Naggy jumped off his seat and disappeared into the storage room. Sparks had only come in to see if he had any extra boxes.

He'd made the decision to jump into this throuple thing. Over the course of the next few days, he would have to pack up all his things, give notice on his apartment, clean it, and move everything over to the sprawling mansion.

Naggy showed up a few minutes later and handed him a jar with gelatinous green goo in it. "You rub a tablespoon of the salve on those burns three times a day. In two days, those blisters will be gone. In a week, you'll never even know you were torched. No scars either. Promise."

"How much is this going to cost me?" After shelling out sixty dollars for a bottle of spelled wine that had been a catalyst for the crazy events of the past week, Sparks's level of trust in Naggy had waned.

"Nah, for friends, I give the stuff out for free." Naggy winked.

"Wow, thanks." Sparks uttered, genuinely surprised at Naggy's generosity. A trait the Clurichaun had never been known for. "That's actually not what I came in here for."

"Do tell. Another bottle of wine? I only have a couple bottles left. Good price today if you buy both!"

"I hoped I could take some empty boxes off your hands."

"Well, I guess so. We got our shipment in two days ago and I haven't broken them all down yet, so you're welcome to them. Are you moving?"

"I think so."

"You think so?"

"Yeah. I need to figure out some details first, but I want to be prepared in case everything works out."

"Are you leaving us?"

"Oh no. Just moving in with Dev and Tully." The minute the words fell from his lips, Sparks regretted speaking.

"You don't say!" Naggy raised a single eyebrow and licked his lips.

"Um, yeah, so, where are those boxes?"

Naggy continued his leer as he pointed to the back of the store. "Go help yourself. The only price on those are details. I want to know all the details."

"Naggy, you're a perv."

Naggy shrugged, not arguing the callout, as he ogled Sparks's backside. Knowing full well Naggy stared at his ass, Sparks wriggled it as he went through the swinging doors into the storage room to pick through the discarded empty boxes. "You still haven't spilled the beans about the Guardians!" Naggy yelled over his shoulder.

Sparks chuckled, but mostly ignored him. After stuffing as many boxes as possible into his beat-up Volkswagen Rabbit, he made his way to his next stop—the barber. After getting pretty, he'd make his way over to Dev and Tully's and have *the conversation*.

Chapter Twenty-Seven

CAM HAD RESTED in the warm water of the hot tub for hours. His skin had wrinkled and pruned. Despite the soak in the bubbles his body continued to ache. His eyes had crusted shut and with his wings waterlogged, lifting himself out of the water required more energy than he had. The fairy mojo juice had run out, and the caffeine levels had evaporated.

Cam resigned himself to death by waterlogged skin.

The back door to the house opened and the *clomp clomp clomp* of footsteps descending the wooden stairs from the upper deck to the patio where the tub lay on a cement pad ricocheted around the yard. Within the confines of the hot tub, the footsteps sounded like cannon shots.

"Oh my Gods! Tully, he's down here." Dev's hand went under Cam's armpit, and he rose a few inches out of the water. Seconds later, Tully's monster arms had grabbed him and hoisted him out of the tub. Water splashed everywhere.

"For fuck's sake, Cam, you scared the shit out of us. The bed in the spare room is soaked with sweat, the sheets are strewn halfway down the hall, and you left the fridge door wide open. You were nowhere to be found...until now. What the hell is going on?"

"I'm sorry, Dev. I don't feel good. Where's Ev?" Cam wanted his wolfman.

"He's delusional," Dev said to Tully. "What the hell are we going to do with him?"

"I don't know. But he's obviously suffering from the sickness Lady Aine had mentioned. Let's get him upstairs, dried off, and hopefully settle him."

For the next hour Dev and Tully pampered Cam, took him inside, kept him warm and dry, while Dev also tried to get him to drink soup, but the only thing Cam craved was coffee. Strong, black coffee.

"Caffeine is not going to do you any favours, but if drinking a cup of joe means you'll ingest some fluids then so be it." Dev made him a pot. Tully had disappeared to the grocery store to get Cam some meat.

After Cam's third cup of coffee, he perked up, feeling marginally better. His brain fog cleared, and he sat upright engaging in conversation with Dev.

"Do you suppose I might have more?" Cam held out the empty mug.

"Jeez, Cam, I don't know if that's a good idea." Dev made a weird face which Cam interpreted as concern.

"Please. It's the only thing I'm craving."

"Okay, well, you know your body best. Speaking of...what is this disease Lady Aine referenced at the Council?"

"I don't know. Something about fae folk who are exiled or cut off from other fae folk. I saw something once in my textbook, but...boring."

"And you didn't learn about it."

"No. I got distracted thinking about Everton. Where is he, again?"

"At the pack house. Today is the full moon, so they've chained him up to make sure he doesn't go all loopy."

"Right—I knew that."

"So, you've been exiled, and cut off from the rest of your kind. Lady Aine delivered a fairly harsh sentence on you. You must have really pissed her off." Dev shot Cam a knowing look.

"Yeah, yeah. I know. Look, her expectations are a little out of whack. I mean, first of all, she wanted me to get her pregnant." Cam rolled his eyes.

"Well, that would never happen."

"This is what I told her, but then—" Cam's eyes popped open wide. "Shit. Dev, where's my hip sack?

"The ridiculous fanny pack you wear? I don't know, maybe you left it in the bedroom. Let me go look."

Dev walked down the hall.

"Found your purse!" Dev returned to the kitchen holding the leather bag lined in fur.

"Gimme?" Cam held his hand out.

Dev passed the bag over.

Cam opened the drawstrings and let out an audible sigh as he pulled out Lady Aine's pretty glass vial.

"I cannot lose this, and I need to return the vessel to Lady Aine." Cam glanced up at Dev. "Can you drive me to the Ancestral Lands?"

"But what about the Council, and Lady Aine's words? You were barred."

"Well, if Lady Aine wants to get pregnant, she better let me deliver this." Cam waved the vessel in front of Dev's face.

Dev made a gagging noise, "Don't tell your come is in there."

"Yup. It sure the hell is. And funny story, Ev and I finally did the nasty."

"What? When?"

"While we were incarcerated."

"You fucked in prison? Oh my Gods. You dirty boy."

Cam waggled his eyebrows, "Yeah, but you know, I didn't even have this vial. Crazy thing, Ev made me come, several times, but I never got...well...sticky. No spooge, no wet spots, the come disappeared! When the Magistrates put the vial up on the table at the Council, the sheen in the glass had a different colour. The bottle is obviously spelled because all my spunk ended up—"

Dev threw his hand up, "Once again, too much info. Way too much info. Why does Lady Aine want to get pregnant so bad, and better question—how come you're the one to do it?"

"Apparently there can only ever be one fertile Royal male fae, and right now, I'm it. So, I have to make sure she can produce babies next spring."

"Good Gods."

"I don't think a good God had anything to do with this. Like, I never wanted to be a parent, or a donor, or...whatever. But this task is the one condition I have to meet. I fucked up on the getting caught part, but maybe if Lady Aine gets this, she'll reconsider my exile?"

"Well, it's worth a shot."

The front door opened, and Tully walked in with several bags.

"Since when does everyone do their shopping first thing in the morning at the grocery store? I don't think I've ever seen that many people there. Apparently today is the day for food. You're lucky the meat selection still had choices." Tully hoisted filled plastic bags and laid them on the kitchen counter. "You hungry yet, Cam?"

"I could eat. Whatchya got?" Cam peered over the counter and tried to get a peek into the bags.

"I didn't know what would sit well for you, so I bought a steak, some chicken, a whole salmon, and a tray of pork cutlets. Take your pick."

"Hmmm, let's try the steak first. Sometimes chicken makes me gag."

Tully pulled out the raw slab of flesh and let Cam at it.

While Cam munched away on his protein, Dev got Tully up to speed. "So, he wants us to drive him out to the Ancestral Lands."

"But what about the exile? Like, you can't ever go there."

"I have to try!" Cam's garbled words flew out in between half-chewed chunks of cow.

The doorbell rang downstairs.

"What now?" Dev grumbled.

"I'll go get it. Why don't you get Cam ready to drive out? It's a long way. If we leave soon, we can still be home before midnight," Tully offered, then ran down the hallway, and out of the front door.

"You sure you want to go today?"

"I kinda need to. Lady Aine insisted I had to get this to her before Groundswell, and she also mentioned something about the weather behaving oddly. There's a distinct possibility Groundswell might happen sooner than normal. Besides, I don't know how long this stays fresh. You know?" Cam lifted and shook the Royal glass vessel.

Dev stuck his tongue out and faked a gag. "Please don't remind me of the contents. But yes, okay, I get it. Important. Do you have anything warmer to wear?"

"No, this is it. A loincloth. Let's face it, there isn't much I can wear with these damn things." Cam fluttered the appendages protruding from his shoulder blades. The membranous wings vibrated, enough to make the point. Besides, beating his wings right now took effort and energy, two things he currently lacked.

"I guess. Well, let me go rustle up a blanket. If you're going to keep being feverish, we need to keep you warm."

"Look who I found?" Tully beamed as he walked into the kitchen with Sparks in tow. Tully had a box in his arms, and Sparks had a couple balanced one on top of the other. "I think maybe we should put these in your office."

"Wait. Let's talk first?" Sparks asked.

Cam propped himself up and put his head in his hands while leaning forward. This conversation was bound to be good.

"Okay." Tully set the box down on the floor.

"I haven't slept much the past couple of nights thinking about all of this. And I still have reservations."

"Well, same, to be honest." Dev leaned against the counter.

"Yeah." Sparks glanced at the floor. "But I keep going back to the fact Cernunnos asked us to be together. And you are the only two people in the world who can hear my thoughts. And vice versa. That's a strong connection not everyone gets to experience, and the telepathy will also keep us honest, right?"

"Agreed. But remember we said we'd work our way through this?" Tully glanced between the two of them.

"Absolutely." Dev grinned at Sparks and Tully. Cam sat quietly absorbing every word. The boys had forgotten he even existed.

"So, I brought over a few packed boxes. Basically, my witch stuff I'm using a lot right now. I'll leave them here if that's okay. But maybe the rest can follow in a few weeks? I also brought over a few changes of clothes and some toiletries in case..."

"In case you stay the night." Tully clapped Sparks on the back, then pulled him into a side hug. "I'm good with this. We'll go at the whole relationship thing at a snail's pace, make sure everyone is comfortable."

"Do you mind?" Sparks asked them both.

"No. I don't. I think it's a smart way forward," Dev said.

"Okay, group hug." Tully motioned Dev over. Tully's massively bearish arms encircled Dev and Sparks, and the three of them hugged it out.

"One small question," Sparks squeaked out, buried next to Tully's chest. Tully released them.

"Sure!"

"How do you guys feel about geckos?"

"You mean, like, the lizard type of gecko?"

"Yeah."

"Why?"

"Well, if I'm eventually moving over here...you should know I have a pair of mating crested geckos. Bernadette and Ralph can be a little noisy, they croak, believe it or not, and Bernie lays eggs pretty regularly. I raise the babies and then sell them. Makes me some extra money, and it's fun."

"They eat insects, no?" Dev asked.

"Yeah, they need the protein as part of their diet."

"And where do you keep these insects?" Tully stared at Sparks, suitably horrified.

"If you're worried about keeping insects in the house, I can have them delivered twice a week. They'll go immediately into their vivarium, and you'll never even know they're around. Usually, I keep them in a specialized container, and they sit on a bookshelf next to their environment."

"I just don't like the idea of the crickets or whatever getting loose." Tully squirmed.

"We can figure out where to store the crickets," Dev suggested, wrapping an arm around Tully. "The geckos are welcome. I think I'm excited to meet Bernadette and Ralph."

"Cool. You'll like them. I promise. They're really friendly, and they like to be cuddled! The babies are super cute too." Sparks sighed.

"Another adventure. Why not? We were just about to leave. Why don't you come with us?" Dev tugged his head to the side indicating the direction of the front door.

"Where are we going?"

"Cam has a delivery to make to the Ancestral Lands." Dev explained.

"But I thought—" Sparks started, but Tully shut him down.

"Yeah, us too." Tully peered over Dev's shoulder at Cam, who watched everything intently. "You ready?"

"Yup. I need a blanket and another cup of coffee." Cam beamed all sharp toothy like.

"I'll never get used to his new teeth," Tully whispered silently but enough for Dev and Sparks's ears only, as he stared in the opposite direction from Cam.

"Still heard ya. Fae thing. Hearing is amazing." Cam winked.

THE BOYS DESCENDED to the main floor of the house. Dev had a careful watch on Cam, as his unsteady gait made him nervous. Cam, being fae, should have been light on his feet. Not this morning. Cam's steps were clunky and uneven, tripping over his own toes. Dev tried to steady him, but his best bud waved and shooed him away. Sparks led the way, and he kept glancing over his shoulder to make sure Cam wasn't going to topple over and take him out.

Taking Sparks's car, even though it was small, and compact, made the most sense. Sparks assured them despite its age, the car performed like a tank and would easily get them to the Ancestral Lands and back—a good three-hour drive there, and another three coming home. In addition, the amount of head and leg room exceeded Tully's Audi, especially considering Cam's horns and wings, and Cam's new propensity for getting car sick, Tully loved Sparks's suggestion.

"I'm going to go check on Uncle Bart before we go. It's been a minute. You got this?"

"Yeah, we're good. Say hi to the old man for me." Dev gave Tully a half grin and redirected Cam toward the front door and out to Sparks's parked car.

Once out to the car, putting Cam in the front became the clear choice, given the horns and wings and tail, not that they were visible—illusion magic and all—but they were still there. The front seat allowed Cam some additional room to adjust should he need to do so. Sparks and Dev stood outside the car, waiting for Tully.

"You've got your semen jar?" Dev asked.

"When you put it like that, eww. Yes, I have it." Cam tapped his hip sack where the vessel lay neatly packed away.

Tully emerged from the house in two shakes, way too fast, and as he approached the car, he had a piece of paper in his hands.

"What have you got?" Dev asked.

"The note from Uncle Bart."

Don't bother me.

I'm fine.

I promise I'll take my meds.

No interruptions for the next day!

Dev read the note, then showed the paper to Sparks.

"Hmph. Wonder what the old man is up to?" Sparks eyed the note.

"Or who!" Tully chuckled.

Everyone gaped at Tully with a side-eye.

"What? He's old, sure, but not dead. The man's got needs. And we all know what he does on his tablet all day. Surely this means he's got a hot and heavy date. Stop looking at me like that. There's nothing wrong with Uncle Bart getting a little."

"Okay, we're getting in the car now." Sparks laughed.

Once everyone had piled in, Sparks revved up Bunny, the name he'd given his car. He made a stop at the gas station to fill her up, and to get everyone snacks and drinks, and to ensure Cam had the largest offering of coffee the gas station offered.

THE LONG DRIVE down the Yellowhead highway seemed even longer with Sparks's choice in music. Cam never understood Country, although Sparks promised his playlist contained a mixed variety of musical styles. There didn't end up being enough music Cam liked.

"Pull over here." Cam pointed to the side of the road as he undid his seatbelt, and in a shimmer of fae magic, let loose the illusion spell he'd maintained the moment they stepped out of Dev's house. After all, he'd been caught once. He didn't need to be apprehended a second time.

"Here? There's nothing but trees!" Sparks slowed the car, unsure where to park.

"Just anywhere. It's flat, put the car in the ditch. We have to go through this tree line."

"Well, I'm glad you remember, I sure as hell would not have," Dev remarked as everyone piled out of the car and stretched. Dev and Tully had taken Cam to the Ancestral Lands with Ev the first time a couple of months ago.

"Come on, it's this way." Cam tromped off, hiking through the bush. The guys faithfully followed.

An hour later, Dev politely inquired on the direction and length of their hike.

"Shh. We're almost there," Cam replied.

No one talked, and the scenery consisted of pine trees and a dirt forest floor. The shedding needles from the coniferous trees made the underlying soil acidic and inhospitable to underbrush. The occasional clearing would crop up, but this late in August the tall grasses that grew here were already done for the season. The landscape featured a lot of tawny brown.

Cam unexpectedly slowed, and abruptly stopped.

"I can't go any further." He took a step back.

"Are you too tired? Should we rest?" Dev asked.

"No, I'm fine. I mean I physically cannot move forward. We must be close."

"Ah, so you are exiled for good. Lady Aine created a barrier so you can't get close to the Ancestral Village. Smart lady." Tully pursed his lips, obviously unhappy about the current turn of events.

"I think it's brilliant, but that means we have to carry on instead of Cam and deliver his goods." Dev frowned.

Cam fumbled with the ties on his leather hip sack until they loosened. He pulled the purse off and handed his bag to Dev. "Here you go. Do not, under any circumstances, drop this." Cam glared at Dev to drive home the importance of the mission.

Dev grimaced as he cautiously stretched out a hand to take the precious parcel.

"KEEP GOING IN the same direction you are going in now. You'll come to a huge mountain ash tree in the centre of a glen, which is surrounded by hills on each side. There'll be a path on the western edge that will lead you right to the village. Two ancient Douglas fir trees mark the beginning of the path. You can't miss it." Cam detailed the entrance to the Ancestral Lands.

"Okay. How far away is the entrance from here?" Dev asked.

"I don't remember. Can't be far though."

"You guys go. I'll stay with Cam and make sure nothing bad happens," Sparks said.

Cam shot him an ugly look. "What do you mean 'nothing bad'? I can look after myself."

"You're exhausted and you still have a blanket wrapped around you. You're pale as fuck, and we know you have some kind of sickness. I think it's a grand idea, Sparks. Thank you." Dev canted his head once and thought to Sparks *Thank you*, then turned as he and Tully took off toward the Ancestral Village.

It didn't take as long as Dev expected, but sure enough, they crested a small hill only to see a large clearing beneath them, with a single tree in the centre.

"This must be the clearing. Look, over there, does that look like a path?" Dev asked.

"I think so, let's go check it out." Tully walked toward a narrow trail in between two large trees.

They stomped through the grass and headed down the path, but as soon as they were both past the guardian trees, the trail through the forest branched in multiple directions.

"Another way to hide the village?" Tully asked.

"Would appear so. Again, smart. Now, which way?"

"Can you use your witchy tracking thing?" Tully suggested.

"Damn, you smart. And handsome. Grand idea. Although I've never attempted to track a place before. People, yes. But people move making the internal compass wacky and hard to follow. A physical location should be easy!" Dev grasped Cam's vessel, as the item had originated from the Ancestral Lands. Having something physical from the area to hold should make dowsing the location far easier.

And as luck would have it, his God-gifted ability came through. The multiple paths in front of them merged into a single way forward, and within a kilometre or so of walking, they came across the most unusual land formations.

Tubes jutted up from the ground right in front of them, wisps of smoke rising in curlicues. Their aroma contained hints of sandalwood and patchouli. Those weren't scents you'd normally find out in the woods.

Off in the distance, a low-grade rumble shifted the ground and Dev and Tully had to brace themselves against a tree as the earth beneath them shook and moved. A section of the ground, less than a city block away from them, sunk and what had once been chimney spouts disappeared.

"Oh shit." Dev's eyes went as wide as saucers.

"We're too late, aren't we?" Tully's jaw hung open.

"Cam is going to be so disappointed. Worse, Lady Aine won't get pregnant. She'll be pissed with Cam. There's no way he'll lose his exile status now."

A chimney pipe poking through the ground in front of them swelled. From the top of the pipe, the rising smoke stopped, and instead, the longest set of fingers emerged.

Gripping the edge of the conduit, a hand appeared to be pulling itself up.

An elbow popped out.

Before Dev and Tully registered what they were witnessing, a long, sinewy, ash-toned fae stood before them. Its hair was a vibrant shocking red. Its facial features were fine and pointed. Its digits impossibly long and slender.

"You are Dev, which makes the redheaded one Tully." The creature pointed. "I am Sen. I am a manservant to your human-made-fae friend Cam."

"Cam spoke of you!" Dev's unease with the strange creature evaporated after learning Cam's friend had come to meet them.

"I'm sure he did. I hear he caused trouble in the human world. I am not surprised." Sen frowned and shook his head.

"Well, he kind of saved the day. He used his fae magic to disperse a wraith."

"He did what? He produced that much light? Impressive." Sen placed a long finger up against his lips. "I did not think his highness would be capable of such a feat. Most extraordinary. Maybe he learned something after all."

"I think Cam learned a lot of things over the course of the last few months. I mean a human who becomes fae? That had to be a huge adjustment."

"Very true. I tried my best to give Cam all the lessons he would need. His talents for academia were, shall we say, wanting. But hearing about his bravery and successes now, means maybe I didn't fail him quite so bad."

"No, Sen, I think you helped him." Tully chortled thinking of all the ways Cam had wormed his way into everyone's heart, not to mention his bravery.

"I must go, now. I had heard you from below, and saw you through our periscope, and I recognized you immediately from Cam's descriptions, so I had to come and say hi. And I wanted news of Cam. Is he well?"

"We think he is sick. He has not been well lately."

"Yes, the separation sickness. We call it *melancholinitis*. Most fae left alone in the world do not survive. Separation hurts. Being cut off from your own kind, especially when you have not learned the ways of your own, is deadly. If you have traditions and customs to cling to, you remember who you are. If you do not have those, you have no way to connect to your own identity when you are so far away from your own."

"Oh my Gods. That's so simple and makes so much sense. Can Cam get better?" Tully raised his eyebrows in interest.

"Possibly. There might be a way. But I cannot just give the answer to you."

"Why not?" Tully furrowed his brows, miffed at Sen's response.

"Fae do not give gifts away. We exchange them. You must have something for me in return."

"Oh, we definitely have a gift." Knowing full well Dev had the most precious gift of all, he retrieved Lady Aine's vessel from Cam's hip sack.

"Oh!" Sen gasped. "You have the Royal vial. Is it...?"

"Yes. Cam filled the vial."

"So, we may continue the lineage. But this is not a gift. The seed is something owed." Sen put his hands on his hips.

"Owed by Cam, who cannot be here as he is banned. However, we can bring it, as a gift."

Sen turned his head to one side and narrowed his eyes as he studied Dev.

"You are a clever witch-boy. I suppose I can live with this exchange. I shall return."

And with a pop of the air, Sen disappeared.

Dev and Tully stared at each other, unsure of what to do other than stand there and wait. Dev handled the vessel carefully, not wanting to break it.

A second later, Sen returned.

"I will leave this here." He pointed to a flat rock. "You leave your gift over there." He indicated a similar stone, but over a ways.

"Deal."

The exchange was made. Sen cradled the vessel next to his chest, raised his hand to say goodbye, and descended into the chimney stack.

Tully held an enormous book.

"What is it?"

"I'm not sure I'm going to pronounce this right. It's called, the *Anatomiae Biological Mediocris de Speciebus.*" Tully cocked an eyebrow, then shrugged.

"Well, the answer to Cam's sickness has to be in there. Let's get back to the guys. We can search the book on the long drive home to Edmonton."

Chapter Twenty-Eight

THE THREE-HOUR ride back to Edmonton dragged. Sparks had to concentrate on driving and did nothing other than watch the middle lines on the highway disappear under the car and keep an eye out for deer. This close to sunset the chance of them making an appearance remained a constant threat.

But the ride proved uneventful, and before he had travelled an hour into the ride Cam and Tully had fallen fast asleep, while Dev poured through the massive tome that had been gifted to them—well, Cam. The book had been a study text of his, and hopefully held the answers that might save him.

By the time they pulled up to the house night had firmly settled in, and the shadows stretched out from the streetlamps.

"You gonna stay over? You've done a ton of driving today and that always makes me tired," Dev said to Sparks as Tully wiggled his way around them, Cam draped over his arms, as limp as a dehydrated plant, destined for the spare room where he had slept the night before.

"Well..." Sparks considered the possibility.

"You can sleep in your office space if you want," Dev suggested.

"I'll stay, I am pooped. But I'm okay sleeping in the big bed." Sparks put an arm around Dev as the made their way into the house.

THE NEXT MORNING everyone slept late.

Tully rolled out of bed first and disappeared from the bedroom. Judging from the clatter down in the kitchen, Sparks assumed he had started up breakfast for everyone.

Sparks borrowed a pair of sweats from Dev and slung them on, then traipsed downstairs where Tully offered him a cup of coffee. Sparks graciously accepted and took a sip. Coffee was not a mainstay in his life. But the piping hot, freshly pressed drink delivered velvety deliciousness.

"Oh, this is good."

"You'll be fine in this house. Coffee is a staple. And a must-have."

"I'm usually not a big coffee drinker, but if you make this every morning, I'll happily drink the ground beans. It's really good. Have you seen where the massive book went? I would like to have a peek at it." Sparks put the mug down as Tully pointed down the hall toward the offices.

"I think Dev put it on my desk, as Cam is crashed out in his room."

A quick glance at Tully's desk revealed the book. Sparks grabbed the tome and brought the weighty beast into the kitchen, resumed his place at the eating bar, and leafed through it.

Tully came around cradling his own morning elixir of goodness, and snuggled up to Sparks, while peeking over Sparks's shoulder to view the book.

There were pages upon pages of writing, and not all of them in English. Detailed illustrations were incorporated on every other page as the various species of fae were listed and discoursed. Sparks had never seen anything so comprehensive on the different branches of classes and types. In fact, he had never heard of most of the beasties listed.

"Wow, the lineages are so detailed. I'd get lost in the minutiae, but, more importantly right now...how do you like your eggs?" Tully glanced over at Sparks.

"I'm not a picky eater. Honestly, you can make them however you want, and I'll be happy to eat them." Sparks smiled.

Tully bent over and gave him a quick kiss, then placed himself in front of the stove and got to work.

Sparks pretended to read the book, but it was hard not to be enchanted with Tully, studying his moves about the kitchen and basking in his morning optimism. He had a way of putting everyone around him at ease.

"Well, good morning, gentlemen. I have to say, I slept so hard last night I didn't even notice the two of you in bed." Dev came down the stairs in nothing but a pair of boxers. He went up to Sparks first and gave him a quick kiss as well. "Sleep well?"

Sparks nodded, then grinned. What he imagined would be weird and awkward between the three of them, living daily life, turned out to be supportive and comforting. He didn't feel like an intruder. Dev stroked his back, while Tully poured a third coffee, piled sugar and milk into the mug, then handed the coffee to Dev with a smirk and a wink.

"Ah, morning happiness." Dev took a sip.

"This coffee is delicious." Sparks glanced up at Dev.

"The best. I swear Tully is a wizard in the kitchen."

"A kitchen witch maybe?" Sparks laughed at his own joke.

Dev chuckled, pointing to the book. "Did you find any-thing?"

"Oh my Gods, there's so much information in here, but I haven't got to Cam's type yet, and there's no index I can see, and not everything is written in a language I'll under-stand."

"I hear you. I had the same issues last night. We gotta keep looking though. Has anyone checked on him yet?" Dev queried.

"Nope. Too busy making breakfast. But I'm thawing meat for him." Tully pointed to the kitchen sink filled with hot water and a package of frozen goods. "You want to go check on him?" Tully turned to his frying pan and sprinkled some onions and peppers into the eggs. He had crumbled bacon and cheese waiting to be added as well.

"Can do." Dev disappeared down the hallway.

"That smells amazing." Sparks sniffed the air.

Dev returned and he looked worried.

"What's the matter?"

"He looks like shit. I gently shook him awake, but we need to figure this out quick. If I didn't know any better, I'd swear he's lost weight. His cheeks look sallow."

From out on the deck a howl erupted, filling the kitchen and Sparks's soul with dread.

Dev clutched an invisible necklace. "What the fuck?"

Everyone glanced toward the back deck.

Everton sat on the other side of the glass and pawed at the door.

Dev walked over, slid the doors open, and allowed the werewolf entrance. He padded down the hallway, following his nose.

"Don't do that!" Dev called after him. "I think I just lost a couple years of my life."

Sparks got up off his bar stool and walked down the hallway. He crept around the door jamb and spied on Cam.

Everton had crawled up onto the bed with Cam, placing his snout overtop of the fae's chest. Cam remained asleep, twitching violently at times, and the fever sweat had returned as evidenced by the beads of moisture dotting Cam's hairline. Everton whined as he licked Cam's hand.

Sparks returned to the kitchen to see Tully and Dev being affectionate with each other in front of the stove. He liked seeing them happy. He had the evening shift at the hospital tonight. A makeup shift for the one he missed while trapped in Byron's soul trap. He would have to leave soon enough and get ready for work, but in the meantime, he decided to spend a little extra time flipping through the voluminous tome gifted to Cam.

The book fascinated Sparks, but he hadn't found any answers before breakfast got served, and then he had to go.

"Hey, before you leave, come here and give me some love!" Tully pulled Sparks in for a hug. "I'm going down to check in on Uncle Bart. You coming here tonight, or to your place?"

"I'll come with you! I love the old man. He's fun. To be honest, I hadn't considered my plans for tonight. I have to feed Bernie and Ralph though, so...I'll probably go home."

"Well, if you want, you can always come over here after. You know you're more than welcome."

"You guys are the best. Thanks. I'll text you later and let you know for sure, okay?"

"Absolutely."

Dev, working in his office, yelled his goodbyes to Sparks as they headed downstairs to Uncle Bart's place.

Tully knocked.

No one answered, but a crash clanged like metal pots and pans had tumbled off a counter.

"That's it, I'm going in." Tully flipped through his key

ring to find the one that opened the door.

Upon entering they were both shocked to see Uncle Bart's place in a state of disarray. He may have been well into his years, but he always maintained a fastidious house.

As they walked into the kitchen, Uncle Bart stood in front of the sink, gazing out of the window, wearing a woman's dress that would have been from the turn of the previous century.

"All right, old man"—Tully placed his hands on his hips—"I don't care what you want to wear, but what the hell is with the mess and why didn't you answer the door?"

Uncle Bart didn't turn around. He didn't even acknowledge the boys' presence.

"Uncle Bart!" Tully repeated louder, although his great-uncle had never had problems with his hearing.

He simply stared off past the window, swaying slightly from side to side.

Sparks leaned in closer to Tully. "Should I call an ambulance? Maybe he's had a stroke?"

"Let's wait a minute…" Tully walked over and gently put a hand on Uncle Bart's shoulder and guided him to turn around to look at them both. "Uncle Bart, are you okay?"

No gleam or recognition sparked in the old man's eyes. He simply stared at Tully with a dead, blank stare.

"Uncle Bart." Tully shook him, carefully.

Uncle Bart's face morphed. What had been a kind gentle old man with an unknowing stare shifted into deep dark eye sockets, shrunken skin, and a skeletal head topped with long silvery hair.

The spectre lashed out at Tully. As he stumbled backward, he tripped over the items strewn across the floor, and fell with a crash. Sparks rushed over and pulled him up.

"Are you okay?"

"Holy shit, did you see that?" Tully's voice squeaked.

Uncle Bart had returned to staring out of the window above the sink.

"I did."

"He's been possessed." Tully's eyes were round. "We gotta help him."

"I think this might be a good time to call my brother," Sparks suggested.

"I think so."

The boys left, Tully locking the front door on their way out, while Sparks had pulled out his cell and dialled his necromancer brother.

WIATT ARRIVED WITHIN the hour.

Sparks had called the hospital and again had to apologize for backing out and missing shifts. This wasn't going to bode well for him at his next performance appraisal.

Dev gave up on the fae tome and joined the other men outside Uncle Bart's front door.

"All right, tell me again what happened?" Wiatt stroked his moustache and leaned in close to Tully who recounted the story.

"And then I shook him, and this ghostly skeletal thing emerged from his face. Damn thing took a swipe at me. I fell ass over teakettle. Sparks witnessed the whole thing. Uncle Bart returned to his spot staring out the window after attacking me. We called you in. This shit is beyond me."

"Okay, well, I'm glad you did. This doesn't sound good, but I doubt Uncle Bart's in any serious trouble." Wiatt pointed at the door.

Tully opened it.

"Before we go in, a couple of rules. Don't be combative or argumentative. That won't help. If anything, we want to stay positive, optimistic, but firm that the ghost is no longer welcome in the house, and more importantly, not inside Uncle Bart. You three need to *push* the thought of the ghost leaving his body, and I'll do the rest." Wiatt slipped off his backpack and unzipped it, grasped the door handle, and opened the front door.

"Uncle Bart, you have visitors!" he cried out. "Which way to the kitchen? He's most likely still staring out the window. Ghosts often fixate on something or someone who held meaning for them when they were alive."

"Down the hallway."

"Let's go." Wiatt fearlessly made his way toward the kitchen.

As predicted, Uncle Bart hadn't moved.

"Uncle Bart, how are you today?" Wiatt shouted. "I hear you are not yourself." He rummaged around his backpack and took out several items. A pentacle, which he strung around his neck, a goat's head ring, which he slipped over his left index finger, a mason jar filled with a blue glowing liquid, and another container which appeared to be filled with black sand.

Wiatt moved toward Uncle Bart, unsealed the jar of water, dipped his fingers in the liquid, and sprinkled droplets in the direction of the old man. As drops of water hit Uncle Bart a hiss of steam rose.

"Yup, he's possessed. Okay. Can you three help me navigate him into the middle of the kitchen floor? Let's move the table over." Wiatt found a broom in the linen closet and gave it to Dev. "Sweep the room, counter-clockwise. We want to rid the area of any negative energy."

Dev did as instructed, then Wiatt took the black sand and replaced the lid with a different top, one that had a funnel. He used the spout to pour the circumference of a large circle. "Before I complete the full circle, can you force Uncle

Bart into the middle? The spirit will fight you, so be prepared for a fight."

"The hell it will." Tully glowered, went over to Uncle Bart, hoisted him up, and slung him over his shoulder.

The rough manhandling did not go over well. The spirit within Bart's body lashed out, writhed, kicked, and screamed. But Tully's big boy stature and muscles kept Uncle Bart securely in place. He held on fast and put up with the flailing arms and legs.

"You're gonna have bruises everywhere." Sparks grimaced as the old man shrieked. The noises escaping from Uncle Bart's mouth were obviously not of his making.

"I'll live. Uncle Bart, though, may not unless your brother can fix this. Besides, I know you'll tend to my wounds." Tully winked at Sparks when a fist slammed into his face. "For the love of the Gods, old man, if we weren't related..."

Wiatt took the opportunity to complete the circle, placing Grimm marks at each compass point, and hex script around the edge. No sigils broke or crossed the original circle.

"Okay, Tully. Put him down, then step out of the protective circle."

"What is the black sand?"

"Oh, it's not sand. It's black salt. Much better."

Tully eased Uncle Bart down, then sidestepped the old man and removed himself from the magical markings. He encountered no resistance or problems. Uncle Bart, on the other hand, screeched and the spirit embedded in him made itself known.

It was not happy.

It lashed out with talon-like hands. A skeletal jaw snapped and bit. Uncle Bart uttered some horrifying foul language.

"I didn't think he knew so many swear words." Dev scrunched his brows together.

"Oh, that's nothing. You've never seen him really mad." Tully cocked an eyebrow.

"Okay, here comes the hard part. Ready?" Wiatt asked as he cued everyone to be alert.

"Wait. What are we ready for?"

"This." Wiatt reached in, grabbed Uncle Bart by the dress's material, and ripped him toward himself.

As Uncle Bart passed through the barrier of the protective black salt circle his eyes grew wide and bulged. The spirit entrenched within him was unceremoniously ripped out of his corporeal body.

Uncle Bart fell and landed on top of Wiatt. The two lay on the floor for a minute. Wiatt held Uncle Bart so the old man wouldn't slip or fall off him. He stared at Uncle Bart. "You okay?"

"I'm lying on top of a handsome man who is easily fifty years my junior, and he's hard and muscley. What do you think?" Uncle Bart's lascivious suggestion quietened the room, then he tried to prop himself up.

"Yup. He's fine." Tully bent over and extended a hand to help Uncle Bart up.

Inside the black salt circle, the spirit spun, trying to find a way out. Despite the ethereal quality, the ghost of a woman from the early 1900s violently fought against Wiatt's circle.

Once Uncle Bart settled on his own two feet he shuffled over to the circle and glared at the spectre.

"Ester, you bitch. We had a deal."

"What the fuck?" Tully gestured toward Uncle Bart with a *What the hell?* glare.

The old man, still decked out in his fabulous time-period dress, explained, "Well, boys, Ester lives here with me." Then he turned to Tully. "She is a long-deceased ancestor, and a witch herself. One who didn't see fit to go to the Eternal Grasslands to be with the Gods." Uncle Bart frowned. "But she's helped out our family for years. This is her house. A house which will one day belong to you."

"Well, the three of us."

Uncle Bart and Wiatt glared at Tully with looks of confusion.

"Ah, Tully…" Dev started.

"I'm not sure we're ready to…" Sparks said.

"You devil." Uncle Bart whistled through his teeth.

Wiatt chuckled. "Wow, dude. Mom and Dad are gonna love this."

"Yeah, maybe we won't mention my relationship status to them just quite yet. Okay?" Sparks raised an eyebrow and glared angrily at his brother.

"Ah, as long as you're all happy, who cares? I think it's hot." Uncle Bart waggled his eyebrows.

"Okay, stop. What the hell is this?" Tully pointed at the ghost. "If Ester is a relative, why would she possess you?" With hands on hips, he scolded his great-uncle.

"She sometimes gets carried away." Uncle Bart shot a dirty look at Ester, who returned the glare. She crossed her phantom arms over her see-through chest. "We made a deal. After your last visit I determined we'd need the witch wood. You're going to want a space for the new coven. Right? I also got Ester to help retrieve some items from Byron's. After all, the Guardians of the Night Grove are defunct, yes? And you boys need those things to start up the next group. So, Ester and her friends helped out."

"Holy shit. Well, that explains why Byron's study didn't have nearly as many items as I remembered. But I don't get it. Where'd everything go?"

"You haven't found the secret passage yet?" Uncle Bart tilted his head to one side.

"Ah, no," Tully said.

"Well then, you haven't had a need for the room yet. You'll find the entrance behind the bookcase in your office, Tully. There's a separate entrance in each of your offices if you are now a threesome. The house will have accommodated all of you." Uncle Bart gave them all a knowing glance and a mischievous look.

"What the hell is with this house? And why didn't you tell me about any of these details?" Tully appeared more put out that his relative hadn't shared any of this information about the magical nature of the structure.

"I'm a witch. I know things. Doesn't mean I share them." Uncle Bart laughed.

The look on Tully's face was the most deadpan, stoic, unimpressed stare anyone had ever seen on the man who always wore a permanent grin.

Chapter Twenty-Nine

A TRICKLE OF magic wound its way through the assembled coven on the night of Mabon. Sparkles and shimmers danced through the night air within the witch wood.

Dev and Sparks had called all the remaining members of the defunct Guardians of the Night Grove, inviting them with the promise of creating a new coven. Everyone enthusiastically accepted.

Sparks had been placed in charge of the decorations and banquet table. Each attendee had brought various items to adorn the offering for the night. Pumpkins, apples, and sheaves of wheat had been placed elegantly in a towering centrepiece. Various bottles and decanters of wine were present, coupled with plump pomegranates, ears of corn, and clumps of grapes. Sparks had even taken to making dozens of corn dolls braided from the discarded husks. They peeked out from random spots on the table like spying imps.

Tully had whipped up a feast that awaited the coven and its guests after the ceremony. A crockpot of spiced carrot soup simmered, a chafing dish full of buttered, herbed yams lofted savoury aromas, while another warmer overflowed with buttered squash. Plates of figs with cheeses and a variety of home-made breads were on hand. A roast mutton, large enough for everyone to have seconds, had been propped up on a spit in the centre of the table. Several berry pies called out to those craving something sweet. A tray of frosted candied apples and drizzled salted caramel had been placed to the side to be served with the honey mead at midnight.

The witch wood had been strung up with fairy lights and candles, Dev had seen to the lighting arrangements. Braided vines of garlic cloves, ornamental gourds of all shapes, sizes, and colours, stalks of barley, and colourful Aztec corn draped the area in festive autumn colours. Woven into the garlands were strings of fairy lights.

Even the Higan cherry tree, so prominent in the witch wood, had participated in the evening festivities. Well on its way into fall, the massive tree sported golden leaves touched with crimson.

The organizers had done a smash-up job. Their first coven gathering would transpire with style.

There were some heart-wrenching moments as well. Tully carried Cam out from the house and laid him near the cherry tree to rest. Discovering Cam's potential salvation had taken dedicated study of the ancient text to finally find the appropriate Eldritch Royal fae entry. The section for males consisted of a few short paragraphs, whereas the mating and progeny outlines had been extensive. Even then, the care and treatment of fae who contracted isolation sickness was nothing more than a footnote buried in an old customs section which would have been missed if it hadn't been for the perseverance of Tully, Dev, and Sparks.

Because of Cam's exile, the tethers connecting him to his fae family had been severed and as the fairy folk are fiercely dependent on one another and their customs, castaway individuals immediately contracted isolation sickness. Only one method to cure the disease had been written about.

For the Eldritch clan, an old tree would have to voluntarily agree to enshroud his body until the sickness passed—basically until Cam's body learned to live on its own. But the merging with a tree would also alter Cam's physical appearance yet again. Diagrams in the book showed the final transformation. Cam would end up with bark-like skin, an additional set of horns, and his wings would change to resemble branches more than the membranous fur-lined ones he currently had.

And so the first part of the night had been the offering of Cam by laying him at the base of the thick-trunked Higan cherry tree that stood guard at the end of the witch wood.

Cam had lost so much weight his appearance startled some of the guests who hadn't seen the fae recently. He had dwindled to nothing more than skin and bones. Everton had never left his side, constantly whining and pawing at his boyfriend. Despite the fact his elongated shifted muzzle wasn't capable of forming words, he still managed to convey all the worry, hurt, grief, and loss he suffered. The crowd surrounding the cherry tree bore witness to the pain in Everton's eyes for the inflicted and exiled fae.

But as soon as the failing Eldritch had been lain at the base of the tree, branches swooped down, gently picked up Cam, and cradled him.

"Well, I guess that's a good sign." Tully grasped Dev and Sparks's hands.

Cam inhaled deeply, and for the first time in weeks his eyes opened, and he glanced around, lucid and aware. To Sparks, Cam appeared to have found a peaceful moment. The constant shine of sweat on the fevered fae's skin evaporated. Cam's mouth ticked up into the slightest of grins as he stretched out a feeble hand and laid it across Everton's muzzle. He closed his eyes and fell asleep.

The cherry tree brought Cam close to its main trunk.

The bark split, and the thick layers of wood peeled open with creaks and cracks until a hollow formed, a small womb.

The tree limbs, moving carefully and nimbly, tucked Cam inside the heart of the wood, then the fleshy wood stitched itself up leaving a fine line of a scar on the tree trunk.

Having Cam be put to sleep within a tree sat well with Sparks. The Earth aspect fit with Cam being Eldritch. Dev, on the other hand, shuddered when he considered being entombed within a living organism. Hope flourished with all the boys that Cam would heal and eventually re-emerge.

The evening's planned events would ensure Cam's safety, initiate a new coven, acknowledge the Gods, give thanks, and celebrate new beginnings.

Everton panted and drooled, glanced between Dev, Sparks, and Tully, and the tree where Cam had disappeared. He found himself a comfortable spot at the base, nestled amongst the roots, where he hunkered down with his eyes focused on the tree's trunk scar where Cam had been enveloped. He never shifted his gaze away.

Dev caressed the gnarled bark of the tree and whispered, "We'll be here for you when you're ready. Sleep well, my friend." He knelt and scratched behind the ears of the werewolf. Normally, a gesture no one would attempt, but Everton peered up at Dev and huffed, agony in his eyes, but solace too.

Sparks found it hard to swallow watching the werewolf. A lump had formed. As relieved as the guys were in figuring out how to help Cam, the resting spot signalled the first step in the journey Cam would have to take in curing the isolation sickness. The rest would be up to him. Hopefully he would arise in the spring, but there were no guarantees.

Dev turned to the rest of the invited crowd, and a few special guests, addressing them. "Good evening, men, and esteemed guests. Welcome to the first gathering of our newly formed coven. This evening marks the night of Mabon. The second harvest celebration and a time for us to look back and be thankful for all the things we have been blessed with. It is also the time to sanctify our home, and the hearth.

Tonight, we look forward to the coming darkness and the cold winter nights allowing us time to rest before the sun returns at Yule. Some fear the dark, for the dark holds things we cannot see, and what we cannot see, we do not understand. So let us embrace that which we cannot know and put our faith and trust in our Gods and Goddesses who guide us. Welcome to our witch wood."

As Dev raised and spread his arms wide, the invited guests moved to the back. Franco and Serge were present, in part to make sure Everton would behave, but also to mend fences with the witch community. Uncle Bart had come to participate, too, sitting in an Adirondack chair and made comfortable with cushions and a blanket. Amna and a couple of her coven sisters were also in attendance, to stand as witnesses to the new all-male coven blessing ceremony. They also wanted good ties to the group who had been mandated to keep Edmonton's city boundaries and its magical community a neutral zone. Dev and his new band of men would take over the job the Guardians of the Night Grove had once held. And a representative from the Montreal coven had arrived only days before, Bastien Toussaint, who had agreed to come help them with the ley lines. His dark complexion offset the myriad of silver pentacles he wore around his neck, a skull ring on his finger, and an interesting ear cuff mimicking the horns of the horned God. He also loved to wear shimmering gold eye shadow, and his thick beard sported silver round clips where braids hung from his chin. Even though he'd only been there a handful of days, he'd become popular with the new coven members, getting along famously with everyone.

Dev nodded to his men.

The watch towers were called upon. Tully, responsible for the North, the element of Earth, called the energy to the witch wood. Phineas deemed himself necessary in the proceedings and helped. He squirmed his way off Tully's arm as his vines penetrated the ground. All around the perimeter of the circle a ripple of tendrils tore through the soil and disappeared again, churning up the dirt, making small boulders erupt, each of them tipped and dotted with iron ore deposits. They sparkled and created tiny prisms as the moonlight and candlelight glinted off the shiny metallic spots.

Sparks had been assigned to the realm of the South, the element of Fire. After all, lightning was a combination of Air and Fire. As he called the flames forth, the bonfire in the middle of the circle burst to life, consuming the air in the vicinity and creating a *woomp* as the blaze flickered and danced. Sparks had practiced for weeks to separate his talent down to one of the basic elements. Dev and Tully had helped him hone his abilities. But tonight, several fire salamanders crawled out of the fire pit and inched their way to the outside of the circle, where they perched on top of Tully's rocks. The result heated the metal within the stones, casting a warmth across the glade. Sparks glanced at his lovers, shock and awe on his face. The salamanders were new.

Dev beamed with pride. Tully's perpetual smile grew larger.

Marcus, who had always called upon Water for the Guardians of the Night Grove, was only too happy to join them now, and as he thrust his hands down to the ground, puddles of dark liquid emerged. They snaked their way in ribbon rivulets toward the circle's perimeter and wound themselves around the boulders. The water hissed as they grazed up against the heated rocks from the fire salamanders, who kept their distance from the writhing water snakes, eyeing them with distrust.

Finally, Scott, another returning witch from the Guardians, called forth the Air, creating gentle whirlwinds, tossing around robes, and gently ruffling everyone's hair. The candles in the witch wood flickered and the garlands swayed. The gentle breeze brought in the aromas from the banquet table and the scent of spices and earthly delights consecrated the protective circle.

Recognizing their watchtowers were in place, and the protective circle glowed with their presence, Dev turned to the altar. All the items the Guardians had once owned had been cleansed and were now in their possession, adorning the altar. The guys had taken a couple of weeks to wash and purify every artifact Ester and her comrades had hauled over from Byron's house.

They also spent countless hours in the new secret library, which had a massive atrium on one side overlooking the witch wood. The guys catalogued and inventoried everything transferred from the old coven to the new one.

Dev struck a match and lit both the Goddess and God candles.

"Great Goddess, maiden, mother, and crone, hear us, and bless us. If it pleases you, be present with us tonight as we call upon you to join our circle as we initiate our new all-male coven.

"Great God, oh Horned One, father, sage, and son, hear us, and bless us. Be present with us as we start anew."

As the flame took light on the God's taper, the spark on the tip of the wick crackled, sputtered, then grew tall and fiery. For a moment, Dev considered dousing the flame for fear of setting everything else around him on fire. But the candle simmered down.

Not before the hedge around the witch wood trembled, and the ground shook. A fog formed outside the circle, making the candlelight halo, casting shadows and fashioning an ethereal ambience.

The hedge creaked and groaned. The wind gusted and blew through the witch wood. From the far end of the wood, behind the cherry tree, the hedge parted, and from the cleaved bramble a giant set of horns appeared. In the fog and candlelight, they glowed.

A shadow formed, and the body of a giant man appeared. The enormity of the Horned One stilled the witch wood. In awe of His presence, a silence settled. Not even the background noises from the city disturbed the grove.

Everyone took a knee.

"Now that's a reception!" bellowed the Ancient One. "Dev, Tully, and Sparks, you boys have been busy." The cloven-hoofed God clomped forward toward the circle, and as He did, He shed the mighty horns, the faun-like legs, and hooves. As He stepped into the circle, He transformed from beast to man, albeit taller, more muscular, and commanding authority. "Now my men, and exceptional guests—" The Ancient One glanced in Amna and her sisters' direction and graced them with a nod to acknowledge their presence. Sparks stifled the urge to giggle at the look of shock on Dev's sister's face. After all, how often is one gifted with the presence of a God? "Come forward, all. Gather around. Let me see who is here."

All in attendance drew in close and no one took their eyes off the Ancient One.

The God glanced at every person present.

"My men, I am proud. You have done well. But our tasks have only just begun. I am pleased to see Dev, Tully, and Sparks are acting as your lead, for they were hand chosen and wed together by myself. They will father your studies, be your brothers at arms, and your comrades in the Shadow Realm.

"But know this. There is danger afoot. The darkness has crept in, and as much as the shadows harbour the beasts of the Shadow Realm we call home, we must do our best to keep them at bay. Remember there is as much light as there is dark in the Realm. All creatures belong, but we don't all play well together. So tonight, I proclaim this coven to be mine, and on behalf of myself you shall be the doers of dangerous things. You are my champions of quests others fear to take. This is the clan who casts the spells most fear to attempt.

"You are my Magus Malefica. My badass magicians—the men I will call upon to do the work others cannot. There will be strife and heartache. There will be death and sacrifice. But I shall also see to it that you are rewarded in kind. Dev, Tully, and Sparks, teach them well. Mentor them and be strong. Kerr, talker of truths, brother witch of sound, Lazaro, witch of the green, controller of plants, Marcus, diviner of futures and wielder of Water, Wiatt, witch of the dead, and keeper of secrets, and Scott, scribe and lover of language, whisperer of history and controller of Air, you are my Magus Malefica. And there will be others.

"As new witches come to you, present them before me so I may know them. But before the night is through, I shall visit each of you. There is much to discuss, to learn, to do, but until the work begins, let us celebrate our inauguration, and to the paths that led us here. Let us be thankful for all we have, and all that shall come.

"I bless each of you, this witch wood, and the home that guards this land."

The Horned One, who stood before them as a man, and yet so much more, raised His arms skyward, and as He did so, He returned to his magnificent glory. A rack of horns grew from His temples and glowed from the crown of His head. The multitude of prongs stretched high into the night sky, tickling the stars above. His legs furred over and His black cloven feet formed. He clomped them, setting off sparks as His hooves hit the granite stones encircling the coven's magical circle.

His head morphed into the wild stag, but His body remained human, taut, muscular, and filled with power. He exemplified the warrior, the hunter, the protector. He was the son, the father, and the sage. The black eyes of the stag stared at all who were present.

He let out a huff in the cool night air. Vapour bloomed into swirling clouds. The fog thickened and condensed, and in the *woosh* of a fall breeze and the rustle of the dying leaves of the Higan Cherry, the God disappeared into the night.

"I love it when he does that," Tully whispered to Dev as he stared at the spot where the God had been with love and peace in his eyes.

Amna came and stood beside her brother. She asked, "Does He come every ritual?"

Dev chuckled. "Nope. Just the important ones, and for important people." He slid his arm around his sister's shoulder. Tully took up one side and placed his hand in Dev's. Sparks came up behind them and wrapped his arms around Dev and Tully.

The Higan cherry branches swayed in the breeze left by the God's exit. A shower of crimson and gold rained down upon them.

Within the sacred circle, the Magus Malefica had been born, and tonight they feasted.

Tomorrow? Well, that would hold a whole new adventure.

Epilogue

SPARKS OPENED THE vivarium and dropped in several crickets and mealworms onto the feeding ledge that adhered to the side of the glass wall with suction cups. The warm humid air inside the enclosure escaped as Sparks inhaled. He enjoyed the smell, reminding him of a tropical vacation he had taken years ago.

Bernadette and Ralph watched the morsels of food drop from above and made their way over to devour their treats.

Tully glanced up from his book and shook his head.

"I'll never get used to that." He shivered where he sat, reclining on a chaise set in front of a large stone fireplace, which currently had a roaring fire. His robe hung loosely, sashed at his waist, exposing most of his muscled and recently trimmed chest. He stared at Sparks and the lizards eyeing the whole scene with trepidation.

"Leave him be. The geckos enjoy the bugs." Dev grinned from behind the desk. He flipped the page of an ancient book Bastien had lent them. He toyed with the idea of memorizing the placement and directionality of the world's ley lines. There were hundreds of them.

Sparks laughed at the two of them. He had moved in only the week prior, giving notice on his apartment, and toting over the rest of his stuff.

They were still figuring things out, and there had been some bumps in the road. But as they had all agreed to talk things through, life went on, as it would, generally going well. Being part of a throuple still made Sparks nervous. A lot of folks would never understand, but the guys in the coven were all supportive. Amna, Dev's sister, had made them each matching talismans for love and commitment, and they all wore them as necklaces.

You guys are the best. Sparks's gaze meandered between his lovers.

"Back at ya." Tully snuck a peek at Sparks and smiled a bit bigger.

Dev didn't look up but he, too, beamed, enjoyed his evenings with the guys, and the lizards.

"I was talking to the geckos." Sparks snickered, then winked at Tully.

Even though Sparks's comment had been telepathic, the three were learning when and how to project their thoughts.

"You sure you don't want to hold Bernadette while I give her a mealworm? She likes you."

Tully looked suitably horrified.

"I'm good. Sorry, Bernie." Tully apologized to the lizard.

The massive windows at the far end of the secret library cast a mirrored reflection of the guys as they attended to their tasks. Uncle Bart had shown them the hidden door in Tully's office. He toured them through the magical addition. The library had been part of the house once before. Each of the shelves and curio cabinets had a purpose and were organized by subject matter or type of artifact. The various relics and witch tools belonging to the Magus Malefica were numerous, and the coven wouldn't be needing much of anything in the near future.

Beyond the windows the purple of the night sky blanketed them, and the witch wood on the other side of the glass lay quiet. Snow had started to fall for the first time yesterday, and everything outside had been dusted in white. A tad early for winter to arrive, but after all, it was Alberta, and snow in early October was far from unusual.

If the snow kept up, as it likely would, Samhain would be chilly. They'd have to build a large bonfire to keep everyone warm. Perhaps the majority of the celebration would happen indoors.

A lonely howl came from outside.

"Ah, Everton has arrived for the night." Dev stood and stretched. "I'll go get him his dinner."

The guys had taken to tossing a raw steak into the witch wood for the werewolf shortly after he showed up. The creature came every night and spent the dark hours protecting the tree where Cam rested. Cam occupied everyone's thoughts from time to time, especially Dev, who missed his friend. He frequently went into the witch wood to visit the tree and talk to Cam.

Samhain was in a couple of weeks, but their task of setting up the neutral zone had progressed steadily. They hadn't managed to get all the wards charged and working in unison. They kept sparking out.

Bastien from the Montreal coven and Scott had been paired together and were working on the problem. Turns out they got along well, and the guys all had bets on whether the two would end up together. If the Magus Malefica gained a new brother in the coven, Sparks already had an initiation ceremony planned. Or would they lose Scott to Montreal? He secretly hoped for the first scenario. Bastien was fun, flamboyant, and amazingly talented as a technomage. The man had an app for everything.

Franco had been spending more and more time with the guys as well, visiting often to make sure Everton behaved. After a couple of weeks of unannounced visits Franco inquired about Kerr's relationship status. Seems an interest had been sparked during the Mabon ritual.

The guys were waiting to see how a relationship between the two would play out as a werewolf and witch pairing would certainly be interesting.

The only thing Dev hadn't managed to resolve was the suspected possession of the boy who had scaled his office walls.

Wiatt worked diligently to find a spell to pull the demon out, but necromancy and demonology were not similar. He had managed to create a hex bag to keep the entity contained, but the child wasn't free from the grasp of the insidious creature. After all, Wiatt's talents were on dead things, not demonic things, and the two were different branches of magic. But Wiatt was up for the challenge and had been working on the problem with dogged determination.

Things were ticking along.

Their coven had formed and gelled well, and rumours were shared in the Shadow Realm community that the Magus Malefica were a boon to the community.

Everything was just as it should be.

For now.

Acknowledgements

As always, Lonny, you get top billing. I couldn't manifest my magical darkness if you weren't there to spur me on. You prop me up, force me to see reality, and set me free to run through the madness I create. Thank you for giving me the time and space to weave words into bizarre tales with all kinds of glorious and hellish creatures.

To Marvin, Glenn, Kevin, and Eric—my own personal version of Magus Malefica—thanks for the venting sessions, the continued support, the encouragement, words of wisdom, and all the laughs. Even though we're scattered across the world, I'm glad our little ragtag group is connected.

My beta readers: Rachel, David, Kim, Brandon, James, Mike, Kari, Katherine, Steve, Graham, and Amy. I know not everyone is involved with every project, but without you, my tales wouldn't be what they are. You rip me apart like the voracious hellhounds you are. But the resurrection rebuilds the story, making it stronger, more accurate, and a better version of itself. Thank you for all you do.

And to my dedicated readers...none of this happens without you. The emails, DMs, and messages I receive spur me on and keep me creating. Thank you for believing in my witches and wanting more. Magus Malefica has many more tales and tails, spells, conjurings, and hexes to unleash. Sit back and enjoy the chaos.

None of the writings I create would be in the hands of readers without the folks at NineStar Press. Raevyn, thank you for all the encouragement. We're two bats from the same dark cave. Liz, here's to many more editing sessions! Thank you for being a teacher. And Natasha, your skill at creating such gorgeous cover art has never ceased to instill inspiration in me to write more stories—you truly are talented.

Thank you, all of you, for supporting me with my strange, twisted, and dark tales (or tails—meh—both).

About J.P. Jackson

J.P. Jackson is an award-winning author of dark urban fantasy, paranormal, and even paranormal romance stories, but regardless of the genre, they always feature LGBTQ main characters.

J.P. works as an IT analyst in health care during the day, where if cornered he'd confess to casting spells to ensure clinicians actually use the electronic medical charting system he configures and implements.

At night, the writing happens, where demons, witches, and shapeshifters congregate around the kitchen table and general chaos ensues. His husband of 24 years has very firmly put his foot down on any further wraith summonings and regularly lines the doorway with iron shavings and salt crystals. Imps are most definitely not house-trainable. Ghosts appear at the most inopportune times, and the Fae are known for regular visits where a glass of wine is exchanged for a good ole story or two. Although the husband doesn't know it, Canela and Jalisco, the two Chihuahuas, are in cahoots with the spellcasting.

J.P.'s other hobbies include hybridizing African Violets (thanks to grandma), extensive traveling, and, believe it or not, knitting.

Facebook
www.facebook.com/jpjacksonwrites

Twitter
@jpjacksonauthor

Instagram
www.instagram.com/jp_jackson_writes/

Other NineStar books by this author

Daimonion

Magic or Die

Magus Malefica—The Coven Series

Summoned

Connect with NineStar Press

www.ninestarpress.com

www.facebook.com/ninestarpress

www.facebook.com/groups/NineStarNiche

www.twitter.com/ninestarpress

www.instagram.com/ninestarpress